WHERE IS YOUR GOD NOW?

James Debens

Acknowledgments

I must thank a few people for helping me complete this debut novel after years of laziness and prevarication.

Thank you to my ever-supportive wife, Emy, whose sleep has, for several years, suffered because I would wake up at 2am with some swiftly rejected idea.

I would like to send my fullest appreciation and love to my family for their support and suggestions; to Tony Jackman, a wonderful editor and playwright, who struggled manfully through a very chewy first draft; to the estimable writer Boris Starling for his advice and Partridgisms; and to every friend who has sailed with me.

Living in the 'livelier' parts of London in my 20s finally makes some sense.

God bless every Luca and Milena, battling the wolf each day. "Here's to the hearts and the hands of the men, who come with the dust and are gone with the wind."

JD

All characters in this publication are fictitious, and any resemblance to real persons, living or dead, is purely coincidental.

No part of this publication may be reproduced, stored in a retrieval system, or transmitted, in any form or by any means, without the prior permission in writing of the author, nor be otherwise circulated in any form of binding or cover other than that in which it is published and without a similar condition including this condition being imposed on the subsequent purchaser.

Published by KDP, an Amazon company.

Copyright © 2021 James Debens
All rights reserved.

Prologue
The man in the Merc.

Round and round the car goes, always in the middle lane, always at 70mph, always on cruise control.

Inside the Mercedes, the sole passenger's fingers are missing two of their nails now. Still, they claw at the tan leather seats; but the car will soon become his tomb. His blood is smeared in the same fan-shaped patterns as those areas cleared by the car's windscreen wipers; in the marks carved in the upholstery run scarlet tributaries.

Beyond the smoked rear windows, the motorway verges speed by. No one can see him behind the glass; and no one can hear his shouts and cries of pain, except perhaps the driver who sits impassively on the other side of the glass partition.

He has been shouting for hours now, and his soft voice has shredded away to a mere husk. Though he begs and bangs on the windows for help, the circuits of the M25 have been uninterrupted.

"Please, please, have mercy on me!" he keeps crying. "I'll be silent this time, please."

However, the driver doesn't respond; this is a man he has met on several occasions, enough to know he won't be leaving the vehicle alive. The driver's boss also has a reputation for silencing people for good; it was in his restaurant that he first met the driver, when the man had been wearing an apron but never offered a smile.

As the man surveys the mangled mess of his hands, from all the blows he's landed on the glass partition, he curses himself. A less greedy man would have survived. Yet here he is, on executive Death Row, motoring towards a final resting place far from his beloved family. He'll be hidden under concrete in a spot not even they would ever know.

Slow train coming.

On the lower slopes of a hill between the towns of Folkestone and Dover lay a cabin, almost hidden from the breaking waves of the English Channel. It was like a soapbox go-kart left abandoned after a long-forgotten afternoon's play. Seven decades ago, my grandfather had crafted the summer home to retrain his war-shocked hands; and thirty years ago, my parents had inherited the cabin over a weekend of Isle of Jura whiskey and weeping. My granddad's great project of 1946 was now waiting for me beside that cliff walk that rose and fell with the shoreline 70 metres below. The cabin would pass on between loving hands once more.

A hundred miles north-west, my train wound its way through the cookie-cut commuter towns past hundreds of little box houses, each with tiny windows in the same spot in their brick walls. I could see their shapes thrown by the greasy windows as a biscuit blur onto the table-top. There was no-one else in the carriage. In the past six months, it seemed to me as if I'd aged from 25 to 38. Someone in the shadows must have been keeping a book on my debts and called them all in with immediate effect.

My back cracked from the 12 hours spent sitting on trains of varying comfort: the efficient engines that skirted Monviso in my home region of northern Italy; the sleek TGVs that fired across the French countryside; and this tugboat with its velour-covered iron brackets masquerading as seats. It was all to give my folks the send-off they both deserved. I'd gone out like a celebratory Chinese lantern over the English Channel in the late Nineties, yet here I was bobbing black on the tide, soggy and burnt, bits of me quite recognisably missing.

I am Sam, and, after two decades of low self-expectation, I feared I'd become the utter derailment of all the human virtues my parents sought to cultivate in me. My sins kept me awake, high above the cobbles, on my dog bed in the corner of Tom's echoing palazzo. I would listen to the shipping forecast on the radio. I would hope to fall asleep as the links of the chain around the British coast were announced – Dogger, Fisher, German Bight, in the shadows of the night – but then would come the random shouts from random scenes in my past to disturb my sleep. Nothing would be left for me to forage through, except the afterglow of the nightmare.

I was a little overweight, but at least I'd kept my hair. It was still sandy blond, if a little less lusty as it swept across my frown lines. My blue eyes were my best feature. Even as Dad grew more patched together with ear hair and Germolene, he had retained the cobalt spark in his own. I hoped he was sleeping soundly now. Just like Dad, the family acres never shrank or grew over the drystone walls and hedges; indeed, they took on the same patched-up air, scars in the meadows from the pale turf and sod torn with tyres and machinery. My father looked tired whenever we chatted on Skype. "Sam," he'd say, "I keep chugging on."

The sparseness of life in Berwickshire, where I had no friends and no distractions apart from my folks, would lead me to suffer epic hallucinations in my room jammed up in the eaves. I would be lifted by ennui into the realm of the fantastic – there was nothing to do around Duns except keep strange converse with the gales, and I had no smartphone, let alone a computer, with which to connect to the material world or escape into the cyber one. So, my universe began and ended at the five-bar gate, although the hallucinations, to this day, would blight my daily life. I still created my own imaginarium, and my inability to divine what was real from my thought-dreams had been the true reason why I'd lived such a cloistered life in Turin. I was frightened by any derailment from my routine, and I was still ridiculously mouse-shy. Reality had too many heads.

Earlier today, I had put down my parents' wreaths in that churchyard spot by the willow and watched as the priest angrily kicked the leaves from the path and banged the sides of his head with his washed-raw hands. He'd used the eulogies to rail against those who seemed to be "on the make", everyone except Alistair and Sandy, his friends for 50 years. God was setting us all tests, and we were failing ourselves, captivated by the shiny and new, our neophyte ways blinding us to tradition and truth. I'd tried to reassure him before he slumped off, but it was in vain.

Now, aboard the train to King's Cross, I was certain that there must be a point to this all. In that seaside cabin in southern England, I'd subsist on whatever the seagulls dropped through the windows; I would cancel out all those debts; I'd regain my sharpness with bracing walks where I would nod at the old ladies, say "how-do?" instead of scorning them for outliving my parents. I'd tell the world how grateful I was still to be struggling along with her. I would no longer be this spent man slumped on a deserted train, trying to get as far away from myself as I could. I would be vigorous and vital.

A child, a boy of no more than six, had passed through the carriage earlier, dragging his harassed young mother along in the trail of his excitement. He had stopped by my seat and he'd stared at me for some seconds before pointing at my blotchy face and asking, "why is the man crying, mum?" You can never fault a kid's directness. His mother, lean under her fleece, perhaps slimmed down from charging after her little blond sparkler, had smiled her apologies.

"It's all right," I said to her. "He's right to ask. I perhaps shouldn't cry in public." Then I addressed her boy, his steam-train T-shirt at odds with his little old man's face and neat side-parting. "I'm just sad because I've had to say goodbye to all my sheep."

"You have sheep?" the boy blinked.

"Yes, proper sheep, with thick woolly coats, just like your mum's jacket. Well, they're my parents' sheep; I am just allowed to look after them sometimes."

"And your parents let you feed them?"

I smiled. "Yes, even the little baa-baa lambs. The baby sheep."

"What do they eat?" asked the boy, picking his little nose.

"Stop it, Giles!" his mum said, embarrassed. "Sorry again."

"They eat grass, but they especially love forbs – plants with broad leaves. They eat them all up, Giles." And I started miming the sheep eating their grasses.

Giles was laughing. His mother slapped his hand away from his nostril. "You're lucky to have sheep," he said. "I can't even have a little baby pork."

"Piglet, Giles," his mother corrected him.

I laughed now. "I am very, very, very lucky to have sheep. And to have parents who let me feed the sheep and the lambs, Giles. Parents are good."

His mother smiled at me and then looked at her boy. "Giles, he's obviously a very nice man who doesn't pick his nose or press all the buttons on the toilet door. Nice people get to have sheep. So, let's be nice, eh?" She turned to me as she pointed her son back down the aisle. "Thank you for being so patient with him. He has ADHD," she whispered. "I hope you have a better day soon." And then Giles hauled her tired bones down the carriage onto a new adventure and more mischief.

From an early age, despite my many moments of incoherence, my folks would let me tend to the flock of 'Lammermuir lions', gorgeous creatures whose lives were so entwined with my family's own, and those of my forebears since the 12th century. The horned Scottish blackface sheep were as tough and intelligent as I was green, easily led and absent-minded. Would anyone in England take a punt on a professional potterer like me, I wondered? Was there any role for this prematurely knackered sidekick after my two-decade yawn in Piedmont? I felt that I was just a solitary atom bouncing around in Brownian motion; my anchors had been lost, and I'd become untethered, adrift somewhere beyond the sentient. I couldn't even get a signal on my mobile phone, a rubber swimming brick I now used as a paperweight for all the death admin on the table.

I closed my eyes and went through the family farmhouse, room by room; I saw the umbrella stand; the sofa with its bruised pout; my parents' racing trophies from across the Scottish Borders up to Inverness and back down; and the Welsh dresser, from which a primrose sailor's cap observed it all, that little patch of fabric, motionless through the years.

My father had seen Sandy standing behind the old Martini advertising boards at the 1966 Scottish Rally. She was adjusting that very cap and looking down the track for the leading car to come tearing by. It was the delicate little movements Mum made to coax the hat to sit just so, these gestures had first entranced Alistair. He had waited until the onlookers were moving to another vantage point, before he crossed the track and asked Sandy whether they could chat. And so that small cap of yellow corduroy would sit on our Welsh dresser alongside their racing trophies; it would sit through all the ring-dances and Hogmanay feasts in that parlour; and it would observe all of the Christmas and New Year's Eves.

My folks were 45 years married – they'd lived and they died, inseparable. Their saloon car had cartwheeled to destruction, somewhere on a lonely road near the family farmhouse, and my parents were found untouched, their heads resting softly on one another as if they were watching television. The Audi was a crumpled mess, but they were together still on that lonely Duns road. Like the sailing boat that had carried them off to their honeymoon, way beyond the sight-lines of the Greek tour guides, the forces of nature had collected my folks and kept them as one in the fury of that final moment. 'Mi Corazon'.

I awoke with a jump, shocked that I had slept even for a minute. All my parents' hard-earned knowledge and wisdom would have been lost in those sharp seconds of the crash. For every person is their own walking Smithsonian and the curator of their own chronicles. These tales might be mighty, or maligned for their mediocrity. We are defined by what we are seen to do and by what we chose to tell, but no one else flies the path of that particular honeybee, pocketing secrets and learnt truths in a flight uniquely our own, manufacturing our own honey-tongued tales. No one else looks upon the world as we do. So, when a soul is lost, that irreplaceable pollenated knowledge evaporates in that very moment, all 21 grams of it cast to the winds as if salt. And it dies, like the honeybee. And the honeybee then becomes a crust, a rock of fuel, as we all must do. New energy.

I was still thinking about what I'd just lost as I took in the twists and turns of Folkestone in a minicab, dropping down through the Old Town as if a propeller leaf helicoptering through the tiniest branches of a maple tree. I then trod carefully at dusk along the coastal path I'd known so well. The grasses were still flattened in dark jade spots that formed the route to the cabin. I wondered if anyone had even come this way in the weeks since my folks had last stayed there. Perhaps their feet had beaten out a path for me.

No one had ever claimed the land around the shack. I remembered that everyone preferred to walk off their lunches on the Leas, the cliff-top promenade designed 150 years earlier by a man with a very Harry Potter-like name, Decimus Burton, the same wizard who had created Kew Gardens. The cabin, perhaps better suited to the ruined boulevards and ghostly dandies of New Orleans, sat off the Lower Leas Coastal Park, with its amphitheatre of sorts and white-faced biddies nibbling sandwiches. It would be far away enough for my memories to stay free from the sickly scent of candy floss and toffee apples.

My sodden aunt Mimi had told me at the funeral that the keys would be awaiting my arrival at the cabin, and there was the Jiffy bag, leaning against the white wood. Inside the envelope was Mimi's Thinking of You card, penned in her whirlybird handwriting.

And then they fell out: two Polaroid photos showing a home that eerily wasn't the cabin. Instead of the pine kitchen units that my father had customised for mum's needs, the first revealed an Eighties counter, pale green cabinets with ornate brass handles.

However, it was the other photo that startled me; it was of a lounge that had been thoroughly ransacked, the sofa on its side, next to a dark-haired man facedown in a red-and-black checked work shirt. I looked at the second Polaroid. None of my relatives were of that age; at a guess, the man was 30 to 35 years old, judging by his frame and the grungy clothes that were his bedclothes. Perhaps Mimi packed the envelope some time after writing the card and, on her fifth or sixth drink, had included some snaps of a friend or colleague of hers; perhaps it was a photo of someone who'd been in the years below me at Chirnside Primary School. I'd call Mimi tomorrow morning and ask whether these photos were intended for me. If I were to ring her now, she'd be pissed. "Apologies, Sammy, for this, that and the other."

The Jiffy bag in my left hand, I opened the front door. The cabin was still brimful of bric-a-brac and junk – pots without lids, pans without handles, all piled high in one corner; old, yellowing car magazines slumped in another, halfway towards papier-mâché. My father never did like to throw anything out, believing that everything would find its use in the fullness of time. Now, the items gave me a little insight into the last stay of my parents.

The majority of my generation all seemed to whizz out from their birthplaces in arcs of sparks, but eventually the winds would blow them back from where they came. My father had very early on decided that he would bend his environment to his own needs rather than finding a utopia created just for him. "Make your home your castle, Sammy;" he'd say. "Just close your eyes and fly."

The wingback chair, with its seat a patchwork of fabric and a little length of gaffer tape, where Alistair had spent hours upon hours taking flight in his books, still stood there tall in the centre of the living room like a superannuated conductor guiding the flow of life. I sat down in it and looked at the spotless kitchenette, my mum's domain. The calendar of Folkestone landmarks still showed October and a panoramic photo taken from the front of the Grand Hotel; if I were to tilt the shiny card in the half-light, perhaps I would see Mum's delicate fingerprints?

I turned away, and there, brought down from the farmhouse, sat that primrose yellow cap of my mother, surveying all the history of the cabin; this little object that started everything, a beacon that enticed my father, called him over to the pretty young thing on whose curls it once sat and whom it had outlived, this curious little flap of material that jumpstarted a great marriage and my very existence.

What would my mother have thought of me that day? She would have straightened my tie and told me not to fuss about the trip. Her main concern would've been the sleeplessness marked in the dark rings under my eyes and the worry planted in me by those Polaroids. 'You'll be wanting to rest now, my babe. Don't worry about us when we're safe. Don't worry about things that have yet to happen, if they're to happen at all. Rest now, son.'

Now looking at the cabin's organic ease, I again wished I'd lived with a little more order. Now was my chance. The sweep of the sea 70 metres below was shushing me to sleep. Perhaps when I woke up, the photos would have been a mirage.

Milena the nail girl.

She finished doing all the daily checks that Tina had put down on an A4 sheet and Blutacked to the counter. The till was locked; the tip bowl was glued down; all the products were stowed away again in the glass display cabinet; and the rubbish was binned in the alley behind the salon. Tina's scrawl was difficult to decipher, though thankfully it was written in Polish. The bin-liner had been leaking something, so Milena had run the mop over the whole floor just in case. The owner had fired a woman that week for leaving the cap off a bottle of nail polish remover and she had not been paid yet for her final shifts.

Milena didn't have to count the takings that Saturday, and the cash was all in pound notes – the owner claimed he didn't trust the girls not to screw up when swiping the debit and credit cards. Milena knew the real reason was to do with money-laundering, but she didn't raise the matter. It wasn't worth the hassle, and she certainly hoped her meetings with the irascible owner would be rare. She'd been told he was a bald Cockney hulk with a one-inch forehead who survived not by breathing in oxygen but by expelling pure hostility.

Milena had worked as a cleaner for her first ten days in the capital before another Krakow girl had bagged her the nail job. The clients who wanted her to tidy up their homes for two or three hours a morning each week were never good tippers, and in just a week and a half, Milena had got to see the very worst of people's domestic arrangements; the rows, the slovenliness, the endless rounds of blame. At least in the nail salon, people came to be pampered for a while, so they brought their smiles and their tips.

Milena had found an ally in an older Polish girl called Justyna, who was a lot more street-wise and a fair bit older than she was, and it was she who had suggested a Whitechapel rooming house only a few miles away that was full of East European girls just like her. There was apparently quite a Polish community now, and this house was the cheapest and friendliest place from which young women could start out, Bambi-like, on their new lives. Justyna was an inspiration. She now lived in her own flat; and she was working part-time at a private health clinic. The nail salon just offered Justyna the cash for clothes that either sparkled or caused outrage or did both.

Milena loved walking around the wondrous Hawksmoor churches in the area. She would send prayers to her dead parents from the pews worn slim by centuries of parishioners; reading the books of well-wishers' prayers, feeling the heat of the leather-binding; imagining the countless pilgrims that had passed through on their way to a better existence.

It was possible to have quite a walk if you were to visit all of the Hawksmoors in one day – ambling past St Alfege's on the main drag in Greenwich; St George's in Bloomsbury; the imposing Christ Church Spitalfields, which almost seemed on the point of transforming into some 200ft tall Portland stone robot; the bombed-out St George in the East in Wapping, a prayer to the lost in itself; St Mary Woolnoth, close to the Bank of England but still spiritual; and St Anne's in Limehouse, which was Milena's favourite, the first she had visited.

Justyna and two other young Polish women, Maria and Dorota, were Milena's entire social life, and the quartet had become very close, skipping to the National Portrait Gallery to hide away from the rain, giggling on the polished benches or chasing one another through the revolving doors. In fact, to Milena, now she had left the bickering and crabbiness of the English households, the whole of London seemed like an enormous playground. It was far from all the sadness and grief she'd left behind in Krakow.

Nobody remained back in Poland to take her to art galleries or have long picnics with her in the parks until dusk called her home.

London truly was the city for her; every street corner buzzed with opportunity and the echo of history, and everything seemed a grand idea. All those inquisitive explorers had, like her, been drawn to its hum and the history. On one Stepney corner, Milena would imagine a horse-drawn cart standing still as its driver chatted to a maiden with roses in her hair; on another, she'd discern a matchstick girl who then grew into a lady wreathed in lace.

Justyna had just texted to say she was having trouble washing the temporary pink dye out of her hair; she had bleached her russet hair recently to look a little more on point, and the new colour made her jagged cut resemble a vanilla and strawberry ice cream in a broken glass bowl. "Milly," Justyna called out as she marched across the salon, the brass bell still jangling with the force of her entry. "It said two washes and I've shampooed my hair, like, seven times. Last time I buy anything from the market. It was ten pounds, and it's shit."

Justyna slumped into the chair next to Milena and her elderly client. "Don't look at me, old lady!" She paused. "Anyway, Milly, there's a party on Saturday, and the three of us want you to come along and meet our friends."

"I would like to," answered Milena as she delicately pushed back the cuticles of her client who was half-asleep. "I would like to meet new people. Here, around here."

Justyna laughed. "And leave us behind?"

Milena grinned nervously. "I will not leave you. You and Dorota and Maria – you are all my family here. All I have. Even in Poland." She stared at Justyna in the mirror's reflection and tilted her head.

"I was joking, Milly. Jesus Christ, you're so earnest, aren't you? This party will be full of men, rich men – we won't have to bring anything. Come, it's a free night for us." Justyna paused and considered her silver trainers. "We could go to the National Portrait Gallery in the afternoon and then get changed into party-gear in the early evening. I'll do golabki, with mushrooms and rice, and we can watch that singing show. What do you say, Milly?"

"I would like that. I love golabki. But I don't want a man. I have to, how to say?" Milena paused, smiled in the part of the mirror not plastered in ads, and completed her sentence in Polish, "skoncentrowac sie na moim nowym rodzinnym miescle."

"You will get to know London soon – you can't spend your free days in the library or walking around dead churches. You're not like this old lady here. No death any more. You have to live to live in London, right? Please come – for your sisters."

Milena sighed. "I will, if you won't talk too fast." And she smiled again.

Justyna lazily got up from the salon chair. "I'll see you outside St George in the East at 1245 on Saturday; bring some clothes for the party. You understand?"

Milena looked up from her client's hand. "Maria bring my nail kit, please?"

"I'll ask her to bring you an outfit too, just in case you turn up looking like Marie Curie again! Laters, my lovely bitch!" And with that, Justyna gave her friend a full curtsy and ran out of the salon door and up Commercial Road.

"My friend, she is little crazy," Milena apologised to her client, "but she is good." And then she returned to the cuticles, smiling at Justyna's sparkiness and spontaneity. She had much to learn about London life; her new best friend, with her red, pink and yellow hair and sparkling silver sneakers, would prove the ideal guide, if she didn't spin off into the sun with her firecracker outfit ablaze.

On a street parallel to the salon, a rumpled man trudged home, burdened by his internal logic. The belt's going,

Luca thought as he felt the leather. The last hole he had winkled out with his kitchen knife had now split almost all the way across. How had his weight ballooned so much? Did his moobs jiggle as he walked? That girl with the mad pink hair and silver trainers had been giggling as she passed him a minute ago. Was she laughing at him?

Luca was never swimming in confidence; he often thought his soggy face resembled a huge wodge of wet dough into which someone had pea-shootered two piggy peepers of dried currant. Maybe the people Luca met at work warmed to him only because he was so docile and unthreatening, a talking teddy bear there to serve them. But what an unholy mess he was. He was built from tinned meats, a repository of cardboard ready-meals, eaten from a tray on his belly as he flicked through the channels. Mama would be so ashamed of him.

Anyway, the belt would last for the walk home. Luca would soon be away from all eyes, and the sky appeared to be putting on a rosy-fingered flourish just for him. This sunset was making worthwhile all the effort he'd made to integrate himself into East London life. It was a sight that made the capital such a beautiful place to live – the pinks and grey-blues racing in the Thames; the same lights sprinting across the mirrored tower-block windows.

Still, Luca was half-expecting the school-kids' jibes. He was often pestered on the 10-minute walk from his post-office stool to the sofa. "Oi, fatty!" "Big man!" And then, home to a comforting emptiness gone with every bin-emptying? This disposable life – plastic cutlery, cardboard meals, three pants for a pound from Sainsbury's. So many nights Luca had passed out on his black sofa in front of the TV that the left armrest held the imprint of his gigantic boulder of a head, all ten kilos of bonce. It once was full of historical speeches; now this had been replaced by late-night chat-show banter. If his body was in slow collapse,

Where is Your God Now?

like a sandcastle left to the rubbing of the sea, then at least tonight his mind was light and free. If Luca remembered to look at the architecture several storeys above him and the ever-changing skies, then he would not sink into self-pity and self-laceration.

Luca felt like the New Year was a time to be embraced, and on the other side, he'd emerge, if not as a butterfly, then as a better man – worth a swipe right from a tipsy divorcée, worth a chance down the local steakhouse and then a "no, but you're lovely". Luca had never been in shape, but his attempts to contour his chin with a little Nike swoop of facial hair were pointless now, a piss-take. He'd lose a little weight by switching to gin and lime and by walking a longer route home over Vallance Gardens, fewer hours to gorge away.

When Luca was trimmer, he would ask out his colleague; she would bring him treats from her cupcake classes and set them down with attractive purpose on the counter near him. Patricia was her name. She did not seem quite as shot away as he was; in her darker power suits, she had a beautiful formalness. She had the confidence to use every last ounce of whatever physical attributes she'd been graced with, and she was always wrapped in bespoke sandalwood fragrances. Yes, he would take her out once he'd shed a little weight.

There would be no shame in becoming another one of Patty's glorious accessories. Patty was such a pretty name in any tongue. It would sit perfectly next to his on the wedding invitations, and Luca imagined the patter of petals on the hot Italian stone. The late-afternoon rays would break through a high-hanging canopy of oleander and aquilegia, and the priest would utter sacred words as the contract was signed on paper and in the heart.

All these things were immediately drained from Luca's head now as the four breeze-block towers came into view, an apocalypse. Everything in front of him rushed onwards in a dizzying blur. Luca prepared to faint against the high hedge to his left. There was just too much to take in, and his breaths spiralled from his mouth into the coldness of the afternoon.

Two men appeared to be kicking around a pile of clothes, which then rearranged themselves, as if a Rorschach test in fabric. The bundle of rags was, as Luca walked nearer, in fact a small, elderly gentleman. And still the kicks came in, causing the old man's white unicorn horn of hair to swing from side to side like a yacht's boom in the breeze.

Luca stopped his breathing; he was winded as well. Why didn't the thugs hold back? The old guy was offering no resistance. A smudge of scarlet ran across the man's hair now, and his body seemed to reduce with every kick. He was gone already. The blows were contorting the old man's form into impossible poses.

Luca was quite aware he was standing there in plain view of the attackers, but his shoes were glued to the sliding pathway. He looked around the quad with tiny movements of his head. There wasn't a soul around, and there was nothing to hide behind; sooner rather than later, Luca would be spotted. He hadn't the breath to run.

Then a saloon car pulled up to the southern end, and the elderly gentleman's bloodied, wet-towel limbs were bundled onto the back seat. One of his assailants bent down to throw in a loose shoe before taking his place in the passenger seat. Luca looked away again to check if anyone else was taking this in. There was no one.

Luca had stopped walking some time ago, but now he ran. And as the Rover sped past, the thug in the front seat spotted him, smiled and knocked on the window. His jet-black hair was greased into a wave crest and his jet-black eyes were too close to a crooked nose; even his smile was wonky. He waved with a camp flourish as Luca stood there, self-consciously open-mouthed, and then the car was gone, up towards Aldgate East.

Luca trembled as he quickly found his keys and, as quietly as he could manage as his heart thumped away and his breath filled with lunch, he opened the door to his block. He then slumped onto the hallway floor, his head on the hard china of a plant pot.

After a few seconds, conscious of his trousers getting dusty, Luca got up, ran to the lift and jabbed at three buttons, one being his floor. He ran as if with sodden clothes to his front door, raced inside, and then vomited into the bathroom basin. He threw water on his face. As then he wet his head under the shower hose, Luca tried to forget what he had just seen in the courtyard. He murmured the first line of Our Father in his mother tongue.

Luca took a deep breath and set about cleaning the dishes in the sink as a distraction. He must have spilt ketchup from his lunchtime egg roll onto the paisley pattern. He was such an oaf, unable to find the approximate location of his mouth-hole. He'd been walking around all day with that red stain, there to tell everyone that he has given up on himself, that here was a man with no direction. Still, Luca thought, at least he wasn't a thug beating an old man to a pulp; and at least he wasn't the poor bundle of bones and woollen-wear thumped into extinction and then dumped into a car. Should he raise the alarm?

Luca had never seen any of the people in the quad before nor had he seen them on the streets. Why didn't he stop to watch the sky's lightshow? A few minutes later, and the car would have been far away. Anyway, fat old Luca wouldn't have been of any help to the stricken pensioner, except as a temporary distraction; he would've been beaten senseless himself. That Italianate beast was huge, as tall as Luca was wide.

Luca went back into the lounge and tried to drift off on the sofa. Thoughts eddied in his mind – what if the old man was dead now? Did Luca's silence make him an accomplice to the deed? As his mama used to say in the absence of anything insightful, "if in doubt, do". The question now, in the Seventies sparseness of his flat, was – do what?

Luca hadn't seen the licence plate of the Rover. He was half-convinced the car had been silver-blue, or was it grey? Perhaps someone else saw the ruckus from a tower-block window and called the police with a far better description of the vehicle than he could manage. The thugs picked the right spot to dish out a beating – there had been a handbag swiped from the middle of the grass court the week before, and the very centre had been found to be off the CCTV's range. All the parents would be waiting at the school gates, and all the adults would be counting down the clock at work. There was no one.

Luca considered his situation. His job was just to sit at Window 3 for the days, weeks, months, years, and deal with all the international mail that was weighed and sorted by size and destination. Luca wasn't employed to be eagle-eyed; it wasn't in his job spec to act as a human security-camera.

He shuffled out of the kitchen and onto the sofa. If someone else saw the beating, then Luca's testimony might confuse things and reorder the timeline. Fact would become fiction. He was tired; he was not a native speaker; he was not a practical man who made notes of street names, faces seen, cars that parked in regular spots. He was just the loser at Window 3, whose eyes lit up only when Patty brought him some delicacy.

Perhaps I'm best off just forgetting it had ever even happened, Luca thought. It may have been a half-dream, something concocted by his overactive imagination. And if he were to tell the police exactly what he has seen, would he be believed, this crazy fool whose life was lonely enough for fictions to be dreamt up?

Anyway, there would be reprisals – Luca had been spotted by the thug with the set-square for a nose. What was the point? The whole scene wasn't something that Luca ever meant to see, so maybe he should pretend it was a trick of an idling mind?

Then the doorbell sounded, and his life was to take a turn for the worse – at the door stood a man who looked very similar to Luca, an Ernest Borgnine fellow, who scarcely fitted into his well-worn grey suit, a human sausage roll that was all meat and no pastry. His white shirt was stuffed full with the memories of one-too-many business lunches, and his cream-and-orange tie, probably fashionable when ABBA were at the top of the charts, threatened to throttle his face from the top of his head.

"Luca!" The man stepped forward and then stood back, waiting for a sign to enter.

Luca took in the fullness of the man's face, his beetling, mud-guard brows.

"Are you Luca? I'm John, Councillor John Wells when at work," he said. "Are you alone? I am a neighbour, your neighbour."

Luca tilted his head.

"And, son, I have come up to invite you to a little soirée I'm having down below. You're alone?"

"It's late," Luca replied, looking down and regretting his stained tie. "Yes, I am alone." What a redundant question to ask him.

"It is late, I know, but I've been meaning to ask you to come over. There are too many young couples here, and you seem to be more my age."

"I'm in my forties," Luca replied with slight offence.

"Well… I'm 57. I've seen you walking through the quad, always smiling. A man at peace, I'd wager."

Luca beamed and adjusted his shirt collar. He didn't feel like a man at peace, but if he could fake looking relaxed, then perhaps he could hide his secret torment. Had John seen the attack from his flat? Why was he here?

The councillor continued: "Luca, please come – no need to bring anything, as the party is already in swing. We have some glamorous ladies there. Hell, I'm sure you are full of breezy chatter for them."

Luca smiled. "I'll try."

"That's it, son!" John clapped his hands and beamed. Luca was thinking how he was often lost in his thoughts on the way back from the post office. The councillor shouldn't count on him to recognise anyone.

"Councillor, I'll try my best. I'll get my coat. Stay, stay please here."

The councillor held out his soft hand. "I'm going nowhere, my friend. In fact, I might be the best friend you make this year."

Luca went to the bedroom, slipped on his finest leather blouson and scooped up his keys from the top of his hallway cabinet. And with that, the two men walked down the corridor to the lifts and the get-together below.

The party was very much in full swing; an extremely tipsy couple were splayed on the carpet outside the front door, trying to toss a bottle cap into the pot plant beside the lift door opposite.

"It's going a bit Matrix now, Fi," the handsome chap slurred to his Ophelia-like squeeze, who was slumped on his left shoulder, her hair fanned on his damp shirt.

Fi nodded with all her might. "That's the best bit."

"It's the best!" came the young man's howl.

"Joe, that's the rush I wait for, darling."

"Darl... Hang onto the green light, and it'll lift us up way above here." She sighed in ecstasy.

"Excuse me," Luca muttered, but the pair were completely out of this realm, cross-legged on the floor, seeing starships. Luca stepped around them in John's wake as if avoiding landmines.

"Don't mind them," said John. "They've had a little too much of the good stuff." He paused. "Do you find you switch into Italian when you get nervous? I have a colleague who does that. A man of great importance and command, but he still does that." John guided Luca through the door. "Come in, come in."

Inside, most of the guests were in a state of undress, with four young cosmetic-counter ladies sitting on the knees of four impassive men in suits. Someone had hung a black trilby on the silver horn of a rhino head on the far wall, and acid jazz farted from the speakers imbedded in the ceiling. Luca looked towards his new best friend, a little petrified at the frivolity and abandonment.

John took the hint to provide explanation. "Just take what you want – drink, nibbles, girls." He motioned towards the four pancaked women. "These are my friends from far abroad. Anyway, may I get you a glass of red? Or should I say, a bucket of plonk?" He clapped Luca on the back slightly too strongly and headed off to the kitchen behind them. "This is my party pad. Mea casa, tua… You're not Spanish, are you? Ah, what the hell!"

Luca glimpsed a trestle table heaving with vodka bottles, just past a corner sofa where a middle-aged couple were hungrily snogging each other's faces, so both their mascaras had made tracks on their cheeks; a barely clothed man was murmuring in prayer by a floorspeaker. The flat was far larger than his, with a lounge separated from the kitchen, and a yellow diner through the double doors. The whole place looked as ancient as John's striped tie; it didn't matter that the guests were spilling drink and canapés all over the light brown carpet.

Luca contemplated the tableau – was this a circle of Hell? Or was this what an orgy was truly like? One of the heavily made-up, punky ladies, almost transparent and wearing just a black bra and jeans, got up from a gent's knee, sashayed over to Luca and held his hand. "Why no drink in your hand?" She led Luca into the diner, with its extending table and dining chairs. "It's quieter here. I'm Justyna; you must be Luca?"

Luca was puzzled why this attractive lady, at least a decade younger than he was, was being so kind to him, and indeed how she knew of him, but he reasoned that if John was a pal to him, then Justyna was also a friend in waiting. Luca took a glass of merlot from the side unit. It tasted bitter; he winced.

"It'll do," he muttered, being careful not to sound too keen to please or unused to such soirées. Justyna was certainly a rung above his colleague Patricia, even though she had not deigned to wear a top and her hair was a shock of sunset yellows and pinks. Punky. "How long's this party been going on for?" Luca looked back into the lounge where the four men were pawing Justyna's three friends, each man copying the moves of his neighbour, looking through one opened eye, like a quartet of octopi moving over pink coral.

"John throws the very best parties – always discreet – and you'll be amazed who you end up friends with. There are doctors and bankers and politicians, Luca. We are all indebted to the Bish for his kindness. He makes all of us feel welcome, and we all enjoy good health because of his clinics. You know all about them?" Luca shook his head, and Justyna tapped her cigarette into a spare glass.

A man sidled over. "Do you want me to drink this ash, mistress?"

Justyna laughed. "Oh, sod off, Kevin!" The guy in the suit shrank back, and Justyna held out her hand for Luca to lead the way out.

"Luca, I've known John for three or four years, ever since I snapped my knee – look at the scar here – and he does this so that none of us gets too lonely."

"That's nice…" Luca smiled again as he navigated the writhing forms on the rug.

"It's nice, Luca! Even with these tits, I can go days without speaking to anyone. It's a long way from Krakow and we can all get lonely, all of us, right?"

Luca nodded.

"And when you come here and your English isn't so hot, don't people pretend not to understand your words? There were not so many Polish when I first came so I would wander around hoping someone, anyone would ask me for directions or ask me where my bag was from, if my titties were real, just anything. Isn't London such an unfriendly place sometimes, Luca? Like a hungry wolf?"

Luca nodded again, and Justyna continued. "Most people are shits – 'look at me with my fat head, talking to my shithead friends about rubbish.' But here, there is a kind of a secret society of neighbours." Justyna pointed to the trio sprawled on the men's laps. "Those three girls are from the 12th floor in the east block, all Polish as well. I bet you haven't even seen them before, yet they've lived here for a month."

"I've never seen them in my life," Luca said, sadly. They were truly lovely-looking women in his eyes. Why were they with those losers?

"Well, Luca, the three of them work or used to work in a nail salon on the other side of Commercial Road, and they are just lovely. Without this party, they fall through the cracks in the pavements. They would be lost girls. The wolf would have eaten them all up." And Justyna then made munching sounds.

She caught Luca's frown, for he had been haunted by similar thoughts, nightmares where he disappeared under the concrete.

Justyna continued: "The first anyone would know if these three women were to disappear would be when the money stopped coming home, to Krakow, to Worclaw, Poznan and Gdansk. That's if they have anyone back in Poland; many don't. The same cracks through which they come, the same cracks through which they arrive here to make what money they can, those same cracks are the ones through which they later fall. The cracks draw in the light, and they suck the light out."

"I see the darkness." Luca was on the verge of tears.

"Hey… It's OK. It's just… My Polish friends would be lost girls. Do you think that these kinds of people ever show up on the census? Do you think the policemen give a shit about these girls when they get lost?"

A cloud rolled across Luca's ever-expressive features, and Justyna halted her rant, placing a hand on the sleeve of his blouson. "Sorry, I'm being a downer. You still have your tie on. Take it off."

Luca fumbled with the garment and put it in his pocket. "I do extra work sometimes because I live alone."

"You're single then?" Justyna's hand was rising up the leather of Luca's sleeve.

Luca couldn't believe that John hadn't informed the partygoers of his availability. "Yes, I'm very single, Justyna. Is that right – 'very single'?"

"Yes," Justyna was staring into Luca's hazel eyes, which made him sweat even more. "Most of us here are single, and even the couples like Joe and Fi outside the door met here at these parties. They are English aristocrats; you wouldn't believe it, eh? They leave their manners in the bottom of the glass, just like Joe's parents over in Turin. 'Niedaleko spada jabłko od jabłoni' – 'the apple does not fall far from the tree'. Joe's father, Ronald, was a friend of John, but he took the piss with the free stuff."

"And he now lives in Turin? That's my home city." Luca smiled. "It's a good place for retirement."

"Oh, Joe's father is now permanently retired. He's dead – and Joe's mama, too. They won't be enjoying the food and the scenery in Italy. Nothing to see but soil and tree roots!" Justyna let out a laugh and then stopped herself. "I don't think Joe's ever sober enough to know that his parents are dead. He's away on permanent vacation." Justyna paused. "So, you're tired? You want to head off to bed then? There are three beds here."

"No, I just need to catch up." Luca twitched.

"Do you ever relax?"

"I can't relax. If I keep my head down, maybe I will see the pavement, you know? It won't eat me."

And then Justyna's hand reached up and turned Luca around by the shoulder, so he could see for himself the last moments of one of the Polish girls, as the four men held her down and suffocated her with a cushion until she stopped twitching and fell between the shoes of the murderers. One of the other Polish girls picked off the dead woman's silver earrings and then kicked her over onto her face, muttering "Dorota, stupid bitch". Then everyone went back to their partying, totally expressionless, except one girl, Milena, who launched herself off the sofa and bolted for the front door, scrabbling across the spilt wine and static carpet.

"Where the hell is she off to?" said one of the male guests. He threw his full wine glass against a wall. Again, no one reacted.

John stepped forward. "She's going nowhere." He grabbed the man by the arm. "Who's she gonna tell? Who's gonna to believe some illiterate Krakow bitch?"

The man with the mascara nodded at him. "I've got ears and eyes on her, John." The councillor smiled and punched his left bicep. "Stay cool, chief."

Luca took Justyna's hand off his shoulder and looked down at his glass, the wine high-walling around the sides like a daredevil rider on the Wall of Death. He vainly tried to stop his shaking with his other hand. Inside his head, that first line of Our Father repeated itself, faster and faster until it became as scrambled as his thoughts.

Luca hoped the woman being bundled into a bathroom by two of the guys was an orphan. Her death had been painless, so, too, he hoped, would be her absence. Luca caught himself in a mirror and looked away in disgust.

"As you can see, Luca," Justyna explained softly to jolt him from his suppositions, "there are reasons for keeping silent. We know what you saw in the quad. Let this be a warning to you. We look after our little gang." Justyna paused. "Isn't that right, John?"

John had ghosted up to Luca's other shoulder, and the councillor's face was now rearranged from free joviality into stone. He looked at Justyna and gave her a slow, evil grin. "Oh, yes. It's a very tight little gang, my darling Justyna." John turned to Luca. "And you, our new friend, you must drink your glass and then another to forget all about your troubles."

The councillor started singing, "We could float among the stars together, you and I. For we can fly, we can fly, up, up and away, my beautiful, my beautiful balloon. The world's a nicer place in my balloon." John nodded to Justyna. "Just take him now and screw him senseless." The wolf had come again.

The lushes.

The salon was bright in its slightly dated, poppy way. There were a few too many Ikea floating shelves holding plastic plant pots, but it looked fresh that day. However, the bedsit at the back where Nena slept was testament to a life lived without any restraint. Pizza boxes formed a side table by her sofa bed, and the sink was full of vodka miniatures that jangled whenever she washed her hands.

Thank god, Nena's parents weren't around to witness all this: her mother's moral rectitude and God-fearing ways had survived the long crossing from Kingston, Jamaica; and her Kentish father would never let Nena forget the privations and flat-out hostility his wife had faced as a dark-skinned woman in 1950s Folkestone. Harry would provide a safety net, a silent force-field, for Maisie for all his adult life until her lungs gave in to the endless lighting of her untipped cigarettes. Then, without its guiding light, Harry's heart had wound itself down into obsolescence, his own work done.

It was down to their legacy that Nena even had this little apple-crate salon that sat at the foot of a hill. As she swept away the hair she had clipped that day, she hid and scanned the walkers at the salon window. Lovers in matching Pac A Macs held hands and discussed a route to the harbour through the ruins of the rain. The drizzle was pooling in the potholes as it coursed downhill to the seafront. Nena imagined the water growing ever more forceful until it was strong enough to sweep the buses sideways into the Channel; his 'n' hers rain-jackets won't help you now, darlings.

The bank's begging letters piled up by the copies of Grazia and Cosmo, though they weren't bills but offers of swanky credit cards. Nena could dismiss all this. Work was going well, in what she called 'funeral season'. This was when the old dears turned blue with the Channel winds that whipped in down Sandgate Hill, and their friends would come to Nena for an elaborate hairdo to send off the dearly departed with some kind of ceremony or swing-band night. Her clients were a good laugh and generous tippers, but they too were dying with every passing month.

Everywhere Nena turned, the boy's absence was there. As her confidant Christian Cadwick had once said, his vanishing act had become a big deal only because everything else in her life was dull. Live your life in a cave, and even a drip of water becomes an event. To lead such a solitary life was Nena's choice, though, and it was her way of convincing herself that she was keeping control of a life once atomising, now fossilising.

Today was just another day; same customers, same cuts, same routine. Nena kept her public life spotless, but behind the bead curtain was chaos. She was 38 now. Nothing much had changed in the previous 18 or 19 years; she still held the outside world at arm's length. She was content to be an observer from her salon; she saw the couples enticed by how many square feet you could buy in Folkestone for half-a-million grand. Perhaps Nena wanted some of that, but what was it worth to her?

The sturdy, shiny chrome handle on this bucket of bubbling ordure was her best friend, Cadwick, a public schoolboy and womaniser. Like the overnourished Scotty dog he closely resembled, he wasn't often awake and could sleep anywhere flattish. Cadwick was rarely sober, but he was amusing. He had inherited a pile of money, but he invested his cash wisely in property, so he went on to make even more.

Even Cadwick was now bored by Nena's obsession with a past he didn't share. He would sometimes complain when he found himself unfortunately sober, but he was playing the romantic long game. He kept on and on like one of those wind-up cars that careens into the skirting-boards and then blasts off in another direction. On and on, he kept at the hard chase, despite Nena's unremitting friend-zoning. So Cadwick chose simply to get wrecked, and this he did splendidly well, slumping into drunkenness with a seal's lubricated slide.

"Do you like my new cap?" Cadwick now stood in the salon doorway, brushing his wool blazer free from the drizzle. His tweed cap was already damp through and perching on his overly large but cherubic head like a slab of butter on a baked spud.

"It's all right, but your eye's going lazy again." Cadwick's left peeper would start having a chat with his left ear when he was tired, drunk or both – Nena assumed he was tired since it was only 11.30am. "Are you shopping without me? Why are you wearing that cap?"

"This cap?"

"Yes, of course, that cap. You look like one of those sad teddies that grannies buy in the backs of the Sunday magazines. For God's sake, Cadders – why the cap?" She stopped washing out the basin and put the nozzle back in its holster.

"The cap's a gift from a girl I met at the property auction…" Cadwick started.

"A gift from a grown-up girl? Or a ten-year-old niece who's dressed you up like her teddy bear?" Nena chuckled, and went to flip her friend's soaked hat. He dodged her.

"No, a real woman. She's Jacqui. It's spelt with a Q," Cadwick announced smugly, but Nena was sure that Jacqui and her Q were fictions. Nena, and everyone around the pair of them, knew he hankered after her affections. "Are you saying you want to dress me up yourself, gal? I have the afternoon free, you see."

Cadders was always free after midday; he awoke with the sunrise and never bothered with breakfast or gym sessions, so he packed his seven or eight hours of property management into the morning. For the rest of the day, he was just on call until the gin tethered his mouth shut and his typing fingers became a mush.

Nena wasn't up for a shopping spree. "We buy enough tat as it is – I'm getting skint again. I'd be twice as rich if wine were free."

Cadwick fished around in his vinyl record bag; there were never had any LPs in it. "Free booze!" he cried, with a gin bottle in each hand. "Join me for a drink?" He cocked his head, cocker-like, and his whole body turned into one little fat question-mark.

"Yes, let's have hair of the dog, Cadders," Nena said. "The old gals aren't picking up their pensions till tomorrow."

"I can see there's no carpet of hair." Cadders looked down at the floor.

"Well, it was busy yesterday. I didn't stop for lunch. I spent ages on the Brillo nape of an old boy; he had the most divine eau de cologne. I couldn't halt from trimming away because the scent was just so beautiful, like mahogany. Any longer and the man would have expired."

"You know, I scour the obituaries in the local press, hoping that God has struck down a patisserie crammed with well-heeled pensioners so you can primp their friends and loved ones for the burial. I've become a serial killer of the elderly, like Harold Shipman."

"Shipman was better groomed than you. And he probably had more friends."

"This is what our friendship has driven me to, Nena. Shame on you." He smiled.

"Cadders, you're annoyingly full of vim today."

"That I am."

"You must be head over heels in love – or still sloshed from last night."

"It's Jacqui," Cadders beamed.

"Who is this mystery woman? Can she dismantle a Mini engine with her pelvic-floor muscles? Does she have child-rearing teeth, gleaming with fecundity?"

"Jacqui has a lovely smile when she remembers to close her mouth."

"Should I be buying a hat?"

Cadwick slumped into the nearest chair to take the weight of his latest hangover off his feet. "No, no hat-buying is needed. We've just had a few nights out – low-level fun and games. I don't know what her grip is like, alas."

"Well, I am all ears." Nena walked over to the door, a little groggily, and turned the slateboard sign from Open to Closed, and the two friends retired to the back room, arm in arm across the chequered floor and laughing at nothing in particular.

Inside her den, Nena began fiddling with her radio, plastered in dust and god knows what – a film? Probably, the detritus of all their lost afternoons and evenings that were gone without count.

"How do I turn this off?"

"Why?" asks Cadders. "This is a classic. A pop-jazz gem." It was Fields of Gold.

"I hate Sting. The only thing he should be mechanically and endlessly shagging is his pointy wife, not my ears." She managed, with no little surprise at her own efforts, to change stations to classical music. The knob still works, Nena thought, under all that chaotic glue.

"Jacqui's trying to sell Rathebone. It's the mansion that Led Zeppelin owned in the Seventies. You won't know it, Nena, but you will have heard of Zep. Song Remains the Same. Lots of hair, lots of denim, lots of fish in unlikely places. Try them.'

"I don't really know Led Zeppelin, though I've always liked the name," Nena replied. "They're a very blokeish band; the songs do all sound exactly the same. I agree with them there."

Cadwick was waggling his little boneless, porky hand around to heighten his words. "This is a fantastic old pile of great, great architectural significance. The mist just sweeps in and covers the whole house with the finest of coatings. It's a lost world, Jacqui says."

Nena mocked his enthusiasm: "Jacqui says!' Jacqui with a Q says!"

Cadders ignored this and stared at the footprint on the wall opposite him, above the sofa. "Have you been shagg..?" He stopped. "When? Who was the shaggee?"

"What?"

Cadders changed subject, artlessly. "I mean, the place is on a vast scale, and the same old poor lady has been scrimping and saving to get the old gal right. She'll shine."

"Rathebone? Or Jacqui?" Nena joked, but Cadders was not amused.

"Jacqui's a good decade younger than even your fair self, so stop taking the piss, miss."

"Yes, father!"

Cadders frowned. "For such a young lady to have the sales mandate for a stately house like Rathebone, well, it is admirable."

"What?"

"I said it's admirable for a young lady to have such responsibility for sale," Cadders repeated. "That footprint is yours?"

"What footprint?" Nena replied, the mark behind her head. She turned around to find a clay smudge. "Oh yes, I was doing handstands last night. Was a bit bored."

Cadders frowned before continuing. "Jacqui has something about her, so maybe she could sort my life out."

"She's not a magician, is she? And if she is, then could she cast a spell to update this salon, pretty please? The old boy said it looked like a 'blushed mausoleum'. Looks grand."

"Nena, shush. Everything's not exactly bloody ordered, is it?"

"You live well, Caddyshack…"

"I live in chaos, Nena. I accept that, I read the contract. But Jacqui seems to be a proper grown-up, despite her youth. She's rather like my mother."

"So, you're about to start dating your mother?" Nena had seen the photograph in Cadwick's wallet – his sturdy mater in a wagon-wheel-brimmed hat, towering over the teenage Cadders in his tweed school uniform at some prize day, her jaw as sturdy as a B-movie cowpoke's. How could a mother so forbidding produce a man so minuscule?

"Jacqui's nothing like Penny," Cadwick protested. "Jacqui's blonde for starters, and she's always in business clothes. Her parting is immaculate, like it's been, I don't know, crafted with a nit-comb under a microscope."

"What the hell are you on about now?" Nena snorted.

Cadders again sighed. "Jacqui has a lofty outlook. It makes a difference from the Folkestone girls I tend to end up with. It's always after getting pissed with you."

Nena laughed. "Oh, I don't know. Despite yourself, you've pulled some aces from these wide, barren pastures. You've gone some of the way with a few thoroughbreds. It's more the case that you fail to complete the deal. You put in all the chat, pay for the whole night and then forget to bring them home to your lair."

"I do tend to pass out, it's true," Cadwick agreed.

"It's like when I came around and you cooked that lovely chicken and tarragon supper you always do, Cadders – and you blacked out on the kitchen tiles. So, I had to tuck your giblets away with a pair of tongs and get a taxi home after putting a blanket on you. It's amusing how you fall at the last hurdle."

Cadders threw another Schweppes bottle-top into the waste bin, missed and muttered. "Well, no more Carry-home Cadders now. I fly like an eagle now."

"Don't believe it…" Nena tilted her head in scorn.

"Look, gal, thing. I've slid off my last banquette, dribbled my last goodbye to the bar staff. This Jacqui is worth shaping up for. I am getting as healthy as a fish. Feel?" And Cadders pulled a flabby bicep for Nena's amusement. "You'll have noticed that I've cut my drinking over the past fortnight or so?"

"Not really," Nena answered truthfully. "I've noticed that you're drinking more slowly, but the amount… the sum remains the same."

"Droll. I drink far less! I'll show you the receipts."

"Cadders… It just takes you an extra ten minutes to drain your tumbler dry. Look," she pointed at her own bottle of Hendricks, "we've both had a half. You're a bit behind me."

"Look, a half-bottle's not a lot. It isn't," Cadwick said. "Medicinal, warming."

"We'll have a half again, and then we'll both flake out. You'll wake up before me and then you'll put the fleece on me and wobble out of the front door. You'll hit each shoulder on the same lamp-post. You will expertly hail a taxi – you will then fall asleep with a full pint of water on your bedside table and an open Miller's Antiques as your companion. Ever think we're a terrible example to one another? Enablers of a daily car crash?"

Cadders leant back into the sticky sofa bed, leaned back up, went down and sighed. "I don't think the time we share is wasted, Nena. It's playtime. Look…"

"Stop saying 'look'! We're lushes. We waste our hours."

Cadders sighed again. "I mean, we may be wasted, but our hours aren't – we act as soi-disant counsellors for one another."

"Soi-disant? You poncey lush," Nena laughed. She felt the hiss of the booze flick up in her veins. Bingo, there'd be no half-dreams that night; she wouldn't sleep and see a future that never would be.

Carryhome-Cadders carried on. "Can you imagine the sheer carnage we'd create across old Folkestone town if we unleashed our true, sodden selves on the unsuspecting public? Me, chatting to a woman who had given up at my very first slurred anecdote?"

"But you admit that you drink just as much, but more slowly?" Nena laughed and brushed Cadders's hair from his moistening forehead. She wiped her hand on the sofa.

"I am trying to change my ways, gal – I realise our life really isn't the world's cup of tea. We're characters, are we not? We belong to a different time-frame, decade. Wevs."

Nena threw a bottle top at her friend. She started gut-guffawing. "Wevs?"

"Shush now. Do you think it's normal for two friends in their mid- to late-30s to get through so much gin every afternoon?"

"It works for us. I don't give a tin shit whether the losers on the high street think we're salting our lives away. Don't you think we might be social Kryptonite to the world?"

"So, after all that time I've been trying to please every Tom and Dick, you and I are outsiders? Really?"

"What am I meant for, Cadders, if not to laugh at you?"

"You could get married? Be a wife? Be the boss? Learn to smile and wear some colour?"

"Cads, my other reality is gruesome, doing laundry, watching the soaps, topping up an Irish coffee or three from a bottle in the washer-dryer."

"Better than being holed up here."

Nena got serious. "I want to laugh; I don't want to be at a mummy-meet. I don't even have the patience for my boss-eyed de Bergerac."

Cadwick laughed: "You mean me?" He paused. "Are you feeling smashed?"

"A little, that's the point. Gin means grins. Grins mean... winning at life. My mother didn't suffer being called the Lilt Lady down the Co-Op for me to be bothered by some bovine shitwit thinking I'm a drunk."

"I'd have liked your mum Maisie, I think. Don't think she'd've liked me much – entitled little posh tit."

"You're really not like that, Cads."

"Well, my mates are. My friends are buying different, vastly costly ways of avoiding their shrew-like wives – 50 rounds of golf a week, 3,000-mile road-trips in their very slow classic cars. Avoidance rather than alimony and a lack of child access."

Nena laughed. "Bit harsh on your imaginary friends." She paused. "The right way would be the wrong way for us. Anyway, everyone should wait until their thirties to marry. I saw it written in some freesheet shit put through my door. Take the crap out when you go?"

Cadders nodded and keep nodding with the weight of his head. "You expect by doing what's expected of you that your life will be great. But really, you have to possess no plans. Que sera sera and all that."

"I have no expectations of anything. Look at my free swim. 'Front crawl. Turn.'"

"Fling your aspirations into the deep blue sea. You can have all the plans in the world, but if you yourself are inflexible, they will shatter and fall. Be an eel. Be floppy."

"Be this, be that," Nena interrupted, "without ever being yourself. When a woman reaches 35, she's not looking for a horny-handed farmboy to drag her into bed and ravish her. She's looking for a little conversation to collapse the blah into something manageable."

Cadders snorted into his beaker.

"And, well, she expects the ravishing and the farmboy, too. Every little helps."

Cadders tapped his foot on the tiles to regain the floor. "I'm open to everything. I don't know what my political or social or religious views are, but I feel like I'll never fall."

"You were schooled to have great faith in yourself, Little King Shit. Your motto?"

Cadwick frowned. He looked again at the foot smudge.

"You have confidence, my lad. Public-school coin pays for that. The rest of us only have confidence until the first sight of the outside world baring its fangs."

"Nena, now... That isn't confidence; it's actually something like a narrowness of vision. I just have fun. I got tired of control, of expectation. Me, a banker? Would Jacqs ever look twice at a drunken little baldy with a lazy left eye if she didn't see my sense of fun?"

"She sees your massive piles of money instead?" Nena chuckled. "She looks past your big old hairy arse and sees your big old pile of cash. When she kisses those monkey ears of yours, she's looking at her future wealth, just over your shoulder. Crisp notes. Piles of them. Fahsands of 'em."

"Jacqs has her own money, Nena. She's not like the women you push my way."

Nena's smile dropped. "What do you mean by that, Cadders? You're hardly Brad Pitt!"

"Am I not?" Cadders was talking at Mach 2 now, just as squiffy as his drinking buddy. "The chicken-tikka-tan ladies who hang around here. Trish, Tania, Trina, Tina, Tits McGhee. Some women like the fact that I am a good listener. I listen and I nod. I am all ears when you drone on and on about this Camelot you had in the 1990s? I wasn't even a part of that time."

Nena smiled. "I'm aware that I'm a massive bore."

"No, no. You're a gem of a girl, but you need to move on. I can smell the dust on you. This salon's like a 1994 episode of some shit MTV makeover programme."

"And you're Janet Jackson?"

Cadders laughed. "No wardrobe malfunction here – well, maybe, the hat."

"My dear balding friend, I'm sure Jacqs knows she has a little diamond in you."

"Really?"

"A treasure, a gem, Gollum's best find. Well, maybe a malfunctioning Tamagotchi."

Inwardly, though, Nena wondered just how different this vision of Jacqui was from the real thing; no martial artist of 25 would ever be entrusted with the sale of a stately home designed by the same mind that had dreamt up the US Capitol. If Jacqui did indeed exist as flesh and form, weaving her Mini cabriolet through the Georgian streets on her way to yet another property viewing and more grinning and handshakes, then she was likely to be 52, not 25, and busty in the Hattie Jacques, matronly sense.

Nena would bet serious cash on Jacqui's only martial-art manoeuvre being the breaking of a chocolate wafer in twain after a hard day's haranguing.

Besides, it was well known in their louche circles that Cadwick could bullshit for Blighty, especially when the booze was shutting down his right eye and the left was glad-eyeing his earhole. This talk of Jacqs had all the hallmarks of premier-cru Cadders, blather and a busload of bollock-wash, but when the little man was being earnest, his hands would form a steeple, as they now were. The lovable lush was telling the truth, damn him.

"Anyway, Nena. What I mean to say, is – do you want to meet her? Jacqs? Do you?"

"Yes, yes! Sounds like she'll bring a little shake to Sandgate…"

"She'll bring more than a bit of shake; she'll rock the shit out of these old rocks!" Cadders exclaimed. "I'm smitten, I'll let you know. I've cancelled my Soulmates account."

"Oh, good," Nena muttered. "I really mean, I'm pleased for you. Yay."

Cadders clapped his hands. "Jacqui is very much what I need. It's only my brief flash of work in the morning that keeps me from becoming like one of your grey-bollocked clients. As I filled out my dating profile again, I realised that I spend an astonishing amount of time just talking absolute bollocks, sitting in my peacock wicker chair, sunning my balls. I finish my errands by half ten."

"Errands? You're not Mary Poppins!"

Cadders brought the back of his hand to his perspiring forehead and then dried it on the thighs of his micro-cords. "Look, I need a woman by my side. My sheet anchor, my lodestar..."

"You sound like Jane Austen. John Exh-austen."

Cadwick's voice fell almost silent. "Listen..." His hands formed another steeple. "Um, I know this is going nowhere, and, try as I might, and I've truly tried, I can't turn your mind. I see a woman who needs..."

"Cadders, we really don't have to discuss this again, do we?" Nena braced herself for yet another conversation about how perfectly the pair of them got on, how it might be worth a try as a couple, before it would all end an hour later with the promise never to jeopardise their wonderful friendship. The pair of them would then studiously avoid the subject for another three weeks until the cycle dropped down from Cloudcuckooland with an elephantine thud, and it all began again.

"No, the game is up, Nena. I should have read the signs long ago. Why bother?"

Nena put her hand on his clammy paw. "This is the booze talking."

"I feel it. I feel what an arse I am. How naïve and powerless I am, despite everything, like a baby crowned king."

Nena closed her eyes. "We talk about this every month. Please stop."

And, deep in his heart, beside his ever-struggling innards, Cadders knew that they would have made for a terrible duo, mired in lethargy until they'd both turned yellow and his leg had to be cut off. Nena would be there, be pushing him around in a wheelchair, the pair of them drunk. He saw how he'd end up stranded on the roundabout by the war memorial; the laughing tourists would be chucking their pennies and beer tops into his crap hat, thinking him a veteran, well, perhaps a veteran of one too many bar fights.

In my time of need.

Milena sat in black among the shadows at the back of St Alfege's in Greenwich. The Hawksmoor church had been named after the Archbishop of Canterbury who was martyred on that very site a thousand years earlier. This time, she was praying not for the memory of her dear-departed parents but for Dorota and for her own survival. In the quiet of the church, she knelt on the prayer cushion, trying to banish the last moments of her friend the night before, the sounds of her struggle for life, spluttering under the grips of those men.

Milena begged the saint for protection from whatever dark forces had been unleashed at the party. A noxious cloud now seemed to fill every corner of every street of a city that had only a day earlier held such promises for her; this blackness had followed her through the back streets of Limehouse, Deptford and old Greenwich as she walked to the church. Everything the cloud touched dripped black. As she walked close to the flint walls for their support should she faint, Milena would now and then look back to see if she was being followed – she would catch only this unholy miasma, leaving the trees drenched in tar and the pavements filthy and oily with its evil, all-embracing presence.

Most troubling to Milena were the reactions of Justyna and Maria to their so-called friend's suffocation. She couldn't run to them now; Maria had even stolen Dorota's earrings, kicked her over onto her face in death. How could her girls be so callous? Were they just playing along to save their own skins? In the absence of a flicker of care, the pair of them must be in on whatever was happening with councillor John Wells and his pack of inspectors, sergeants and detectives. Milena had nowhere to turn; her family had revealed themselves as the molls of murderers.

The only partygoer to show any degree of shock or concern for Dorota's fate had been the strange, tubby man in the blouson. He'd been led away by Justyna almost at once, but Milena had caught his face collapse in on itself, his hands shaking until the wine sploshed over the sides of his glass and wetted them in crimson. His appalled expression was unforgettable; its contortions were everywhere in her nightmares. This man was clearly not one of John's immoral gang; he was the only other person who shared her revulsion, and Milena would keep walking and walking the toxic streets until she came across the face that was haunting her so. She would not rest until she spoke to the man who might lend a friendly ear to her horror and lead her out of her nightmares.

Anyway, Milena would not feel safe in her Whitechapel rooming house – she couldn't go home again after escaping the party and collecting a bag of belongings, her passport and her visa. That unholy gang knew who she was, but they would only know where she was if she stopped walking as quickly as she should, hugging the cold walls of the loneliest streets, head down and wrapped in her darkest shawl.

And if we meet again.

I'd fallen asleep in the wingback without drawing the curtains, so the very first flash of morning slapped me awake in the chops – the dawn here always was a treat for the early-risers in their windcheaters and cable knits. I ate half a pork pie from a paper plate, so I didn't have to wash any crockery and I could spare myself the recurring thought of my mother standing there with her Marigolds on. All those days I could have made a surprise visit and waved hello to her through that kitchen window, gone.

Every time I attempted to shut down my thoughts, I'd see the sleeping bearded man in the photos. Perhaps the Polaroids were connected to the life I had in Piedmont or maybe it was just a prank, something to startle me back to an irresponsible existence. It would be just like Tommy to make a serious point with a jape or a joke. After twenty years in one another's pockets, there was sure to be some fallout from the change in our circumstances.

The trouble with the theory of a prank was that the room, the lounge, in the photos didn't look Italian – this room was carpeted, not covered in marble, a shocking green carpet. The sofa, too, spilling its intestines, was as mumsy as an angel finger.

I put the kettle on the stove and flipped a teabag into the old British racing green Jaguar mug into which my father would pour morning cocoa. The radio warned that the bright morning would turn into unrelenting rain, which the wind would send arrowing almost horizontally into the slats of the cabin, threatening to bust the nails out from the century-old pine.

I reached over to take the photos out of the Jiffy bag, praying that the image of the grungy, bearded Jesus laying across the nasty carpet had been an illusion manufactured by my exhaustion – but, no, the guy was still face down on the floor, this lumberjack picked up by a Deep South typhoon and dumped there in the lounge of a blank suburbia. There was no one else in shot. The chap seemed like a ghost figure transported from the early 1990s. He'd be pissed off to hear that Kurt Cobain had left himself dead in the same prone position.

And even now, nothing in the photo suggested this was a joke by Mimi either. Indeed, there was no evidence that she'd ever been there – there was no Dubonnet aperitif, no pile of frilly scatter cushions clogging up the spots where one would hope to sit down, and no dollified Westie dog in the corner farting himself to sleep – it wasn't her cottage. One could sniff her booze fumes even in a photograph; the Dubonnet would make the corners curl up. Although a trail of destruction often followed in the wake of that one-woman Waco, Mimi was incapable of tossing a sofa over with enough force to tear it until its cumulonimbus filling poured out.

Ah well, I thought, enough sleuthing; I had a whole town to reacquaint myself with. Perhaps some forgotten face would gift me another memory of the way my parents had been or bolster my own recollections of Alistair and Sandy. I would have to brave Sandgate anyway for supplies at some point. I would try to scour the teashops for a light lunch on a chequered tablecloth, overlooked by crap local paintings of pierrots. The village was such an agreeable place, so unburdened by the relentless charge of modernisation, I now felt like a fool for abandoning it in favour of Turin. It was like leaving your Nan at a rainy bandstand to go and chat up some busty sort.

Sandgate was only 30 kilometres from the coastline of France, but it could not be less cosmopolitan. There were two pubs, a post office-come-car boot sale, a butcher's, three grocers and a dry-cleaner's run by family friends –

the usual spread of small businesses. It had been that way for centuries. Nothing ever happened. The newspaper had long since gone bust, ossifying through the lack of drama, and the most excitement came when the sea waves breached the thick stone walls and turned the high street into a paddling pool. The water would put the no.16 bus out of action and kiss the stone skirts of Sandgate Castle.

With Dad's old blue Barbour flapping around me like a windsock of sorts, I set off back on the way I had come the evening before, along the flattened grass paths back to the stile that was, these days, covered in lovers' graffiti.

A mile away, Nena was on a mission to complete all her errands that morning. First off, she would suck on a breath mint to mask the gin fumes and then pop around to the dry-cleaners to drop off a dress that she had torn when falling off her couch. The large-eared couple who ran the shop were always kindly to her, although she suspected that they had built up a very sound picture of exactly how derailed her life had become. The Coupers would just bicker with one another about the mundanity of their work, thinking no one could hear them in the back room. Their bulldog Bristow had an especially careworn face for the breed, as if resigned to his fate as a mute agony-uncle.

Yet Nena had once hoped for a co-dependent life like that of the Coupers, with their ears like tubas full of wheatsheaves blocking out any nonsense from the world. Nena sometimes imagined a life with a fellow hairdresser who would share her bed and the salon and help her with all the tedious admin that accumulated around even such a tiny business. One could build a tower 15 storeys high with all the paperwork that was shoved through her door from the Inland Revenue and Folkestone District Council, and she kept an overstuffed ceramic pot full of her many receipts. Please, Nena begged, please, someone, come and share in this shit-shovelling; at times, she spent more hours tallying up and logging her earnings than she did cutting grey-white hair.

Nena took the ticket for the Zara dress off Mr. Couper and headed off to the butcher's along the uneven cobbles from Napoleonic times, always cleaned by the little green electric wagon. Here, the seagulls stood on the pitched roofs like elderly generals, wings tucked back in observation, twitching their wing feathers like itchy trigger-fingers; here, the talk was reassuringly bland and soft-edged – minimum info, minimum offence.

The swift-approaching weather squits made it vital that Nena got everything out of the way. She would sit and watch a film on the old movie channel and grill a lamb cutlet for supper, the one she was going to cook for Cadwick before he had got too drunk even to sit up, let alone hold her one serviceable pair of cutlery. A bottle of merlot would then send her sweetly to the land of nod – and much of the grape would no doubt end up on another dress to take to the ever-discreet Coupers. Maybe Nena should just begin to squeegee her clothes into a goblet and save a fortune on plonk and laundry bills. The coming squall would cloak Nena in silence, inside her salon, at the back behind the beads. This was how she liked it. The less human contact she had, the less chance there was for a faux-pas.

And then Nena saw him, her mystery boy, the cause of almost all of her heartbreak, the ghost who flitted around her life's periphery, the subject of 10,000 hallucinatory afternoons. He almost didn't seem the same person; his blue eyes pushed into the centre of his face by chubbiness so they appeared reduced in size; his once-strong, dark-blond eyebrows sparse with age; his hair swept across his forehead to disguise its thinness; and his body bulkier, bursting at the buttons of his pale blue shirt, his gut rolling over the top of his dark-tan cord trousers. A tatty old wax jacket fluttered around this corpulence but couldn't hide it. He looked as if he hadn't slept for the 18-odd years he'd been gone; deep, dark rings were under those famous blue eyes. Then Nena noticed that he was smiling at her.

It was half past ten in the morning, and the pair of them stood without a murmur on the pavement, gunslingers without firearms, both wondering why the other remained stock still. The pavement, to both, appeared to be shifting, sliding down the hill and off into the sea.

I studied the lines of Nena's face and her chrome-brown eyes – with age, her features had closed up and softened. She no longer resembled some well-fed Caribbean heiress with her cappuccino skin and ski-jump nose, but a wholesome schoolmistress, with not a spare ounce of fat remaining in the pursuit of healthy mind and body. Her eyebrows no longer seemed to belong to someone else, tamed flat with a little too much Vaseline, and the puppy fat had shifted from around her jawline. I thought of my own paunch, a sandbag I had been humping around since stopping any nod to exercise.

"You haven't changed much," I told her, although she was markedly better-looking, and Nena replied without a breath, "Well, you have. All those years breaking you down at once?" Ah, she was as intuitive and direct as ever.

"I've been thinking the same," and I smiled weakly, though any goodwill wasn't returned.

We were standing on the cobbled pavement, just across from the shop that appeared to be about to take off with all the silver-skinned balloons tethered to the pale-blue weatherboarding. I could feel the breath of a storm rolling in from the way of the Imperial Hotel some two miles west, and the sycamore leaves whirled around the drain cover every few seconds or so, like children busying themselves with play when their parents begin to quarrel again.

"You know, the last thing I would've expected, aside from Hailey's Comet destroying us – the last thing I would have expected was you standing here 18 years on. But here you are, alive and plumpish. Where the hell have you been? And why bother to return? I thought this place was never big enough, too mousy for the starboy?" Nena stretched that last word out to accommodate a full vat of scorn. My insides gulped.

"It's been 19..." I stuttered, disputing the facts in vain hope of heading off Nena's imminent assassination of whatever character I had left. It was futile.

"No, it has been 18 years, 18 long years."

"Ok, 18…"

"Where have you been? Off to Kabul with an Olivetti typewriter on your back and a Triumph between your thighs?"

"No, I-"

"Why bother returning to these folk like the Coupers and me who are too little for the vast expanses of your dreams, eh? You bloody deluded idiot."

"I've been working away…"

Life had got in the way in my twenties, and then a lethargy had been dragged in from the streets by my thirties. Into the cast-iron lift to the first floor, it had come rolling into my pit like an overstuffed beanbag; it had pitched into Tommy's apartment at the darkest hour and onwards into the tomb of my room, and it smothered me in my sleep. 'Here lies Sam, suffocated by lethargy until he forgot even how to breathe.' And yet, what good are anyone's ambitions in the face of life going on all around them?

Nena carried on: "No one said a word about you after a while. Even your parents had lost any care they had for the starboy…" Her soft voice trailed off. She stared at me with an unwavering scowl.

I could feel my eyes darken from the centre outwards as they always did when I was angered, my pupils growing enlarged until my whole eye was a ball of bitumen. "Let's leave them out of it, shall we? You do know they passed away?"

Nena's face fell. "No, no, I saw them only the other month?" She paused. "I keep myself to myself. How did it happen?" She was no longer stern but saddened, and her shoulders slumped into slopes. "For god's sake. I liked your parents. What happened?"

I took in a breath. "Car crash. Their car flipped into a ditch. At least they died together and just like that. Just me left now." And I started to well up at the bald facts I'd just said. The whole weight of existential foreboding made me feel as if I were wearing a rain-drenched overcoat. It was dripping coldness on this still-bright, summerlike day.

Nena couldn't stay angry with me any longer. "My folks died too, quite a long time ago, just after you left."

"I'm sorry."

"Yes. It all went a bit black; I cut off all my hair, wanting to get away from anything that had touched the past. There was too much dead skin; too much death. Believe me, I'd read every bullshit pamphlet the NHS can get rid of. They had the knack of pumping them out faster than I could go to the recycling bin."

I tried to flatten my shirt and hide my spread, but it was futile. "I need to tell you why I left and I've only ever told my folks and Tommy. Remember him?"

Nena nodded blankly. I continued my story, unburdened now. "All those years ago. I was only 19, Nena. Please remember that. Then the weeks became months, and the months rolled into years, and I had been away for a decade."

Nena lowered her eyes. "Your dad was most cryptic and evasive for the first 18 months or so. Everything he said to me seemed to have been memorised and then repeated in parrot fashion. The poor sod wasn't really a very good spokesman."

"He always stood off-screen as Mum and I chatted," I smiled.

"We all thought you'd joined the Foreign Legion or the clergy, but that wouldn't explain Alistair's sadness. It just appeared on his face."

I looked up from the cobbles, caught her blank expression and looked back down. "I'll tell you everything, Nena, when you've decided whether you want to reconnect. I mean, your opinion of me will change, of that there's little doubt," I cautioned.

"I doubt it will. I just want to know things, however bleak," Nena whispered.

"I can't escape that night, even in my sleep. I try, I try…"

"Well, I'm not one to sit on old grudges. I've seen how short some lives are, and how easy it is to fill in the gaps of a narrative with poisonous supposition. There were plenty who believed you were doing time at Her Majesty's Pleasure – you were really quite a weirdo in your last months here."

"Really?" I rubbed away at my right brow. "My life has been so mundane."

"Everyone has their reasons – let's see if I believe in yours. So, start by telling me everything with all the cymbal crashes included. Speak to me."

I grinned with the relief of a man who had moments earlier been subjected to the full 'hell hath no fury' experience.

Nena smiled. "I need adventure. There's only so much chatter I can muster about the weather and the farness of the superstore and the nearness of the sea."

"The Sandgate trending topics."

"Most folk here think that Twitter is a bird-watching society." Nena smiled, and her face lost a great deal of its forbidding tautness. "Come. Let's go to our old pub and dodge the raindrops. If we walk quickly enough, we can step in between them."

We walked slowly over the glossy cobblestones and once almost touched hands. My reawoken feelings for Nena grew with every old memory we stirred up on the red velvet banquette of the East Kent Arms pub. Nothing much had changed in the place, and so it was possible for me to squint and fool myself that it was the late 1990s again, far away from the rips and destruction of the present-day. This timelessness also helped relations to thaw out between the pair of us.

"I used to sit in this exact same spot and wonder how it would be like to come here without the threat of an exam hanging over me, how it would be to go to the bar again and again until I'd tasted every single optic and not to worry about sneaking back into the cabin, shoeless, at closing time."

"And how does it feel? Adult?"

"Now I'm sitting here, it feels like an act of rebellion. But then I remember that my folks won't be silently waiting up for me."

Nena moved to hold my hand at the exact moment I reached for my beaker. I brought it back, and she coughed. "I spent a whole month living off gin from these disgusting Ocado orders – five litres of value spirits and half a litre of clam chowder."

"Jesus, Nena. Did you get help?" I asked.

"No. I was paralysed. I couldn't break it. I mean, I could see the delivery driver shake his head as he walked off. He came twice a month, and I prayed that someone else would turn up with the order. But it was always the same wire-thin guy, an emaciated Einstein. The salon was no longer my place of work. It was a Prohibition gin den."

I now grabbed her tiny hand. "And there I was, wandering around Turin and the Strada del Portone, and not a single person could see me. We were both lost. What a shame."

"Hush. It's all hindsight. Can you imagine the chaos if you had stayed?"

"I can imagine the rows."

Nena chuckled. "I figure we would have torn the salon apart."

She closed her eyes. "All this is so… transportative. Same scents, same you."

I studied the room. "The hops still look out of place, though – we're miles from fields – are they the same hops? This place contains so many of our memories, doesn't it?"

"We use pubs as cocoons – I reckon we all do."

I sighed. "If they switched off the Spotify, it could just be as things had never happened – we are teenagers again."

Nena rested her chin on my shoulder. "We had to go somewhere to get here."

"Our worldviews have altered for the better, Nena."

"Life should be less frightening."

"Well, exactly." And I clinked my glass against Nena's.

After hours at the East Kent Arms, I felt heady with the drink and the chat. Nena may have felt the same as she followed me back the way I had come on my own that morning. Now we were two. The sky seemed sharper now, the condensation trails like chalk in the blue. Over the stile where we had kissed at 19 and past the flattened grass where we'd spent a night or three, Nena seemed to walk slowly as if lost in these memories as well – or maybe it was because the grasses were starting to glisten under her pink suede heels.

The pair of us had talked about the aches and pains we were both feeling, in the lower back and the depths of our psyches; we ruminated upon the state of the nation, the fate of my old car, the Flying Pig, last seen as a rusting geranium of sorts on a travellers' patch of mud. With every topic discussed, I felt closer and closer to the magnetic pull of Nena's healthy cynicism; there were no saints in her world, but every sinner had at least some claim to penitence. She had still possessed an abhorrence of binary thought, of static sentimentality, of 'those whose mouth champions one thing while their heart holds another'. Good old Nena. I hoped that my sunny side would be enough to dispel any memories she had of my dark places. Nena had somehow retained only the most admirable aspects of who she had been at 18, chiefly her ability to look at herself and laugh. We had kept memory of our old way of talking, too – it had been impossible to lose our rhythms completely, but would she still consider me worthy of her?

I unlocked the door to the cabin, and the pair of us slipped in. Nena sat on the handwoven piano stool and I relaxed into the wingbacked chair. She tapped on her knees as she took in the found objects and bric-a-brac. "The cabin hasn't changed at all. There's the primrose cap to which you owe your life, Sammy."

"It's good to leave it all as it was. I'm turning into Dad, I guess, but it's like all this is there to be used at some distant point in the future."

"What in the hell's this?" said Nena to break the morbidity, holding up what appeared to be a miniature shepherd's crook wrought in iron. "Is it a cosh?"

I squinted. "I think it's for cleaning out the hearth. I don't know – Dad picked it up at the antiques fair at the Grand. Everywhere you look, there's a load of old junk."

"Oh, Samuel, you know, I have been wondering where you were. I'd given up going to Folkestone and scanning the sea of faces for you, but I never convinced myself that you'd age, too. You were frozen in time, like one of those early Everest climbers that are found in a pair of sandals, a century after dying. I had this feeling – it was as if my tongue had turned into paper and I couldn't form the words. You'd have always been 18 years old if we hadn't have bumped into each other today. It was like you aged 18 years in one second, in that moment."

"You feel like you can touch the past." I looked up at the primrose-yellow cap.

"We see former versions of the same person with our own filters." Nena looked at my ragged fingernails and round gut. "Do you still nervously scratch at the back of your neck?"

"Yes, I do. A few things don't ever change. My neck is raw. But you, you look so much healthier now." I smiled and tilted my head sideways. "You have a tan."

"I think that's the merlot," Nena joked. "Everyone was slightly lo-res in the Nineties. I watch those old episodes of Friends or ER, the big old popular shows – everything looks a little fuzzy around the edges and far away. We looked like we were made of cotton wool."

I replied, sadly. "I don't have any photos. I had some on an old phone, but I didn't back them up and it fell into the river."

"Well, you should have told me I resembled a murderous Victorian doll."

"You were gorgeous; you still are."

"I had a face that could scare a soldier." Nina relaxed and let out a little sigh.

I agreed: "I was more than a little scared of you in those last few months."

"Were you?"

"Yes, you had a plan, a focus. I was so lame. There's a river out in the country around Turin, one that Tom still jogs around, and I would stand there as he ran, skimming stones into the brickwork around a water pipe, wondering how we would have coped with growing up as a couple. That sunny decade before everything turned to shit in the global crash, you see, we might have turned it shady."

Nena laughed. "We're always impatient, Sammy. That's why we talk rubbish – to make the hours collapse."

"So we do, but my folks survived through patience."

Nena grinned. "I don't think either of us was really ready for a life of no surprises. At 18, you should have high hopes, while your energies are similarly so – you should aim for the moon and use all your rocket fuel to reach it." She paused. "Christ, that sounds like something stencilled on a theme pub wall. Or even worse, it sounds like something Paolo Coelho plopped out for a fat cheque."

"You don't get that nonsense in the East Kent Arms, just odd photos of old Irish poets like Behan and Yeats. Always hung up at a slant," I murmured. "Jesus, I'm the same age as Dylan Thomas was when he keeled over in New York after 13 doubles."

"That's hardcore chugging, Sammy."

"I've always asked myself why a pub presents this wall of famous creative types utterly destroyed by the demon drink. It would be like McDonald's having pictures of Mama Cass and Elvis next to their doughnut cabinet."

"'Eat yourself to death like The King!'"

"It's one thing to do around here, Nena. Or drink the cellars dry, like the old soaks with eyes like pickled eggs."

"The Peperami people – tanned from the wine, thin from malnutrition, yellow eyes and teeth. Sam, you needed to have your Italian adventure. I'm just relieved you are not dragging along some Italian babe with two bambinos."

"Sod all chance of that!"

"Imagine that. Talk about puncturing my daydreams – to see some Italian goddess following you with her hatboxes and her adorable, doe-eyed children. And then she'd clap her hands, and a dozen Milanese servant boys in thongs would appear in a golden cloud to do her bidding."

I rested my palms on Nena's shoulders. "There's a lot to be said for watching your best friend live out your romantic what-ifs."

"Tom?"

"The rollercoaster of his love life acted as a natural antaphrodisiac for me."

"Fast-food loving."

"I didn't have the energy, Nena – I was struggling even to exist, to get along."

"You did-not-a-speak-a-the-lingo, Sammy?"

"Allo Allo. My bumbling attempts at learning Italian were my only contribution to the Piemontesi. It made them laugh. I did this course at the old church around the corner every Tuesday evening for three years. No one stuck at it for half as long, and everyone else sounded like a Romance poet or like Dante. "A mighty flame followeth a tiny spark." I was so shit. I was just this sullen Scotsman, picking away at the table's laminated surface."

"Speak some Italian, for me," Nena flicked my nose; it hurt a little.

"Due chili di patate per favore, signore."

"Beautiful."

"It's about two kilos of potatoes."

"Oh." Nena paused. "It's beautiful, though – and useful."

"Well, thank god, my job meant I could rely on Tommy's language skills – I'd speak to mainly English people. Laconic types. Grumpy."

"The ex-pats?" Nena asked.

I continued: "Very frail colonel types looking for a sunset goodbye. We helped them out. I found suitably stunning homes for them on Lake Maggiore. They got their home with a view from the veranda, a perch on which to rant at the imported Daily Telegraph and moan about how the beautiful sunset was hurting their eyes. It became almost robotic, like ten thousand weeks washing the same heads, I'd assume."

"That's my life," Nena sighed. "That was my life without you. We both ended up far from what we imagined. You're not a dashing war reporter; I'm not a stylist to the stars. We are consolers of the grey and lonely. Hope – it's an evil thing. Dreams? To hell with them."

I joined in: "See it this way. We were two near-hermits, but two thousand miles apart. We were mothballed to be ready for this very moment in time."

Nena laughed: "There is always much to be thankful about. Change works like a sushi conveyor belt – the same dishes appear within reach if you wait long enough."

"And get stale?"

"Well, Sam, what I meant was; everything comes around again."

"And you didn't want children?" I asked.

"Just because I have the tools doesn't mean I want to produce the goods?" Nena picked up the Jiffy bag from the rug. "Hey. What's this? Incriminating evidence? Is this a print-out of all your social media postings? Will give it me a quick summary of your life for the past 18 years?"

"Sod social media."

"Always a people person. Were you working for the Turin tourist board?" Nena laughed. "Or is it like that old tin of smut you had in your desk, Sammy boy?"

I took the bag and put it on my lap again. "It's just an envelope with two photos. Polaroids. Have a look – it's just a ransacked room. There's just a broken sofa and table, with some Jesus-looking dude passed out on the floor." I handed the bag back to Nena and settled back in the wingback. "It's just mad Mimi, no doubt, my mad old aunt; she's drunkenly posted them to me." I didn't believe this.

Nena grinned. "Does Mimi still love the sauce?"

"That she does." I pointed to the pink and purple monstrosity facing away on the Welsh dresser. "The card is up there. I mean, Mimi gets a sniff of Dubonnet – she's keeping them in business – and suddenly it's a marvellous idea to send these… these random found objects in the post, fragments of a drunk's day-sleeping. Then she wakes up on the sofa, quite unaware of yesterday's bright spark, and I come along to the cabin and find this package on my doorstep. It's always been the case. Mimi's inebriation means those around her have to walk the extra mile."

"So the Polaroids were with the card in the Jiffy bag? And where was the bag?" Nena asked.

"What? The photos were with the card in the open Jiffy bag. It was on the step – the rain had got to it."

"Any marks?" Nena asked.

"The postal stamp was from Mimi's local post office. Case closed." I hunched up.

Her hands fell from the Polaroids. "What if someone slipped the photos into the Jiffy bag after it reached the doorstep? You said the envelope was open? That could be another option. Was the Jiffy bag open?"

"Yes, it was," I replied, and the floorboards started to slip away below my bare feet as if they were skis. I rubbed my nape and couldn't look at Nena any longer. "I thought the footsteps in the grass were those of my folks."

"Maybe." Nena looked worried.

"You're saying there's a chance they belonged to someone else, an oddbod wanting to put the fear of God into me?"

"Well, someone may have popped the Polaroids in there then. You must see that, Sam?"

I held the photos in my clammy hands and still didn't realise what Nena was saying, or rather I refused to accept that, out there beyond the brambles, heather and gorse, was a person who wished to pour more misery on me. More weight, more sadness.

The old Palazzo.

Councillor John Wills would wake up at seven every morning, duetting with the coughing of his teas-made. He had to see that his troublesome Gracie got to school instead of hanging around Greenwich Park with her equally punkish friends. She'd been served a drunk-and-disorderly penalty for having sex in the kids' playground near the National Maritime Museum; the tips of her blonde hair were now blue, as if a litmus test for her gradual slide into wantonness. John had swiftly made sure his friends high up in the police force quashed the penalty sum, but now he dwelt upon the fact that he himself had never been afforded such protection. He was the grit, she the oyster. She was taking the piss.

And so, though John doted upon his Gracie, leaving a little something on her pillow on Present Tuesdays, he couldn't wait for her to leave for university; he'd had her late in his life when his energies were flagging. Soon, thank the dark lord, he wouldn't have to wake up so early to cook her an omelette; he wouldn't have to guide her into the Merc away to her A-Levels up in Highgate. She had been an angel when his second wife had died, but over the last two years, she'd lost her wings, torn off probably by that floppy-haired bastard in Hackney she was 'seeing'; well, that was the politest term for them going at it in his power-shower.

This constant texting wasn't the courting of John's teenage years, when you'd go to a film at the Rio and then treat the lucky girl to an ice-cream sundae. That was all passed down from the 1930s, love in the matinee glow; this was illiterate, text-speak humping.

John didn't understand modern romance. He had left that all up in Soho as a young man. The smog cloud of

AIDS had claimed so many of John's friends, once-strapping men who adored Grace Jones and Marvin Gaye as he did, men whom John would see shambling around Dean Street, emaciated, confused and skull-headed until they disappeared. Then came Jeannie's death and the late Noughties rise of that horrible dance music that Gracie would set up on the speakers through their Royal Hill townhouse. There wasn't a single room from which John could escape the cacophony; he'd stupidly had speakers set up even in his en-suite. Back in the day, they had vibrated with his beloved soul tracks, the music with which he had courted Jeannie. Now, when alone, he'd rest his head against the vibrations of the speakers and dream of her.

John had made his money from his hobby, beat music, and the live gigs in clubs where everyone got dressed sharp and things got hazy. John had entered the business by using his raw printing skills to produce flyers for the bands he went to see at the Four Aces Club in Dalston, East London. There was a lot of reggae and ska music most nights, but John could also catch all the new black soul artists in the UK and some of the more famous names; Stevie Wonder had once dropped in to play. From the inky kitchenette of his bedsit, John had done the promotions for a young soul singer called Steve Dunbar, who had then asked him to become his manager. John's white skin would act as an entry card to certain establishments that would not accept black acts with black managers.

Dunbar came up with the name Robbie Jewell, and constant gigging and John's entrepreneurial mind soon saw the cash flood in. John invested his money in an ailing club in Soho, which he ran singlehandedly; Dunbar snorted most of his and ended up back living with his mum in Kingston, Jamaica; he was stacking supermarket trolleys by 1990.

As Jewell faded, so John became a club boss, not a talent manager. Even now, as he put on his towelling robe and kissed his bedside portrait of Jeannie, the old Soho club sign for Palazzo was there hanging on the bedroom wall next to the ensuite. It reminded him of his journey – that first, but not last, successful nightclub – and the word Palazzo became in his mind a lucky charm and a reason why he'd sought out Italian investors for his business propositions. The guys from Turin didn't know of his past in clubland, and they were two thousand miles away. John was on free swim, except when they were on his Skype feed and the nagging dragons were on his shoulder, reminding him of his commitments.

That morning, Gracie was, surprisingly for a school morning, up and about. John could hear her slam the crockery cupboard shut – she made her morning cappuccino to go with his inexpert ham omelette. Eight years a widower, and John still hadn't mastered the kitchen – everything was created on the hob, not the oven, which probably had packed in long ago. The kitchen itself had been installed sometime in the late 1980s.

John would always shower after Asgar arrived and Gracie had left, and then he would settle down with his copy of the Daily Mail and heat up a croissant in the microwave, in defiance of his physician. John might rely on doctors to staff his clinics, but he was damned if he would take their advice after they'd misdiagnosed his Jeannie's cancer. Working medics into the ground was John's own little revenge act for what they'd done to his girl. He'd pursue them like a hellhound.

"Gracie, use the cutlery!" John shouted as he caught his daughter sliding the omelette straight into her mouth off the plate. Asgar then came in and picked up the car keys from the bowl on the kitchen island. Gracie left, moaning as usual about the disruption caused by her father's business meetings at home.

John muttered to himself: "I should have married an Algerian." He would wait for Asgar's return, to then be whisked under the Thames through its sooty road tunnels. He would hear the progress reports on the construction of clinics and weekly updates from his adjutants on the success of those already up and running. He wouldn't stop until Gracie was meant to be home, but often she would stay at The Boy's flat in London E5, and John would carry on conference-calling in his leather captain's chair until the wee small hours; his beloved Geno Washington blasting out 'Alison Please' or 'Hold on Momma' to keep the late-middle-aged man from the uselessness of sleep. Gimme pills, John would ask his employees, for he had to please his own taskmasters, and the chicks' mouths never seemed to be satiated, no matter how near to the morning John worked.

There were six clinics now set up in London, all of them primarily catering in eldercare, well, making sure that wealthy seniors had access to GP services during the day. The one near Liverpool Street, the old betting shop, was the least hassle to run and most profitable – there were plenty of old folks able to afford the consultancy fees and only a few drunks mistakenly coming in to place a bet – but it had all been a roaring success.

However, scarcely a third of the money was John's, which is why his office light was the only one on throughout Royal Hill at 1am. No matter how much revenue he made, how often he turned over a profit, or spirited the cash away, the chicks would keep him awake at night; the chirping grew louder; his benefactors lost money to other ventures and then tried to milk his success to pay for their own failure. In his lonely hours, John longed for the devil-may-care Saturday of another soirée up Whitechapel at his party pad. He reached for the pillbox on his bureau. Cheer up, lad: you can always find people to do your bidding, if you can't clone himself. Flutter the cash, or finger the cosh – people will listen up.

John had long held this idea of a co-operative, a secret society sharing favours as the Masons did, but without the right-wing traditions and all that. There would be tradesmen to fix a boiler or a car in return for emergency health care; there would be police officers to provide information and security against those who opposed the greater good; and, of course, there would be parties that echoed those of Eighties Soho, parties drenched in the spirit that had been extinguished by the chain pubs and executive flats popping up in place of the speak-easys, trans bars and nightclubs.

Just as the areas around Spitalfields and Shoreditch had harboured the Jewish, Huguenot and Pakistani outcasts over the centuries, surely they could now house the co-operative, this collective of skilled workers, funded by the clients of the clinics?

For the many, from the few, each member was as vital a cog in the machine as the next person; well, John sat at the tiller, holding the course. This was the way to get things done quickly and efficiently in these times of public-sector bloat and private greed. John just needed his medicine to keep up the pace, to stay on track, and to satisfy the little chicks. Pills, pills, lovely pills – take me up, bring me down.

The two men sat in the corner of the Pride of Spitalfields pub, just off Brick Lane. Luca the Italian was too stunned to speak, a clay dam forming in his mouth, yammy; and John was smiling as he studied the quivering of Luca's sweaty face, all cheeks and doughy concern, the councillor understanding that he had the upper hand. Luca's expressions were immediately readable like a weather-vane, manipulated by a foul wind. John found it pleasing to watch Luca's thought-processes scroll across his face.

At last, his amusement waning, John spoke. "Do you actually think we would hurt you, Luca?"

Luca said nothing.

"I mean... You're part of our casa, my friend."

"Am I?"

"Yes, son. That grants you an awful lot of protection from the nastiness all around us. People get shat on all the time. Look at the wasters in this place: that guy over there by the serving hatch – do you think it was in his ten-year plan to be nursing his sixth pint of bitter at midday?"

"He doesn't look happy, John."

"No, he doesn't, Luca. We all get shat on – it's how we cope with the shit that's flung at us that defines how we are. I've got a pity story. Let the bad guys bury their dead, and just be thankful your friends will keep you away from all that. I saw a man running down Mile End Road with a knife in his leg last month. It's a hard, unforgiving world," John explained, although he was talking to little more than a mask. "You see, this is a form of insurance for you. Premiums protect you against the damage done, but we can protect you from any damage happening in the first place. We're proactive, not reactive in the protection of our pals. I like my friends to be hale and hearty, and they like to see me thriving. I could have been a sad case like that pissant drinking over there when my Jeannie died young, but I was proactive and I got going again."

"Why did the old man and the girl have to die?" Luca blurted out. He looked into his untouched but heavily stirred cappuccino. He needed anything that he could find to focus upon, but everything he set his eyes upon – the old lone drinker, the cushions in the window seat – everything brought him sliding back to the murders he'd witnessed, sliding back as if he were on a toddler's rubber reins. "Why did the two have to die? It was not a natural thing. I can't..."

His words were failing him; his English skills often did when he grappled for them up on the highest bough, but the poison word 'inutilmente' mushroomed in his mind. It was all useless.

"Would it make you feel better to know that Dorota was the old man's daughter and he was sleeping with her?"

"Was he?"

"Yes. Come on! Would it help you to learn that she was blackmailing him and that all of us in this special club were at risk from outer forces?" John grinned again, the smile of a father explaining an act of nature to a fearful son. "Would that help you? Does that perversion disgust your Catholic morals, eh?" He was now serious. "It disgusts me. Father sleeping with daughter… making a hussy out of her. It's unnatural. It's unthinkable."

Luca went to drain his cappuccino but put the cup back in its blue-and-white saucer. He had little time for those whose aspect flickered so swiftly between congeniality and coldness. Maybe councillor John had a variety of faces for every moment, shedding off mask upon mask like the commedia dell'arte players who toured Italy under the aegis of the dukes. Maybe he just lived to please those who could aid him. Would councillor John ever show his true expression, or would he just unpeel a succession of disguises? How could he not feel anything? What was his involvement?

John broke the silence: "Listen, Luca. Loose lips sink ships. All this blathering is a danger to us; it destroys the ecosystem in which we live. The delicate ecosystem is what protects us from outside. We are only ever as strong as our weakest link. We can't let even a tiny crack in the dam we've built. The girl Dorota was telling a story that didn't need to be heard. She embellishes it, and the tale snowballs and becomes solid fact, like a boulder that flattens everything in its path. We just rolled away the stone, out of harm's way."

"I don't believe…"

John cut Luca off. "Your forefathers had a word, 'fama', or 'rumour'. Fama begins as a shy creature, not predisposed to using its many tongues to spread what its multiple eyes may have seen or its many ears might have heard. But Fama grows large when the evil and the misguided feed her, and, soon, tall tales that are best left at home are winging their way across entire continents. I get four hours' sleep a night, making sure the best medical services are available to our elderly. I fight every day on the council to secure the futures of the good people; I was there past 10 o'clock, pushing through new machines for the New London Hospital. What were you doing at 10?"

"I was trying to sleep but thinking about the two dead people," Luca muttered. "I walked around in circles until I thought the carpet was going to catch fire."

"Very droll, dear boy, very droll. But… You have to understand why these things happen; they do not occur in isolation, just as Rumour doesn't grow without collusion or the loose lips of a condoner." John picked up Luca's cappuccino and drained it. "You read Virgil?"

Luca watched the councillor put his cup down. "Not since school. I don't read too much; I like to watch things instead. I try to learn that way."

John got up from his chair, vainly tucked his shirt into his long-suffering trousers, and smiled at Luca. "Well, what you watch: it's your choice to either remember what you've seen or disregard it. You can choose how you look upon things – is Brick Lane a melting-pot that, for centuries, has housed the dispossessed and disenfranchised like the French Huguenots and Ashkenazi Jews, or has it become oversaturated with human carrion feeding off those cultures, these cultural appropriators? The Jews and now the Pakistanis motor this area, but are they the ones enjoying the pop-up shops and brew shacks? Are they bollocks? There's the disgrace – that's where your anger at the other night should be directed. Luca, listen to an old man who's seen it all from Soho to Stepney and back – I've been here in the capital for six decades. I was a friend to the Jews in the post-rationing days, to the Pakistanis who made their homes here in the Sixties – and I have seen it all, way before the Kray twins and the Richardsons were around here. So, Luca, my boy, trust in me that you are master of your own destiny. I'm not lieing when I say I see good things for you – you have no poker face, and you seem discreet. Be that and have fun. Please, enjoy your afternoon; don't sit here moping like that sad bastard at the bar. I'll see you around."

Councillor John walked to the door of the Pride of Spitalfields and was scooped up by the same Rover into which Luca had seen the old man's inert body being thrown. The circle was complete, but did Luca step within it or call attention to it?

He would spend the whole night and the next few days working out which course of action was best, sleepless on the edge of his sofa with the TV buzzing away incoherently.

In the black and white dots, whizzing around like a moving magic eye, Luca could sometimes see the girl; he could sometimes make out the old man's broken form; but most of the time, he saw his own unshaven face, lost in the loneliest confusion for all time and fixed in a howl of the blackest despair.

The way we were.

The mottled interior of the East Kent Arms resembled a murky jar of pickled onions – what windows there were in this hoover-bag of a hostelry merely threw the scantest light on the constellations formed by the dust, forever altering their shape with the outside breeze and the wheezing of half-a-dozen tertiary-stage alcoholics.

In this town pub hung wave upon wave of dried-out hops that shut out yet more of the sun's rays and engineered yet more clusters of dust particles. It was an asthmatic's hell. The Victorian mirrors, into which curlicues had been etched, had not been polished in such an age that one could well picture certain fingerprints belonging to the glass-fitters themselves. And what scenes had those mirrored surfaces captured? Of walrus-moustachioed men sinking their final pint of mead before being recalled to the Boer War and of chattering, whalebone-corsetted ladies taking a revivifying gin after the mile-long constitutional on the Lower Leas?

A hundred years on, those mirrors reflected teenagers enjoying the end of their exams: curtain-haired boys in lumberjack shirts and carpenter jeans, and girls in thrall to hippy chic, all pretending to be of age to buy in rounds of beer and cider, with Jack Daniels chasers. Nena and Sam were old enough to get drunk and have their usual Saturday afternoon tiff. Things had been heading south for a while, largely because the young man was only a visitor to Folkestone, and Nena knew she was going to lose him for good to the flatlands of Berwickshire, hundreds of miles away. Both felt the inevitability, but they shoved any real discussion of it into a deep ditch, like the meaning behind last night's dreams.

"Get me a sausage sarnie, not the bacon. Ta!" Sam shouted from across the bar, from the bar billiard table lined with empty shot glasses. Tommy was absolutely crucifying him this Saturday; normally Sam won, but he was finding Nena's presence in a pair of pink corduroy cut-offs a distraction – well, that and her moaning about the self-predicted awfulness of her A Level results. It was tiresome really, as she had no ambitions to go to university, unlike Sam had earlier this summer. "Two more Jagers, Nena. I'll reimburse you." Sam turned back to the bar billiards. "Tommy, we're going double or quits, matey."

It was nigh-on impossible to play bar billiards when half the bar was stacked up on its edges: empty shot-glasses, half-empty pints of snakebite, Tommy's bacon sandwich and Nena's car keys for her 15-year-old Metro with its odd-coloured doors.

"Sammy, young Samuel, we're stopping." Tommy was quitting in the lead.

"You can't go, wanker. I need a chance to claw myself back."

"Young Samuel, enjoy your sausage sandwich and accept your thrashing. Tomorrow, we can play another tournament. You can regain your pride then."

"Ah. Come on, Tommy!" Sam urged him.

"No. Take your girl home – she looks bored as usual." Tommy signalled over Harry on the other side of The East Kent Arms. Harry was the new owner of a VFR750, thanks to his PR job at the council, and he chucked a second helmet over to his drunken friend, before the duo disappeared into the Folkestone sunset.

Nena came over with two shots. "Fifteen minutes for the sarnie."

"Cheers, darl. I'll need a lift home – I'll pick up my car tomorrow. I'm not fit to drive."

"The Flying Pig's staying here?" Nena joked. She hated Sam's Austin 1100 for its Seventies brown paint job, but to his eyes, the old gal was like a stately galleon, never getting flustered, a design icon of the 1960s, when its silhouette appeared on many a road sign. "I can run faster than that shitheap," Nena chuckled.

"I feel unusual." Sam was beginning to awaken from excess with red and sorrowful remorse, and it wasn't even closing time.

"No wonder you feel as sick as a pike. You and Tommy have been caning it all afternoon. Look at the capillaries on your nose – bright red and popping." Her birdlike face turned into something of a scowl. The two of them had been together for all of secondary school, but she was beginning to waver in Sam's affections. It wasn't just the constant fretting about a future she kept resolutely unfocused upon, despite expecting him in the same breath to make up his mind about possible further education; it was that she was becoming extremely bossy, a schoolmarm like her mother. Sam wasn't going to go without treats, just because she was embracing the prevailing trend for the waifish look. This meant no boozing for Nena, no bacon sarnies, and no benders that started on Friday night and finished sometime on the sofa on Sunday afternoon.

Nena wasn't much of a laugh any more. Tommy was right, Sam thought – these girls make sure they're indispensible to you, then they drop anchor and start barking out orders from the starboard bow. They're on a mission to get you ship-shape. They would rather turn you into the image of how they'd been imagining a boyfriend to be since pre-puberty than let you just be. Times were crazy enough for Sam, what with his true home being in another country, yet Nena was always swirling in the four winds like those damned hippie scarves she wore, scarves she wore "because Winona does".

"You've left the bar-billiard table an utter mess, Samuel." Nena's nagging now cemented what he had been thinking. Where had the breezy girl of three years ago gone? The world wasn't such an inimical place that they, as teenagers free from the ennui of examinations and vivats, should suddenly turn sour and snotty.

"Give it a rest, Nena. We'll have a chat when I am sober again."

"You're never sober."

"I really need to get back to the cabin and sleep in my crib, you know. We'll have a chat."

"And when will that be?" Nena snapped back, still fiddling with the third or fourth scarf that was throttling all the joie de vivre from her.

"Come over to the cabin – we're not leaving for Berwickshire until the weekend. Come over and have mum's lasagne, and we can go to the stile and look out over the Channel and you can apologise to me for being such an arse." Sam smiled weakly, but to no avail.

"Normally, I'm heartbroken to wave you off to bonnie Scotland, but I couldn't give a tin shit this time. You're impetuous, you're aimless, you're swollen – the state of you, with beer stains all over your rugby shirt. Look, you've got shit all over your chin." Nena moved to wipe off the ketchup mark, but then stopped herself. "Should we just take time out?"

"Ah, come on!" Sam folded his beer mat in half.

"Boarding school's over – and you don't have to come back here. Seriously. You can sleep with your sheep back home; you can play with their tartan kilts and leave me the hell alone. I have enough on my plate without having to shepherd my man-child boyfriend through life."

"Ah, come on!" Sam pleaded.

"No. I am not your mother, Sammy."

"My mum's more fun!"

"You've chosen to be a lad at the exact time you should be getting serious about which path you're taking." Nena paused for breath. "Blitz your tiny brain until tomorrow comes, and keep doing this until you're on your own, with no way back here."

Sam drunkenly headed off at a tangent: "This isn't a shared history; this is my story. I get one tale to live out. It's mine to edit, and mine alone to relate."

"What the hell are you on about? And what do I do while you're being wilful?" Nena asked Sam, cocking her head slightly.

Sam was on course for a brick wall, but he was rather enjoying his boozy gabbiness, despite the impending impact: "I can't sit here waiting for spring to turn, for you to make up your mind."

"What?" Nena was itching to leave the bar and lay in her bubble bath for a few hours.

Sam continued his babble: "My history exists alongside your own, perhaps, but even if we were to live, and die, together, we'd never share one destiny. We would share a co-dependent life, but we'd always see it from a different point of view."

"So, what's the point of trying to understand one another?" Nena asked.

Sam frisbeed the beer mat into the table opposite: "The point is to make living easy. You'll always be disappointed."

"I'm very disappointed now. I'm despondent." Nena looked over at the bar. Her friend Rhona was listening in on the lovers' tiff.

Sam carried on: "You place too much importance on everything. You will probably tell me now all about potato ring rot, as if the past ten generations of my family haven't worked the soil. You. Just. Go. On."

"What's your point, Sam?"

"You think you hold the world on a little diamanté tether. You believe everything you read in your glossy magazines. This princess life – the glamour, the boyfriend, the clothes are all on your list. You are living by proxy." He looked at the bar absentmindedly. "Where's the hell is my sarnie, Rhona?"

Nena had had enough. "Listen, I'm not going to sit here and soak up your shit just because your best mate's gone home with another boy and you're plastered. Get Rhona to call you a taxi, please. I'm not your drunk wagon, Sam." Nena stormed out of the pub. "Battling period pains and Captain Gobshite – what a day."

Rhona looked at Sam from the bar and mouthed, "Do you want the sandwich?"

Sam shook his head and looked at the door, but Nena had gone, with her jangly bangles, scarves and silly orange velvet muffin cap. He wasn't going to blow a tenner on a taxi; he'd sit it out until closing time, nursing a jug of water, then drive the Flying Pig home, around the back lanes. The road would be all his – then and for ever.

Sam wasn't feeling too shitty, certainly not as bad as last weekend when he was chundering through his nose, when Nena was holding back his floppy blond hair, his aquiline nose red with the effort of vomiting. The sandwich would have been a great call, some stodge to soak up all the shots he had necked with Tommy. Bastard had buggered off with Harry. Now Sam had to take care of himself, without his sarnie. Sobriety now, please.

Sam drank jug after jug of water. Rhona had stacked them around him, fearing Sam had taken a pill on the sly in hope of combating the boozing. Leah Betts and the crusading that her death had initiated had been in the news for a couple of years now. It was all a bit redundant to Sam and his friends – the guys from school were now of an age to go pubbing, rather than slinking off to Radnor Park to drop acid and neck a few pills behind the breeze-block toilets. But Rhona was keeping an eye on him from behind the bar.

After Sam had finished off three jugs of water, Rhona called over to him from the bar: "You want to go easy on the water, Sammy. Don't drown in your own body."

"I need to sober up, Rhona," Sam whined, pleading from behind his barricade of glass. "I need to pick up the Flying Pig and get myself back to the cabin. It's only a short ride. I can do it. I can drive safely."

"Sammy, you're going nowhere, mate. You'll be twice over the limit at least, mate." She was the girlfriend of Tommy's sister, her fine blonde hair up in pigtails and dyed blue for some late-night showing of some execrable sci-fi film. "I'll book you a taxi now. Stay here. Please."

Sam would take the taxi, but he'd get it to lap the block and ask the driver to drop him off by the harbour. A brisk walk up the narrow, cobbled Old High Street with its one-in-five gradient would sober him up enough to get the Flying Pig and its driver home in one piece. He'd soak up the booze with a lovely battered sausage or two from the chippy; he could have a cheeky tinkle up the side alley if all the water decided to make a run for it.

"The car will be here in a couple of minutes, a grey Ford Sierra," Rhona called out from the phone.

"Thanks, Rhona. I'll pay you back tomorrow."

She crossed her arms against her chest and puffed out. "No trouble. Hey, help me here. I've got a film to get to. Fetch me those empties, mate."

"There's a load of them," he replied, obviously.

"God, you and Tom were on a mission today. Who won?"

"I lost. I lost in every way." Sam smiled as he collected the whiffy glasses until the tables were clear.

"Night, Sammy," she added. "Have another glass of water before beddybyes! You look a bit red-eyed."

Sam snorted his disdain and headed out of the door, past the umbrella stand full of walking sticks no one ever used, not even in the throes of an angry confrontation. He concentrated on walking in a straight line and plastered on a fake smile. The taxi was already there; thank god he didn't know the driver. Everyone lived off Folkestone Taxi Co while they were all struggling to pass their driving tests, and Sam didn't want news getting back to Nena or Rhona that he'd driven himself home.

If they saw that the Flying Pig was no longer parked haphazardly in the centre of town, he'd tell them he had got up early to caress the old gal home. Anyway, one could walk almost anywhere in Folkestone if one had an hour to spare; the Flying Pig spent her days bespoiling the views along the gorgeous avenues around Clifton Road. She truly was jolie-laide, a riot of rhomboids from her hunchback to her apologetic muzzle.

Sam got in the taxi's passenger seat next to the young lad sat on his beaded pile. "Just go to the bottom of the Old High Street, mate. Change of plan."

"Ok, my friend."

Sam tapped his shoulder: "You can still charge the pub for the usual amount, mate. I'm getting a lift home from my missus…"

"Sure you are." He smiled over at him. "It's only a few hundred metres, mate."

"Yes. It's fine. I'm going to the pay and display, you see. Frees up a bit of time for your other fares, doesn't it, if I get out here? Write me out a receipt for the trip to Sandgate, though, yes?"

The handsome Arab nodded and focused on manoeuvring his Ford Sierra into the hushed road. There was some jangly guitar band on the radio, one of those faceless Britpoppers, and a horrid vanilla and coconut air freshener in the shape of a palm tree swung from the rear-view mirror as he pulled out. A minute later, the taxi came to a stop at the curve before the hill began its winding ascent up to the newspaper offices. Sam unclipped his seatbelt and took the paper receipt. "You have a good evening, brother."

Sam started chugging his way up the steep wind of the ancient hill, past the hobby shops that were closed or closing and the kebab huts where the drunkards were inhaling their dinner in one go, ketchup everywhere but on the white paper napkins they held scrunched in their hand. The pavement was covered in potato smears, chips trodden into the ground.

What did Sam care anyway about anything? The hoofbeats in his head were fading away at last, overtaken by the race of his heart. A little scamper up the hill would blast away the little viper in his veins – it had seemed such a good idea to let the booze snake its way in, but now it was shaping up to be a weekend-ruiner.

Gaggles of giggling girls in barely-there eveningwear were floating downhill, trying to avoid the chuntering bulk, if not the eyes, of lads in football shirts. While the ladies were making up their faces, the boys would have been watching the Saturday soccer results roll in. Now pissed up, their plan was the same as his; a little stodge to soak up the booze before kip and a lazy Sunday on the cabin's sofa. Sam's folks would be at church with the Coupers and then taking tea with the vicar in the corrugated hut over the road.

Tommy would always talk, in that Hemingwayesque manner of his, about 'surfing your hangovers', but Sam derived no pleasure from feeling like the entire world was strobing to the pulse of the hoofbeats. He always had to have a pint of water at his bedside and a bottle of Lucozade for breakfast. There were no guts nor glory in your guts feeling gory.

Towards the top of the hill, the crowds of the cheerful young thinned out. Sam's breathing became laboured as his jogging slowed down. The Flying Pig was parked on a plot the teens distastefully called "Three Rape Alley"; it was by the newspaper offices, where the land flattened out and the chain shops and bookies started in earnest; to Sam's knowledge, no one had been assaulted there, but there was a soggy single mattress covered in dubious stains in one corner of the land, and one could tell the state of the weather by the colour it took on. If it was turning green, then the rains were setting in; if there was a taupe hue to it, then the sun was out. It was that colour now, so all was well.

The grateful dead & the kings of convenience.

Milena's bows had fallen from her curls. Her black jumper and her Gap jeans were streaked with dirt. She had been sleeping rough for several days, now her money had run out. Her face was gaunt from living off the soup that was handed out every other day by church volunteers in front of Christ Church Spitalfields.

Milena had been walking for more than a dozen hours daily, venturing as near as she dared to the quartet of tower blocks where her little Dorota had been murdered. None of the free newspapers had mentioned her passing, of course – no one would know that Dorota had ever been there, running up the steps of the National Gallery as she laughed with her new friends, poaching shifts at this salon and that for cash in hand, living off the grid before sleeping in a bunk two rows over from Milena's.

On the fifth day of her endless circuits of East London, Milena had spotted a guy who might have been the blouson man at the tower-block party, but when he turned around, she had noticed he had a full red beard – he wasn't clean-shaven. Justice for Dorota kept Milena striding through the slicing rain, always bundled up in all the clothes she had managed to take from the boarding house. Sometimes, there would be a bed at the women's refuge if others were out boosting drink at all-night off-licences; at other times, she slept in a bus stop until the service started at sunrise or around the back of a bench in front of St George in the East. Once, she had woken up to find a fellow homeless person trying to mount her while ripping off her jeans; on another occasion, she had been punched hard in the face for taking a guy's spot in a dank alleyway of cardboard and rags. She never rested in the daylight hours.

Where is Your God Now?

A week had passed, and Milena was approaching the post office on Whitechapel High Street when she saw the man in the blouson coming out. He was whistling and undoing his tie. She ran up to him, her steps hesitant through her hunger. Milena tried to flatten down her dirty hair. Then she grabbed his arm.

"Sir, sir!" She manoeuvered herself in front of him.

"Please, I don't have any…" He tried to walk around her, avoiding her eyes, but she blocked his way.

"I was at party, sir," Milena cried out. "I saw you. I saw you – Dorota die. She was friend of mine. Sir, please."

Luca dropped his tie to the pavement. "You… I thought that you were part of it? The monsters."

"No, no." She looked into his eyes. "I've been living on street. I run, try to find you. You not part of John's gang. Good man."

Luca looked her up and down. She was a mess, with dirt across her delicate features and a cut on her cheek, but she had been one of the punky girls at the party, yes. Luca put his hand on her damp wool jumper; she flinched. "Don't worry, child. I am on your side. I am afraid; you are afraid. Come with me. Please."

Milena tilted her head and tried to smile, but it wouldn't come. "I am Milena." She held out her hand for him to shake, ashamed at the dirt under her nails and the cuts on her palms.

"I am Luca. Let's find you some lunch in the warmth, Milena. Come, poor girl." And he put his hefty arm across the bones of her shoulder and shepherded her down the late-morning high street, almost hiding her from the passers-by.

At the back of the most rundown café he knew, screened by a window full of Day-Glo, misspelt cards advertising basic meals, Luca gestured for Milena to sit down. He then poured her some tap water from a jug before scooping a menu from the counter next to their booth.

"It's silent here. We have quiet. Choose anything you want. I'll pay." Luca smiled at the woman scanning the dishes as if they were lost photographs of her parents. "You won't have to run any more, Milena."

She looked up at Luca's warm hazel eyes, and finally, after a week of pursuit and begging, she managed to grin again. It was a beautiful smile, more than enough to cheer up Luca himself inside in this frigid café.

"We are not the best English speakers. Talk Polish into this, Milena," and he held up his smartphone to her across the table. "Tell me everything you know. This will translate everything into Italian. I need to know about John. He is watching me."

Milena suddenly made to leave, but Luca gestured to her to sit down. "John doesn't know I'm here. He is trying to win my friendship." He pressed the screen of his iPhone. "Please, Milena – speak in here. It is an app. Tell me everything."

Milena spoke fluently for ten minutes in 30-second blasts of Polish; Luca would then nod along to the robotic Italian as Milena wolfed down eggs, toast, liver and mash. She told Luca how she had arrived in London, how she had befriended evil Justyna and Maria and poor Dorota. She apologised for how she looked. Milena revealed that a handful of people in John's orbit had died, folks who would be at one party but not the next. Everyone seemed grateful to the councillor for easing their health worries and introducing them to very useful friends, but some went missing. One semi-famous lawyer had been found dead in Poplar from an overdose, days after Milena had talked to him at the pad about his London Marathon training.

It was all a little askew. There never were any arguments at the evenings Milena attended; no one ever badmouthed John, but there was a heaviness in the air, a layer of menace that tramped down the hashish smoke and held everyone trapped as if under glass. "These people, they do what's convenient, not what's right," she sobbed in Polish, "so you suddenly find yourself all alone, dodging all these piranha people. I'm so tired, Luca."

"You don't have to feel alone. This will be our own society, just you and me. As long as Councillor John thinks I'm his friend, you are safe, because I am safe, and we are together, Milena. You're not alone."

Back to the present.

Nena was sitting on the vinyl bench in the back room of her salon, trying to fashion a glass shampoo bottle into a candlestick holder. She was still processing Sam's reappearance as she whittled the wax with the edge of a bottle opener, and she had already managed to shave off the very tip of her left ring-finger. While Nena was very glad of Sam's return, she feared whether too much time had passed and whether Sam was bringing trouble with him to her quiet seaside haven. Of course, he was; but it was an electric thrill to embrace danger.

That pair of Polaroids could be linked to both his disappearance and his re-entry into her life. It was not the sort of surprise package that wends its way to folk who would never suddenly bolt into the night; Sam had left behind a caring, close-knit family; friends who'd give up hope only after several years; a promising set of A Level results; and all his possessions. Neither the sudden exit nor the sudden entrance nor the sinister photos seemed to exist in isolation.

There had once been a local couple, thirtysomething accountants who lived higher up on Military Road, opposite the very first bend when the incline begins to ease off. They had moved to north-west France to live The Good Life; all hens and cows and living off eggs and milk, theirs was an attempt at autarky, but it was hampered by the fact the marriage had been dead in the dirt for years.

The pair had simply transported their real problem from the cradle of Sandgate to the unforgiving harshness of a gîte where they knew neither the language nor any of the region's residents. Their relocation had carried their dislocation with it, and there they were, trapped with each other's own worst enemy on a tiny patch of nowhere land that was plastered in chicken shit. The hope and expectation had been futile – trying to live off a handful of small eggs and a pint of milk for two days while avoiding each other's gaze and all the thrown crockery.

The woman, newly divorced and with wild corkscrew hair and baggy eyes, had popped up again in Sandgate a year later; she now worked stacking trolleys at the big Tesco superstore in Cheriton. God knows where the husband had fetched up; perhaps he was still stuck on that muddy part of Normandy, trying to turn chicken shit into biofuel or calvados. You drag along past problems, sometimes unawares, the problems are like a length of soiled toilet paper that glues itself to your heel.

Nena remembered that quote – "My lifestyle is a consequence of my wounds. I'm the son of my history." We can all pretend that we're hard done by, Nena reasoned, but usually, the catalyst for any hard fortune lies in small or grand mistakes made years ago. The way someone sleeps, for example, might over the course of several years lead to the persistent neck complaint that means they must give up their job, and unemployment might set in train a medusa's head of troubles – alcoholism, a hermit's existence, poverty, homelessness.

Cadders was right – the little otter always spoke sense when not too far over the limit. Nena would wait for Sam to reveal the reason for his flight from Sandgate: she wouldn't ask, because forcing the issue might stem the flow of revelations: she wouldn't prod him for an answer in the muggy after-sex; and she wouldn't ply him with drink. However, she wanted to know everything in every colour and light, even if the filter, given Sam's nature, would be grey and tarnished. That meant traipsing over to his cabin and leaving the elderly gents to thrash their ear hair and pension books against her closed salon door. Now she truly wished she hadn't made the walk through the gorse.

I rocked forwards in my father's patchwork chair and buried my head between my knees; someone told me this would help in times of crisis, but I was hyperventilating. "I didn't know what to do, Nena." I could see the grasses bending as if to hear my confession through the window. "I didn't know whether to call the police or to flee. I ran him over. I did. Drove to Tommy's in panic. I know now that I should have stayed with the boy. I should've just stayed a while in the hope that a car would come, but it was desolate out there. It was pitch-black, half ten on a Saturday. I panicked."

"Couldn't you have called someone?" Nena asked me, perched on the footstool without much on her. I kept my eyes on her tapping feet. It was far too early to start shagging again, however much I wanted to.

"Remember, we didn't have mobiles, Nena? I've sat for hours and hours on my own in that room in Turin. I sat hoping to find a door that would slide me back by chute to that night so I could fix things."

Nena stopped tapping her foot on the scuffed pine boards. "Please don't do this."

I kept gibbering away. "I may have been over the limit, I don't know; it had been a couple of hours since my last drink and I've gunned my way through about six pints of water. I know the kid was OK; he just had a lot of cuts, but he was aware of things; well, as savvy as a boy drunk on vodka who'd been hit by a car can be."

"Sounds like it was his fault."

"All mine, all mine!" I thumped the chair. "You know, I used to sit alone and listen to the voices of the people in the piazza below; they all seemed to be talking about me, this wanker who'd left a boy injured in a country road. I couldn't understand much Italian, but all those folks in the streets seemed to gather below my window, muttering away." I raised my wet eyes to Nena. "I would pay all the money I have. I wish I could go back and rewind it all. I've thought about it every day for the past two decades." I looked away from Nena, but she dragged my face to hers and cradled it.

"That boy was rescued, though. It was probably best you drove to get help, wasn't it?" she countered. "No help would have come if you'd just stayed with the kid in the middle of Alkham Valley Road."

"I drove to Tommy's, not to the cop shop. I couldn't tell if I was over the limit. I shouldn't have been over; as I said, Rhona kept filling me jugs of water. Tommy rang 999, I remember, and I rang my dad. Darl, I'm not very good in such stressed situations, you know that. It all went shit-shaped." My voice quavered and I put Nena's hands down by her side, as gently as I could. "There was a lot of blood, but the boy was talking to me, though the cut to his left cheek was like a second mouth... He was babbling." I looked away again. "What the hell was he doing crawling about in the middle of the night?"

"So, you stayed at Tommy's family farm and then he drove you back down to the cabin the following morning?"

"Yes, then dad took me back to Berwickshire the next day. Tommy said the boy was in hospital overnight for his stitches, but then his mum discharged him the following evening because she could care for him better."

"The mother was probably thinking her boy would be taken away by social services, Sammy."

I sighed. "I didn't even know his name, but you know how small this bit of the country seems at times; you can't even cut your hair without some mad old biddy moaning about it two miles away. I thought there'd be huge repercussions, especially if he was from the traveller community around Dover. I recall his hands were dirty, absolutely caked in mud, and there was vodka on his breath. I remember this thick dirt under his nails. What was he doing there? It wasn't very helpful at all, Nena, you know?"

"Yep. So how did you get to Italy? We didn't see your folks down here for a while."

"That was just happenstance really, and of course I'd left school here; A-Levels were over, and I wouldn't need the results. Dad was doing a lot of volunteer work at the rallies up near Duns. Then I got a call from Tommy that he was flying to Italy to work as a paralegal out there. So I went with him. I didn't have any other options left open to me after our blazing row and the hit-and-run. I heard nothing except what my folks reported back, and, a year on, no one really asked that much after me."

Nena checked her watch, stood up from the foot-stool and went to the Welsh dresser to put on her dress. "Sammy, you overreacted back then. You always do."

"Do I?"

"Yes. And you're sweating yourself into a soup. You overthink yourself into a course of extreme action. You weren't escaping a crime scene – the kid was jackassing around on a country road, pissed out of his head, and probably fell into the path of the Flying Pig."

"I was to blame!" I despaired.

"You cannot take on the responsibilities of other people – I mean, where the hell were the boy's parents at half ten at night? Probably shagging; maybe they had got him hammered on vodka at the local – what is it? The Marquis?" Nena went over to the kitchenette and filled a glass of water. "Anyway, Sammy, have this. Sack it off."

"Where are you off to?" I asked.

"I've got to meet my mate Cadwick's new woman. You'll meet them both soon, I hope – if you don't run away to Piedmont again because you swatted a wasp."

"Stay!"

"Change your T-shirt, Sammy; you reek of tinned hotdogs." Nena opened the cabin door and turned back towards me. "You're your own worst enemy, you know – this form of self-hate is hard to watch, and it always has been."

"What do you mean, Nena?"

"You crucify yourself; it's like a Calvary complex you have. You cut and re-edit the past like an obsessive trapped in their own little museum."

"I don't just sit in this cabin…"

Nena coughed. "Live in the present. I'm just extremely glad you're back, and if I'm a bit saddened that it took nearly 20 years to happen, then that's the price of having you return here at all. Keep me near now, Sammy, and don't you ever drift too far. And calm the hell down, soldier."

"Ciao, bella," I said, locking the door behind Nena. I didn't want to close it. Through the kitchen window, I watched her slowly trace our footsteps back to that old stile past the centuries-old mile-marker. Nena wasn't walking with her usual balletic gait.

Then I could make out the misty forms of my parents, following a few steps behind her. I put my hand on the kitchen window and bowed my head to the glass – my hallucinations, coming to me again…

Oh, to have been Cadders; sitting there on the velvet couch between his two girls, a mack daddy in country casual he'd picked up from the garden centre; a beautiful navy Barbour quilted jacket, a cream-and-chestnut checked shirt and cherry-red cords. He had ditched his floppy cap from the other day, after it had provoked Nena into giggles. Instead, he was wearing a black beanie in a desperate attempt to hide the baldness playing peekaboo between his cherubic curls. This was Cadwick's idea of heaven. The toffee vodka would soon be out; then it would be a game of truth or dare until passing-out time. Nena was odds-on to be the one pouring Cadders into his usual taxi.

Shockingly, Jacqui was rather more like Cadwick had described her in his hormonal breathlessness and rather less like the 50-something emotional wreck Nena had envisaged during all the hyperbolic waffle. Jacqui was a good deal younger than the other two; her Chelsea Blonde face had yet to suffer any sun damage from the Sandgate micro-climate.

But for the absence of logos and a name-tag, Jacqui could have been wearing a flight attendant's uniform, such was the formal air and blueness of her twin-piece. She had a tendency to laugh from her shoulders up, wrenching the chuckle from her very core, so Nena resolved to keep any wisecracking to a minimum until she was too tipsy to be bothered by it. How dare Jacqui find life so fun?

"Yes. Nena, tell Jacqs about your blast from the past." Cadwick's nickname for Jacqui was beginning to mither Nena, but she gamely told them about the elusive Sam, in return for a gin and slim. They fuel me with drink, and I'll play raconteur, she thought.

"Anyway, Sam was telling me about why he left – seems he had knocked down a young boy."

"Oh, God!" exclaimed 'Jacqs'.

"No, no. The lad was ok, but Sammy was mortified. He thought he'd be done for drunk-driving; he got his best mate to drive to the scene and sort it out."

Jacqui wrinkled up her nose. "That poor boy was left all alone?"

"Only for about half an hour, maybe even twenty minutes, Jacqui," Nena responded. She wished Jacqs was necking spirits rather than nursing a white wine spritzer she seemed to have had beamed in from a neon cocktail bar in 1985. "Sammy's not the sort of guy to abdicate his responsibilities, and the boy was out of hospital within a day. His mother came for him. The boy had been very drunk. I mean, what was he doing crawling around the farm road in the pitch black?"

"Sam did the right thing, Nena," echoed Cadwick. "He went and got help, and he saved his own neck, too. The boy got proper care."

Jacqui sighed. "But the police…"

Cadders continued: "The police can't be trusted to make the right call, especially now. All those cutbacks put so much stress on them. I feel sorry for the sods. It must be a case of prioritising need, and it shouldn't be that way in the modern world. Anyway, what the hell do I know?"

"The lad was apparently absolutely plastered on voddy and crawling down the lane on his hands and knees like a dog," Nena reiterated. "Poor Sam is in the cabin sweating himself to death and pacing around, even now."

"Don't take the blame away from this Sam of yours, Nena," Jacqui interjected. "He should've stopped and taken the boy to the hospital. Those minutes are crucial. And Sam probably didn't stop because I just know he'd been drinking. It doesn't matter that the boy had been crawling in the road. You'd stop if you'd hit a dog."

Cadwick felt it time to join in. "Well, Nena, at least you know now – Sam didn't just run off because you'd gone all Mommy Dearest on him that night, eh?"

Jacqui wouldn't let things lie, however. "That poor boy. What if he'd been bleeding internally during the 30 minutes he was on his own, dazed in the road?"

"He was talking perfectly normally for a drunk kid…" Nena corrected Jacqui again. "Anyway, he was on his own for about 20 minutes. He was compos mentis."

"That's no sign. You're just covering for your boyfriend, Nena. My mum's friend bashed her head on a swimming pool wall and died a day later in Guy's Hospital. She was only 43 and left three kids. It's just like that actress Natasha Richardson – you know, Liam Neeson's wife. She was fine after a skiing tumble and then, a few hours later, she was dead from a brain haemorrhage. If someone gets whacked in the head, you might be leaving them for dead. I wouldn't leave anyone who was bleeding from the head. No right-thinking person would. It's savage." Jacqui was not making any friends here. She was truthfully on a mission to blow apart the cosy friendship between Christian Cadwick and this lithe brunette he appeared to worship.

"It's all right playing devil's advocate, Jacqui," Nena hissed, her gaze set unwaveringly on the new girl in her starchy royal-blue suit, "but this all happened in a blur to a boy of 18, who was very scared himself. See it through his eyes. He was, he is, a naïve worrier, completely unworldly."

Cadders was not smiling now either. He undid a shirt button. "The real issue, Jacqs, is that Nena here lost her soulmate for nigh-on two decades – Sam suffered enough – and poor old me has had to listen to her interminable prattle for the past 12 years." He could never resist a punchline; his right eye was closing and pulling away from the left as the alcohol did its magic. Jacqui was quite unsure which eye to look into, Nena had noticed, much to her amusement. "Still, Nena, Sam's back now. You're keeping him hidden over there on the cliffs or shagging him into catatonia."

Nena sighed. "He's sleeping – we've been compressing 18 years of history into the past 18 hours, Cadwick." She paused. "There'll be a time when we can all have dinner at Rocksalt and rake over old coals and guess at how things might have been. We can all spout off then." Nena shot a poisonous look at Jacqui that Cadwick caught, but his girlfriend thankfully didn't.

"Let's have another drink," Cadders piped up. It was always time for a drink when the thirstiest man in town was around. "Jacq, be a doll and get another round in? Here's twenty." Cadders gave Jacqui the note with a wink and turned the other way, facing to Nena as if he were a justice of the peace delivering his measured opinion on matters. "You never know what would've happened if you and Sam had been stuck in this dull perch on the coast for the past two decades. What's the point of replaying the past until the film breaks? And you don't want to slide back to the place you were in. You used to barricade yourself inside a wall of gin bottles at the back of your salon."

Nena rattled the ice in her tumbler and shook the lemon slice onto the tiled tabletop. "It is annoying me how a simple event – well, a quite major event that blew out of proportion all those years ago – has essentially put my happiness on hold. I've lost my 20s and most of my 30s to this grand wait, and was it worth it? Now Sam's back, will it work out? I was worrying this morning about what troubles he's dragged across from Turin. Am I strong enough to deal with a damaged man with a grieving and worried mind, no matter how much I love him? Do I have that in me? At times, I haven't. How could I have coped with both my parents dying when I was so young, and yet I haven't been able to deal with Sam's absence? How can it be? Life is short enough without having to wait for misunderstandings to be resolved. That's if they ever truly are. We have to make the best of what we're left facing. Life is survival, Cadwick. You know that; you taught me that. Surviving, well, often that's the extent of our control over God's unknown plans…"

"Nena, you do more than survive, old gal. You run your business, and you have done for 18 years without any real help. Look at all the places that close every day. You've achieved it all as an orphan, as a single woman." Cadwick now had his hand on Nena's right shoulder, something Jacqui noticed from over by the bar. "I haven't taught you a thing."

"It's okay, Cadders. I probably wouldn't have the salon now if I'd stayed with Sam back then. There's no guarantee that we'd still have been together after 18 years. We – we were both a bit fighty."

Cadwick smiled: "Were?"

Nena continued: "Well, at least we're together now, at an age when we can make a better shot of it. We don't have money worries, or children to cart around."

"It's the same with me. I mean, I thank the Lord my fertile seed and love of the ladies haven't brought a mucoid urchin knocking on the door of Castle Cadwick."

"Cadders, please be serious, just this once. Why always act the arse?"

"Ok, I shall be serious." Cadders loosened his smile and frowned.

"Maybe this hiatus has meant Sam and I will grow old and grey together…"

"Just take things slowly, Nena. Sam may be dragging back a ton of issues. The Italians I know are mainly cokeheads."

"That's nice…"

Cadders continued: "And people who suddenly turn up from nowhere are often running away from somewhere."

"Again, nice."

Cadders smiled. "It's only been a couple of days that he's been back and, as you say, there's a quarter of a lifetime to catch up on for each of you." He paused. "For as sure as Jacqs will tear a strip off me later for some infinitesimal slip of my tongue, or just for being a pube-headed dwarf whose money she can't resist, and how she hates herself for that, just as sure is the fact that the past is treading on all our toes. Your Martin Guerre may not be divulging his true history."

"What do you mean, Cadders?"

"I mean – beware the past. The truth is revealed in its various forms, once all our storytelling and bullshitting are over. Does anyone really know anyone? If one goes up to the East Cliff and looks over across the harbour, does one see the architecture of The Bayle and think, "How beautiful are the narrow streets of Georgian architecture!" Or does one instead think of the many hundreds of crimes committed there over the centuries? Perspective, gal."

"Meaning?" Nena looked most baffled.

"Oh, I don't know. Maybe Sam was a nightmare in his twenties. Maybe you've avoided all the shit the young man may have brought to you. Maybe he was a drug dealer. Maybe he served time."

"Nice, nice, thrice nice!"

"Well… Maybe he spent years working in a soup kitchen as penitence for spending a while in one of those Italian gangs where they all wear biker leathers and buzz around on scooters, dishing out drugs. Maybe it's all a question of mood and perspective. Maybe the only thing that matters is the present day. Maybe someone else has been suffering from Sam's intensity all these years, and it was a poor signorita who broke him in for you. Maybe that signorita pines for Sam now, as you have pined for him. But I bet she wouldn't channel her directionless rage and emptiness into a successful business."

"The salon's hardly threatening to become a franchise, Cadders. Steady on."

"Put it this way. If Jacqs is indeed The One, and that's highly improbable, then maybe she'll one day consider sending a bouquet of thanks to each and every one of the poor gals who've scooped me up and poured me into a waiting taxi. Men need a lot of breaking-in and life-coaching from women; and there are a lot of ladies who wish to play a mother Madonna role of sorts. It's in the genetic make-up of both sexes. But you, it's not in your nature – you are as maternal as that wild phantom in the bingo hall on Grace Hill. You seemed to exist on merlot and no sleep. You don't have to be a Madonna woman. You're just a great person."

Nena stared off into the drizzle outside. "I don't want to play mother to anyone, not even you, my loyal Cadders."

Cadwick winked at her: "We always see the same things from a different point of view – your position is a bit more lofty than mine, though."

"That's my heels," Nena laughed.

"Sam will have his reasons; aren't we all correct in our own minds, eh?"

Nena flicked the lemon slice into Cadders' lap. "Our weird and wondrous ways, dear boy – forever forged in the furnace of our desires."

After drinks, the trio decided to walk to the beach, sit on the shingle and watch the waves as the booze kicked in. They never got there.

"Join arms with me!" The sixth spritzer had sent Jacqui into the stratosphere, aboard her own out-of-control airliner, pointing wildly at the nearest available exits, mascara riverletting down her pampered features.

Only half-an-hour before, Jacqui had been describing the Greek Revival architecture that graced Rathebone Park, the country pile whose sale she had the mandate to oversee. Nena had been impressed by Jacqui's passion for the Grade I-listed house; she was obviously hugely knowledgeable about antiques and architecture, and she was almost demonically predisposed to succeed as a property agent, granting Nena and Cadwick a room-by-room guided tour of Rathebone, its cornicing, ceiling roses and Coadeware plaques, the harpsichords, twin pipe organs and pianos on which occasional concerts were given. But now... now Jacqui was well away, all her professionalism having been sunk beneath the waves of white wine.

"Link my arms, Nena!" Jacqui had been hollering for half an hour, and she was dancing to her own invisible disco; the old ladies with the blue hair, bright pink cheeks and chattering teeth had craned their necks as they sat waiting for the no16 bus. "Dance for me, Nena!"

"No, I can't. Dance alone, Jacqui," Nena replied.

Cadwick, whose right eye was now completely shut, stopped. "What's up? You're not still worrying about Sam, are you?"

"Feel shit…" Nena had indeed been fretting about Sam. Was he pacing the lounge in the cabin? Was he imagining his mother placing the crockery in the drainer of the kitchenette? Was he endlessly replaying the crash on a loop in his mind, until the tape began to warp and new horrors crept into his imagination – the boy now dead, bleeding out on the Tarmac, the police cars parked in a circle around his dented brown Austin, and a dozen officers racing to pin Sam against the bonnet of his car?

All these things Nena knew were happening in the cloistered hush of Sam's cliff-top cabin; he was slowly becoming a prisoner of his mind's eye. Nena had to make her exit. "You know, guys, I'm going to the cabin. I need to check on Sam…"

"Don't go!" Cadwick and Jacqui screamed in unison, but Nena had already turned back towards the way they came, walking past the brown-bricked council offices, the enormous mini mansion halfway up the hill with its Doric columns and pool-house, and the church at its bottom that had been converted into luxury homes.

Soon, Nena found herself jogging back to the cabin to find out which wraith Sam was running from. Within ten minutes, she was there.

"That piano stool was not there. It was here," I screamed. "You were sitting on it, remember? Damn. When I was telling you about the accident? You were sitting right in front of me, and I was in Dad's wingback chair. That footstool has always been there. My Dad used to rest his slippers up on it. You see – the scuff marks?" I was pacing around. I was plain terrified.

"Calm the hell down, Sammy, or I'll have to call for an ambulance." I was drenched with worry.

"Someone has been in here, Nena. They came in while I was sleeping in the wingback chair – they have moved certain things around."

"Really, Sam?"

"I can't see anything missing, but nothing's in its right place. All the trophies on the dresser have been shifted around, but the dresser is where it was."

"Are you sure?"

"Why would someone do this? My wallet is here, my driving licence and passport are in the dresser, but the footstool and the ornaments are not where they were two hours ago."

"Serenity, Sam."

"What in the hell is happening? Did I move them? Am I losing it? Am I?"

Nena was still breathless from her jog over from Sandgate. She was tracking my hand movements, taking it all in. She could see the scuffmarks from where the stool had been dragged out of place. She'd been sitting on it that very afternoon, trying to calm me down from the endless onslaught of my eddying memories.

"Nena, I'm not making this up." I was still wearing the grey marl T-shirt, and the sweat was pouring from my forehead, down my face, and forming darker grey rings around the neck-hole of my top. I just wanted to shower.

"I know, Sam." Nena replied instantly. "I had a hunch something was up. So, I came."

"You had a hunch?" I asked.

"Yes, I left Cadwick and his annoying tit of a girlfriend. I ran here. You're having a panic attack, but, yes, someone has rearranged things. Why? I don't know."

"Thank you. Thanks for running here."

"Calm down, please."

"I'm scared," I replied. "I was only asleep for two hours, three hours tops. I suppose the intruder only needed a few minutes to reorder everything."

Nena frowned her little kitten-nosed frown and blew out her cheeks. "You have to calm down and let your thoughts rest. Were you asleep all afternoon? I left at 3pm."

"What time is it now? 7.30pm? Yes, I've been asleep most of the time."

"Then they must have done it in the past three or four hours."

"I was asleep, in a deep sleep, in the wingback, and I awoke. I haven't touched a thing since you left. Not even the junk, not even the dirty dishes. In fact, I've left it all as it was when I first got here down from the funeral – look, Mum's birders' book is still on the dresser. I didn't move the trophies, the footstool, the magazine rack." I paused. "Why? Why would someone do this to me?"

"The Polaroids, Sam. I told you so."

"What's with the photos?"

"Sam, it's all very random to us, but to the person who's doing this, there'll be a perfect plan."

"Such as?" I cut in, knowing I was being rude.

"Well, you hear all sorts at the salon. Some of the greybeards act like the oldest teenagers in town. You know? They're always pranking each other."

"Pranks. For God's sake!"

"People play practical jokes to alleviate the boredom that is Sandgate life. It's childish, but it happens." Nena shook her head, and the kittenish frown fell away.

"Who would possibly prank me? Only you and Alan Couper know I'm here. The others are hundreds of miles away... Mimi can't even walk most days after 11am." I laughed. "You know what she's like – all the days, weeks and months just elide into one big slosh."

"No, not Mimi." Nena moved the footstool back to where it had been. "What about Tom, or Tommy, or whatever the hell he's calling himself this season? What about him?"

Nena had never liked Tom. As she had become steadily more saturnine in her teens, so Tom began to craft his Flashheart persona, all flying jackets, "fillies" and flights of fancy. Now, the revelation that he had offered me a job in northern Italy and, in her mind, lured me away all those years ago, like some pissed-up Pied Piper of Piedmont, was enough to make her suspicious of someone she hadn't seen since the last millennium.

"Tom's too busy fleecing widows."

"But where is he?" Nena asked.

"He's in another country. Probably doing a lap of a lake before an evening of roistering," I closed my eyes in the vain hope this suggested weariness would stop Nena's line of questioning. "I doubt he's in the country."

"What a tired game for a man approaching 40 to play! Sorry, I meant 'man-child'," Nena smiled. "Tom would probably fly all the way over just to mess about with you."

"He's not bored. He's not like your old buffers," I replied.

"He's a shitbird. Like when he booked me into a stud farm to 'get me loosened up' and gave them my poor folks' contact details. He was always a loon, except I never find much to laugh about when he was telling one of his tall tales."

"He's got a steady girlfriend now. You haven't seen him this century; things have changed. Claudia would break his balls if he flew in to muck me about."

"He'd find a way," Nena snorted.

I raised my voice. "Tom barely has time to take a piss these days. He does these insane jogs around the River Po to buy himself a little space, some time when he's not fielding work calls on his Blackberry, driving Claudia to some fashion fitting or doing up the ceiling in his mini palace."

"The higher a monkey climbs, the more he shows his tail," Nena countered. "And the older this particular monkey gets, the harder he'll fall off the tree."

"What does that even mean?" I asked, slightly fed up that we were focusing on my erstwhile friend's foibles rather than the immediate concern of finding the intruder or prankster. The rearrangement of objects was far too subtle for Tom's tastes.

"I mean, the guy needs to calm down. I mean, I never understood why you venerated Tom and not dear Harry." She was hovering near the dresser and the Jiffy bag.

"Harry killed himself on a superbike," I countered. "Tom is a very rich bloke, super fit, and he has a lot of work coming in. Probates, wills – they never go away. Anyway, I'm my own man. I'm not Robin; Tom's not Batman."

"I'm not saying that!"

"I haven't told you yet about what went on in Turin. I wasn't some butler to my adventurous best friend."

"So, what were you, Sam?" Nena asked.

I ignored this. "If I ever had a hero, it was my dad. God bless the old boy."

Nena looked down. "Yes, sorry. I was just mocking the way you guys get together – blokes always chain themselves to the biggest idiot out of their friends."

"Not too much wrong with Tommy. Just a juvenile tosser," I smiled.

"It's almost as if you want to give yourself the hardest life to prove you're a man by hitching yourself to some broken-down best mate. You haul a hundredweight of wanker along with you. It's a bloody mystery to me, male friendship." Nena laughed.

"You don't have to understand it."

"It's just a mystery, that's all."

"Well, it's just as much a mystery what kind of wrong-nut would break into someone's home just to mess up with their heads. It's all messed up, Nena. Everything is broken."

"That it is."

"Nothing really makes any sense this week." I looked up at Nena from the wingback and wiped my eyes free of sleep. "I don't know if I'm grieving, or if I'm severely sleep-deprived, but I just can't see why someone would do this."

"This bag holds the key to the madness." And Nena shook the yellow padded envelope. "If we find the bearded man in the Polaroids and the house he's kipping in, then we'll probably discover why you're being messed with."

"God, people get so bored these days," I murmured.

Nena nodded. "I was waiting for Cadwick and Jacqui and just scrolling through Facebook, and it's wall-to-wall cat videos, rants about world politics, selfies and boast-posts about how wonderful life is. In the meantime, you see none of those things. It's just life out there, and life only."

I smiled. "And how do you pass the time?"

"Well, I try to wear you out now, don't you? I try to shag the sadness out of you, bury all your concerns at the foot of your bed," Nena winked. "Before that, I slept. And I drank like a shoal of fishes, of course. And I cut a lot of grey heads, trimmed a lot of ears and waged a one-woman war on white nasal hair."

"So, shall we go to the bedroom then? Leave the Jiffy bag there – I don't want to think about it."

Nena agreed. "Let's forget about it until the morning. Let's hibernate. We can pretend it's 1945 and we're doing our little bit to rebuild a war-torn world, bed first."

The dark lord revisits.

This kind of prickly heat didn't agree with Councillor John at all. His pale-blue linen shirt clung to his skin via the corona of sweat around his nipples and the beer-mat moistness of his lower back. The flight had been a mess of incompetence; the transit bus had been waiting at the wrong side of the airport, and then the old French heap broke down. John had ended up swearing at the driver in full Cockney. He was thankful that this visit to the Sacra Di San Michele was to be mercifully brief; any more exposure to the Torinese sun, and he'd be poached like a slab of red snapper.

As he braced himself against the rear flank of the Lancia taxi, he adjusted his tired eyes to the thousand-year-old abbey that stood atop the craggy Mount Pirchiriano. Was Asgar keeping an hourly eye on his errant daughter? Were the foundations setting all right over in East London? Why was he here? John needed to be everywhere. Skype was not enough. Soonest meet his business interests, soonest home, back to the breakfast omelettes and his owlish hours in his study. Gracie would bring her drama, the slamming of doors and sofa-slumping, regardless of when John returned. She was a whole carnival in teen form. Maybe she should elope with that floppy-haired tosser of hers. She could be his burden. He was young and fresh; that boy didn't need amphetamines.

What John and his confreres shared, aside from the steady accumulation of money, cash with which to slip through life's snags, was a fascination with the other side of the mirror, the occult, the pre-religious state of the world.

There had been no messiah to comfort the witnesses of eruptions, earthquakes and lightning strikes back in early times, just the elemental earth and rain. The water washed away the grime; and it revivified early mankind. Sacra Di San Michele was the portal to this prehistory; from certain angles, it resembled a stone sculpture of a kneeling Greek Orthodox priest, but from others, it crouched on the mount like a hell-dog primed to sprint off and ravage every land.

In his grief, Councillor John had come to accept a fitful nihilism. He had let the blackness into his midnight study and he'd sunk into the void, a swimming pool full of tar in which his tears and fretfulness wouldn't show. Weakness was not allowed.

At the mount, at the abbey site where St Michael had warred with Lucifer himself, John would feel the lick of a dark tongue and a surge of power course through his spine. He'd read the Chronicon Coenobii Sancti Michaelis de Clusa and rejected the idea that the abbey was as new as the year 966 – this edifice belonged to the ages before time itself, long before Christ and other consolers of the weak. Early man had no time for platitudes and placebos in his harsh times.

The devil himself had come to Mount Pirchiriano for a reckoning with the archangel; they had sparred on the French west coast at Mont Saint-Michel, this battle between dark and light that straddled the globe in a daisychain of almighty dust-ups. John had followed the trail from station to station, across the latitudes and, at every stop, he'd met kindred souls recharging with the energies of the elemental.

Many of these fellow travellers were now benefactors in John's clinics; again, failure was not an option. On the morning John had buried his wife Jeannie, he'd been expected on a conference call to explain away slow growth in the East London interests. The chicks always needed feeding.

An athlete in grey Lycra skipped past John at the foot of the mount. The councillor turned to watch the young man slalom up the hiking paths with the ease of jogging on the flat and remembered a time when he possessed boundless, non-chemically assisted energy. In the end, we all end up at the mercy of medicine, John mused, no matter how deep our faith in the archangels and the Benedictine monks. The spirit to survive comes from within; the hand-holding lasts only for as long as a Sunday service. You're on your own, kid, for all the good that running up inclines will do you; there might be a switch, a genetic twitch, that runs down your heart when you reach the top of the mount. Then you're screwed.

John padded over to the bench; he was 15 minutes early for Don Paganino. The last translator had been appalling, turning up on a shonky folding bike that had completely punctured the entrepreneurial air. The Where's Wally lookalike had then pissed around with his cycle clips for an eternity, grease from the chain on his slacks and Converse shoes. "Are you trying to tell me my own surname is Willis, not Wells?" had been the councillor's final words to the translator, and Paganino had bundled the guy back into the rear of his Maserati Quattroporte. It was now up to the Don to bring someone who knew the etiquette that geared such lofty business meetings.

John sat down on the bench and freed his shirt from its clammy fastenings; the slats of the concrete rubbed into his backside. He wanted home. The shades from the mount made even the successful man feel miniscule, but he was no longer trapped beneath the sun. John fiddled with his iPhone and looked up as Paganino's Maserati pulled into the car park with a swaggering curve. It was time for business; Paganino, you bollock around with my minutes and seconds, and I'll spend a lifetime shafting you sideways.

Far above the streets and houses.

Nudging the verges that act as an approximate guide, my Austin wobbles across the undulations of the country road, sending the moonlight scattering in the puddles that have formed. It's raining with a passion now, and a low mist hugs the broken Tarmac, so it becomes almost indistinguishable from the miry laybys. Alkham Farm Road has always been a dog track; the craters have already punctured my offside rear tyre that summer.

What am I doing on this circuitous route to the Leas? I've added a couple of miles to my journey back to the cabin, all to avoid any police cars scouting for Saturday drunk-drivers. Am I still tipsy? I don't know. Thank god I feel sharper than when Nena huffed her way home a couple of hours ago. The water has worked its wonders, I think. My heart isn't fast-spinning to oblivion like a short-geared clock any more.

Like my father, I prefer older vehicles; there's less to go wrong, and the steering is more direct and true. I can feel the imperfections in the road through the steering wheel, with its boss looking like a black cummerbund. The tramlines on the road are pushing the thin Austin tyres to the left, though, and I am rueing the day I'd ripped out the radio's wire to tie the shoogly exhaust pipe in place. I could use a little night music to keep my mind alert; I'm flagging and I've been up for 16 hours.

Then, there's a low booming sound, and the elderly Austin shoots right towards a muddy lay-by. I brake immediately but in vain, and my vinyl seat is sent upwards as if on the Leas Lift, the funicular that falters and shudders from Folkestone seafront to the promenade. Up, up and up, my seat climbs steadily through the still air until I am sitting at a point some thirty feet above the front of the car, my bare feet dangling in the chill summer's night. I flex my toes.

I have a bird's-eye view of the scene now, down towards the offside front bumper under which the crumpled body of a boy lies. He is moving and groaning, almost lost in the cocoon of his blue parka coat, trying to form a ball, twenty seconds too late. I can see his curtained brown hair glued with blood to the road, a few dark guy-ropes tethered to the ground. He is calling out, but I can't hear what he's saying. I lean as far forward as I can without falling the 30ft from my seat.

All these unending years I'd been castigating myself for leaving this young lad in such a state, but what was the point of all that soul-searching? He'll be fine. I can see him on all fours, scurrying into that lonely road for some lost reason, the snap contact with my left bumper then sending him spinning, his limbs spreading out as if they are linen clothes riding the breezes on a fast-revolving washing line. He rotates to a stop, and a foamy chalk outline forms around him like a grey-white aura. He won't die.

I float down out of the seat and land softly on the balls of my feet so I'm standing over the boy. There are cuts to his left cheek, the largest one being by the side of his mouth. I can smell Smirnoff on him, sweated out in fear, mingling with the damp and murk, and his hands are tanned by dirt; it has collected under his fingernails like he's been clawing the roadside. I look up at the single Victorian streetlamp and then to the lay-by, which has the marks left by the boy's hands and knees. Has he crawled into the road, his addled mind turning him into some feral beast?

Then he launches at me with his soiled hands, tearing at my throat until he grips tightly and throttles me, his boozy mouth foaming at the sides. He's snarling, and his thumbs press into my windpipe with all his strength. I black out. When I awake from the dream within the dream, I'm back in the cabin, but the place has still been raided.

Saving his skin.

Luca was face down on his trusty sofa; during his half-week off from the post office, he'd taken to swapping day for night, 'la nuit americaine'. He lifted up his head to catch the television still buzzing away. There were no faces in the static. There was another day before he was due back at his window, and he had hoped to sleep it off and remain in his dreams, but there was little chance of turning another day of worrying into much-needed rest. Luca looked at the TV again. He wondered if the oceans of Barolo he was drinking were helping or hindering his thought-processes; he seemed to be turning hours into minutes and minutes into hours. His mouth was a red mulch. Time had fractured itself. These were broken-backed days.

If Luca was now part of this secret society of councillor John, then the threat of suffocation was something he could readily avoid, unlike the poor Dorota. If there was the option of sex in return for his silence about what he had seen, then he would be mute for ever more. Luca was trapped; he might as well bend the circumstances to suit himself, allow himself a little sunlight from above, even if his feet were shackled to the floor below. Luca knew he couldn't now soar away like a mountain eagle back home to Lake Orta and the Sacro Monte, so he might as well adapt the surroundings he found himself in. Most days, he didn't speak at all outside of working hours anyway. Silence for sex might just become an easy trade; a monastic vow of silence in return for more carnal pleasures with Justyna.

Luca had helped Milena escape all the darkness. That was his good deed. She now had cash in hand after their café meet-up to buy a flight back to Krakow; she could stay with a great aunt, who had doted on her parents. To help this fragile foal of a woman evade councillor John and his set had eased a fragment of Luca's own guilt at playing pals with a man whose friends were rumoured to disappear and at whose flat Luca had witnessed a murder. Milena was a pure drop in an ocean of noise that was far louder and more invasive than the television's angry buzz.

What other choice did Luca have, if even councillors, police officers and judges were part of John's brotherhood? Who would listen, especially in these uncertain times? Luca could imagine the police officers pretending not to understand what he was trying to explain, about the Rover motor car, the old man with the horn of white hair, the blood-spray on his tatty suit, his form becoming just a ragbag of fabric and bone being kicked around the muddy grass of the concrete-fringed quad, kicked into nothingness, kicked into an immobile mound. And then there was the girl Dorota, this bird-like creature whose last moments Luca couldn't think about without welling up. The police officers were in on it all, in exchange for good health, good career opportunities and good head.

No, Luca was better off clasping the crag, rather than being shot out of the skies. He would befriend John, invite him into his flat for little chats, and hoover up all the perks that then would come his way; sweeter wine, lovelier ladies, fewer weekends of paranoia and sleeplessness. Luca's conscience would remain clean now Milena was safely back in Poland.

Councillor John Wills had left his embossed black plastic business card in Luca's pigeonhole. None of this paper nonsense for Councillor John, of course; this was not a man who microwaved his Sunday lunch. Luca imagined that John's Greenwich townhouse probably boasted three bedrooms, a stainless-steel kitchen, and a marble floor, staffed by a diligent maid and a discreet butler. John definitely didn't own a telly that needed a lolly-stick jammed into the on-off button. His television set was very likely a wall-mounted flatscreen larger than Luca's bed.

How would Luca win over a man who had everything on tap? All he could offer was his time and his silence. He would run errands for John, and maybe he'd catch a few of the cherries falling off the councillor's overflowing plate. Luca tapped the plastic card on the hallway shelf and set it down next to the stack of the takeaway menus. It was time to feed now.

Extracurriculars.

The man spoke sharply into the hotel pay phone, scrawling a stick figure on the paper pad on the shelf. "No, I'm not calling you from a private line. I don't have one. I don't even have a mobile properly set up here. I'll call you rather than vice versa, but you can PM me on the Facebook page. Yes. There might be a problem here, but I need to work out a few things." He paused. "Listen. There's a fat mudskipper trying to use the phone. Yes, I'll PM you tonight. Yes. Bye."

He hung up the receiver and mouthed "Off you go" to the panting chap dripping in his waterproof clothes. Then he ran up the swooping rise of the hotel's art deco staircase to get ready for the company he'd hired for the afternoon. He was going to start revelling in the dividends of orphanhood, instead of riding out panic attacks in solitude.

By the pricking of my thumbs.

Nena had left me snoozing in the cabin bedroom but not before swiping the blonde kisscurl from my forehead and the Polaroids from the Jiffy bag. Having bored the shit out of her with my neuroses, I'd drifted off, thanks to some breathing techniques she'd learnt herself when her parents died – four seconds of deep breath in, seven seconds of holding it in and then slow exhalations for eight.

And now, in the back room of her salon, Nena set out the photographs on her tiled table for Cadwick's appraisal. She studied his response – the cap was back; and the black beanie had been banished. He looked like an abysmal Seventies singer-songwriter, the kind who got one shot on Top Of The Pops, something to brag about for the rest of their days, all those hours teaching one-fingered guitar to bored rich kids.

"I thought you might be able to help me out here, Cadders," Nena began. Her balding lieutenant nodded. The cap slid down. "You see, that lounge window? It's metal-framed and very distinctive. There can't be many of those still about, can there? It's definitely something to work on."

Cadwick hummed. "You'd be surprised, darling. There was a period when not very many refurbs were done here; Folkestone was a bit of a forgotten place, wasn't it? It was just too far from London."

"You can never be too far from that hole," Nena replied.

"Well, you've never been to the capital, have you? Then, of course, money was pumped into the old town by Roger de Haan and Saga, and art deco features came back in vogue, so there are a few examples. Are you sure this is from around Folkestone?" He leant in further to peer at the

Polaroids with the same expert eye that scanned for antiques every weekend and twentysomethings every other night.

"No, we're not sure if it's here," Nena replied, a little crestfallen. "How would you go about finding out if the house is local? Help."

"You assume it is," Cadwick sighed.

"If we can find the place, then Sam and I agree we might get to the root of who has been messing him around."

"What?"

"These Polaroids were waiting for him on the cabin step, so it must have been someone who knew that Sam's parents had died and that he would be returning to Folkestone. Therefore, we must assume that the person is local, and the house is somewhere in the Folkestone area, no? Or are we jumping a step too far, old man?"

Cadwick whipped out his smartphone and rapidly took snaps of the Polaroids. A few taps later, he beamed. "The photos are on my WhatsApp group. The guys will tell us if they've viewed this place; I have contacts in most of the estate agencies."

"Lucky you!"

"The market is very febrile at the moment, lots of turnover of properties, Nena. Some houses are bought and sold three times a year." Cadders paused. "You ought to see if Sam wants a few introductions to agents; with his experience and presentable manner, he'd be a smash hit."

Nena's smile returned, and Cadwick caught it. "Nena. You were a smash with Jacqs, you know? She sees you as her elegant sister."

"Really, Cadders? Elegant? Women usually get pissed off with me; they always have the impression that I'm playing up to the boys by dressing down."

"Hush, now," Cadders said.

"'A hairdresser who doesn't wear make-up? And we never see her at the coffeeshops. And did you see the state of her own hair, piled up like a drunken bird's nest?'"

"You're not a girly girl by any measure, Nena."

"I just prefer boys' company. It's so much more uncomplicated and less judgmental, usually, but maybe that's just the reprobates I've hung out with, like your good self."

"How do I let you talk to me in this way? None of the investors or even high-net-worthers speak to me like this."

Nena looked at his hat. "The cap's made a return, I see. You no longer look like MC Hammered."

"The beanie was worth a go."

"A go? I'm glad it's gone."

"I gave it to a homeless man on Cheriton Road." Cadders smiled. "Well, Jacqui liked you a lot. I managed to pack her off into a hubcapless Toyota Carina before she started running around the golf course half-naked. She says sorry for the dancing – she blames a lack of dinner – and for going on about the hit-and-run."

Nena frowned again. "It wasn't a hit-and-run. Cadders, you must correct her."

"I shall, I shall," the little man harrumphed.

"Cadders! This isn't a historical cold-case. And anyway, I doubt Jacqui remembers very much of our night on the tiles."

Now it was Cadwick's turn to frown. "She remembers everything in its completeness. She's under a great deal of pressure to complete the Rathebone House deal, so she likes to let loose when she has the opportunity for a duvet day the morning after. Jacqui means no offence. It's simply she has to compartmentalise work and play and to pack all the latter into a single night. She does have a boss after all, unlike us." Cadders paused, realising the mood of investigation could be shattered. "Listen. We can always check to see if this house is Listed."

Cadders had become an expert in diversionary tactics, given Nena's propensity to swing from Little Bo Peep to Big Bertha in a matter of seconds. It had come in very handy since Sam's return, which had triggered a veritable flicker-book of emotional responses in Nena. In worrying so much about Sam's sleeplessness and worry, all his pacing to and fro, she hadn't asked the question of how all the upheaval was affecting her. Her old friend could see the rings of insomnia under the same chrome-brown eyes in which the moon would swim. After all those years of unrequited affection, Cadders felt a duty of care to see Nena kept herself well. She always did the same for him.

"Can we check to see if the property is listed?" Nena asked.

"Yes. Give me two ticks." And Cadwick started tapping away at his phone once more. "You know, you ought to see if Sam wants to go away to someplace like Rye for a spa retreat. You can leave me to hold the fort here."

"He won't leave," replied Nena. "What fort?"

"Well… It's going to take the whole weekend to glean even the tiniest bit of info, and I don't want the pair of you sitting on the edge of your sofa, phone in hand."

"Any news would be good," Nena sighed.

"The agents are very overworked, and there's not much to go on really. The Polaroids might have been taken a while ago."

"But the window would be the same, no? Why would the bearded man or whoever go to the trouble of sending Sam photos of an interior since renovated?"

"No, Nena. I doubt the property has been changed. If the photos are more than three years old, then the estate agents probably weren't working the area then. They would have no knowledge of a sale or purchase. Just as the turnover of properties on the markets is rapid, so the agents too tend to come in and out of the revolving door. The upshot is: Don't wait on answers, get some rest – you look a bit run-down."

Nena sat bolt upright on the vinyl. "I don't want to look shattered. I want Sam to see me as box-fresh, even after all these years."

"You look marvellous but…"

"So, let's reconvene in a couple of hours, Cadders, and I'll grab a little sleep on this faithful couch of mine. I'm just impatient for everything, and Sam's the same."

"Well, nothing comes to the impatient, except panic and insomnia, and certainly not answers." Cadwick got up, buttoned up his green check blazer and gave Nena a full bow. "Sleep the sleep of the just, dear lady. Answers will come soon."

The lone soldier.

Joseph took off his brown suede jacket and threw it in a ball at the bare wall under the bare lightbulb. His best-laid plans had been utterly atomised and would have to be redrawn; he wouldn't give up now, no matter how forbidding the roadblocks that prevented him from getting any further along. He had to keep pressing on.

Women, women — why must they intrude into his solitude or ruin the very balance of his plan? Who was this new girl? Where had she sprung from? How would she change things? Nurturers they might be, but he had lived so sparely and been so alone that the love of a woman would materialise as sharply as a rock through an Austen picture window. Romance was something that would change the sketchy view he had of himself and the strong one he held of his destiny.

His scars acted as a barrier anyway to any woman who might have found him eligible; they weren't noble marks but ugly carvings in a face full of sensitivity. He would warn aggressors when he felt threatened that he hadn't earned the cuts by playing chess, but, in truth, his coffeebean-brown eyes betrayed the fact that he was more of a Romance poet than a street brawler by nature, even if a mother's nurturing had always been roughing him up inside, making him intractable to the outside world.

Joey had earned his scars not by fighting but the stitches had been clumsily applied late at night, so a Y-shaped red crevice ran down the left side of his face like a funnel to collect his tears. He still slept on his right side, and with the cold winds whipping in, he could often feel the scars contract in the chill. He was perpetually grumpy because of the pain and because he knew passers-by would recoil at the red marks. His mum would rub silicon gel into his face before and after school, but the scars looked even angrier, and now her caring hands were no longer around.

Still, as long as he was the sole passenger in his boat, he could claim to be its captain, and the course that stretched out before him was his and his only to chart. Destiny was now staring him directly in the face, and it wouldn't shy away from the ugly traces of his past. Through force of habit and the daily weights sessions, his body was everything his face wasn't.

He had his lonely room in a house that stood like the last thin slice of cake; the rest of the street had been flattened by a single Parachute Mine dropped by a lone German bomber in the summer of 1941. Inside, there was his sofa bed, a single chair and a small kitchenette with a gas hob. The bathroom was shared with two garrulous girls, ironically from Dresden. Each day, they phoned home, dragging the phone outside on the stairs, so he could hear harsh arguments all night in a tongue he didn't understand.

Above his dumbbells was a map of the whole area, some 15 square miles, and he would stare at it for hours, learning every street and hillside, as if undertaking The Knowledge. The dumbbells, as well as absorbing some of his welling anger, built up his once-weedy frame; the map built up his always-phenomenal mind. And now he would use both to wreak an awful revenge, as destructive and unforeseen as that parachute mine of June 1941.

There deserved to be a reckoning.

But now he sat down on the side of his bed, exhausted; his arms cramping up from the repetition of loading tray after tray into the bakery ovens, and his legs heavy with the trudge of miles he walked every day, figures of eights up and down the steps of the East Cliff, across the Bayle and into the town centre, often at a time when the whole world was asleep and even the postmen had yet to rise. Repeat once more. Joey knew every street, every alleyway, every cut-through in Folkestone like the cracks in his bedsit's cornicing.

Then he lowered his back onto his duvet, and with his workboots still flat on the carpet, he looked up at the high ceiling rose, taking a deep breath. The German girls had been quacking away all night once more, some crisis in Dresden coming in on the telephone that woke them up and drove them to demented shouting on their favoured spot on the stairs; Joey had recurrent fantasies of smothering them, one by one, using the duvet left damp from the wash – it smelt of cress under the sweat of the Febreze. There was always a cacophonous party going on downstairs in Joey's mind. And sometimes, the vapours drifted upstairs through the clints and grykes of the floorboards and darkened his thoughts.

Joey could feel through the single window that the draught had picked up. The Post-It notes on the map fluttered; bank statements and solicitor's letters flapped away on his bedside table. No sleep would come to him.

Joey closed his eyes and concentrated on the breeze blowing across his face. He always needed rest before working at the steel-fronted ovens; he was not getting burnt again. He rubbed his wrist. It wouldn't have happened if he'd been more awake. He wished he could jack in his job, but his mother's money only went so far; the death taxes ate away at the inheritance stack, and her house just wouldn't sell in the state it was in, some Seventies relic in avocado green and cappuccino.

Everywhere was so damn expensive to rent nowadays. All that foreign cash had turned Folkestone around, but those born and bred on the Kent coast were being forced out to the less-salubrious parts of south Kent – Romney Marsh and Dymchurch. These places were still tatty, like the strings of grubby, multicoloured pennants that flutter outside the empty beachfront, enticing no one. The tourists were all over drinking beer in plastic pints on the windy beach in Thanet, forty miles north, or along the curve, eating whelks with a tiny fork and playing pitch n putt golf in the rain at Hastings. Here, in the Nineties, the highspeed had brought the down-from-Londons, if not as many tourists. In Folkestone, six hundred a month used to get you a two-bed flat of your own; now, here was a bedsit in the Cultural Quarter with a broken window and a pair of garrulous German bitches going off at all hours like air-raid sirens. You had to pay for your prime spot, even if your bills were thrown in.

Joey grew up here and his dad had never been around, and mum's stories about him used to shift in tone, the facts eliding to the point where the young Joey believed the man had never been her boyfriend at all, just another shadow she'd taken home in her wild days. Now, in his early thirties, Joey knew that his mother used a sperm donor. Sometimes, over the course of his childhood, this phantom father had been an aeronautical engineer; sometimes he'd been an ambulance medic; but always he had represented some distant figure who might inspire his son to become similarly erudite or heroic or full of care. The erstwhile figure became this exemplum of a perfect manliness, when he was probably not even a clubber with commitment issues and a workable chat-up line but a student who needed a solid hundred for jacking off into a beaker.

If he'd lost a father he could hug and play football with in the rain, then Joey gained a mother who was extremely attentive, and as such, he never felt starved of affection. Joey was a disciple of Newton's third law – for everything that he had ever gained, there was some loss to be expected in return. And so, his mother died bit by bit, but he acquired a workable, if rapidly diminishing, set of accounts; and just as he gained an exoskeleton of muscle and mental fortitude, so he lost his poetic naivety. As long as Joey drew breath, he knew that there would be few constants, and he found comfort in that.

In dreams, he would see himself being pulled into a crowd of people who'd embrace him and tousle his hair and then withdraw again with the motion of the sea, leaving him swimming in the vast whiteness of loneliness. There was a chaos to living and a definite ending to all human life, so Joey focused on having total control of his precious hours. When he wasn't working, he was working out; and when he wasn't working out, he was working out a plan, one to correct past injustices, the same imbalances that now kept him awake, fuming at a fixed point on the ceiling to focus on a rage he could one day use.

It was a pity now that Joey was unable to sleep the day away. In only a few hours, the metal hammer of his alarm would sound, and the cycle of his long day would begin again – churning away like the clothes dryer in the shared garden four floors below. In his weariness were hatched his plans for revenge, the quiet and starkness of his room incubating his thoughts, the minimal human interaction letting him focus on just the people that mattered – him, his mother and his nemesis.

Just as the self-help CD had urged, Joey had removed any extraneous information from the banks of his memory, leaving only the facts vital to his design for living. His mind was the most useful muscle. A certain sparseness in his diet had kept his once-puffy frame lean; a certain sparseness in his life had kept his thoughts clear, constant, undimmed.

The lovers so entwined...

The first time we slept together after 18 years, it took a lot of getting used to; I had forgotten just how much space even a lithe ballerina such as Nena needed as she sprawled, a rock climber pinned to the sheets, and I hadn't any real practice at sharing the bed in Turin. There is a certain art to it all, the science of getting a couple of near-six feet tall humans to interlock in a queen-sized bed. Because of the poor state of my illiolumbar ligaments, I liked to sleep on my side, riding an invisible scooter; Nena stretched out like a crown-of-thorns starfish on a stretch of Indo-Pacific coral. I remembered, though, how late Nena liked to chatter until the BBC shut down to a dot. When she was in deep sleep, Nena made tiny parping sounds from the side of her mouth – I found it adorable.

Now that I had been shocked into insomnia by the strangeness of recent events, Nina's natural wakefulness was a true comfort. The pair of us had more than enough waking hours to work through every single scenario for the break-in the day before. What and how it had happened was no mystery, yet there remained no why, and the reason for the rearranging of the cabin seemed lost to the squalls outside.

Hours earlier, I'd scattered a cup of salt on the doorstep in the hope of showing up any footprints that might appear overnight. I hadn't told Nena about this, or that my sleep apnoea was developing once more, brought on by the sheer terror that some maniac out there in the whistling thrift and whipping grasses had it in for me. My general creeping paranoia felt like the photo negative of that dream Dad always used to describe, but instead of the canvas cushioning my fall, it wrapped itself restrictively around me, like the bindings on a mummified corpse. At certain moments, I couldn't exhale – my chest was forced inwards by the strictures of the canvas, and my mouth was gagged. Ascending arpeggios of dissonance rang in my ears, seemingly linked to my shortening breaths.

I was cocooned; I was entombed. I knew that the break-in would prove to be only the start of what might well develop into a series of unfortunate little inconveniences. It was an unappetising entrée. I had talked myself into thinking it just a prank; Nena had already convinced herself, it seemed. When I ran through her breathing exercises with eyes closed and nose side-on to the pillow, Nena slept sweetly, parping into her invisible trumpet.

Nena was now banging on about Tom pranking me, trying to persuade his old mucker to return to the apartment and our immature existence. Tom knew the cabin well from their teenage days, when my mother used to try to fatten him up. Over endless rounds of cheesy beans on toast, Sandy would ask him about how the family farm-shop was faring. The arrival of the express supermarket was ruining the attempts by the farming community to sell their produce directly; the local councils were aiding and abetting the men and women from Tesco and the like, who would whizz around the undulating town of Folkestone and the surrounding greenbelt in their fleets of Ford Sierras, their cars and their actions slowly choking the air supply of folk such as Tom's dad. Sandy believed that the young boy needed all his strength to fight the bastards from the big superstores.

However, back in the present, I was finding it impossible to square why would Tom go so far out of his way to scare me. Wasn't he my best friend? I knew him well, his rebellious energy keeping him chugging away like one of the family tractors at idle. He might rig up an explosion in the cabin; he sure as shit wouldn't just shunt things around.

For my first few months in northern Italy, I had been flapping around the cafes set in the vicinity of the Mole

Antonelliana in Turin. As a waiter, I was all fingers and thumbs, unable to master the Italian language or the simple act of tearing off a paper receipt or dropping a wafer onto a plate with a pair of tongs. After my most recent sacking, dished out by a hairy-bellied groper called Nicola who had once offered me a lift home and then locked the two of us inside his rusting Fiat Punto, Tom had suggested that I would be an asset to his burgeoning business interests. I could handle the written English, while Tom schmoozed the elderly ex-pats and those drawn from Blighty by the lakes and the Nebbiolo grape.

I was loth now to criticise Tom, even if that was Nena's plan. However, as dear Sherlock often remarked, "once you eliminate the impossible, whatever remains, no matter how improbable, must be the truth". Nena and I had to eliminate all those explanations for the break-in that hovered on the borderline of and in the regions of improbability – the intruder couldn't have been Mimi, for example, as two hours before the home invasion, I had called her on her landline and heard that tuneless Westie of hers whining for a biscuit.

So, sadly, I couldn't quite rule out Tommy; he was devious and tricky. He wanted to be the catalyst for something, anything, so long as he had been the instigator, the agent provocateur. The other morning, Nena rang nearby Lydd Airport to check whether Tom's Cessna had landed there recently. No, but Tommy was a clever bastard, with a mind always dreaming of an intricate and pristine scheme.

Like Nena's own lieutenant, Cadwick, Tom had an eye for the long game, and his ability to cover his tracks was legendary. He was fond of inventing a whole new agenda for himself, scattering facts and photos on social media to give the impression that he was somewhere other than north Turin. And never once had Tom been caught out;

the only other person in the know was always me, his brother from a blonde mother. Tom's Twitter feed was the home of the original fake news, his tweets tossed like breadcrumbs to send any carrion from the shadow of his front door. Tom didn't believe anyone truly needed to know where he was at, other than the people he chose to hang around with – me, Claudia, an ebullient gorilla of an Englishman called G.

I turned over to the other side of the bed. Nena tossed off her towel and sat naked on the edge of the bed, running a cotton bud between each of her toes before flicking it into the bedside bin. "You haven't slept again, have you, Sammy?"

"I was thinking." I wished I'd feigned sleep.

Nena turned to me. "It'd be just like Tom to fly Claudia over to show her off to his old mates and to show off to her that he remains as free as a bird."

"In what? His Cessna hasn't been seen. Did he flap himself over here?"

"You arsehole. He might have borrowed another plane, a Robin, or flown to Shoreham, Headcorn, or anywhere in between."

"And the point? To move a foot-stool a metre to the right?"

"The most important thing would be shocking the shit out of you for rejecting him, for coming home. Tom treats life as if he's on a perpetual stag, with all the carnage that involves."

I sat up in the bed and rubbed the wetness off her slender, sloping shoulders, the riverlets racing past the god-awful star tattoo under her right shoulder-blade; the rest of her was just so exquisitely crafted, like a viola fashioned from smoked glass.

"I just want to work out what happened, Sam," Nena sighed, leaning back into my palms. "I feel it has relevance to our happiness. Why let another outside force shag things up for us, eh? I sometimes feel like one of those seaside grabber-machines took you up and away from me. I felt that helpless. Fate reached in and took you while I was completely unawares. I don't want that happening again, my 'carino'. I will fight Fate herself if I have to keep you within my orbit. I'd give her a kick in the crotch." Nena brushed her downy pubic hair with her fingertips.

I laughed. "If you're itching for a bit of hairdressing work, I need a trim myself. I look like Bob Geldof on a Van der Graaf generator, darling – this mop of mine."

Nena stopped her primping and again looked over her shoulder at me. "You need to get serious about finding a suspect, Sam. I'm anxious to work out just what is happening here before we both get bitten again. Look at the state of both of us – dark rings around our eyes, and you've lost about 5kg since I saw you in that tatty wax jacket on the high street. We need answers and we need to make sure the person mucking about is or isn't your so-called best friend. Have you called Tom to check he's definitely in Piedmont?"

"Yes, and there was no answer." I'd called Tommy twice since I'd arrived in Folkestone. Tom was rarely available for a chat; he let it ring through to a voicemail he never checked. He was always scared of not having time to edit his words, so he enjoyed text rallies on WhatsApp instead. Even a smooth-tongued wanker like him could at times get caught out in the course of a phone conversation.

Nena nodded. "Well, there's your answer. Let's find out where the cock is staying. He'll be at the Grand or the Imperial."

"So, I've got to ring hotels? I've got ten thousand things to tie up. The farmhouse…"

"Tom's probably splashing the cash around and ordering girls up on room service. Fit a tracker to the comeliest brunette hooker in town, and you'll find him beneath her. Some people never change, especially when they're allowed to get away with being a fool for so long."

Nena got up from the bed and dropped a dress over herself in that insouciant manner that women can; the clothes just fall onto their frames, glad to be of service to such pulchritude. I took in the show. Nena pulled her coiled curls back into a ponytail. "Need to wash my hair, straighten out the 'fro. It's OK up like this?"

"Yes, it always looks good."

"Sure, sure. Come. Let's get some food in the village. Let's go to Loaf. They do a mean mac n cheese."

"Sure. My shout this time." I looked down at her thighs. "You're not going to wear any scanties?"

"Hey there. It's all right; I will," and she went into the kitchen to fish a dry pair of knickers from the airer above the tumble-dryer.

At Loaf, Cadders looked quite surprised at how bonny I looked; well, he'd only seen an Instagram selfie of me with Nena wrapped around my chest, posing at the foot of the Leas Lift funicular. 'Déjà vu' read Nena's caption. From that photo, Cadders had told Nena I had the air of someone subsisting on a diet of Guinness and pie. In the snap, I looked tubby from the best of times, like some twin of King George IV; but, in the flesh, Cadders later informed Nena that I resembled a Germanic prince without a kingdom or castle. The charmer. I seemed to have wandered in from the eighteenth century, he declared, my right foot always pointing out ahead of my left as I stood and my blond hair swept from the side as if I'd been riding my estate horses all morning. God, Cadders was a great bullshitter.

Nena came over to her friend, almost bounding over. "Cadders! This, this is Sam." She pushed me towards his lap; I was almost ten inches taller than Cadders, so the latter remained on his bar stool, very conscious that his loafers were dangling some distance off the scuffed wooden floor of the café. Cadders would tell me later he used to feel similarly downsized when his father, Hubert, would present himself in the drawing room after his son's return home at the end of every term. Pater would then disappear to his Caribbean mistress, and Cadders would only ever see him on TV, ruddy-faced above a mustard-and-plum tie in the crowd at Lord's cricket ground.

So, this was Cadders, said to be always dependably present, known to rattle around all of Folkestone, waiting to bump into a friend or an acquaintance who might join him for a tipple or three on his slate. Just as a swift lives on the wing, so Cadwick lived to flit among the bars and coffee-shops of Sandgate and Folkestone, a pocket-sized boulevardier always desperate for a chat about something or other, knowing all the best spots to engineer a supposed chance encounter. He told me that it was lovely to meet the man who had re-ignited a light in the lantern of Nena's face. I half-believed it.

Cadders was coming off a busy old night down in the harbour – a bunch of property agents were turning an old chippy into an art gallery. And it was easier to buy a shipwreck sculpture in Folkestone now than a soggy cod and chips. Cadders told me the old lady had changed in the past 18 years – she was wearing new threads, though if you were to go up Black Bull Road, he swore I would see the same decrepitude as in the Nineties and the same sort of druggies, pickpockets, tarts. "Even a strapping lad like you would get stripped and eaten in seconds," he said; but he, he would be tossed like a baton, all 5ft 3in of him.

We then agreed how single days of hangovers could chain themselves together into these imposing blocks of three, with 72 hours of feeling like death bringing the ruin of those nearing 40 – the mounting dread, the shakiness, the volcanic evacuations… and Cadders joked that the night-times might belong to the young and firm of flesh, but the lunchtimes belonged to us.

"What's the other option – to give in?" Nena chuckled. "I don't want to be slumped like sludge on a bench on the Leas, waiting for nothing, looking out to the sea but seeing nothing, wrapped up in endless layers but silently begging the winds to whisk me away."

Cadwick hiked up his eyebrows like an aggrieved bullock. "Nena, we kill care with booze, so it'll be three gins then?"

As for me, I hoped our trio would act as crash-mats for one another, keeping at arms' length a world that seemed to be growing ever more straitened yet nasty. Reactionaries roamed the roads in their monster pick-ups, coked to the gills, snorting their petrol fumes, desperate to catch wrongdoings on their dashboard cams; while everyone else scoured the internet messageboards and micro-blogging sites for the smallest slight, no matter how retrospective, to hurl a toddler's tantrum at. Abandon all hope, seal up the vault behind you, and load up on liver-compromiser.

And as for Nena, if Cadders had indeed failed to capture the heart of that ebony maiden, then it was clear to me that he'd resolved to make damn sure that he continued to enjoy the soul-charging warmth of her presence, this electric jolt when one knew she was focused solely, intensely, upon oneself alone.

Anyway, they were drinking buddies from years back in a way that Jacqs and Cadders would never become – he would tell me later that his new girl had a towering intolerance for the sauce that turned her professionalism inside out, the very orderliness that so attracted him to her – no matter how he tried, Cadwick couldn't kill the image of Jacqui's balancing act on the low wall beside the shingle of Sandgate Beach. It was not very Cadwick – he was a slumper. He couldn't tolerate manic drunks, not even pretty ones.

In his most hush-hush voice and with his right eye shut, he confided to me and Nena over his third large gin that he had news. "Guys, I've got hold of a list of all the art deco or 1930s houses sold in Folkestone recently. It's a start, isn't it?"

Nena clapped her hands, but I was a bit confused. Cadders had this awful habit, reader, of forgetting that others couldn't read his thoughts or divine his gestures, and so he often acted as if everyone was in the know. At this point, I was not party to Nena's request for help. I was tired, a bit tanked up. I must have looked most unamused.

"Sam, I was asked to make a few in-roads into where that house in your Polaroids might be." Cadders saw me stare at Nena. "It's really no problem, Sam. I know all the property agents around here. I have done so many of them so many favours in the past that they'll help us now find the house. Your situation needs a prompt solution; you can't have someone coming into your cabin as you nap, and you can't have some lunatic playing around with your things."

I untangled my hand from Nena's. "I'm not sure it's worth any of our time, this let's-play-detective piss-about."

"Sam," Nena interrupted angrily, but I was not having any of it. I felt my face slump downwards to the floorboards. I lacked the energy to haul a sheet over my irritation.

"I'm not wasting any more time on wishy-washy old shit. I've already lost a good few years of my life to my inaccurate guesswork," I replied. "I'm sorry, Cadders, but I'm sure that this is all a prank or a mix-up."

"Be grateful, Sam!" Nena hissed.

"Guys, I'm just very tired, and all of this has come at the worst possible time. I'm knee-deep in worry and grief. I have to sort out the probate for my folks. I have a large farmhouse in Berwickshire that nobody's going to want to buy."

"It'll sell," said Nena.

"Oh, yes? You'll put in a bid using the mountains of dosh from returning your empty bottles?" I rubbed my leg as Nena muttered a sod-you. "My head is so heavy that my neck keeps cracking; my parents are fresh in the ground and not here to guide me. I'm utterly exhausted and careworn. I haven't the time to play piss-about Poiret." My hands shook.

"Sam, we won't let you become bogged down again. Listening to bloody Radiohead on a loop." Nena looked at Cadwick. "Does breaking into someone's home and rearranging their earthly possessions sound like a prank to you, Cadders?"

I stopped supping from the old school tumbler. "You were the one saying it was a prank this morning, Nena?"

"I was trying to calm you down, Sam," Nena replied to me, condescendingly. "You've not been sleeping, Sam. I've heard you stalking around in the middle of the night. You can't outpace your anxieties. I've seen the salt you poured on the doorstep. It doesn't escape my notice that you're firing up your laptop all night to search for an explanation. It'll drive you batty, Sam. Sometimes, you're nearly finished with the puzzle and you find that the last few pieces are missing."

Regretfully, I snapped, hissing close to Nena's face. "All the pieces are missing! Why, why can I never be just left the hell alone, especially at this time? What draws people to intrude into my silence?"

"Cadders is trying to help you!"

"Why do others just think they can dive-bomb into my life? Why can't I find tranquility?"

"You are never tranquil, Sam. You never rest. You'll soon be just a huge mess of panic attack after panic attack. I bet you've been suffering from flashing visions again, haven't you?"

"No," I lied.

"Bullshit," Nena roared. "Hyperventilation, nausea, numbness, feelings of escaping? Imagining things, like you've done for the past 25 years."

Cadders, feeling awkward because of our brewing domestic, sought the middle way. "Sam, if you don't want me to do anything more, just say, but Nena's right – it sounds like some random nutter is trying to provoke you into either leaving again or lashing out at those nearest to you. I saw it all at boarding school – we used to call it 'stigging' – you'd try to rattle the new boys, or the geeks in the year below, and you'd try to get them to become loners, or Stigs of the Dump. You'd play pranks, capers, rags on them, to weed out the losers."

"Delightful people!" Nena exclaimed, with huge sarcasm.

All this chatter was becoming tiresome, riding on the back of the insomnia. "It's no big deal, Cadders. I feel like I've been up since the dawn of time." I put my hand on Nena's shawl. "I appreciate how both of you are trying to discover what it is that's behind these events and stop it from affecting me. Here, let's have a look at that list." I took the piece of foolscap from Cadders' hands and scanned the names jotted down like spikes in a cardiogram.

"My writing's a bit cack, I'm afraid," Cadwick apologised.

"No worries, Cadders." I peered down at the addresses. "There's nothing here that I recall, though I'm very rusty with the area."

Nena murmured. "Sandgate only gets excited when the sea bites back and hurls its salt at the houses. It reminds the old lovelies here that, in Napoleonic times, troops marched down the hills and brought blood and murder with them. The castle is skirted in crimson."

"Steady on, old gal," I said, gripping Nena's thigh again. "Do you want a chamomile tea perhaps? Something soothing?"

Cadwick then chipped in, his loafers swinging again, this miniature Michael Flatley. "The elderly are drawn here, because, as your wits and senses start to decline, you cling to the comfort of the unchallenging and familiar. Then the sea's spitting wakes you up for cream tea, I suppose. When everything starts shutting down and/or falling off, I'm going to live in a ground-floor flat here; in 30 years' time, the only thing that'll have changed is me."

"And your liver will finally be football-sized…" Nena added unnecessarily.

"Yes, I remember how Sandgate's like that, Cadders," I agreed. "Though this list of addresses seems to be mostly drawn from the Cheriton area? No?"

"Yes, there are a lot of inter-war houses, chained together like a Rubik's Snake, and you'll find those metal-framed windows dotted about. They'll be around Cheriton and then down Hythe way, dropping down the hill to the sea and the bit between Sandgate and Hythe, just before the Imperial Hotel. It's all golf course there. You know it?"

"I remember it."

"Well, the same. There's always a bloody burger van or three blocking up all the road, and all these seagulls watching some bloater hoover up his chips." Cadders was looking at the back of the paper; Jacqs's number was scrawled on there. She might be useful in narrowing down the search area, if she wasn't still schmoozing or whatever the hell she did at the Rathebone pile. Perhaps Jacqui was learning the harpsichord.

Nena caught Cadders' eye and then mine. "I had an idea…"

"Go on, darling," I said.

"Well, was there anyone who was expecting a cut of some of your folks' money? I mean, I know you're an only child, but are there cousins, any uncles and aunts aside from Mimi?" She traced the vein in my right wrist with her right ring finger. "People can become bloody grabby around a family inheritance. Everyone gets sniffing. You see these grandsons with slicked-down hair gamely listening to their granny Agatha prattle on about Sandgate in the war and the rarity of a good Yorkshire pudding. They come down every month on the fast train for a roast lunch on Agatha's slate and make small talk for a maximum of two hours. They have one eye on the free supper on the chequered cloth and another on securing Nan's townhouse on Sandgate Hill when the old dear is finally reunited with her late Maurice. Money makes people commit desperate acts, deeds far more wanton than accepting an elderly lady's luncheon invite. It lures out the hungry and immoral. There are plenty of hearse-chasers. Maybe some distant relative is peeved that you've received an enormous farmhouse in Berwickshire, a charming cabin on the cliffs and an outbuilding full of classic cars. People get jealous and then they leave their sense at the doorstep."

I gathered my thoughts for a second, and the edge of my scarf dropped to the floor as I rubbed thumb and forefinger together. "No. I'm afraid there's no one else. It's just Mimi. I mean, I've thought the same, about there being some long-last relative after my folks' money, but it's just Mimi and me. It was hardly like my parents were like King Edward VII and Alice Keppel swanning around the Grand Hotel, waving over their scones and fizz at the well-wishers peering in the windows. And anyway, who'd hate my folks? They were like Father and Mother Christmas."

"I know, I know. Bless them," Nena put a consoling hand close enough to my groin for Cadders to look away at the Loaf's sandwich board full of squiggles. "You know, darling, maybe we should hold off from doing anything but getting you back on your feet in England and maybe finding an upgrade for that useless rubber brick of a phone you have?"

"It never breaks," I countered.

"You can sit in my salon reading your Don DeLillo and overhearing my natters with the old gents in blazers. You could sweep up the nasal hair into pretty avenues. We can get you enrolled at the swimming baths on Radnor Park Avenue. A little exercise will relax you. I can't even begin to imagine how blanched out your mind must be, Sammy. I'm exhausted just watching you try to find your peace."

Cadwick turned his head back towards us. "I'm sorry for your loss. I didn't know your parents, but they sound like an adorable pair." Cadders pursed his lips in a vain bid for compassion; I laughed to myself. It wasn't a strong look. "You'll find that wearing some kind of sports jacket softens the attitudes of Sandgatians towards you. It also pays to have at least £100 of cash in your wallet as most of the shops around here are still acclimatising to decimalisation. The old lush at the antiques shop thinks chip-and-pin is a golfing term."

I smiled. "My folks were not the kind of people to rock the boat and they hated sticking their oars in." I paused again. "Sorry – too many nautical metaphors. I'm pretty certain any lunatic would be after me, not them."

I drained the last inch of my drink and set the glass down on the rustic table-top. The booze was firing me up, the viper in my veins biting me awake. "Let's have a ramble. Let's see if we can find that lounge window from the outside."

Nena nodded: "Let's be proactive, instead of worrying that the world and his whippet are trying to get at our throats."

I was getting swacked on the gin: "I'm going to walk and walk until I either sleep standing on my feet, or I satisfy my queries. Hell, I'm not going to sleep anyway."

Nena was half off her stool. She seemed happy I was regaining a little of my spirit and not sliding into the slough of despondency she knew all too well; earlier that day, I'd stumbled into the bedroom chest of drawers; the same sleeplessness that carried me sideways into the furniture was also stopping me from feeling the bruises.

I excused myself for a moment, eager to use this new vim from the gins while it lasted. "Excuse me. I need to call the guy selling the farm for me."

I got up and walked to the back of the bar. As quietly as I could, I spoke into my big old mobile: "Yes, it's the Scot here. I'm being stalked here. No, I don't know who, but when I do, I'll need your help, Bishop. Yes, stay connected through the Facebook page. Tired, tired and ready to gut someone like a fish. Bye, Bish." I hung up and walked back to the others. "No offer as yet," I lied. "Only been a day. Let's go and find that metal window, and that house?"

However, Cadwick was going nowhere. "I'm going to chummy up with my estimable, delicious, liquid-skinned friend Mr Hendricks and wait for Jacqs to come back from Rathebone. She's got another fundraiser there. I don't know why she doesn't just pack a sleeping bag and kip on the sodding grand piano. It'd save her the commute."

"Come!" Nena pleaded.

"No. You have fun, kiddies. We'll still be here, slightly growling at one another."

"Ah, the fissures of young love. I know it well." Nena elbowed me and winked. I then shepherded Nena and her brown-suede kimono out of the café, and the door shut behind us.

And Cadders, well, I looked back and saw him rubbing his temples at the window. He must have been wondering which version of Jacqs would enter Loaf; the one who had taken her Seroxat and was charmingly playful, trying to scatter what was left of his curls over the bareness of his bonce, or the other Jacqui, the one he said was nuttier than squirrel shit and would rail away at him like a bird-scarer for his obvious, undying love for Nena.

I saw Cadders gird himself for a battle with a Hendricks gin n tonic. He seemed ready to step into the arena again.

Garibaldi in a foil hat.

Luca opened the cupboard, half-knowing that he'd drained every single box of Tesco merlot. He vaguely remembered punching them flat until the silver bag squeaked. In the maelstrom of his emotions, that sac had ended up on his head, as a tricorn of sorts. Underneath it, wobbling like a mattress on a bottle of wine, he had recited excerpts from Giuseppe Garibaldi's call to arms to his soldiers in 1860 – except Luca was orating to a kitchen-towel holder and a microwave.

Hours earlier, he felt impassioned and roaring with eloquence, but he now felt horrendous and foolish; his aching brain slopped around his head like a shaken tank of fish shit. The foil tricorn had been in the bin, mocking him, until he'd nipped outside in his boxers and sent it down the universal waste chute. Had his neighbours heard him bellowing at 1am in his fully ornate Italian? What did it matter; they all were part of John's swinging safari of late-middle-aged lotharios and young beauty technicians. A little recital of Garibaldi meant nothing at all, compared to the bacchanalia of Saturday nights in the block. How did Luca ever fail to notice the noise of two-dozen people pouring all their frustrations and fun into a few hours in a flat just below his, every weekend without fail?

In the cupboard, Luca espied a prehistoric bag of seaweed crackers from Wake Up Little Sushi. What a sad life he was saying sayonara to. Everything would become a great deal more fragrant, rhapsody-smooth, under councillor John's aegis; he would be "farting in silk" apparently. In return for his silence, Luca would claim the finest of treats. In Piedmont, they would say, "You don't eat anywhere better in the world, but you always eat the same thing." Well, Luca planned to run a hot bath of

Bagna cauda fondue and bathe in the anchovies and garlic until he sloughed off this skin of shame.

In his latest nightmares, Luca would see the old man's head, detached and planted on the handlebars of a brass steam-punk tricycle. With no one else around, the contraption would chase Luca endlessly through the narrow streets of Spitalfields. He saw the black vapours rising from the old man's bloodied forehead; he saw his tongue lolling out with every turn taken. The pursuit ended only when Luca woke up, face down on the sofa, the cushion turned from vivid red to dark crimson by his sweat.

Luca closed the cupboard door and looked back into his lounge. In the fierce rays of morning light, it transformed back from misery den to the place where he felt most secure in this sprawling capital. How strange was life that, some 48 hours after believing his days were nigh and a couple of Italian heavies were marching across the quad to kick his door in half, a pair of empty wine bottles at his feet and a pot of Paracetamol in one hand, here he was contemplating the winding road to his own personal Valhalla, no longer staring at the dots of the detuned television set, delirious with fear at his similarly ill-defined future and the coldness of the recent past. He promised himself he would never again feel so inclined to suicide. Life was too richly variegated for too much lily-hearted what-if-ery; his happy countenance would act his passport. Hadn't John said how his smile felt like a big cuddle? Luca would endeavour to remain breezy, even after a night of being pursued by phantom heavies and dead old men on steam-trikes.

It was only when his lift passed the floor where the smothering happened or when Luca gazed out upon the scruffy grass square that he realised his own happiness had been secured by means of others' misfortune. No one really deserved to die like that, kicked around into obsolesence or choked under a cushion, no matter if they were a 'grass', a pervert or a prostitute. The elderly gent was some mother's son, after all; back in sepia times, someone would have packed him off to school in his worsted uniform and little cap, sandwich box tucked under his arm, and that somebody would have wished for him every success in the whole wide world. The fate of Dorota was even sadder; she had barely started out on her life.

If one sees a man in the street beaming from ear to ear, Luca thought, then you could bet your last lira that his carefree ways have come at someone else's expense. The truth was that somewhere, at some time, someone else was paying for whatever freedoms you enjoyed, just as the old man and the girl were expendable makeweights in the buying of Luca's silence. Your hand might well be waving free, but far away somewhere in the half-light, another soul was feeling a choke-hold on their neck.

In his new life, Luca wouldn't be the chubby dolt at Window 3; he would become a well-dressed, well-fed man of leisure. The Rubinacci tailored suit from John's old mucker on Commercial Street would speak for him; Luca could remain silent, his face expressing bonhomie, his threads shouting with confidence, con brio.

A walk among the pining.

"My knees are still sore," Nena moaned as we walked up the severity of Military Road, which snaked through clumps of chalets and recreation space. "You've shagged me bandy, you little bastard."

"Shush!"

"My left patella feels ready to spin its way through my jeans – like Oddjob's hat." Oh, Nena was lean, but not fit enough for the one-in-five gradient of a mile or more.

I was no better, but I was hiking in front, scanning every side road for those metal-framed windows; I could feel the hammer of my heart, my eyes were twitching. I looked back at Nena. "You know, let's start walking around here each day so I can get to know the place again."

"I have my business to run, Sammy."

"Business!"

"Shut it. I've already slipped well behind on my hours. The salon should be open this week; the elderly around here will have been swamped by their hair, bumbling around under a cloud of white and grey locks, bumping into the postboxes, distressed under their crash helmets of out-of-control tresses. And it's all because of you. You steal my hours, Sam. Shagging me bandy."

I kept walking. "And you wouldn't be just sitting in the back room getting slotted with Christian Cadwick, would you?"

"I run Sandgate's second-busiest salon. I get through a pair of scissors each week."

"Pull the other one, Nena. The hairdressing just stops you from being permanently plastered. It just gives your jaw a rest from all that causerie and chitter-chatter."

"Causerie? Who are you – Miss bloody Marple? Causerie! For God's sake." Nena was shouting up the incline at my striding. "I am the one chatting with the elderly, not you."

I changed tack. This was the point I wanted to make. "Well, when you've built up your walking endurance and found your fitness again, you should come see the mountains of Piedmont. The Alps are on its three sides. Monviso will get your glutes cooking."

"My arse is already numb, thanks." Nena paused. "Can't we just slacken the pace a little please? I'll be of no use to you tonight. Come on, Sam." She was some 15 feet behind me now as the road continued to rise up towards the chain fences of the military complex, horrible prefabs, and balding patches of grass among the crumbs of tarmac.

"No, you come on, Nena, for Christ's sake." I was getting a little annoyed by Nena's diversions; the semi-detached house with its rusty brick wall and metal front window could be just around the next bend; and perhaps I would come face to face with my persecutor, the bearded sleeper, under the darkening sky. We'd passed only one guy on the whole walk, a hulk with a scar that made us pick up our pace. "Is everything just a game, a time-waster between your bouts of boozing?"

"No, Sammy, sir!"

"Can you just be serious for once?"

"Yes, I can," replied Nena with mock contrition.

"Well... Stop farting around then." I angrily shoved my frozen hands into my padded blue overcoat. "Pick up the pace. Hut-hut-hut!"

"It's slippery. Look at the brown sludge everywhere – the autumn leaves are just mulch now the rains have been."

"Hark at Alfred Lord Tenalady!"

"Hush, bedwetter." She paused. "The whole pavement's coated in sadness."

"Just press on – be stoic for once in your life," I barked, but what a prat I was, so I smiled and playfully whip

Nena's backside with the end of my black bobbled scarf. "This is better than a thousand gym workouts. Come on, old gal."

We rounded the last corner, and the road – and my mood – levelled out. We neared the end of the military base across the road and the start of Cheriton, a russet-bricked enclave for families, investors and student sharers alike. There was a little something for everyone, but nothing life-changing for anyone, and the place remained forever bland because of its functionality, a palate-cleanser beside the sorbets and patisseries of Sandgate and Hythe. Cheriton was the worker bee to those twin queens, and everything looked tired; the bricks, the tarmac, the concrete, even the trees sagged. The wind couldn't be bothered to shake them.

"Everything here is convenient, but nothing is compelling. Plop, plop, plop. I mean, I couldn't live here."

"It's not your place, though, is it?" Nena said, rightly.

"It's just this collection of tissue-box houses surrounding a little park or a local shop – how dreary an existence. You're tucked away from the sea – you can't really see it from up here." I looked down a side road of red-brick terrace houses for my mystery house. My frustration spilt over into a dumb rant. "The public gets what the public wants, and it wants regimentation, and a pretty 4x4 on the driveway."

"Well, it's a place for people to use as a base, just like the military use it as a base. It's like a rack on which one can hang one's baubles and trinkets. It's a starting point for other journeys, a place where you can buy anything for your trek ahead: a can of beans, a woolly hat, some plasters, a packet of mints, a pint of milk, maybe a pork pie if the diet's off, an A-to-Z, chicken stock, a stale quartet of croissants, some candles you'll never light, a card you'll never use to write…"

"Are you just going to list the entire contents of Co-Op? Why did I invite you along?"

"Well, thank you, kindly sir, for such a beneficent invitation. I mean, this is what every love-struck maiden wants – to walk for two miles in the drear, watching her beau's fast-disappearing, well-upholstered rear. Reader, her patella starts to disintegrate." Nena chuckled. "I shall be quite the focus of envy from all those at the debutantes' ball." She stopped again. "Where's the pub, Sam?"

"Pissant…" I joked.

Nena stopped walking, so I did, too. "Listen, let's just grab a cab."

I chuckled. "Grab a cab? Grab? This ain't Kansas, dear."

"Oh, sod off, Sammy."

"There's another five minutes to Cheriton High Street – and it's going to rain its arse off soon; you know, I don't want to be stranded in this soulless hole for too long." I picked up the pace as yet more rows and rows of 1930s suburban red-bricks unfurled in the distance. Under her wheezing, Nena thanked the Lord that the ground was now flat.

On the other side of town, Joey let himself into his building, wiping dust off his hands onto the back of his trousers and bounding up the communal stairs. His nemesis, one of his Dresden-born neighbours, a Hitchcock-blonde beauty of about 22, was sitting on the steps, loudly talking in German on her phone.

Joey snarled. "Do you want to take your shouting match inside? Rauss!"

The blonde was having none of it. She switched to flawless English. "Screw you, nutter."

"Oh, yeah?"

"You're the one coming in and out at all hours, not me."

Joey leant over her. "I work nights in a bakery."

"Why carry a knife with you?"

"What?" Joey muttered.

"I see you sharpening your knife outside the building. I have enough on with my mother ill. I don't need your threats." The girl looked at the phone.

"What business is it of yours?" Joey was staring her right in the eye.

"My sister and I feel threatened. We've told the landlord about you and your knife."

Joey hissed in her ear. "I know. I'll slice you both up. There's a threat for you!"

Joey bounded up the stairs, leaving the girl stunned. Al the landlord was the type of guy who would charge a tenant for denting his tin utility-room roof with their dead body – "Your suicide took me £50 to fix," he would no doubt hiss at their ghost before pointing to the online estimate. "I could've billed you for wasting my time, but I appreciate you're dead."

Once inside the sanctity of his tiny bedsit, Joey rooted around for his leather bag of tools under the bed frame. He leapt up and began picking at the lock on his door, scratching and scraping away at the metal, quite unperturbed at losing his cool with the German girl.

"Love thy neighbour?" Joey muttered. Their assurance in the light of their ignorance of his life was astonishing. What did they know of him? Nothing, and Joey wished to know nothing of their lives; them jogging down the stairs for a 5am run around the Bayle; and getting enormous amounts of fresh greens delivered every day by an emaciated farmer's lad with a bum-fluff 'tache on the world's screechiest scooter. They knew nothing about hard work and toil.

Joey put his tool back into his pocket. Practice, practice, practice – he wanted to be a man for all purposes, a living Swiss Army knife. No rust would ever surreptitiously grow on him if he remained vital, always becoming better and sleeker, a hymn to ever evolving.

In his darkest moments, as thoughts fluttered down to him from the coving as he waited for the world to wake up with him, Joey had wondered whether he would have been more content killing himself slowly with meds at the same pace as his mother's decline. His life had always dovetailed with hers; it was if the umbilical cord remained there, binding them together and nourishing him via a tube impermeable by evolution's design.

And now she was gone, posted into the ground in a pine box for all eternity, Joey was well aware that he dragged around his heavy, inert jukebox full of memories, making himself ineligible to any girl. The power he shared with his mother travelled down the cord into his heart and gave him just enough of a spark to keep him suffering on in a material world he didn't understand or trust, a world of shouting and virtue-signalling.

Meanwhile, as our taxi pulled up into the fresh puddles outside Loaf, Cadders seemed most relieved that it was Nena and I, and not Jacqui, who emerged from the Prius, both of us laughing at my graceless attempts at leaving the car. Cadders hopped off his stool just as indelicately and scampered up to us. He didn't get any bigger as he came nearer.

He bearhugged me, almost hanging off me and soaking up the spots of rain from my blue coat. "Mon ami! Any news on the property?"

"None, I'm afraid. No window." I said, slightly stunned by the fulsome welcome.

"We went everywhere," Nena confirmed. "Then, it started spitting and my stomach began to yawn."

"We'll get some food, darling."

"Sam, I'm so tired. You kind of forget how far Folkestone sprawls. On and on it goes; there's a big sod-off hill stretching from the beach. My patella is so sore."

Cadwick showed Nena a stool. "Come and sit down, gal. Rest your knee." He pointed at the blackboard above the counter. "There's a feta and pomegranate salad special this afternoon. I'm a bit leathered, to be honest. Six gins down."

I scanned the board. "Looks good, Cadders." I paused. "I kept trying to flip the bloody photo so I could picture it from the outside rather from within. We were just walking down the same parade of red-brick boxes. The residents must get lost and walk around for hours trying to find the station or escape. Still-rotten pumpkins from Halloween, and so many bricks."

Cadders patted a stool. "Well, you're here in the warmth now. My lieblings, sit here, next to daddy."

Nena surveyed her friend's face for any telltale slippage of an eye. "I mean, we've been gone for about four hours, Cadders, and you're still in the same spot, supping."

"I was following the cricket on my phone! The West Indies! New opening bat! Captain at 4! Easterlies! I mean, I must have a snifter when England are batting, what-what!"

"And your lover in the Sixties Pan-Am uniform?"

"I've been gathering up enough Dutch courage for a face-off. I've been working out what to say."

"Say the truth, Cadders."

"Jacqs will be wearing her gin gilet of infallibility; she'll have been drinking with potential buyers of Rathebone. Her confidence will soar as her motor skills swan-dive."

"Yes. Her confidence will be on the surge, Cadders." Nena examined the detritus of his long afternoon alone; the spent glasses, the new bar-girl looking fearfully at his back.

"So, will I get the gorgon or the goddess, Nena? It's becoming tiresome, so verr tarsome, not knowing whether I'll face the angel or the ass. Do I give in and play lapdog?"

"Well, we were the same at the same stage of things – having a blowup and then a bunkup. Now it's just the latter." Nena looked at me, as I ordered the three cappuccinos. "Actually, Sam's being a bit of a prat today. Barking out orders like an angry arse. I like Cheriton. Feels safe. Sam the snob doesn't like it."

I waved back, quite aware of what Nena was muttering.

Cadwick sighed. "It's just shouting for us. No sex, a few tired gropes at night-time. Jacqs actually threw her own shoes out of my back window last week. I mean, what the hell was the point of that? At least throw my brogues and get me into the courtyard in my socks. I had to get the stepladder and fetch her heels from the lower branches, and then I got a bollocking for leaving the stepladder out on the patio. It's my stepladder and my patio, and I was fetching her shoes, which she had thrown."

"Is she learning her habits from reality shows? Slovenly Island?"

"Love Island? I don't know. People are sometimes very strange, endlessly peculiar, and I feel as if I'm speaking in a different tongue and existing to a different beat. Do I exist on the other side of the mirror? Jacqs is like Alec Guinness playing all the D'Ascoyne family at one – she flicks between all nine characters, and the only ones I can abide are the reverend and the lady – and I never know which to expect."

Nena laughed. "I suspect there's a reality-TV team somewhere around; she certainly acts as if her life is on camera."

Cadders sighed. "Oh, sod it. What's the point? I don't want to lose what's left of my cherub's curls. I'll let her just roam free."

"She's not Black Beauty, Cadders!"

"It's getting a bit weary, to be honest. I might just sack it off after Christmas, Nena. I might give her the little festive gift of no longer having to pretend to like me. I thought ghosting was a terrible dating habit, but I might just try it out in the new year – spin around in it as a resolution. The Three Musketeers are a better use of my time."

"What? The Three Musketeers? You mean, you, me and Sam?" Nena spluttered. "You must be Porthos? Honest, ever-believing, gout-ridden." She scanned Cadders' face in vain for a glimpse of a joke, but his steepled hands again denoted that he was being 100 per cent truthful.

"I would very, very much like for us three to become the Musketeers – one for all, and all of that. It might be good for us to be a little escapist for a while, what with all our crap. It would certainly drag Sam out of the fug of grief and the confusion of being pursued. I mean, we could assume aliases and monkey around town in velvets."

"But…"

"It's all right. You won't have to dress up as a 17th-century Béarnaise gentleman; you can still wear your apple-press shawls. Is that OK with you?"

"It's more than fine. I'm just surprised, Cadders."

"Why surprised?"

Nena cleared her throat. "Well, you've warmed to Sam so swiftly; he's not the easiest chap to get to know – big eyebrows, griping and saturnine glances."

"He's a thoughtful chap, better that than some grinning fool…" Cadders laughed and then stopped, conscious that he himself was about to grin. "Well, yes…"

"I always think Sam is forward-planning for the next decade," Nena continued. "He'll know what he's going to eat for breakfast next week, except at the moment he doesn't seem to want to eat even a crumb. And he's always so pallid, he must glow under a black light. He's a human prism. I mean – was he living in a bunker in Turin for 18 years?"

Cadwick held her hand; his loafers swung. He tilted his head. "He's Scottish. I like Sam because he doesn't fill the air with the same amount of bollocks as we do."

"Speak for yourself, Cads! You keep quacking away for the very fun of it. Are you paid by every single letter?"

"I like his laconic ways. I have time enough to chunter away. And Sam listens to my mechanical chat and grinding charisma without reproaching me."

"I like how his eyes seem to go into REM every time he has a thought; his eyeballs do this little shimmy before he speaks, as if he's wiping his feet before making an entrance into the conversation. Can he hear us?"

I could, just, above the clattering of the coffee-making.

"And Sam has brought us such a marvellous puzzle to try to solve, hasn't he, Nena?"

"Well, ask me tomorrow once I have seen the state of my left knee. It's turned to hot gloop." Nena rubbed the denim softly and winced. "But it's very sweet how you see us as a little gang, this little green gang."

"Like the Muppets…" Cadders added, excitedly.

"I'll take anything. I've spent 19 years praying for something, anything to happen. So, I shouldn't now be afraid of change, should I? Aside from the crazy man who's terrifying my partner with photographs and break-ins…"

"Life is sweet. This place is warm, your boy is back, Christmas is roaring up the tracks."

"And we can investigate your list properly," she said, ending his joviality as she picked up his notes on possible houses, "but, Jesus, your handwriting is terrible, Cadders. Did you write this when you were on the power plates?"

"No. I have the scrawl of a man who writes a great deal…"

"Anyway," Nena continued, "yes, we have a start. It's not in west Folkestone."

Cadders looked at the rain hurling itself against the café's white-bordered windows as if trying to eavesdrop. "I will flag up the list on my WhatsApp group, get the chaps involved in the search, but I'll say it's a list of houses I'm looking to buy for future letting." The trails of raindrops joined together into little riverlets that branched out like the veins on the backs of a hand. "You know, Jacqs will be able to help us there, if she sees fit, but, Christ, I hope she doesn't turn up now. I'm half-cut, and she'll turn me from happy soul to arsehole. I'm going to text her and say I've had to go home and do some admin, eat, pray."

Nena laughed as Cadders jabbed his lie into his latest gadget, some slab of hard plastic that was bigger than both his hands. "The honeymoon period is well and truly over for you, Cadders."

"Nena, we former public schoolboys are like criminals – we've never had anything in our lives we cannot walk away from in under half an hour."

Over by the cabin, Joey was pacing away in the wet grass. He'd seen the three smug tossers in the window-seat of the Loaf café, getting pissed and braying, the little one swinging his legs around like Kermit the bloody Frog. It was time to once again puncture their buoyancy aids, break up their little drunken bonhomie. So, Joey had just plunged his hunting knife with full force into the side of the wooden-slatted building. And, as he did so, he felt a release, imagining the blade splitting the ribcage first of Samuel and then of that Dresden bitch. This is the effect of staying hungry and lean.

Try laughing now, muppets.

Odd Thomas.

Tommy is still the Tommy of all the tales, or Tom to those clients too geriatric for him to bunk up with. The name Tommy keeps him feeling young; there remains the gymnastics of avoiding the crockery and glassware Claudia throws during her histrionics and then the gymnastic make-up sex. He still spends nights on his recumbent exercise bike in front of a DVD. The truth is, his dark features appear to have been given a rushed colour-wash of ash-coloured paint, thinned out with a greyer glaze; his strong brown brows have sunk lower as his hair thins out from front to back. Tom is turning into his father, who had the air of a melancholic manatee contemplating the slow rub of the seas.

"Tommy! Tommy! Too much burning of the midnight oil, eh?" His friend Gerald is being his usual ebullient self too early in the day. He himself has slid into middle age like a walrus slides into the subarctic seas; he glories in his bulk, not even bothering to stretch his red Fred Perry polo over the expanse of pale and hairy gut. Gerald's dark hairline is trying to colonise every last square centimetre of his tiny forehead; he'd apparently been so hirsute as a child that the midwife had jokingly offered him her lunchtime banana.

"Mate, lay off with all this fun-time twattery. I feel like my insides are being pulled out through my arse." Tommy motions up from the sofa on which he lies. "Give me a glass of Barolo. Come on, come on." He shifts across the buttons of the fake leather, trying to find a position where the knitting needles may cease typing away at his stomach. "Give me the Barolo. Give me the whole bottle, G."

The older man obliges, his magnificent proboscis even redder than the rest of his pock-marked face. "For you, a million glasses of Barolo, a thousand bottles, a vineyard –

we shall be millionaires many times over because of you. You crafty little bugger." Gerald unscrews the bottle top and fills the mug to the brim once more. He hands both the bottle and the mug to Tommy.

"Gerald, you have to keep silent from now on. Except when you have to explain away what's happened. Put it all in different clothes."

"Right, chief."

"This is not England, you know? The Piemontesi eat a lot, drink a lot and talk a lot – that's the bit you need to remember." Tommy grimaces and so drinks another mouthful of the red wine, which fizzes on his tongue like an Alka Seltzer. "In Piedmont, we can't blab. Brothers marry pairs of sisters, and so on. And someone will cotton on what we were doing up in Switzerland, and those millions flutter away like a flock of starlings. We don't want any prying for the next couple of months, no matter where we find ourselves."

"I get it, Tom, I get it," Gerald smiles, but Tommy is on one of his barrel-rolls.

"No, you don't get it. I flew you in only four days ago, and you've been roistering around the place, acting as if this is your manor, fluttering your money around like confetti. Claudia told me you got thrown out of the Slot Club In The Alps. The favour I did for you can always be undone, and you just try booking a flight out of here in the next few days." Tommy drains the last inch of the mug and holds his churning stomach.

"So, what do I say?" Gerald stops smiling and sits down next to his old friend.

"Apart from day-to-day chat, you parrot only what I tell you to parrot. Every face you see is that of a stranger who might take a shit on your hopes and dreams. I do not want the Piemontesi police to have even an inkling of our money-washing. The pair of us will get trapped in Turin for months and months until we agree to pay off the right people. Even Claudia can't help us there."

Gerald shifts on the sofa, and the thick rings of sweat under the polo shirt's fabric give off their stale scent. "I'm only a house-guest here on holiday. I'm no one here. I'm the ghost under the pavement."

"Right, G," Tommy says, sarcastically.

"Everyone thinks I'm improving my handicap on the golf course – don't worry. Switzerland never happened."

"Good. So, I don't want you getting coked up, trying to screw Claudia at The Beach on Via Murazzi, and dancing the Macarena, and I most definitely don't want you quacking away like a duck down the local trattoria. You stick out around here – like you stick out everybloodywhere – and you sound like a bad copy of Michael Caine."

"Italian Job? Zulu?" Gerald smiles, rubbing his chest.

"The Cider House Rules, you soppy melt!"

A criminal estate.

Nena fumbles at the lock of her salon, cursing the rough cut of her spare key; I peer in through the flyers on the front window and laugh at the ripe pinkness of the interior; and Cadders shambles down the street, his drunk Shetland pony legs sending him weaving across the pavement. His tracking is off. All told, we three are swacked after a few hours at the Loaf window seats; the three unwise monkeys. Well, Nena again is the sensible one. Cadders catches up with the two of us at last, Nena unable to guide the key into the Yale lock.

"Open up, girl. I want to get my hands on our secret stash. I'm starting to sober up," Cadders roars, with his Arran jumper wrapped around his waist like a carpenter's apron and its arms swinging loosely in front of him.

"Yes, open it up, Nena." I am just as inebriate as my new friend, and Nena seems to be rueing her offer of midnight gins in the backroom bunker. I am in no fit state for any romance, and Cadwick is likely to let slip to me all the secrets of Nena's past decade. If everyone did indeed have three lives – a public life, a private life, and a secret life – then Cadders is curator of Nena's cupboard of skeletons. He is now woozy enough to open it up to the one person she truly doesn't want to be prying inside.

"All right, all right, boys. We're in, we're in." Nena shoos away my slobbering mouth from her shoulder. "Sam, get off me. Cadders, switch on the back light while I lock up behind us." Nena pulls down the door's blind and takes a full breath.

Then, the three of us race across the salon floor, bundle through the bead curtain and pile onto that hardy vinyl bench. There are four bottles of gin chilling in the mini fridge, but Nena takes just one and pours four fingers into each of the mugs that rest on the red shelf beside the seat.

"Sam, Sam – here, take this one. Cadders and I always use the other two. I can't be arsed to wash the mugs out. Here, take it, Sammy." She brings the drink into my hand. I grin at the cup. Nena wishes she were as buoyant as I am, but she is too busy playing mother to her two errant boys. It must be strange for her to watch me regress to that summer before I left, but better than watching me fret or fall asleep at random points of the day. Perhaps tonight I will slumber for the whole night in my gin bivouac.

I stand up and, swaying, raise my Tintin mug high above my sweaty, gurning face. I can feel my fair skin being poached in gin sweat; and my kiss curl is plastered to my forehead like a question mark. "And here we are, we three, perhaps the last island of beauty in the world. Would it be in bad form to plagiarise a toast?"

Nena interjects. "What the hell are you on about now?"

"He's quoting Withnail and I! Great film!" Cadders then frowns. "This gin tastes a little woolly. You know what I mean?"

"Woolly?" I ask. "It's fine. WOOLLY BULLY!" I stand up and start belting out the old song, with a wiggle of my hips. This version of Sam is fine for a night, Nena seems to be thinking; but it will grow extremely tiring, even in the medium term.

Just then, there is an almighty crunch, a seismic ripping, as if the entire salon is sliding backwards towards the sea, shunted by the thigh of an invisible giant. Through the bead curtain comes a shower of sound, a huge whumping wave that carries shards of glass in from the front window and scatters them against the back wall like rice grains. A cloud of plaster follows in its wake, microparticles that turn the entire back room sooty and white and the red shelves a dusky pink. It is as if an airbag full of chalk and glass shards has enveloped the entire salon.

I fall across Cadders and Nena, with my flying coat-tails wrapping around them in an armless cradle of support. Still the crunching tear continues until there is no sound apart from the glug of the gin bottle emptying itself onto the floor and into its fine flour of dust. The boozy batter mix pools around our shoes.

"What in the hell was that?" Cadwick mutters from under my armpit.

"God only knows," I reply. My mouth tastes of flour. "Earthquake?"

"Sounded like a tsunami or the cosmic tearing of time itself," Cadders says. "Are you both all right? I am." He tries to wriggle his body free from mine, but I can't move. Truth be told, it's a little bit amusing.

"We're too far from the sea for it to be a bloody tsunami," answers Nena from under Cadders.

"No, there aren't any tsunamis in the Channel…" I say.

"I wasn't being serious about a tsunami, guys."

Nena rolls herself away from under Cadders. "Stop being a jester."

Cadders sighs. "I could just hear metal being crunched up. And where's the water?"

"I just feel the gin seeping into my shoes."

"It's like a wrecking ball slammed into the salon, and all this dust…"

Nena coughs into the bench. "The whole place is coated in stuff. What is it?"

"Sam, can you get up please?" Cadders lifts up my left arm and smiles at me. "The gin will definitely be woolly now, old bean."

I get up, now the shock has gone, brush off the diamonds of broken glass from my brown sweater and padded coat. I help Nena to her feet as Cadders rolls away from me. "At least we are all uninjured. We're all good?"

The three of us part the beads and peer at the scene of devastation in the salon. Where once were Nena's purple velour sofa and her two pink barber's chairs, there is now a very mangled Skoda estate, lifted slightly by the furniture now jammed underneath its loose bumper and crinkled grey skirting. The black-and-white floor has various car parts as its chess pieces; a column of vapour rises from the car's buckled bonnet; and the front left wheel hangs out at the horizontal like an indicator paddle.

No one is in the driver's seat; and there's nobody in the salon bleeding out or brandishing a knife, thank god. But the shop is, to all intents and purposes, now outside; not a single sliver of glass remains in the front window, save for the lower corner where the board of prices is keeping a tea-tray-sized square of shattered glass in place. Some of the rubbish – burger trays and empty Heineken cans, the old flyers and ketchupy serviettes – a few moments ago bagged up beside the front door, is now sliding into the salon on the gusting wind and dancing around the broken metal monolith at its centre. I blink away the dust.

"What a shit storm."

The car has missed the telegraph post that stands to one side of the shop front, but it has knocked over the heavy metal street bin that once sat directly in front. I walk around the car and through the salon's glassless front door.

"Guys, there are no tyre marks out here," I report. "There should be tyre marks if someone was trying to brake. Why didn't the driver brake? Where are they?"

"What do you mean, Sammy?" says Cadders, from beside the Skoda.

Suddenly sober, I speak through the open mess of the window. "Cadders, there are no skidmarks. It looks like the car outshot the T-junction and ploughed into the window here. It must have come down the hill at speed and just not stopped. It must have come down Military Road." I look up the steep incline towards the streetlights in the distance. "I doubt the car even slowed down. But why would the driver not try to stop, or lessen the impact? A drunk?"

"999?" Cadders is on his phone as he leans against the silver-grey front wing of the Skoda. "Hi. It's Christian Cadwick here, and a runaway car has hit the salon opposite Military Road. At the bottom of Military Road." He pauses and looks at Nena who is rubbing her forehead and staring at the crumpled pair of chairs under the car's number plate. The furniture now acts as nothing more than a ramp for the vehicle. "Yes, it's called Nena's. N-E-N-A. Yes, call this number. Thanks, cheers." He presses the home button and shambles back around the front of the car to where Nena stands trembling. "They'll be twenty minutes or so, they said. So, make it at least three-quarters of an hour."

"Where's the driver?" Nena asks us in shock. "Where's the driver? I mean, where is he? How did it-?"

I gingerly step over the lower frame of the window and the missing bricks of the low wall beneath it. I speak through the emerging fug of my hangover. "Nena, I don't think there was ever a driver. They'd have been badly cut up by the glass from the shop window and the windscreen. There's glass everywhere. Look – it's sticking out of that wall, a hundred daggers of the stuff."

Cadders joins in. "I don't think it was a case of someone just forgetting to put the handbrake on. I mean, no one ran after the car, and if you follow the track of the car, it came from right in the middle of Military Road. Look," and Cadders points directly from the car up the sharp slope with cars parked on either side. "It would have been impossible for the Skoda to pick up enough speed if it had been last in the line of parked cars."

I nod. "It could only have come from the middle of the road and from a way up the hill."

"The estate was really travelling when it came through the window. It got through a two-brick-high wall under the glass. Thank the Lord, we weren't in the front of the salon."

I nod again. "This was a deliberate act." Thinking of the break-in at my cabin, I go around the back of the Skoda and show the others two hand-sized clearings in the dust and grime on the estate's hatch. "Someone's pushed it. Silly twat's forgotten not to lock the doors either, though the number plates are missing. We know that no one was in there, you see."

Nena jabbers away in shock. "I need a crime reference number. I need action. I need a reference – I need to get one off the police to claim my insurance on the place." Nena is hysterical, rubbing the end of her scarf between her thumb and ring finger. The chairs she bought at 19 are a crumple of metal like the legs of a crushed spider; all in, it will take months to repair the shop and her haven.

"At least we're all safe, eh?" Cadders reasons, but Nena's face is like rolling thunder. Oh, no. Don't, Cadders. You can tell he rubs most people up the wrong way.

And here we go. "All safe!" Nena chimes in, sarcastically. "All safe? Is my shop safe? You know, is my livelihood safe?"

"No, but ten minutes earlier, and we'd have all been marmalised at the shop front." I look out from the wreckage and up the hill. I can't see a soul about in the early-morning mist; only the immediate foreground is chaos. In my fuzzy mind, the lines of parked cars all seem set to join the Skoda estate in crashing into the salon.

"I want all this craziness to stop now, Sam," Nena murmurs. "Yes, I want it to stop. I want to know why I've been targetted – this isn't exactly a slight rearrangement of furniture. We could have been seriously injured. This is an escalation, and I want answers now. What's been going on for the past two decades in Turin, eh, Sammy? Cosa

Nostra? Camorra? Whatever you brought with you from Piedmont is dangerously wild," Nena snarls.

This is wrong. I hold up my chalky hands. "I didn't bring…"

"Enough, Sam. This has come after the break-in, and this is no bloody prank either. This is my livelihood – this is all I have left from my parents." Nena turns on her heels and catches sight of her family photos, untouched above the beaded curtain. "They're looking down on us, looking down on the carnage of our lives – the physical and emotional carnage – and they must be disgusted. Do you think this kind of shit happened to Alistair and Sandy and to my parents too? It just didn't." She bends down to pick up her rack of tongs and scissors, which have been shunted into the skirting-boards with enough force to leave an imprint in the pine. "Do you think this disorder happens to those who live with a certain measure of order, and not wasted days in bed with a laptop and a pizza? You've lived out of a sports holdall for 18 years, and Cadders and I bounce from hangover to hangover." Nena begins to weep again, and the tears roll down her cheeks and into the pink wool of her rollneck. "We never learn; we just mock those who've found peace with the world – those rows and rows of happy families sleeping in Cheriton – while we scrabble around in this war zone."

I see Cadders stepping towards her as she kneels, and I wish that I'd done the same. "Everything can be replaced, Nena," he says. "I can loan you the money to get all this cleared and fixed. The insurers will then step in. We can make an early start; we can begin tomorrow and make this salon even better than it was."

"I don't want your charity, Christian," Nena sighs, wearied by the knowledge of all the work and admin that lay ahead of her. "Not everything can be replaced. The floor and the chairs and the walls and the windows will all be different – they may look the same, but they won't have the age, the signs that I've lived with them for the past two decades. My furniture has picked up the markings of my daily life for all those years. You know, that time when estate cars didn't smash through my life…"

Another single tear runs down Nena's cheek, collecting the foundation and powder until it reaches the corner of her mouth no longer clear but a cloudy pink.

"You will have to let the restorers do their thing, and you'll have to start afresh," I say. "Begin anew. These things are just possessions. Are all your memories really bound up in the things you've bought and had cleaned, or are they somewhere inside yourself?"

I am trying my best to mollify my partner's towering rage at the injustice of it all, but I am signally failing. I bend down to pick up a Braun teddy mascot covered in broken glass and the dust from the wall plaster around the front window.

Nena rubs her head. "My memories are just like yours, Sam. That cabin of yours is unchanged. It is your cocoon from other aspects of your past – a flotation tank into which you can escape at any time. You've chosen that cabin as a time-capsule and your only physical touchstone to the past. It's something you've selected; for all your talk of a fresh present-day, it's only possible because you've rejected huge swathes of ties that stretch back all your life. If that cabin were to be shunted off the cliff-top by a runaway car, what would you have left? You'd have no souvenirs; you'd only have the people who survive – me, Mimi, Tommy. Your little Tardis would be gone, and you would have to rely just on what recollections we could come up with for you. And your nearest and dearest can sometimes act as unreliable narrators. You'd ask, was the cabin sofa a light red, now you can't see for yourself that it was indeed a bright scarlet? Your world would collapse in on itself or blow out like this window – you'd be reliant on an ever-diminishing mental capacity, with no photos and diaries. You'd be as adrift as I feel now. So, don't dare tell me, either of you, that everything can be replaced. You can pretend that to be so, and you can pretend that everything can be forgotten too, but through the mind's window, all those people peer in, and all those conversations will be a loop while you remain sane. The past cannot be replaced by the future, and the past cannot be renovated."

Cadders and I look at one another, and we then throw our arms around Nena, who is sobbing away in front of the car that has carried away her belongings and, with them, some of her memories.

The queen of Torino, its fallen prince.

If Gerald represents a containable problem for Tommy, then Claudia, his firecracker of a girlfriend, is like a rogue spirit, 'Claudia degli spiriti'; she seems to drift into his apartment like white smoke before the commencement of her technicoloured tantrums. Perhaps she has learnt from the fashionistas she hangs out with in Milan how to move without a sound?

Tommy has long given up on appeasement or trying to split up with Claudia; the locals have treated her from girlhood as if she were Gina Lollobrigida, so nothing has come to her with any effort. As long as she remains unapproachably beauteous, the world will continue come to her. Any criticism of Claudia is off limits.

Tommy acts like her manservant, and he's curbed the extremes of his swordsmanship, the excessive girl-chasing, yet still it isn't enough for Claudia – Tommy can always see her right hand fiddle with her earring as she races through her memory for an excuse to fulminate. Tommy tells me it is all part of diva act she owes everything in life to; whether it is enough to constitute a recognisable human character is another question altogether. And one I wouldn't ask. Tommy says she's uncommonly bright and caring, but to me, Claudia seems to simply mirror whatever it is you are to her. I feel that Tommy is simply the errand boy for her wandering desires.

His apartment in the right-hand corner on the first floor of a fine palazzo on the Via Carlo Alberto is perhaps worth around four million euro now, but Tommy has been tinkering with it for some 15 years, in between his work duties. For five years, he has tolerated Claudia gradually moving in her roomful of haute couture, all of it gifted by the fashion homosexuals of northern Italy for whom she acts as petulant muse. Her clothes spill over the sides of the roll-top bath Tommy's salvaged from a bombed-out palace; they sit on the table, joining Tommy for his breakfast of poached eggs on toast; they swing on hangers from the backs of the heavy rosewood doors as Claudia glides around the palazzo. However, once inside, and with me sent packing, it seems Claudia is rarely clothed, believing garments will sap her life force if worn for too many hours of the day.

Tommy tolerates all this because he tells me he loves her, the sex is unimpeachably fantastic, and for the very sound reason that her contacts have brought him almost all of the legal mandates that have paid for the arterial work to his home. There is not a scintilla of maternal instinct in Claudia's ludicrous form, a lacking that is remarkable for a woman who has never left the matriarchal Piemontese society; as Tommy once joked to me, his old friend Sam, why would she leave her adoring public, or abdicate her responsibility to light up Turin with her dazzle? Isn't Tommy always told how lucky he is to have possession of the city's most exquisite gem? Often, this seems to Tommy to be a disgusting thought; he wants Claudia to be so much more to him than a trophy girlfriend, to show off her phenomenal knowledge of her country and to teach him. But, no, that is not her persona. Claudia seems to have been dreamt up in the pages of di Lampedusa's Il Gattopardo, being a carbon copy of Angelica Sedara, radiant jewel of the Risorgimento and destroyer of men. Claudia should be running an empire, not sitting on a foreigner's knee, taking out rogue white hairs from his eyebrows with a set of tweezers.

From the cellar where he prays that he's taught Gerald a little restraint, Tommy attempts in vain to walk off the cumulative hangover of four days of partying. His head ticks, his neck cracks, but his heart is light. Gerald is correct – these are halcyon days, after all. There's a porcupine's-back of irons in the fire. Gerald's wife, Fenella, a blousy heiress to a Kent property-developing fortune that has been built on extremely dubious practices, is transferring the bulk of her wealth into an offshore account in Gerald's name, and the burly St Bernard is in the process of transferring the funds to Tommy. All the money washed and saved is to be spent on Fenella's folly – a multi-level Italianate garden in the west of Kent – but the fees are almost as much, and Gerald and Tommy are to divvy them up over the coming year when the cash has been cleansed of its Kentish dirt. The problem is, Gerald has started the party early, snorting cocaine off the headrest of Tommy's Cessna before they'd even left the airfield tarmac and mouthing off about the intricacies of the deal, even to the woman in the control centre of the regional aeroporto.

Tommy is still shaking from the chat in the cellar, and the cold sweats are telling him to cut down on the Barolo for a wee while. This is a hangover that he won't sweat out on his jog out of the city; nor can he leave it as steam on the sauna floor of Palestre Torino. He has a call with Claudia's ferocious father in an hour. He must stay sharp.

Without me around, Tommy spends his leisure hours jogging up and down the banks of the Po, ever winding about until it disappears in the flood plains below the city. At times, he tells me he feels he's trying to outrun his predicament, his strides taking him further away from his gradual absorption into co-dependency and commitment. Tommy listens again and again on his iPod to the same trios of Nineties tracks, songs that take him way back on his pilot's wings across the Channel to east Kent. Tommy doesn't feel he is built for anything more than the making of new friends and the symbiotic relationship with his best mate. If Tommy can just keep jogging until the Po hits the Adriatic, perhaps he can find a portal back into the past, when everything was so much simpler, with less weight to drag around.

Tommy wonders why he can play the notes expected of him beautifully 99 per cent of the time, but why that one inevitable, discordant clang is all the audience ever seems to remember. He sounded depressed on our call the other day. He asked why he ruins all his hard work in a mindless moment. A certain wilfulness appears to be the killer of his hopes. Tommy sinks into despondency – the lonely runs lengthen, and some mistake, a bum note, sends him hurting down the serpent's tail to the very bottom; only then can he look up and see all the treasures he possesses. Perhaps Tommy is his own destroyer by design, to prevent himself from becoming too content and entitled. He ought to settle for comfort, but he just sees the next hill, the next deal.

What I don't know is that Tommy has his own ghost. On his runs around and about the ever-changing topography of Turin, Tommy obsessively dwells upon that horror night, every incident real and imagined. The jog starts with my car, the Flying Pig, crawling up his family farm's long sweep of a drive, alongside the brown, corrugated cold store with its grains and apples, stopping just before the gnarled oak of the porch; the jog ends, as Tommy's heart rate hits 160 beats a minute. He sees the boy I hit, crawling on all fours in a pig mask, on the road out towards Alkham.

On that single carriageway, a bootlace between the hills, only a maximum of two cars pass in the hour before midnight. Tommy imagines the stricken boy dislocating his own jaw with his muddy hands, half in pain and half in a vodka hallucination, trying to close up the cuts and reset any fracture. The boy's cheeks are tracked in dirt and tears. The knees of his carpenter jeans have been rubbed away, so the mud can be seen in the bright blood-red rawness. Tommy is the condoner. Tommy is the concealer. Has he wrecked my life, and his, by helping me?

Logic returns only as Tommy recovers from his run. His sports top is soaked through. He rests his back against the stone arch that stands alone in a field of peas – his fifteen-kilometre jog is complete. Then, after a breather, Tommy can correct his delusions and see the boy sitting on a red plastic chair in triage at the Royal Victoria Hospital, a few cuts to the left side of his mouth, the dirt making his hair appear like a brown hessian mat, and the smear of blood across his forehead exaggerating his injuries.

Why have all Tommy's memories of his teenage years been bundled up into the chaos of those few hours? Is it a repeating trick of his oxygen-starved mind, triggered by those old songs? As consciously as he seeks to free his recollections from the hysterical adornments brought on by his aerobic exhaustions, so does his subconscious request the same scenes from his internal jukebox, these phony tableaux of horror. The false memory becomes more muscular. It shunts away the truth.

Tommy may have his treasures, but the fear is very real that he will end up telling his tales to a roomful of empty chairs. Tommy will end up summoning up the ghosts of somehow-forgotten friends from the floorboards. The boulevardier is still doing his act, but the audience has left long ago. Tommy is running out of time; soon, his looks will completely fade under the heavy sag of time. He has closed himself off to almost everyone, and now the door is closing, too. One day, Tommy will unload a single chamber into his head. It's in his contract, he believes.

Music triggers real memories, not false ones inflamed by lonely bellows at the midnight hour. Music is his light, and it is transporting and transportable. Tommy has his jukebox in his head, the memories dancing around it like unbreachable holograms never to be decayed by time. There is nothing in Tommy's world as comforting as the strange daydreams brought on by his playlists. Music alone calls his angels to their table.

But it also calls his devils.

Where is Sammy to talk him away from any false memories? In acceding to Claudia's desire for a palazzo in which her wardrobe is the third, bulkiest resident, Tommy feels he has turned his back on his oldest and stoutest friend; he hasn't, I tell him repeatedly. Tommy needs the same change in purpose that I have made, otherwise the self-administered gunshot behind that closed door will happen sooner rather than later.

Something has to give.

The aftermath of the crash.

"I mean, for God's sake. That achieved the square root of sod all, didn't it, boys?" Nena turns to Cadwick and me after waving off PC Stuart. After a volley of robust Anglo-Saxon, she has managed to fish most of her possessions from the Vesuvian detritus of the salon.

The young constable had been making a supreme effort to display thoroughness, but the closing of his notepad betrayed his lack of interest, and I saw he hadn't put down more than fifty words in handwriting that resembled the telemetrics of a poisoned daddylonglegs. PC Stuart looked the part, but he was either too tired to be of any help or judging us three friends for the fumes of gin on our breath and the puddle of the stuff on the backroom floor.

The copper has repeated almost exactly what the three of us had concluded hours earlier: that a runaway Skoda estate, stolen from Folkestone's East Cliff area that night, had ploughed, driverless and fingerprint-less, into Nena's sanctuary. The policeman said he would now be crossing town to speak with the car's owners and would then run through the station CCTV from all the possible crosstown routes. And that, sighs Nena, is all, folks.

"Did you see his writing? Like a baby's," continues Nena. "They're not going to find footage of the bastard beaming into the cameras, giving it the double thumbs-up, are they? He's not going to Instagram his handiwork."

I have been hearing this cavalcade of criticism for the past two hours, and it palls. "No, whoever did this was canny. I bet the plates are in a hedge up the road. And he- ... they wore gloves and probably a baseball cap..."

Cadwick is sitting on the counter before us, swinging his tassiled loafers. He has been back home to pick up his

Where is Your God Now?

iPad Mini, to shower and to change out of his powdered clothes. "The hand-marks were man-sized, though, Sam."

"I don't know, Cadders. The marks were smeared all across the tailgate," I walk over to the counter to hear him better. "The Skoda got in here with more ease than it came out, you know. I thought the tow-truck was going to snap in two."

"Half a shitty car and half a shop," moans Nena. She turns to me and cocks her head. "I'm hungry, Sammy. Take me somewhere, please. Take my mind off this all. I feel dehydrated from all my crying."

"Oh, come now. Don't you want to sleep? Don't you? You've been up since yesterday morning." I ask, but Nena shakes her head; she looks dead to the world, her eyes shadowed with tiredness, her shoulders no longer held high but slumping into her chest with the strain.

Cadwick jumps down from the counter. "I'll leave you two to it. I'm knackered."

I nod.

"I'll transfer the cash online, Nena," says Cadders. "We'll get started today; the sooner we begin, the sooner you'll be back to a certain normality."

"No, Cadders, come along," Nena pleads. "Now we know that someone is wreaking revenge on us, so we Musketeers should redouble our efforts. Come on!"

"I thought a shower would wake me up, but I'm still schoonered."

"This is the kind of thing you were born for, Cadders. You can bring all that organisational flair of yours to this mess; just treat us like your fags at school."

Cadwick laughs, hoping he will soon see the mocha freshness reappear on Nena's face. The white face from the cloud of powder that came in with the Skoda accentuates her careworn appearance. He can't leave her now. "Yes. OK, Nena. Let's go to Loaf. I'll see you two in 20 minutes. I'm just going to see if my brother was on duty last night."

Cadders already has his smartphone clamped to his ear as he leaves the pair of us in the dust and odds 'n' ends of the shop. "Ru?"

Cadwick's brother, Rufus, is a slightly boss-eyed, melancholic concierge at The Grand and has a thousand ears. Dressed up like a chocolate-box Napoleonic cavalryman, if some 25 kilos too obese ever to see active service, Ru sighs at his mahogany lectern as his sibling gives his usual breathless outpouring of information. However, this request from Cadwick will prove to be another well-meant long-shot in a life spent currying favour.

On the other side of town, Joey fishes yet another angry note from his pigeonhole. He throws the German girls' crumpled warnings about noise in the hallway bin without reading their latest crimes against politeness and the English language. In last night's dream, he stashed the sisters away under an oak tree with roots in Radnor Park, where he could treat them to electric shocks from his machine, watching their thin bodies jerk.

After his walk to East Cliff and then his stealthy drive to Sandgate, Joey has worked until mid-morning at the bakery, cleaning up after the crew on the shift before him. Their finger- and thumbprints have been all over the stainless-steel doors as usual; Joey is sure that none of his was on the estate car that disappeared an hour earlier into the front of the salon. From the hill some 100 metres away, he saw the vehicle swallowed up with a hungry snort in a pastry cloud of dust and broken glass. "Now you see the car; now you don't." Joey smiled all the way back into Folkestone, walking up Sandgate Hill at the dead of night and looking back near the top to see the sporadic lights as Hythe curved away in the distance.

And now it is time to demolish the white bloomer he's brought home, with a little butter and a large stripe of ketchup. Plenty of matters have played on his mind at work that night as he wiped down the doors and stacked the morning loaves on the half-dozen trays in the three-decked ovens, but nothing is troubling him now in the quiet cocoon of his bedsit. Often, the stillness makes his mind race around like a laundry drum, but any storm to come is far off; he is quietly satisfied to be nearing the end of the first act of his neatly penned revenger's tale. With every action completed with efficacy, so Joey removes a splinter from under his skin. He is dragging out the darkness, cutting out the cancer that has been left to spread within, and the light is gradually returning to him. Joey has addressed and satisfied the twin sides of his Gemini soul.

The week to come will bring the anniversary of his mother's passing, and Joey has been turning his mind to how to honour her memory. Every month keeps winding on, the passage of time marked only by the additional annotations on his wall map and the lessening of his inheritance fund. However, the memories will never recede. This morning, his room is calm, private and sequestered from the outside world; at other times, it is mournful, but always the special moments he shared with his mother flutter like ghosts among the eaves, high above the hubbub and avenues of oak trees and Victorian townhouses once ruled by the Earl of Radnor.

The voices of the ancients come through the lime plasterwork to console Joey, and he can feel along the dado rails for the sweep of the history of his home. Joey finds comfort in the certainty that other lost souls have passed in and out of its panelled white entrance hall. The long-dead might remark upon how the leaves are beginning to parachute onto the pavements or how the frost has begun to finger its way along the architrave above the front porch. Dozens of residents have been cloistered within since the mid-1860s. Joey can picture them committing deeds far more nefarious than his. He's sometimes kept awake during the daylight hours by his own bodyclock and indigestion, but never by pangs of conscience.

Everything will be levelled out in the fullness of time; Joey just has to survive for long enough. Virtue is cyclical, in Joey's world, as is what constitutes moral cleanliness. Just as the Victorians who constructed this robust dwelling with precision had found fault with the shallowness and appetites of their Georgian antecessors so the Edwardians in their gaiety had laughed at the corseted lives of Queen Victoria's subjects. Regency green gave way to Victorian mourning black, and that in turn had ceded to the pale blues of the playboy king Edward VII, who had set up his imperial shag-pad at The Grand.

History grants Joey's transgressions a certain leeway; his are not serious crimes after all. His deeds will not cover the front page of the local newspaper; they won't incite a phalanx of ragged protestors to shake their smartphones, those modern-day pitchforks, high in the air below his fourth-floor window. Way up above all the hot fuss and the melée of modern life, Joey can close his eyes and return to the past. The sludge people will leave him be.

Anyway, Joey is training himself to do the time if necessary, ready to swap his four bare walls for another box somewhere away from Folkestone, where he won't have to work for his crust so much. He's learnt to subsist on extremely little; he has almost nothing to lose. All of his valuables are locked away in his memory, always accessible, always portable. He's becoming truly invisible, and it warms him up.

In Turin, Gerald is glued by drool to the paisley pillowcases, face down as if starjumping into the bedlinen. Rather than barking bollocks around the bars and bistros in the shade of the Cattedrale di San Giovanni Battista, the property developer has taken to one-man drinking sessions 10 feet below street level, bored to tears and extremely homesick. Empty bottles of Barolo stand at the side of the bed, next to a very tatty copy of Mayfair. The party has been forced to come to Gerald, on Tommy's instructions; at least, he has understood the warnings and stayed underground.

Gerald has told Tommy he's been having a nightmare in which the cellar's walls turn into a trellis of waggling ears and staring eyes, the network of Turin spies listening in to wreck the plan that Gerald and Tommy have formulated with such precision. The only way to blot out this monstrous vision has been to get thoroughly slotted and to tug himself to sleep – oenophilia and onanism, the missing Austen novel.

"Tommy?"

"Yes, Gerald." Tommy bends down over the back of the older man's boulder-like head and recoils at the stench of sweat and tannins.

"I'm ready for home. I miss The Crown. I can't get a signal in this cave."

"OK, mate. You're right, mate." Tommy pats his friend's matted hair.

"We've done what we wanted to do," murmurs Gerald into his pillow," and I can't go on living like a hermit down here under the ground. I need my people."

"Yeah, it's time for you to head back," Tommy replies. "By the way, thanks. There'll be a time when we can hit the West End and have a proper session."

Tommy always dreads a night on the tiles with Gerald, which invariably involves hours dropping pound coins in the pint pots at the ropey strippers' pub near Holborn where all the dancers look like Mick Ronson. They then search for the largest steak in the West End; if a place offers at least a 16oz rump, regardless of the zero-hygiene stars on the window and the amphetamine-hollowed waiting staff, then Gerald paws his way inside.

Tommy goes over to the sink and fills up a mug of tap water for his slumbering chum. "Bit of a tug you've had, eh?" He looks back at the static lump on the Z bed and gestures with the cup towards the open porn magazine. "Cleaning out the pipes, eh?"

Gerald laughs and then breaks into a cough that threatens to become a belch. "I had a little bit of stress relief. I'd rather be dreaming of Keeley's tits than a dozen angry Italians forcing their way through the walls of this shithole. I could see them coming again, and they were stretching the brickwork like it was rubber sheeting. Your warning properly shit me up, Tommy." Gerald mumbles into his pillow. "This place reminds me of when I got locked up for the night in Islington – same painful pillows, chipped sink, lack of telly, same feeling of dread, like the world wants my goolies and is pounding its way in. I wouldn't put this place on Airbnb, mate. It's a right shithole." Gerald sighs and tries to roll over onto his back. It isn't happening.

"It's just a holding pen for John's people. The Who could play a gig down here, and the folks up on the pavement wouldn't hear them." Tommy pauses and sits by Gerald's side. "We'll be fine."

Gerald speaks. "Anyway, are you going to stay on in Blighty, Tommy?"

"Yeah, I'm going to go and check in on Sammy, make sure he's behaving himself down there in the motherland."

"He always behaves. He's like a facking choirboy next to you, Tommy."

"His parents died both at once, G, as you know. Sammy's not one of nature's sunbeams. I'm going to recharge him with a few nights out. We both need it. I've been doing two jobs, one for me and us and the other for John. I'm just tired, G. And then I've got Claudia to contend with. And Sammy's not here. I'm starting to have those hallucinations again. It's happening, G."

"You're missing him?" Gerald replies, stone-faced.

Tommy sighs: "Oh, I suppose, yes. Things turn to shit when Sammy ups and leaves. I went down to that trattoria in the Milan quarter from the other night and just sat there reading The Times on my little smartphone until the battery ran out. I was watching all the happy couples coming in and out, parking their Vespas up outside and giggling arm in arm. I've been fooling myself for too long. I'm invisible in this country. I haven't got any friends of my own here."

"What about me?" Gerald looks very much like a St. Bernard who's discovered his cask is half-empty.

"Gerald, mate, you'll be homeward bound in a few hours – and anyway, you quack away like Daffy Duck when you've had a bit of beak. Be on call when I need you." Tommy rubs his eyes and blows his cheeks out. "We've got a bit of a flight very soon, so fix yourself up smartish."

Gerald looks over at the sink. "I'll give myself a five-point hospital wash and I'll meet you at the trattoria in an hour, capitaine."

"Good man."

"I've said it before, Thomas, but you and Sammy make a great duo. There's something complementary about you two. Maybe try to sweet-talk him into coming back to Piedmont, eh? You have it all set up here for a couple of rich guys in their late thirties – you obviously don't want or need to settle down with a wife and a couple of mewling shits who'll knacker you out more than your missus. I have seen it this week; I've seen all the complications and all your mad duties – you run about like a rabbit on PCP. That Claudia will be the death of you; her family require regular maintenance like they're a garden of rare flowers;

and the business you have here won't matter anyway when we coin it soon."

"I was thinking the very same, Gerald," Tommy mutters. "I don't see myself here in six months' time. This little jaunt is coming to an end without Sammy around, and if I can't persuade Claudia to leave her fans and join me over in Kent or Katmandu, then that'll all be over as well."

"Just let the lovely one know this."

"She'll be the very last person to know – you think she'll let me go easily, without a hundred carbonieri chasing me down the autostrada? So, if I call you, G, it'll be the sign for you to use your pull to whisk me away somewhere warm under cover of the night. Got it?"

"I got it, Tommy." And then Gerald finally rolls onto his back with a groan.

A power nap and a few hours later, Tom's tiny Cessna touches down at Lydd Airport, ferrying his ursine business partner back to the south of England, the raindrops sloping off the 172-SP's windscreen with Gerald rigid in the passenger seat. He has taken two Valium pills in Piedmont and has been drooling little riverlets of spit onto his bearded cheek for the past three hours. Tommy looks over.

"You overcooked it again on the pharmaceuticals, mate. We're home."

Gerald comes to. "Bloody Valium. I gobbled them all like Smarties."

Tommy takes off his headset and sighs. "How do you manage to make millions when you're barely awake all the time? For God's sake, if I slept as much as you do, I'd be sleeping in a caravan on Camber Sands."

"God knows. Can I sleep a bit more?" Gerald asks.

"No, get up, you shitbird."

"I feel grotty. I need the medicine to make my world go around."

"You took enough to stun an elephant. Are you going to be up and at it if I come to call you, Gerald?"

Gerald wipes his mouth and then smears his hand onto the leather seat. "It's all – er, part of my charm, Tommy."

"And you're ready?"

"I'll be set up to whisk you away from Italy."

"Yeah, well, I hope so. Let's see how my little visit to Folkestone goes. Hop out here, mate."

"OK, right you are."

"There's a Central taxi here, a Prius, to take you to north Kent."

"And you?"

"I'm off to Folkestone in my own cab," huffs Tommy.

"I'll ring you later this afternoon." Gerald burps.

"Keep up the pretence of a golfing week. Don't fall asleep in the taxi. You'll have to direct the cabbie for the last bit of the way. And cover your lap; you've got a patch of piss down there."

"You're a saviour, man."

"Speak later, G."

"The exit's through there?" Gerald points to the passageway out.

"Yeah. Don't shamble around." Tommy hops out and runs past Gerald with his leather shoulder bag and into a waiting Mercedes minivan. He has a little something to do down Folkestone way.

When you say nothing at all.

It's that time of the week when Luca and councillor John meet for a chat about silence and all the wondrous treats that it will bring. The Italian has been using Google to check the local news for any mention of the old man and the Polish girl, but as he was told at that first party, such people come with the dust and are gone with the wind; nobody checks the cracks in the pavements for the folk who never were. Luca has wondered how many phantom people wander around the capital.

"Luca, my boy!" He is getting used to councillor John's unflagging bonhomie, and the clap of his hands that accompanies every exclamation. "Sit down." John looks across the ever-empty café and winks at his employee in the apron. "Asgar, get the usual for our friend and me." John sets out his mobile and a small plastic container full of five-spice on the formica table.

The ever-surly Asgar busies himself with what is, at half noon, very likely his first order of the day of any kind. The Bright Café is just as lazy as its name; even the Cash Only notice by the old-fashioned till has been inked on a scrap piece of white card, free of any penmanship. In the half-dozen or so Monday meetings, Luca has not seen a single customer; much of the time, Asgar looks moodily out of the window.

John brings his hands together once again and shifts his wooden chair nearer to Luca and the table. "So, Luca – tell me about your week. How's the post office? The festive season is keeping you honest, I trust?"

"I'm always honest, councillor," Luca responds earnestly.

"It's a phrase we use, Luca. I know you can be trusted, my friend."

"Yes, yes. Work has been very busy; we get triple the numbers of cards and packages. I missed the Christmas party this year."

"So, there's no more romance with Patty?" John leans even closer.

"No, she didn't show up at the post office the day after the party." Luca's face crumples. "It disgusts me. This people are work-shy, and I have to work much harder, John. Instead of the beauty treatments, she should stop the eating-out and drinking, you know? I've changed my way of thinking. My life is different now."

"Well, we have a group of ladies interested in you, so don't worry about that Pat, eh?" John slaps Luca on his bicep. "You have seen the class of lady we entice to our soirees. These are girls who work very hard because they came to this country to work; they didn't just plop out here and expect the moon on a stick like that Patty."

"Patty's nice, but yes, I feel happier with my new friends, Justyna's friends." Luca looks over at Asgar flipping his eggs. "I don't get this country sometimes; the English are so casual with work – you know what I mean? The English all still think they are kings of the castle, and immigrants are the servants who look after them."

"Luca, I'm English, but not many of my countrymen know the value of things; how hard work is behind everything that's worth owning. Asgar has this place open seven days a week; he only takes two weeks off a year to go back to Algiers. He fears losing his job if he's away too much to see his wife and kids. But his boy, Mo, will grow up proud of him; he'll know why Asgar was absent for these years. You can trust a man who toils away all week not to chatter all over town about shit that's not theirs to spread. That muck-spreader, Dorota, the Polish girl at the party, got too sloppy with her hours and, more importantly, it meant she got sloppy with her mouth. She's just another forgotten tart. Everyone's replaceable." Councillor John smiles. "Except you, me and Asgar, of course."

The Algerian stops flipping his eggs and looks over. He reaches into his apron and stares straight at Luca, a glare that suggests he's only being civil for the moment.

Luca looks away and sits up straight. "I've been thinking about your own offer of a free flight and I'd like very much to go back to Turin before Christmas and New Year." Luca returns the councillor's smile. "My shifts are covered."

John thumps the table instead of clapping his hands. "Great – that is good news! I'm so glad. You deserve it. You'll be able to see your brother and go to that winter concert. Verdi, yes?"

"Vivaldi, sir," Luca coughs, "though Verdi is a very important to me, too. He felt the spirit of unification in Italy, and that is my specialist thing about my country."

"Yeah, yeah," John mutters with boredom.

"Verdi was born humble near Parma. I am humble born. Yes, I love Verdi, I love Il Triovatore, but I'm going to go to see The Four Seasons with Gianfranco."

"I don't know very much about classical music, my friend," John confesses. "I used to run some nightclubs in Soho in the Eighties, big old boxes of music and light, but that was new wave and soul music, you know." John looks a bit bored.

"Nightclubs?"

"Yes, long before I entered politics and public beneficence, I ran the clubs, and I mean really ran them – I did the posters, found the DJs, poured the pints, ordered the taxis, scored the drugs… You didn't hear that, OK?"

"No. What did you say, councillor? Something about rugs?" Luca smiles.

"Good boy, good boy! What a keen sense of humour you possess!" John laughs, insincerely. "Yes, I had two clubs that were a bit rundown, over on Dean Street in Soho, but had lots of young crowds, mainly new wave, New Romantics, new music but old floorspace and speakers…"

"Those were good days, the Eighties." Luca keeps checking on his egg and chips.

John whoops. "They were the best days, and Soho was the pumping heart of the capital. I bought the Bright Café and my Roller with the cash from the northern-soul nights. I would find a space, kit it out with big speakers, set up a dance-floor that made you feel special. Everyone lived for Saturday," John clapped his hands, "and, boom, you had a hot night spot for almost nothing. You could make a mint under Thatcher very quickly, and the property was so cheap. I bought this gaff for ten grand, thanks to Maggie. God bless her soul."

"There was dance music in Torino, everywhere, back then."

"I'm not talking about all the beeps and whistles. I don't like that shit that sounds like a microwave going off or a washing machine full of cutlery going down the stairs." John frowns. "It all sounds like a ringtone before it even hits the charts and then it becomes a ringtone, you know. My daughter, Gracie, listens to all that shit on the radio everywhere – it's partly why I can't wait for her to sod off, hopefully to Brunel University." John pauses. "No, you know I love my little Gracie. She gave my life its texture and purpose after my second wife died." The smile returns to John's face. Luca has noticed the councillor is less grey and his eyebrows are less bushy than last time, and he resolves to get Justyna or one of her girls to give him a makeover before his trip to the motherland. Good luck with that, girls.

"Excellent, Asgar. Good job!" John follows the two plates as the young Algerian stalks over from the counter, his tea towel swinging from the belt loop of his bottle-green jeans.

"Luca, here. And here's your breakfast with the extra mushrooms, sir." Asgar sets the lunches on the table, fiddling with the cutlery until the plates are centred.

John looks up from his full English at his employee. "I was telling Luca here how hard you work here, Asgar, and in my other businesses."

Asgar doesn't look up. "I am grateful for what I have been given, and I expect nothing without hard work." He walks back to his perch at the counter. He moves with street-smarts, like a seasoned jailbird crossing the prison yard. He reaches into his apron pocket and fiddles with what Luca thinks are dice.

John starts his patter again. "You see, Luca. Someone like Asgar is very important to me because he's like a multi-tool-kit. He seems to run on very little, and yet he works every day. And I used to be the same when I was in my 20s, running between my clubs in my suit and Adidas trainers. But you and I are older now, so we need our downtime. I'm very glad you've agreed to go back home. You must be shattered, but you look in great shape."

Luca laughs. "I've put on weight with all the parties and the wine."

"Rubbish! There may come a time when I'll need a favour, but I'll give you plenty of forewarning. The clinics gobble up staff all the time, and it might be that I need your Italian skills for a project I may be launching in Turin with one of the city grandees. He's a man of culture and a real presence. You could be my man in Piedmont, but first of all, you must relax yourself and settle into the new order of things." John leans in and whispers to Luca. "There can never be enough fun – for life is brief, my friend."

Luca chuckles, though the very notion of its brevity gives him chills.

"Did you hear about that other girl?" John asks. "She'd ODed."

Luca stops eating and sets down his cutlery. "What girl? You mean drugs?"

"Yes, she was found in the gardens, Vallance Gardens. Drugs. Heroin, they say – she had a ligature, track marks. Dead on a bench at sunrise. The detective sergeant told me; you know the guy who always has mascara on his face, some kind of glam-rock thing from his love of Roxy Music. The Bryan Ferry guy at the parties, remember him? He's a strange guy, but a very useful chap to have around our people."

Luca is staring at councillor John; he can see his mouth flapping away, but he can't hear what he is saying. "But who was the dead girl found in the gardens, councillor?"

John chuckles and sets down his own knife and fork. "One of the Polish girls. They like their fun. Not Justyna, don't worry there. A friend of hers, though. Called Marlena or something. Pretty young thing. Worth a wank." He pauses. "Sorry. Did you know her?"

Immediately, Luca stands up and runs to the toilet, alongside Asgar's counter. He throws up several times until he is empty and raw, before collapsing around the toilet bowl, shivering but fearful of crying or making a sound. So, Milena never made it home. She never made it to the sanctuary of her homeland – the bastards got her. They had hunted her down and dressed her up as yet another homeless druggie. After composing himself and washing his face, Luca returns to tell John that he's been sick because of all the rich meat and Malbec from the night before.

"The appetite on you! Like a Ferrari!" John beams. Luca gives him a thumbs-up, afraid that his voice will break. His world has just shattered once again.

The return of The Three Musketeers.

Nena and I reach the café well before Cadwick, who has changed outfits yet again after his fruitless questioning of brother Rufus. There has been no blip on the radar of the concierge; not a single one of his soused informants has heard anything about a stolen estate car or even about the crash at Nena's salon. It is as if the Skoda materialised on Military Road and torpedoed into the glass shop-front at Mach 1.

One can only wonder what PC Stuart has unearthed. I suggest to Nena that the policeman spends two hours a day ironing his pristine uniform in front of re-runs of Prime Suspect. At last, she laughs – good girl. Cadders returns from the bar.

"Cheers, Cadders," says Nena as she takes the drinks from him. "Another costume-change, J-Lo?"

"Oh, do please sod off, you ninny. I had a popcorn of dust dans ma nez, Nena." And he points at his round nose.

"I guess you heard nothing from your brother's circle of spies, eh?" I look at Nena as if to warn her about talking too openly. She sticks her tongue out.

"Not a peep, Nena," Cadders replies. "Bill the Sandgate postman thought you were simply finally doing renovations to the salon; he saw it all boarded up."

"There's a car-shaped hole!" Nena snorts.

"Ru will continue to ask around, but this isn't the place for midnight ramblers."

I pipe up. "Yes."

Cadders sips his espresso macchiato. "I've been thinking about the strangeness of it all; it's scarcely believable for Sandgate, our little museum hideaway by the sea, wreathed in mists and nebuliser fumes."

"It's strange, it's sickening..." Nena interjects.

"When I was freshening up earlier, guys, I came to the conclusion that we're dealing with a pro, a mystery man." Cadders gulps down the last of his espresso and smiles at me. "If Rufus doesn't know what happened, Sam, then that bumbling fool-child of a police constable has next to no chance."

"I said the same to Nena," I smile.

"In fact, Sam, my brother Ru probably knows the where-abouts of PC Stuart's superiors last night. They were probably at the local Masons, comparing cufflinks and all that shit."

Nena taps me on the thigh. "Rufus has his own massive gang of informants, Sammy."

"Yes, and he pays them off by giving them free board or breakfast, and drinks, at The Grand." Cadders laughs and rubs his good eye.

"It's like a crappy version of the Baker Street Irregulars, you see," Nena adds, "but made up of alcoholics and horse-racing nuts in boxy blazers and combovers."

Cadders laughs again. "Irregular boozers. They're always slumped at the bar with a copy of the Racing Post and cough sweets to mask the whisky from the missus."

"So, Rufus is rather like Sherlock?" I reply, an eyebrow raised.

"No, Ru's more a fan of gossip. His fella works there, too," Cadwick answers. "Ru likes to think he's the beating heart of this elderly town and while that's not the truth, he has saved me several times, especially from giving my heart to certain chancey women." His quip makes Nena laugh, for it is true. I later learn Ru runs these character checks, as he calls them – his irregulars have most of the school years covered in the local area from about 1949 onwards, so any name can be cross-checked informally. "In fact, I'll have you know that Ru vetted Jacqs and said she was a good grammar school girl, paid grammar school, that is."

"Oooh, 'posh grammar'? You simply must wed her – ignore the stiffness and the sudden high-handedness. Make a woman of the gal! Because she's posh grammar!"

Cadders doesn't laugh now. "Ru's super-well-connected around here, Sam. But, yes, he has the air of someone who's running the US Embassy rather than front-of-house at an old hotel in a geriatric town for elderly soaks."

"He's married to the job," Nena agrees.

Cadders laughs now. "He carries his clipboard as if it contained security codes for the war rooms rather than simply breakfast orders."

Nena puts down her mug. "Damn, this coffee tastes like a sock. Have a taste?"

"Er, no, thanks," I say. "Mine's fine, old gal. I'll get you another if you bear with me." I slide off my stool and walk to the counter, keen to give the two friends a little catch-up time.

Cadwick shimmies over to the empty chair. "Nena, I'm having a bit of a WhatsApp ding-dong with Jacqs, so I'm going to have to head off in a little bit."

"Really?"

Cadders leans into and whispers. "She's a bit snappy today."

"Jacqui always seems to have sand in her gladys... Sorry, but it's true." Nena looks down.

"Well, Nena. I got this text that just reads, 'I'm trying to forgive myself for liking you'. I'm going to head her off before she talks herself into splitting up with me for the fourth time this week. I'm going to hold onto her for as long as it takes for her to unearth some nugget of information, but I fear the end is fast approaching and I may be provoked into it today. So, I have to head off."

"That's OK, Cadders. I'm going to cook Sam an early dinner at the cabin."

"Very nice."

"Well, he's really not eating very much, and he bought a lorryload of veg and stuff that's going to go off," Nena replies. "And me, I feel better about the salon, but I can't seem to face all the paperwork and claims forms. The departments at the insurers don't seem to liaise with one another, so I receive a dozen phone calls requesting very similar information and the completion of identical forms. You know how it is; the arse is barking, and the mouth is muttering. But the salon is getting there at least."

"It's only been a short while, and you've done the initial work," Cadders says. "For god's sake, that is your home and place of work. You're still in shock, so take the day off from any thought of insurers and cook Sammy a meal before he becomes a spaghettini."

"Spaghettino," Nena corrects him.

"Well, whatever. I'll get my gang over to start work on the restoration. Terry will buzz in tomorrow afternoon with his Luton van and begin on it. This is temporary, and what you have regained with Sammy is permanent. You're making new memories to coexist with the beautiful ones you have as teenagers. Everything's going to be as smooth as a rhapsody. Trust your slightly dog-eared old mucker Christian Cadwick."

I come back with a fresh Americano, just as Cadwick's phone begins to repeat-ping with texts from Jacqs.

"Just saying, Sam, that I'm going to have to head off back to mine as Jacqs wants a chat with me."

"Best to talk it through, face to face."

"I'll just nod and try to listen and understand what she's been briefed to say by her witches' coven. She met up with them for lunch yesterday, and they'll have filled her head with the meaningless platitudes that she is right and that I am wrong and must be corrected."

"Good luck," I say. "Count to ten, then down to zero. Chuck in a few blandishments."

"Tell her how blue her suit is," Nena jokes.

"Oh," sighs Cadders. "It'll all be easier with a cocktail in my hand."

"We'll have a ring-round of people to sort out the salon anyway." I clap Cadders on the shoulder. "You've been a real friend to us over the past 20 hours."

Cadwick smiles. "I'll transfer over a few grand tomorrow afternoon to your account, Nena. It's the one ending in - 357?"

"That's the one."

"Take the day off, guys – have a duvet day. Happy cooking." Cadwick winks.

Nena smiles. "Good luck with Jacqui – send me a text to call if it gets too overwrought. I'll try to reply." She kisses her friend on the cheek and we watch him shamble up the street towards the Leas.

"Right, Sam. Let's finish these coffees and then I'm going to cook you a lamb ragout." Nena touches me on my knee. "We can continue canoodling in front of the woodburner and put Gainsbourg on the stereogram."

"I should be cooking for you."

"I'd rather not be shitting through my eyelids, thanks. I remember your chicken roasts used to practically flap onto my dinner plate." And then we gulp down the coffees and follow the hunched figure of Cadwick in the mist. Hunched as he always is, he appears to be five or six miles ahead.

We get to the stile before our happiness is torn apart.

"For God's sake. Someone's got in again." I've glimpsed that the pale-blue cabin door is open. The pair of us jump over the stile. Nena slips in her heels but steadies herself to see – yes, somebody has broken in. My heart seems to burp, and I can hear Nena herself let out a whimper. Will I be able to protect her and myself? What in the deepest hell is happening to the calm of Sandgate?

"They might still be in there. Stay here," I put my black gloved hand on Nena's shoulder. "The kind of crazy who sends a Skoda estate thudding into a shop won't think twice about attacking us."

"Thanks for that, Sam."

I shrug. "Well. We have to remember that; this person is likely to be very dangerous indeed. We could have been in the salon. Stay here."

"Are you going to go ahead yourself? Sam? Are you going to be able to defend yourself?" Nena's eyes begin to moisten, and the wind seems to be scouring at our backs and shoulders. I wipe my forehead.

"Yes, I can defend myself, but I'll be super-careful – don't worry. I won't go through the front door, just in case. I'll go the long way around." I have taken to carrying a metal torch in my coat pocket that can double up as a heavy cosh, and now I pull it out in readiness, slapping it into my left palm.

"Should I call Stuart?" Nena asks. We are both suddenly aware the pair of us are a good half-mile from any human help, 800 metres of muddy grasses, with nothing to be heard above the whistling winds. Even the gulls have disappeared, like a Western bartender who knows a fight's a-brewing. The piano-player has left.

"The guy PC Stuart's as much use as a chocolate radiator. You won't get a signal anyway. Just stay here." And I begin to quietly approach the cabin from the back, leaving a large semi-circle of jade bootprints in the light green of the dewy grass until I am beneath the bedroom window and hidden from Nena's view, to the back of the building. The grass is completely drenched as the bathroom outpipe sends water directly off the decking that skirts the cabin. A red plastic bucket with a set of my dad's shears is full of murky water. There seem to be no other footprints than mine, so the intruder must have come to the cabin before the mists of dusk rolled in and wet the grasses. I slow down my breathing.

Where is Your God Now?

I inch around the clapperboard edifice, wall by wall, peeking into each window for some 10 to 15 seconds and then ducking back down, until I reach the open front door. I look back towards my Nena, who is pacing some 30 metres away, her eyes fixed on the cabin, even though her shoes are slipping in the dew. Nena's hands are up by her face, though her frown is dragging her features to the ground below.

"No one's in there. Come over, darling," I beckon to Nena.

"I'm coming."

"Watch the grass in those kitten-heels. You ever check the forecast?"

Nena laughs; she has always dressed inappropriately, and it has worsened from being her own boss when she was just a teenager. Her pink shoes are now caked in mud. She couldn't run if our survival counted on it.

I duck into the cabin and tiptoe in my Timberlands across the lounge floor, past the wingback and the Welsh dresser. That cap looks down at me; I make the sign of the cross, and hope my folks are safeguarding me now. I hold my breath and kick off my boots as the woollen rug runs out by the end of the lounge. From the doorway into the hallway, I espy something I haven't seen during my sortie around the edges of the cabin.

I sink to my knees in despair. For there in the hallway, hidden from the windows, lies a vintage blow-up doll, dressed in the chiffon scarves and velvetwear that Nena favoured as a teen. My mood swiftly transforms from fear into a towering rage. I stand straight up, and my right fist slams into the pine frame of the hallway door.

I reach down to pluck the rolled-up note from the pouting mouth of the pneumatic doll with the bob. 'Sammy, I didn't know if you had any spank mags here, so

I got you A Blast From The Past to keep you company. It's a true likeness. T xx.'

"Don't come in yet, darl!" I call out, scrunching up the paper, but it's too late. Nena is standing in the lounge doorway, with a face that looks as if she is on the verge of punting the mixed-race doll through the bedroom and its window. "Hand me the note please!"

"Nena, it's really not a good idea – it was only meant for my eyes. Silly bastard."

"I know this doll is meant to be me." Nena smooths out the note, and her shining eyes turn coal-black, which I always find entrancing, though it isn't the place to say so. "The little wanker. How did he get in? Can't we shop Tom in for breaking and entering?"

I look at her and shake my head; my right hand is throbbing. "He knows where the spare key is – under Dad's red bucket. But I couldn't see any sign – Tommy ghosted in here before the mists came." I pause and check my breathing again. "Look – I'm just relieved it wasn't the car guy. Tommy's not going to attack me with an axe, no matter how juvenile he is." I realise I am on a very sticky wicket here, but commonsense has to prevail.

"Really? You can't see the shame of it? After the week I've had, I scarcely need your jackass of a mate lampooning me in such a... such a grotesque way. Is that all you and he saw me as? A pair of legs between which you could unload your teenage angst?"

I raise myself up and put my arm around Nena, her shoulders damp with sweat. "In Tom's mind, which has barely developed since he was 11, stunted as it has been by video games and rap music, that might be how he views all women – he's squiring a lass who doesn't bother to speak more than 50 words of English. But in my mind, you're the best friend I can rely upon, my soulmate through all the shit-flecked trials of modern life. God must have loved me so dearly to send me someone as fine as you. You're a trillion times my ideal woman."

"Did you say a trillion times?" Nena whispers down into the lapel of her fleece as if it were a radio mic. "You did, didn't you?"

I chuckle. "I shall never let you go again. I made that promise to myself back in Piedmont if I were to ever bump into you. I wrote it on a pizza box as if it were the American constitution. The line was cut, but it wasn't the end – we've picked up the thread and the line has been recast in yet brighter colours, in stronger definition. Even as a drunken 18-year-old, I knew you were the one."

"You left, though?"

"I did. I did back then, but I now choose you to live out the rest of my days, in total solitude if need be, in constant flight if need be. I choose you."

Nena puts the side of her head upon my shoulder. "I just wanted you to say again how I've always been the one."

"Needy Nena," I whisper, "but I feel the same."

"Well, yes, I am very needy. I am very in love with you with the same intensity that makes me so very, very annoyed with Tom."

I position myself behind her and wrap my forearms around her waist and kiss her nape. "The guy bounces around listening to Pearl Jam and playing air guitar in his £100 boxers. He spends more on underwear he wears, tears and discards than most families spend on monthly food shopping."

"Sounds a sad and sorry existence…"

"It's an air-packed and unreal existence, like a reality TV contestant trapped in a prison of plasma screens and press cuttings all showing their televised disgraces from two decades ago. Tommy thinks he's Tom Cruise in Risky Business, living it up, but really he's Tom Hanks in Cast Away, with a smartphone instead of a basketball called

Wilson." And it was all true – life went on all around Tom, outside the shutters of his palazzo, in the open city of Turin where the scooters weave in and out of packs of friends growing old together. And little Tommy stayed up in his garret, his windows shut to stop real life flooding in, trying to relive 1997 or trap it inside. "When I catch up with him, I'm going on a truth attack; I'm going to eviscerate Tommy with verbal shears. Tell him how he really is." All this is also true, because I have almost two decades' worth of evidence piling up against him, stacks and stacks of shit that should wake him up to his stunted reality.

Nena chuckles and punts the sex doll in the hospital parts before racing into the bedroom.

I follow her, sliding in my socks on the smooth wooden floorboards.

Nena starts taking her purple fleece off. She looks over her dropped shoulder and naked back. "Can you close the door please? I can see the doll, and it's like my doppelganger is about to rate our little dance to come."

I kick the door shut with a solid bang.

Some thirty metres away, flat among the gorse and grasses, Joey puts down his birding binoculars and gets up, shaking his head and brushing down his combat trousers.

A little less conversation.

Cadwick sits in his Arne Jacobson egg-shaped chair and kicks off his brogues. The summoning by Jacqui's WhatsApp does not bode well – the text has not finished with the usual, pitiable "xoxo" – and he's already removed those chuckable trinkets and items of his, those purchased from Kent's myriad antique fairs and fusty old hobby shops off the cobweb people. Cadders once considered a life of sedentary seclusion after he'd qualified as a valuer and auctioneer, but decided he was at least 20 years too young to be a human statue, sitting fused to a red leather captain's chair in the corner of an unlit curiosity shop, measuring out the chugging hours with slugs from his silver hip flask.

As he imagines himself as some Gollum of gadrooning, his lion's-head door-knocker sounds out. Cadwick pops out of his egg, slips on his loafers, does a quick sign of the cross and answers the door to a surprisingly benign-looking Jacqs.

"Come in, come in! Welcome to my Folkestone home." They kiss each other on each cheek, but with their midriffs held some distance apart, so there is an awkward, frontwards wobble. Jacqs recoils slightly at the scent of gin, half-masked by spearmint chewing gum. She has resolved to keep her new man to an unseen three-line whip. She is what he needs; he is what she wants.

When Cadders pulls back from the clumsiness of their embrace, he sees that Jacqui is beaming. A pure joy lights up her fine, unblemished features, the counterbalance to her flaky, cracked moods. "My god, Christian! There are so many sights, I don't know where to look first." And there is much to take in, from the Queen Anne drop-leaf desk in the 13ft tall entrance hall that boasts a hand-painted ceiling frieze to a brushed-gold Armani mirror with its riot of curlicues that makes the otherwise richly monochrome hall appear to stretch for twice its actual length.

Cadders smiles. "Where others may go to the football, I potter around seducing the old buffers who sell such treasures. I love to see them, raising a sprouting eyebrow as I enter their lair. Then the game of bartering begins – I see it like a tussle over the chessboard, a game of wits and suggestion." He pauses and redoubles his smile. "As my home suggests, hopefully with a low whisper, I am an inveterate shopper. And I take fierce pride in loafing around." It is at times like these that Cadwick forgets all about his failures and his physical ill-favour and just fully drops into his Fifties cad persona.

Jacqui is scanning every corner, and Cadwick wonders whether she is in her professional, property-agent mode or even picturing herself as lady of the house, rolling forward to a time when she might monitor a maid's polishing of the Edwardian candlesticks as she reclines in full repose on the hallway chaise longue.

Understandably keen for the lady not to entertain too many daydreams, Cadders then leads Jacqs by her left shoulder pad into the enormous inner hallway that doubles as a dinner room with its glass table and quartet of elegant tan leather and chrome chairs. Cadders points at his pride-and-joy, a moss-green marble plinth with a bust of Kipling. "I picked that up there last year off a lady with a beehive hairdo. She was out for £450, but I got her down to £300 cash. Then I treated myself to roast duck breast and mash in the dining room. Magnificent day, just magnificent."

Jacqui taps the plinth. "I have cream tea with my gal pals in the tea-room at The Grand." Cadders recoils slightly at the term 'gal pals' but continues shepherding his paramour into the sitting room. She is trembling with excitement, probably at the glories to be won once she has Cadwick's hand; all of the treasures would then be shared, but Jacqui would become the new custodian of her own mini Rathebone. "God! This is an even bigger room." Her eyes light up. "It's even more regal than Rathebone, Christian."

Cadders hovers by her right shoulder pad and whispers: "Wingback or lovers' seat? I shan't share the latter with you, don't worry." Jacq settles into the Chesterfield wingback and puts her Harrods tote bag down by her boots. With her happiness, she becomes ever more pristine, her blonde chignon like a delicate pastry upon the fine china of her face.

"Should I have taken my heels off?" Jacqui asks, but Cadwick shushes any such idea with a swish of his right palm. "Anyway, I have some very good news, Christian. I showed my colleagues the Polaroid photos you sent on WhatsApp – and Wendy, you know, that girl I play tennis with, well, she was trying to sell the house last year and she says it's still empty because the vendor died and her son is a bit, you know, simple, apparently. Can't get him to do anything with it, hence the horrible kitchen. It's a vacant possession, almost, but he's been seen by the neighbours, going in and coming out all distressed. Poor lad, I suppose."

Jacqui shivers slightly as Cadders jumps out of his lovers' seat of purple velvet and races over to the walnut drinks globe in the corner. "Such fine sleuthing deserves a libation! Sherry?"

"Sherry!" squeals Jacqs, and she ruins her loveliness with the very same demented seal-clapping that has made Cadders most sure that he will not be consummating the relationship, even after a month of squiring the lady around. He's even fixed the shower at her costly Sandgate penthouse, getting drenched in the process. And yet he thinks the flat a ringer for a Premier Inn suite, all watercolour prints and Habitat occasional chairs of the kind that fill out the show homes around the coast. Jacqui has lived in that tissue-box apartment for three years, and still it carries not an ounce of her soul or character – where are the trinkets and the antique finds? It is pristine yet almost completely unlovable. Just like... her. Oh, God! She's an exquisitely bland penthouse, thinks Cadders. He then considers that he truly is an awful person; his father was right for once.

Cadders hands Jacqui a large glass of Amontillado Seco Napoleon Hidalgo, not his best stuff – that is for his real muckers, the Musketeers. "Tell me more, tell me more. This is an astonishing breakthrough, Jacqs. It will cheer up many people."

Jacqui sits forward in her wingback, revelling in the usefulness of her information. "Well, Wendy says the vendor knew she was on the way out but couldn't sell the house in time because, as we know, it's in a rotten state and there's the new three-per-cent stamp-duty levy on second homes, so she died of diabetic complications before she could hand cash from sale to her only surviving relative – her son. He's called Joseph and he hasn't done anything with it since he took it off the market. He's a moody sort, according to the team at Ward and Partners, and he's not even tidied up the hedges, so it's gone even more on the unsaleable side. If Joseph ever decides to pick up the sale, well, I will be shocked. Wendy says he got his money anyway from her savings account. The lady was a Miss Harkett, a single mum. God knows where she made her cash, but she seemed to spend most of it on Joseph – or on cats. Place stank of cat. Wendy almost gagged the first time she went in. Joseph was just sitting almost catatonic on this ratty sofa, as if meditating, except there was a patch of cat muck right in front of him. He just doesn't care. I think he needed help a year ago. He must be well on the way to craziness now."

Cadders wants more. He feels a desire to decant the contents of Jacqui's mind into a flask so he can swill them around at his leisure. He could hold her chignon like a teapot handle and pour the information into the cut-glass punchbowl on the console table. With a fluttering right hand, he beckons her to reveal more. "So where is the place? It's Folkestone, right? The window was a big clue. It's a Thirties semi. We Musketeers thought Cheriton."

"Musketeers?" Jacqui pauses, before returning to the main thrust of her revelations. "No, no, no, Christian. This is on the East Cliff, tucked away next to Warren Way, near the primary school. You know, the one where there's been the development? All the lorries and cement mixers?" She brushes down her skirt and puts a hand on the Chesterfield's leather as if to stop the giddy rush she feels at becoming information-provider to a man who lives like an earl. "What's the Musketeers? You said "musketeers"? Are they your property mates, the one you went out with to the harbour?" Jacqui knows the answer isn't that. She has already sunk the sherry, and the glass sits precariously on the Chesterfield's restored arm. Cadwick half-expects her to brush it with force into the black marble of the hearth.

Cadders gets up and retrieves the glass. "Refill? The Musketeers are the gang of Nena, Sam and myself; we thought it suited the fact we've been on the trail of..."

Jacq crosses her legs and pulls her now-uncomfortable-looking thick skirt down her thighs. "You can't just keep filling up her bank account, Christian – Nena has a fella now to do all that for her. Let him pay for the salon repairs."

"Sam is..."

Jacqui's voice winds up the octaves. "He must be rolling into it since his parents died. I mean, did you see his watch? That's £7,000 on his left wrist. He can flog that and pay for her thirstiness. Leave her well alone, Christian. You're like a little terrier always running around her, trying to get her attention – except it's you who dishes out the treats. She's not your girl – she'll never be your girl, so give up the ghost and let that guy Sam take care of her. She's trouble, she is. I've seen her wobbling down Sandgate High Street at 10am with a jangling bag, if you know what you mean."

Just to make sure that there is to be no wheedling back into the relationship by either party, Christian Cadwick has always been fond of placing a mortar bomb under the gang-plank at the point of separation. He renders himself as objectionable as possible, so there will not be any way back, no matter how often he is to see the old love on the far horizon.

This course of action at times leaves him rueing the casting-off of yet another fragment of his history, but it also protects him from being seduced by the rose-tinted memories that piggyback his loneliness and might restore him to the beds of several unsuitable women. So, right now, he's about to give Jacqui the full 21-gun farewell, an almost-operatic display of male bitchiness that she can gleefully relay to her gal pals over a pitcher of Long Island iced tea as proof of his callousness and black heart. Everyone's a winner, baby.

"You're saying Nena's an alcoholic, Jacqui? Well, all of us are in that merry band, for God's sake. Pay for your ticket and don't complain. Je t'accuse, je m'accuse, and all that shit – shit is what it is. Trouble is, you believe your drinking is normal, because you have a gaggle of over-tanned arseholes backing up your every witless word with a cry of "You go, girl!" You all act as if each one of you is a member of Sex and the City, rather than some trolley-dolly promoted beyond her skill sets by an office manager who takes you out for Friday drinkies in the vain hope of bedding you."

"Don't bring my girls into this," Jacqui counters, "because when you decide to twist again, having stuck with me for a whole month in your game of stick 'n' twist with all the single women in south-east Kent, those girls will be the only ones who'll pick me up. One of those 'arseholes' was subjected to your crap pick-up lines in Rocksalt last year apparently."

"Stop saying 'apparently'. Yes, that was me. So what?"

"Well, she said you came into the bar after a liquid dinner with Nena and you were giving it the "Big I am" – 'yeah, I own two big-bollix houses and I have this pile of money and won't you have a little champers perhaps?' and all the time, Trina didn't have the heart to tell you that you had this huge bogey going in and out of your nose like a cuckoo-clock bird. Sod all use having a Paul Smith overcoat if you have a bogey playing hide-and-seek in your nostril and you can't fill your clothes in the right places, you odious little man."

Jacqui is shaking with rage and gripping the arms of the wingback, and still she's not finished. "Trina said to me, 'that little man you're dating slides into Rocksalt like he's on rollerskates and starts talking to pretty girls who are 15 years younger than him until his eye starts falling shut, then he either passes out in one of the booths until his friend comes to wake him up or he slinks off home without tipping me because, no, I don't want to shag a 5ft2in curly-headed tosser'. Right little charmer, aren't you? The posh voice, the limitless wallet, they won't work much longer – your nasty obsessions will make you ugly inside and out. And get your eye looked at, because no woman wants to kiss a guy whose left eye is checking her earring and whose right eye is looking at the bedroom door."

Cadders closes up the globe drinks cabinet and leaves Jacqui's glass inside. "Stop being unfair. Look now…"

"No, you look, Christian – there's only so many times I'm going to stand for getting the scraps of you. Nena gets the best of you – she gets all your thoughts and concentration. You really try with her – and I have to scoop up the slop after she's left you maudlin and pissed in

Loaf or The Grand or wherever you've taken her. And screw her shitty little salon! I've seen someone had the good taste to drive a car through it."

"Have a little empathy for once!" Cadders crashes back down into the lovers' seat and looks at his scuffed loafers. They'll need a shine today.

Jacqui slams her hand into the armrest. "It's 33 Chambois Close. I'm done. We're done. Sad sack – you're a sad sack, despite all your lovely houses and your money. Don't WhatsApp me; don't call into my shop. And don't pester any of my girls for a hook-up. Bye!"

Jacqui stomps off out of the sitting room and down the inner hall, her boots clattering against the white-painted floorboards. Cadders hopes from the sitting room that she hasn't scuffed them. The tradesman who treated the wood was a dozy nightmare to deal with, forever going off for ciggies in his Transit or moaning about his 75-year-old squeeze, how she'd left him at a Simply Red gig for a younger guy.

When Cadders hears that heavy front door slam, he blows out his cheeks. He is free again. No doubt, once the happiness of being single once more subsides, he'll feel a tinge of regret at another failed relationship, but the much-searched-for bit of information is his now. '33 Chambois Close' is his currency to pay for the company he so craves, the good people, his happy crew who don't judge him for his thirstiness at pub time, just for his sad headgear, and who value his loyalty and his belief in the sanctity of companionship.

Nena will be extremely grateful when he texts the names and the address to her, but it is not only about just her now – his new compadre, Sammy, will also be delighted to know the details of the person who is slowly destroying his sanity. In Cadders's liquor-coddled mind, the Musketeers are all that matter, and he will have more time with them now that Jacqui has slung her handbag over her big blue shoulder pads. Good riddance to bad couture; here's to fair fortune.

Cadders sets himself the task that his gin will barely get acquainted with its tumbler, a whole bottle of the stuff chilling in the fridge. There is plenty of whistle-wetter to sup while he waits upon the joyful text responses of Sam and Nena. Salad days, halcyon times indeed. His friends are his family, and his family will be so very proud of him. "Are you watching me, father, from hell below?" Cadders mutters.

As he falls asleep in his wingback with his smartphone pressed under his chin ready for the texts of congratulations yet to come, some half-a-mile away, Tommy is pacing around the concentric carpet of his room at The Metropole, raging at himself for once again bollocksing up his own plans at the eleventh hour. His prank has backfired horribly, and his medium-term goal of cajoling me into coming back with him to Turin lies smouldering and slammed flat in the trouser-press; he'd have more chance of becoming the next Pope in St Peter's or of convincing Claudia to wear sackcloth for all eternity.

I have called him, absolutely pissing steam, and told him to grow up or get the hell out of my life; when I am extremely irate, my voice sinks down to the substrata as if the words it carries are too heavy for the earth and sod to support. It is no longer "all right" to act like we all did back in the Nineties, an orgy of bars and clubs, pranks and sports, horseplay and putdowns. Not only has Nena issued me with an ultimatum, but the prank has also scared me witless, coming only days after the break-in. My words piled up at hurtling speed like a stack of slung-out, broken chairs until I hung up with the hissed sign-off, 'you abject bollock-brain'.

Tommy had tried to convince me that he'd known nothing about the rekindled romance with Nena nor about the break-in, but it was rather akin to attempting to calm down an angry bull with a wet sock. Bloody playboy.

To calm his own fears at the fracturing of a 25-year friendship, Tommy had chatted to Claudia on Skype. She had been worrying about his diet – she'd seen an English cookery programme where the chef, boasting two Michelin stars, was urging viewers to add dark chocolate to an already-inauthentic bolognaise. And so the video chat descended into promises that Tommy would eat only at an Italian nestled just above the loveliness of the high street and that he would check in every three hours for the very brief time he would now spend in his mother country. Claudia seemed to genuinely fear that her beau would end up on a drip after a bout of malnutrition. Her knowledge of food and fitness was astonishingly vast. He had blown her a kiss and quoted a little Catullus in Italian to send her off to her dreams.

Alone on the creaking floor of an authentically Victorian bedroom, Tommy now switched on the hotel room TV and selected the pop radio channel before throwing the remote onto his four-poster. "All is lost," he muttered to himself. "You've screwed the goose again." He would leave it a couple of days and then trudge to the cabin past the stile, monkishly contrite among the silent grasses; Tommy would offer a peace-making bottle of the Isle of Jura single malt that we all used to drink at Radnor Cliffs on Saturday afternoons. He might even offer to help fix up Nena's salon; I had confirmed that some nut had driven an estate car into it. The tiny shop front had been all boarded up the day before, and Tommy had half-guessed this patchwork of MDF was not by design; perhaps there had been a break-in by one of the ne'er-do-wells who lived up the hill.

Tommy had no rush or reason to fly his tiny plane back to Turin, only to be confronted by a shoe mountain of a flat, although Claudia was in a remarkably stable mood; Tommy could spend a fortnight making it up to Nena by restoring her sanctuary. He would leave her a card explaining that he'd work for free for the rest of the month to tidy up her memories and so remind her of all the good times the teenaged trio had spent on the cliff tops.

Right now, unable to fall asleep on the creaking Victorian bed and unwilling to drain all the miniatures in the mini bar, Tommy would scroll through Gerald's Facebook wall and make sure his wayward business partner truly was keeping quiet about the 'golf trip' to Turin. Tommy wasn't even sure the Piemontesi played the game – was Constantino Rocco from that part of the world? Why was Tommy unable to marshal his own mind and stop such discursive thoughts? It couldn't be helped now; Gerald would have been doggedly sticking to the script for a couple of days.

Past Gerald's videos of Russian drunks falling over in public parks and of dogs playing the piano, there was a brief, illiterate status update – "Back in GB da motherland after a round or two with me old mucker T @ Turin. Birdys galour – say no more!!". Tommy smiled. It was a good enough effort from the big man, who regarded golf as his weekly cardio fix. Gerald dressed well on the courses, with his pink Calloway polo shirts and blue checked strides, but his game was hampered by his well-upholstered figure; he couldn't get a swing going around his tits.

Maybe Tommy would ring Gerald later and tell him about the backfire and the fear he had that after years and years of perfect fellowship, he had deep-sixed his bind with me, all for the sake of a crap prank; maybe Tommy would head downstairs to the dark-wood lounge and chat up the prettiest waitress; maybe he'd just sit in the uncomfortable, round-backed desk chair and watch Gerald's Russian drunks stagger backwards into puddles and coal slagpiles; but certainly, anything would have been better than staggering over to the cabin, half-cut on the mini-bar bottles that were hanging out of his Evisu jeans, in a vain attempt to make amends to his friends.

Listen to what the man says.

For all his great love of London, with its endless energies to remake itself for each successive generation and to absorb those souls of every single colour and creed keen to taste its vibrancy and vastness, Luca always obeyed the call of the motherland. There, he was regarded as a gentleman of high tastes; indeed, with his brother Gianfranco, he would hold court at La Taverna dei Mercanti, off Via della Consolata, and talk of many things, but chiefly their love of opera.

Moving through the gears in his first day back in Torino, Luca's language became ever so slightly archaic and formal as he re-adjusted to the rhythms and music of his native tongue, that which he almost always thought in and would dream his dreams in. His English was a means to try to get by in the pell-mell of capital life, his lowly language in the high-rise Square Mile.

Ever since Councillor John had gifted him a return journey to Piedmont, Luca had been planning his suitcase; he'd been throwing out the supermarket jogging bottoms and marquee-sized sweaters and hitting the family tailors of Commercial Road for cut-price three-piece suits in eye-catching fabrics a businessman would not dare to sport. The councillor seemed to know everyone, and all the best tailors.

Just as Luca saw himself as an ambassador of sorts for the Presidente della Regione when he scratched out a living in the East End, so he felt honour-bound to impart to his countrymen his knowledge of London. Its rate of change remained a thing of wonder to them all. It was not the city it had been five years ago; it was wholly different to the place where Luca had arrived all those Christmases ago,

Where is Your God Now?

the capital shedding its whole skin as it adapted and survived, if seldom thrived, as a 21st-century super-city.

Luca would tell Gianfranco of all the grand building schemes, the chrome apartment blocks that seemed to rise overnight like classroom sunflowers, chameleonic as they took in the changing colours of the day and season. Sometimes, the Commercial Street yuppie towers would appear slate-grey as the winter murk set in; at other times, they shimmered like the mirrors that plunged into the apartments' basement pools. London would cast off every imaginable colour in God's palette, Luca would enthuse, in its unending quest for relevance.

And so, in the days before Luca would take off from Southend airport, he would scour the London Evening Standard newspaper for facts and opinions he could recycle at the taverna for his brother's amusement. Then, his tongue would be free once more from the strictures of English and fuelled by rounds of bottles of Barolo, Barbaresco and Moscato d'Asti. Their friend, Andrea, would keep the wine high on the walls of their glasses, lock the doors at closing and help himself to what little risotto was left after the brothers had sated their enormous appetites.

It was only when Andrea's wife would bang on the floor above with her slipper that the trio would bid one another farewell and agree to reconvene the following evening.

On nights such as those, Luca felt like he was enthroned at the very corner of the universe. He would look across and over his brother's shoulders, through the ribbon-like letters on the taverna's elderly window, and see the history of all unified Italy there, piled up with the leaves in the darkening streets outside.

Luca could see the sturdy Piemontese farmers trooping off in their muddy boots to stand shoulder to shoulder with Giuseppe Garibaldi in the uprising of 1834; he could hear the **Father of the Fatherland** and the King of Sardinia and then of all Italy, Victor Emmanuel II, calling upon the deputies to form the first Italian Parliament in Turin, almost three decades later. The streets still sounded with his exhortations and the politicians' energised support.

Here, in 1861, in what was once the capital of Italy, the Piedmontisation of the whole country had happened, as predicted by Vincenzo Gioberti, the philosopher and fifth prime minister of Sardinia. Gioberti had been born nearby and studied as an orphan for his theology doctorate at the 15th-century university, filling his lonely heart and soul with the dream of a confederation of Italian states, free from foreign modes of thought and any strict command, and ripening under a benign papal leadership. Luca carried a second edition of Gioberti's book, Of the Moral and Civil Primacy of the Italians, wherever he went, as a tribute to the seer who had died a decade or so before the reality of unification; it was a reminder to Luca that the biggest of dreams could act as a comforter to those who might not live to watch them made real. The journey and the hope were everything in his mind; the result, the cherry on the top.

As Gianfranco often remarked, sometimes teary-eyed at his own observation, Luca belonged very much to Turin, but he was made for the city as it was 150 years ago, in a time when one could earn oneself a polenta dinner simply by lustily re-enacting Garibaldi's speeches. How could such a romantic man hope to survive in such a hard-headed city as London? No, Luca, 'Londra' didn't slough off its dead skin every few years to remain vital, Gianfranco believed; rather, it retracted its metal scales and became another species of gluttonous monster, feeding off hope and devouring innocents lost in the temporal jump-cuts of the universe, innocents of whom his brother was by far the most out-of-time.

Luca had wandered into modern life from around the year 1850 through a glitch in the matrix and had survived by daydreaming and by virtue of his limitless geniality. Sooner or later, Luca was bound to go the way of all historical innocents.

Recently, Gianfranco would pretend his Skype video feed was playing up, so as to hide his tears and fretfulness from his elder sibling. He was thankful that, in another few days, Luca would be once more where he belonged, showing off his shiny houndstooth-check suits and reeling off a compendium's-worth of high-minded tales and pithy observations. Until then, until he wrapped his forearms around his brother and held him like an anchor to the Italian soil that was his, Gianfranco was staving off insomnia with whisky and Wikipedia.

At the same time, Luca lay on his sofa two thousand miles away, urging sleep by reciting the London boroughs in reverse alphabetical order. If Luca could store up enough facts about the English capital, then surely there would be less space in his memory banks for the murdered to intrude into his sleep? The information would shunt the nightmares off the mountain-tops once and for all.

A few miles south-west, councillor John's gargoyle-like face was being lit from below in the 2am darkness by a banker's lamp. "Listen, listen," he barked into the speakerphone atop his leather-topped desk. "I am in control of all situations, not just the one you seem to be fixated upon."

He paused as a blast of heavily accented English came through the device. "No, I have your countryman on a very short leash, trust me. I live at weekends in an apartment just below his, and we have ears and eyes on him from dawn till dusk; I even know at what time he takes his morning shit. So, don't tell me that he's a loose cannon, because this particular cannon has had his balls removed. You should…"

John stopped again and scratched his crotch through his dressing gown as another volley of irate words poured out of the speaker like bonfire smoke. "You have to trust me on this. You're not in this country, and you sitting in Turin dishing out orders to do this and that is all well and good, but what you're repeatedly suggesting I do is simply not practicable. Certain people can't just be spirited away at a downward point of the emperor's thumb; here in London, we need certain human resources to provide certain skills for certain upcoming situations. This age of technology, these conference calls, video-chats and Skypeing, Facetiming – it all means sod all if it leaves me with a couple of bodies shoring up the foundations of a clinic. Two's fine, three maybe, but I can't just work my way through a football team. I can't turn people into smoke or pipe them in gas form into the Thames."

He pauses to receive another verbal shellacking. "No, you listen… We were very lucky that the witness to the shit shambles that happened in the quad was a loser with barely a friend in Italy, let alone London. What we are achieving here in the east of Europe's greatest capital city will last for centuries. If Luca squeals, then I will not let the wanker see out the hour, trust me. You must have faith in me; I'm micromanaging the shit out of the situation, as I always do. Until things start falling down, you must judge me only on my results."

John paused. "Hang on. I'm patching in Signor Tallardi. He wants to know about Sam." He tapped another large button on the silver-plated face of his telephone. "Hello, signor. I have spoken to Tom, and Sam is knee-deep in his family tragedy – sorting out the wills, probates, the sale of his family home up in God-knows-where – but I expect him to return to Piedmont in a month or so. We must be patient with someone who has worked with great skill and enthusiasm for 18 years. And we all agree that his discretion is his finest quality of all. Tom is in Kent right now, and Sam is his usual self. He called me with a very thorough run-down of what his movements have been, even a chat he'd had with the local dry cleaner, for God's sake."

John stopped and took a sip of tea to wash down another Benzedrine pill. "Now, Signors, tell me if you're satisfied with the accounts and the new client list at Liverpool Street..." And then John rocked back in his captain's chair and closed his eyes as the Italians rattled off figures and gave him by-rote praise in halting English.

John could hear his own heartbeat tick and rise, and he smiled at the thought of the renewed energy that all the pumping blood would bring to him; he didn't need it down below any more, but his brain would be on high alert throughout the night, like a beacon of business sense firing away on that Greenwich hillside.

The pair of Torinese tortoises wittering away in the darkness of his desktop didn't know who the hell they were dealing with. The former king of clubland, The 'Bishop of Wells', that's who, baby – and John looked up at the framed photos of him with Geno Washington and Percy Sledge on his study wall.

Friends disunited.

"Tommy, please go away!" Nena called out from the hallway through the closed door of the lounge. Our raised voices had woken her up from the haze of midnight lavender, a few minutes after Tommy's tapping on the kitchen window and his jangling pocket of gift miniatures had disturbed me. Now we two old friends were in the middle of a near-physical altercation on the wool rug in the front room, broken bits of accusation coming back to Nena, who stood with her head against the pine-clad hallway wall.

"Well, maybe we've outgrown each other, Tom," I shouted.

"What d'you mean?"

"No one's timeline is exactly the same. Friends come along; friends disappear, like smoke."

"No, no. Those are acquaintances. Who cares about them, Sammy?"

"Even the best friends drift apart, despite the best will in the world. People have families, they get sick, and they are called away to foreign jobs. It's unnatural to think that there's an Eden where no one ages or ever really dies, where you can call your best friend and he'll be right there around the corner, not a single day older than when you clapped him farewell on the back. That Eden doesn't exist. Even the best friends might one day discover that, despite the greatest will in the world, they're splitting apart."

"You're the same. You look the same. I'm the same," Tom pleaded. "It's only been a couple of weeks… we're the same." Tom held his lower back with his shaking right hand. "I thought it'd all be a good surprise, not a shit-storm. I didn't plan to scare the bollocks off you, mate. That was not my aim. It's obvious."

I tightened the belt on my red dressing robe. "A lot's happened in a fortnight. The funeral, coming here, meeting Nena again, her shop, the break-in – I've tried to tell you about it all – well, not about Nena, because that's my private life."

"I just wanted to see that you were happy here. Mate, things are a bit dull in Turin. I thought this cabin would stir up unhappy memories." Tommy looked immeasurably forlorn at this. "Your mum was an absolute saint to me, you know. A saint. Cooked me meals I sometimes didn't get at home. And I don't get why you'd come back here alone when I can't imagine the cabin without them both. Your mum used to make me toasties over there. And you, you're sitting in your dad's chair with his magazines where they always have been. How, mate? I, I would feel his presence on my neck if I sat right there. Damn. How are you living here alone?" Tommy shook his head, and a drop of sweat caught itself at the end of his long dark locks like a cliff-diver at the drop.

"I'm not alone, Tom. I have Nena here now. I'm surviving here. I'm 38 now. This isn't 1997; I've grown up since then. 1997 was a long time ago – no good Blair, no bad Blair, no 9/11, no Osama, no Obama, no Facebook, no Twitter, no Harry Potter."

Tommy laughed to himself. "Ah, come on. 1997? You've lived with me since then! You can't go to the computer shop down the road and get your laptop fixed on your own. You, you can't tell Tino how to fix your MacBook with your sign language. Tino with the nose hair? In braids. Remember him?" Tommy dissolved into chuckles. "Everyone still thinks you're in Turin, just hiding away because it's been sunny and you don't want to burn."

I hated the sun, but I was having none of this. "Tommy, stop skirting around the real issue. We were flatmates; we never had matching aprons or a joint account."

"But..."

"You know, Tommy, I lived perfectly well when you'd piss off on some business trip abroad for two months, or when you had one of those great flights of fancy of yours and you'd decide to fly to Africa in your airplane. All you were doing was trying to escape reality. I was living the day-to-day life, getting the flat fixed when the old lady we called our home starting leaking water from her radiators or when her boiler broke. I managed. I wasn't a hermit, but I was running my life, and quite often, yours, as well. Have some respect. You make it sound like I was some invalid mute you had to push around the piazzas in a bath-chair."

I was now sitting in the wingback, my head flung back with exasperation and exhaustion. I just wanted to sleep again. I looked at the primrose cap.

Tommy countered my claim of independence. "You were struggling to keep that fat man's hands off you, struggling to find a job, struggling to make your tips, struggling to follow the football, struggling all around, as well you know." His speech was fast but slurred, barely keeping up with his tumbling thoughts as he swayed in the centre of the rug, the miniatures sticking from his jean pockets like screwdrivers and spanners in a tool-belt. "I gave you a job, a home, flight away from the disaster you found yourself in. You never once dug in your pockets, your wallet, to pay me back."

Tommy offered up his palms in supplication, as his powers of persuasion declined and the spirits worked around the rollercoaster of his worn-out body. "And that's fine – it really was. You'd have done the same for a mate like me, but come on, Sammy – you don't belong in this hut, living in the past. This place is like a museum. I've bought a 75in telly; it's coming next week. Imagine that…"

Nena now thundered into the room, her long Minnie Mouse T-shirt promising a playfulness completely absent from her expression. "Tom, leave. Now!"

Tommy turned around clumsily and took a second to focus on her. "Oh, here, we are!" He started grinning goofily at the lithe figure standing to his left. "We're all three here now, aren't we?"

Nena was sparer than she had been all those years before, her fine, half-Jamaican features more pronounced, and this was for the better, as her puppy-fat cheeks had reduced. The thinning out now made her appear taller than ever, almost six feet in height, an exquisite, stem-like diagonal in the doorway, wrapped in her baggy nightwear. He could well see why I had been drawn to her once more; certain women just improved with each passing year, rosy-cheeked innocence being replaced by the delicate geometry of high-boned refinement. The ditzy kook had grown into an elegant, athletic lady; just the cartoon T-shirt remained. Even her straightened mid-chestnut hair framed her face more kindly than it had in the 1990s.

But this was now, and Nena stared Tom down, noticing the miniatures falling from his pockets onto the tweedy cushion of the tub chair and threatening to drop onto the rug. "This is Sammy's home." It is a madhouse, Nena. "He doesn't expect you to turn up without notice and scare the living shit out of him. Juvenile and thoughtless as always, that's what you are. What kind of friend is this? Eh? Who brings pain and problems to a guy who's just buried his true best friends, his parents? You come bobbing back like an unflushed turd and expect everyone to bow. I'll ask this again – what kind of friend is this?" Nena looked down at Tommy's muddy Air 97s and snorted. I was more worried about him falling over.

"I'm a good friend! I'm a best mate. I'm the friend who picked him up when you shoved him out of his country!" Tommy plucked a vodka miniature from his right pocket and necked it before tossing the empty bottle through the open front door some ten feet away.

Where is Your God Now?

"I drove no one out of here!" Nena looked as if she was about to grab Tommy by his jacket lapels and send him flying the way of the miniature. "Whatever problems we had as a teenage couple didn't force Sammy out of the country. You're drunk, you're making no sense and you should just piss off out of here. Go to the strip clubs, get back to your hotel, and leave us be. We're not young any more. Your mind is playing tricks on you."

"You sucked all the joy out of my friend's life – you, you throttled him and tied him up with those bloody scarves of yours. You throttled his dreams. You tried to tie him to your dull life as your plus-one."

Nena shouted: "He wasted his life in your sad jocks' house instead."

"Haha. Sam wouldn't have even got on my plane if he thought he had a good and easy life here. He was your little old man. Don't you think it strange that Sam left everything so easily? Left his folks, left his good grades? We built a better life out there. Why would he have been here? In Folkestone? He'd have been in Berwickshire. He would be just as far away as Turin. You know that."

Nena didn't really have an immediate answer to that, so she concentrated on the shapelessness of Tom's life in Turin. "A better life in Piedmont eh? I bet you have a candyfloss machine in the kitchen, eh?"

"I don't."

"Well, a popcorn maker then. One of those keyboards from Big? You see Sam growing old gracefully and you want to drag him in the hole you're in – you need a batman and a mate who'll put up with you being the oldest teenager in town. You know what I'm saying. You're going to be 40 soon, and you take days out, whole days, to fly over here to play a teenage prank on your supposed best friend. What kind of bodge-wit does that?"

She paused: "This 'hut' is Sam's memory capsule, you know – and it's sure as shit not a place where you can barge in and be a shitwit. Have you even asked how my shop is? How Sam is coping with losing both his parents at once? Eh? No, you haven't because you're dicking around in that stupid flying jacket of yours."

Tommy collapsed into the tub chair by the woodburner, head forward, his sweaty, floppy dark hair mussed up and almost touching his knees. "I've, I am always asking Sam about his health, how he's coping. We had a long chat on the phone a few days ago. He called me from the hotel."

"Tom, shut up now," I quickly interjected. I looked across the room at a momentarily confused Nena.

Tom burped. "Yeah, I will shut up, Sammy. Anyway, Nena, I didn't even know you were around. I haven't seen you for years, and Sammy didn't mention he'd hooked up with you." Tommy was growing a bit green around the chops and he was letting the empties fall around his muddy trainers.

I nodded. "Nena, I was really just telling him how I was doing with all the death duties and the funeral and all of that. I popped into The Grand as my mobile reception is – well, you know, it's crap." I smiled at Nena and she winked back.

Tommy sank even further forward. His right foot stirred the bottles around on the rug. "Listen, I came here to offer you my services in repairing your shop because I know you've had it for about 20 years, and I wouldn't like my home to be damaged like that. Destroyed by a runaway car. We have to hold onto our memories, even if we can't, I mean, sod it…" He stammered, drunk, "… even if we can't keep hold of the people we made them with. I get it. The world has moved on. I was offering you help, Nena, but I'm going to leave you together. It'll please you if I go. I know, I know."

Nena went to the sink of the kitchenette and brought Tom a tall glass of water, which he drained in one. "Just get back to The Metropole and sleep it off. I'm fine for help. But, Tommy, you can't keep crashing into our lives…"

"I-, I only did it twice. And I thought really long and hard both times. If I had managed to drop off and sleep through the night, then I wouldn't have come, but sleep wouldn't come. I tried everything, and then I tried the mini bar. Bollocks."

I must have appeared asleep, but I was just resting my eyes and listening to the verbal to-and-fro. "Go and get some sleep, Tom. It's the middle of the night now and I'm shot away. We all need to sleep because a lot is happening out there. We need to be sharp enough to handle all this shit."

Tommy had already half-tumbled out of the tub chair and stood in the front doorway, half-turned towards Nena and me, swaying. "The walk will sober me up and then I'll sleep soundly." Tom paused. "Sorry, both. I'm so sorry."

Nena closed the door behind Tommy and slid the bolt. "That bit of thunder might just have cleared the air, but Tom needs to stop dragging us into the past."

I nodded. "Tommy's unhappy enough to mess up the present for the past."

"Poor boy. He needs someone."

"Don't worry – he'll be flying back to Turin on his own. And as for us, we have stuff to do – I have things to take your mind off the salon."

"You'll stay with me?" Nena asked, sleepily.

"Yes. I mean, of course."

Nena patted the velour dressing-robe on my backside. "But, first, listen up. You're coming back to bed and warming me up. It's truly winter now, and this is a 'hut' after all."

Where is Your God Now?

And Tom was out in the wind, struggling manfully to stay more upright than horizontal, the moon in its first phase. As he fell over the stile, facing away from the cabin, he saw a balaclavaed man with night sights, lying flat to the grasses. "Here, you! What the hell are you doing out there? Come here, you twat!"

And, without answering, the prowler hopped straight to his feet and ran at full pelt along the fencing, sprinting away from Tom and his friends in the cabin. "Perv," roared the drunken man in the flying jacket, before fishing another miniature from his trousers. "Some blokes have gotta screw the duck, feathers an' all."

The museum to mother.

Joey let himself into the family home he knew so well, grabbing a handful of lavender buds; again, as he turned the key in the front door lock, his forearm caught the thorns of the rose bush that needed friendly shears after months of autumn mists. Any gardener would alter the character of the place, though, and, worse of all, they might trim a branch that his mother had touched. Better to leave it all to wildness than to take away any pathway to the past.

Joey had been coming back every other day, always on his own; he was always alone, anyway. Once inside, and once the pink velour curtain had been pulled back across the stained-glass entrance and the hardwood door, he would sit cross-legged, his breathing slow and measured, on the settee on which Eleanor Harkett had spent her final months. The diabetes had slowed her to a standstill, and then she had resolved to live a horizontal life, enjoying the westerns she had obsessed about since she'd been a little girl in the Brecon Beacons.

In life, Eleanor had tried to do everything with grace, so, when she perceived herself becoming a burden to her darling son because of her illness, she resolved to stay still, where he could always find her; she didn't wish to be carried or wheeled around, or to provoke worry with countless tumbles down the supermarket.

Instead, Joey would visit her every day with a new DVD he would order from LoveFilm and maybe a takeaway salad. It did give him huge peace of mind to know where she was – there, on the settee, with a pair of reading spectacles on her nose, and another pair for TV viewing balanced like a red tiara on her black fringe. It was a habit she'd carried over from her days as a reviewer of films and books for the local radio.

Eleanor had ordered her life for the sole aim of being the perfect single mother; she would not accept any job or friendship that took her away from the east cliff of Folkestone for even a night, and her chief hobby, aside from Fifties film and the works of Patrick Hamilton, was home-schooling Joey. His education went far beyond whatever was in vogue in the nation's classrooms, so he became exceptionally computer-literate, an early adopter, at the same time as possessing a forensic knowledge of the classical world. Together, the pair would sit in front of the television and work their way through The Guardian newspaper's annual top 50 films of the year, Joey writing a critique of every one of the movies on their many lists, the Oscar nominees, the Cannes Film Festival prizewinners or those in Sight & Sound magazine's all-time pantheon.

Eleanor had no use for acquaintances or gentlemen-friends; her mind and her character were not wired in a way that took much solace from company. She was happiest when she felt she and her son had learnt something that day. They were in a constant state of bettering themselves. Idle chat simply got in the way of their latest intellectual challenge, and every person invited to 33 Chambois Close was expected to deliver a new take on an old film or play, a recounting of their travels, or their verdict on whatever had been reviewed in The Guardian's arts section that week. Those who turned up with blithe chatter about their humdrum lives were never invited over again.

Eleanor had approached the concept of securing a sperm donor in the early Eighties with the same precision and efficiency. There was no chit-chat; just exhaustive research and data-gathering until little had been left to chance. Her much older sister, Meghan, had been thrown off her life's course by a legion of male suitors and the call of Cardiff's bright lights, which, some say, had sapped any radiance the valleys girl once had. Aged 40, Meghan had reappeared for Eleanor's 21st birthday party at the local village hall, her hair prematurely grey, her eyes a yolky-yellow and her figure betraying half-a-dozen miscarriages to unknown fathers. It had been quite the wake-up call for Eleanor, and she made a pact with herself that she and her son would live as in control of their destinies as possible. That said, Eleanor had often wondered whether the retreat into homeliness and solitude was fair on her young boy; they shared friends, meaning the teenage Joey was always surrounded by fiftysomethings and their attendant cynicism and caution.

Joey had never complained about the absence of children his own age; to be a kid surrounded by adults was all he'd ever known, and he found this version of self-sufficiency suited him. Even now, as he sat alone on the settee and closed his eyes, he dreamt of scenes that brought him happiness. Joey remembered everything with crystalline precision and with huge affection for all those who had sailed with the pair of them and shared their world of learning. There were enough memories forged in that home of light and laughter for Joey to fill every other afternoon with transcendental reminiscences until he himself was elderly and unable to assume the lotus position on those cushions. Eleanor had left him with the greatest gift – a veritable museum of moving images and happy tableaux – and all he had to do was close his eyes and wing his way there.

A little birdie told me.

"For Christ's sake, Nena. Why didn't you reply to my texts, WhatsApp messages and calls?" Cadwick was as vexed as he ever became, and he quite forgot that his robe was open and revealing his Armani trunks and little pot-belly of downy fluff.

"Are you going to let me in? And yeah, I would prefer it if you tethered yourself in first." Nena was amused at the mismatch of her friend's expensively sturdy underwear and his distinctly infirm stomach.

"Yes, come in, come in." He drew the cord of his dressing gown around his waist and ushered Nena into the entrance hall. "Where's Sam? Do you want a coffee?"

"No. He's over at The Metropole."

"Having a treatment?"

"Nah. Long story. Tommy, his errant best mate, turned out unannounced from Turin and scared the shit out of us twice; the first time by breaking into the cabin and leaving some hideous Nineties doll of me in the hallway; and then, secondly, by turning up absolutely bollocksed at midnight with a fistful of miniatures to make amends. Sam was very, very unhappy; he was muttering about never speaking to the fool again, but I managed to get the pair of them to meet for a burger and a chat about ground rules."

"Good girl; there's your one good deed for the winter chalked up."

"Well, let's see,' Nena sighed. "Tommy's trouble."

Cadders trailed a finger on his drinks globe. "Now what about a snifter of gin – or are you fancying something more seasonal, like a mulled wine or an eggnog?" This would not be a rerun of his contretemps with that Rathebone girl.

Nena stopped. "Jesus, Cadders – it stinks like a brewery in here. Crack open a window." She looked around the familiar room and counted at least four empty bottles standing on the parquet flooring.

"Yes, I've been rather locked in since the bust-up with Jacqs. I need to restock the globe. I might have had a thimble or three of the hard stuff." Cadwick's hands formed that tell-tale steeple.

"You've polished off the contents?"

Cadders looked down. "Not hearing from my fellow Musketeers and suddenly wondering if Jacqs was correct to call me a 'sad old man' led me to this. I've spent the past 36 hours set adrift on a galleon of self-inquisition and sodden melancholia."

"I know, but…"

Cadwick brought his right hand up to her left wrist. "Dear, don't chide me for taking on a weight of water. I did the right thing in dismissing that halfwit Jacqui. I simply didn't want to face anyone until I'd heard from you, that's all."

"It's only been a couple of…"

"Hush, Nena. You know how we both like to sequester ourselves in our bunkers of choice whenever reality seems to be bearing down on us…"

"And we always remind one another that it is society's fault, not ours, that we become so withdrawn. Look at the cavalcade of shit that's outside your bow window. I saw a man throwing his Tesco shopping at someone's front door down the Bayle."

"Well…"

Nena shook Cadders' greasy paw from her forearm. "You're not implying that Jacqui's accusation had any merit to it, are you? You're certainly not a sad little man…"

"It was 'sad old man', Nena," Cadwick interjected. "She definitely called me a 'sad old man'."

Nena collapsed into the wingback from which Jacqui had delivered her diatribe against Cadwick's character. "So you're now taking the advice of a property hustler, who dresses like a Sixties Avon Lady; and who, when in her cups, is a screeching dignity-phobe who is barely able to find her own way home?"

"Dignity-phobe?"

"Yes, I loathed her. I'm glad you're well shot of that insult to womankind. Please don't say you are dwelling upon what she said? Sod her inexpert, mitten-fingered dissection of your good character, Cadders. Be tougher."

"Don't chide me – please!" Cadders handed her a beaker of eggnog. "I feel perfectly dreadful."

"That's your age, old man!"

"Nena, I don't consider myself to be 'old', though I'm certainly on the little side."

But onwards Nena continued. "Only last week, you were reminding me of the importance of remaining true to our very specific mission – to keep at arm's length the sober world, the straight world, you know. Remember that?"

"I do, I do!" replied her friend, holding his sorry head in the vain hope of stopping the metallic knocking of his hangover.

"Well, you have to have the strength of your convictions. 'Never explain; never complain.'"

"That's right," Cadders whimpered.

"What harm have you done to Jacqui, except in the course of standing your ground? Didn't we agree that as long as we didn't cause a bother to any other soul, then we could quite happily just carry on with our own behaviour? Do unto others, and all that shit?" Nena sighed and tilted the yellow liquid in her tumbler, back and forth. She was thinking about Sam – and Tommy.

"You speak the truth. I didn't initiate the barney – I merely responded to Jacqui's wildcat allegations about my supposed behaviour. The worst thing I ever do is drop off asleep or bitch away. I do not chase teenage quail. That is a slur." Cadwick went to the globe and fished about for what liquor remained within the veneered dome. "You're right about our pact. I know, I know."

"Please stop saying that! You don't seem to know; you seem to be drenched in the booze blues, accepting all the sins of the world as your own. Cadders?" Nena leaned forward and pointed to the bracelet on her right wrist. "You remember what this bracelet signifies? You do, don't you?"

Cadwick shook his head mournfully. "It means we renounce all the expectations put upon us. But what if we're just selfish arseholes? I mean, Jacqui described every drunken trip I've made to Rocksalt and how I'd come on, pie-eyed, to a friend of hers who works there as a waitress."

"Recently?"

"No, no. The other year, well before I'd made the mistake of squiring Jacqui around the town." Cadwick poured three fingers of his special eggnog into his finest crystal tumblers, the ones that had come with the 18th-century drinks cabinet. His right hand was trembling after his solo session on the pop.

"Well, what's the problem then?"

Cadwick walked over to the wingback. "It's just... We live without any responsibility and without any concern for how we appear to others."

"And?" replied Nena.

"Well... Is that a good way to behave as we approach 40? I mean, are you bothered by the fact that Jacqui saw you the other week with a jangling bag of booze at 10 in the morning?"

"I don't give a tin shit."

"You don't?"

"No. She's the one who should be worried, with her late-night star-jumps and show-tunes; I keep my quaffing behind closed doors. Lots of people buy their wines in their morning shopping, anyway. I don't make a habit of going to the store to buy four bottles of Pol Remy and some chewing gum; in fact, I've never done that."

Nena looked at the shaking hand of her friend. "For Christ's sake, Cadders, have some hair of the dog. And stop this soul-searching. You always act the gentleman with the bar staff at Rocksalt or wherever. Jacqui was the one tottering, smashed, on the high street there and screaming out Born Free at the top of her voice." Nena paused. "How dare she chip away at what little confidence you have left!"

"You would tell me if I ever act the arse, wouldn't you? As my best friend, as a Musketeer?"

Nena had downed half of her eggnog. "I swear, by this tumbler of exquisite liquor, that I, Miss Nena Morrison, shall always inform you, Mr Christian Cadwick, if you are being a mammoth pillock." She paused. "By the way... You, Christian Cadwick, are being a mammoth pillock, as well as an extremely slow drinker, which is even more unforgivable, my friend." She raised her tumbler and gave Cadders a wink with her heavily mascaraed right eyelid.

God, she is wonderful, thought her friend – he would fashion her a cape that sparkled with a thousand iridescent pearls from the deepest ocean to keep her from the squalls. And then, at once, Cadwick remembered Sam and the fact that he couldn't deep-dive or even sew. "I'll see this drink away, my dear. I promise to shape up and go for my afternoon constitutional. But, first, I must tell you what it was I called you here for."

"Ah yes, the great mystery," Nena chuckled. "Our friend, PC Stuart, has still been unable to find the man behind the wheel of the Skoda estate."

"Quelle surprise!"

"And he hasn't picked up a face through CCTV at two points between the East Cliff and the Leas. There are plenty of action shots of the car, but there's nothing of the driver – the Skoda might as well have been Herbie, driving on its own around town in the dead of night."

"That would make more sense." Cadders winced at a stabbing gut-pain.

Nena laughed. "PC Stuart says they're waiting on fingerprint matches to come back. Great, eh? What are the odds that the driver had no fingers?"

Cadwick downed his eggnog and collapsed into the lovers' seat. "Well, apart from lambasting me with a force I didn't think she had in her, Jacqui also told me – as a parting shot – something that will cheer you and your beau up no end. I always put my faith in contacts rather than the police. This is yet another example of the power of the people."

"Cadders, spit it out!" Nena was heading to the globe for a refill. "You always address a situation like you are Orson Welles introducing his latest theatrical sleight of hand."

"This is a true revelation, though. Jacqui has found the address of the house in the Polaroids," Cadders revealed, "and she told me who the owners of the mystery house are."

"Success!" Nina turned and beamed at Cadders. "Now there's a breakthrough worthy of dear Poirot. How did that awful woman manage that?"

"She has a friend called Wendy who was handling the sale of the house last year, Nena. Except the vendor died, and the property went off the market. It's in Chambois Close – you know, on the east cliff?"

Nena walked over with her replenished glass and slumped back into the wingback. "I know that area well. Lots of building work, lorries, school runs, blah blah. Do you have any more info?"

"There's the house number over there, written on that pizza box on the windowsill." Cadders lifted his arm to point but groaned. "The property had been owned by an

Eleanor Harkett, a single mother who left it to her only son, Joseph."

"Our lone nut?"

"Nena, I suggest we do a little Googling tonight and then reconvene at The Grand to quiz my brother about the Harketts; again, he'll know more than the police constable, unless the Harketts have been tearing up Kent like the Corleones." Cadwick went over to the drinks cabinet but then turned to face Nena. "We could scoop up the boys from the Metropole dining room and then go to The Grand?"

Nena set down her tumbler. "No, no, we should leave them to patch up their 25-year bromance over a beer and then chest-bump their way to the sports bar."

"And the rest?"

"Well. As long as Sammy doesn't hump a stripper, he's on a night-long pink pass." She smiled. "But we should tell PC Stuart that the driver of the Skoda lives at Chambois Close."

"Tell that wanker?" Cadders snorted.

"Well, what are we going to do? PC Stuart can bring the residents in for questioning or something. Show them his big-ass, polished boots."

Cadwick laughed and poured four fingers into his glass. "Let's go to the Grand. We shall try the halibut my brother has been raving about."

"Sounds good, Cadders."

"And then we can come up with a plan that may or may not include the young PC but will certainly mean a stake-out in black rollnecks. Starsky and Hutch!" He walked over to Nena, and they chinked glasses. "I think I'm more excited about dinner, to be perfectly honest."

"Me too. I'm starting to get bored of sleuthing. Though I would so like to find the reason why that Skoda slammed into my salon."

"How's it going?"

Where is Your God Now?

"It'll take another two weeks to fix up, nothing really, but God, do I remember just how angry and upset I was – I want 15 minutes with the driver…"

"And give the wrongnut a kick in the jaffas?" Cadders asked.

"Oh yes. I want him to feel his bollocks ascending into his gullet." She looked up at Cadwick. "You and Sam will pin him down and allow me that? I want his blood!" And Nena cackled with an alarming, if cartoonish, intensity that rather scared her hungover sidekick.

Just down the coast, Tommy and I were getting reunited.

"So, she's all right, but Claudia's taken to laying out every single garment she owns on your old bed. The whole apartment is like one big dressing room now. I was hoping to persuade you to come back to Turin before my entire life gets buried in a mountain of uncomfortable-looking scanties." Tommy had finished his cheese and bacon burger and had been filling me in about the last month.

"Man, I am never coming back, even to rescue you from that sea of clothes!" My eyes confirmed that I had made my mind up. "I wish you all the best. You must leave Claudia and not be afraid of being alone or losing her Rolodex of contacts."

"Easier said than done, Sammy."

"You surely know enough people to strike out on your own? I mean, we have had dozens of clients over the past two decades."

"Fresh ones needed. You know, old age and death and all that?"

I chuckled. "Well, I'll send you some more thoughts about ways of targetting clients without her network and family ties."

Tom raised an eyebrow. "I would have a lot of clearance work for you if …"

"It's never going to happen."

"Oh, come on, you wanker!"

"Tommy, I worked for two decades for you. Sooner or later, I was going to get sloppy and trip up, and I don't want to let you down."

"You never would, Sammy." Tommy leant in. "Never."

"Forget what I said last night – you have been the brother I never had, better than that, and my Mum recognised that as well. But you have to go it alone now." I pleaded; he sighed.

"It's just taking that first jump, Sam. I really live in Claudia's world, no matter how I try to integrate into Turin life."

"Meaning?" I replied.

"Sam… There are little words and phrases that you know only if you're a native, and the last few pieces of the puzzle are always eluding me, even after all these years. I am going to slip up if I stay in one place."

"So you're drifting back here, Tommy?"

"No, that'll never happen – you know how many people rely on me to tidy things up for them, but just as I can't come back here for good – I have no anchor here, now that my folks are gone, so I have to change things up."

"What do you mean?" I asked.

"Well, we're all trying to keep one step ahead of the persecutor within us, let alone the ones outside. I've ridden my luck, and without your counsel and calmness, I'm going to get caught. I don't have the organisational skills to remain in the daylight."

"You're going to be like me, Macavity the mystery cat?"

"I'm going to lie lower. Look, I'm a farmer's son from a sleepy hamlet on the fringes of a smallish town. So is it any wonder that I feel like a squash ball ricocheting off the walls in Piedmont? Last Sunday, I jogged past the Church of San Lorenzo, and there must have been five generations spilling out into the streets, the toddlers in their white suits weaving between the sticks and walking frames of their great-grandparents. I felt like I was watching *Cinema Paradiso* on the sly through someone's kitchen window – do you know what I mean? You can't wheedle your way into a society like that; you and your parents and your parents' parents and their grandparents all have to have lived it. It's like a long folk song of kings and cabbages and beautiful princesses with diamonds in their tresses." Tommy laughed. "You know, I only came to Turin on the promise of work. It would set me up financially for life and mean I could set my own hours and use my Italian when I wished. I didn't realise that even the business players here are guided on short strings by the old, old families, so you're not dealing with just one guy in his Berluti loafers, but you have to make provisions for his cousin and his wife's aunt and so on. Being a fixer, fixing things, in that part of the Continent is like trying to clear up a spillage in Fort Knox without all the passes and privileges."

I tapped Tom's forearm. "You might want to not talk shop here, mate. Rufus, Nena's best friend's brother, has a network of ears on the Leas – here, at The Grand, among the police force, the taxi drivers, even the woman who brings me my newspapers."

"Ok."

"That's why I've been calling you from the booth here – it's well away from all the guests and rabble. I haven't met this guy Rufus yet, but he's very connected. The glassy-eyed alkies in their suits and ties at the bar are all under his command."

"Message understood."

I smiled.

"Anyway, Sammy, it's all East London this season – that's the fashion. Nothing big is doing in Turin since you left, if you catch my drift? You're not missing out on the latest haute couture, or your cuts." Tommy winked at me. "The jobs from Papa John are tiddlers."

I rested my right arm again on Tommy's forearm. "Not even speaking in code is going to help here. Let's finish off these Peronis and find some dancing girls. I have been given a pink pass for the night, and I want to use it in full." He returned my wink, and we bumped fists.

Tommy whispered to me across the dining table. "It'll be the perfect sending-off gift for me. Nena will be pleased to know I'm flying out from Essex tomorrow night with a friend of our friend – on the hush hush. I'll leave like a thief in the night – well, maybe an errant lover."

Homeward bound.

Luca rolled his two enormous trolley bags into the block's lift. It had taken him six days to buy and pack all his provisions for the five-day trip, but he now smiled to himself at the riches contained within his Antler luggage, all bought with the flight money saved through Councillor John's beneficence. Gianfranco would be viewing The Four Seasons through a set of 1960s opera glasses, courtesy of the finest antiques shop on High Street Kensington. It would cheer up his brother, who had seemed unusually sullen during their last Skype chat on the Saturday just gone. Luca hoped there wasn't a problem at home.

Just as Councillor John had promised, the car, a black Mercedes S350 no less, was waiting outside, its driver even wearing a peaked cap. This was reward for his silence. Luca had been most circumspect for six weeks now, chatting only to John and his many friends and shunning Patty and the gossipers at the post office.

"Loose lips sink ships", and Luca had convinced himself that the old man and the Polish lady had secured their own fates by endangering the lives of good people like his friend John. Hospitals and clinics were being built in the borough, and Luca had met dozens of ordinary folks at the councillor's swinging soirees who were benefitting from John's bright thinking.

People were getting the medical attention they'd been starved of; one lady in her late Sixties had told Luca that she'd been on the waiting list for an ankle operation for sixteen months, and the wait had gradually turned her into a hermit, chained to her armchair and forgotten by her friends. All of John's plans could have all been derailed by two deviants – all the shiny towers to come were nearly brought down, and all the parks and play areas almost remained under the earth and sod of Tower Hamlets.

Luca pushed such grim thoughts out of his mind as he settled into the Mercedes's leather back seat and watched the driver fuss with the two trolley bags. Luca's iPhone read that Southend airport was 35 miles away, or 54 minutes in the car. His holiday started here. For the first time in a decade, for the first time since Mama had passed away before her weeping sons, Luca could see his destiny rising like Caesar's storied shield against the sun.

Somewhere down the clogged motorway, past the rolling fields of the Weald of Kent, Joey slept. He had fallen asleep on that sturdy old sofa yet again, his mouth pressed airtight against the armrest on which Eleanor's head had rested only months earlier. If he took a long and deep breath, maybe her essence would enter his lungs and spur him on through the final stage of his mission. Whenever Joey managed to have a siesta at Warren Cliff, in the few hours afterwards he would feel energised by the dry-powder inhaler of that front room. It would be a shame to auction off the only home he had ever known, but he had to press on now that a year had passed – his mother had always said that people who never changed their minds never changed a thing. She was right as usual, for Joey was fast becoming entwined in a web of solitude of his own making. He had to break the cycle of afternoons at the house, visiting under the pretence that Eleanor was somehow still part of the physical world, a place so much more compromised than the realm of spiritual thought.

The day before, on the way back from loading dozens of Christmas puddings on the bakery pallets, Joey had stopped at the cemetery and tended to his mother's grave, on the first anniversary of her death.

Joey had placed the bold bouquet of red chrysanthemums and light orange germini against the black marble headstone he'd fetched all the way from

Birchington on the north-east Kent coast. In stark letters of gold inscribed across the top third of the slab, it read: "Eleanor Harkett, 1955-2018. Mother, polymath and writer. 'Wherever truth, love and laughter abide, she is there in spirit'."

Not a speck of dirt was ever allowed to settle within the inscription, for, four times a week, Joey would brush down the headstone with a velveteen cloth.

Patting down his hair and removing the sweater with the bakery crest embossed on it, Joey had knelt down on the grass, wearing his finest shirt and tie, and recited their most-treasured film quote: "We were both maladjusted misfits. We still are. And we've loved every minute of it."

With those immortal words of Stella from Hitchcock's Rear Window, a film that the pair of misfits had watched every Christmas Day since 1991, Joey had poured out the contents of a vial of Eleanor's most-loved scent, Hermes Elixir des Merveilles, the woody orange incense firing up the grass with its citric notes. It flipped the fuse switches of his senses, so he could feel something akin to an electrical charge rising out of the soil. It would be enough to power Joey for another year until the next anniversary wound its way around.

He had asked his mother for guidance now all he could do was wait, and in response, he had felt an orphaned breeze race round the marble headstone and kiss his neck above the collar of his white shirt. All would be well. Joey had then reclined back onto the perfumed grasses, half-wishing that Eleanor would drag him tenderly down into the warmth of the soil and into her embrace to rest alongside her. Joey looked up at the thin, white sheets of stratus clouds that moved across the grey sky. It was as if they were drawing a curtain close to this sorry chapter in his life.

Eleanor had always convinced him that he had more to lose than other boys by giving in to his well of rage, but in her becalmed last months, she had conceded that closure was even more important than containment; if the valves were left open, all the poisons of the past would seep and corrupt Joey's bright future.

Now that his plan had implicitly been countenanced by his mother, Joey had begun its planning and execution over the past month. The deaths of Alistair and Sandy, announced in church and in the local newspaper, would bring the bastard back to Folkestone. It was ordained.

Now, a day on, with his mouth against the fabric of the sofa, Joey muttered "all will be well" to himself. He could still smell the dark orange Hermes scent he'd poured over the grasses the day before. Only a mother knows the metres measured out by your heart, and how the trials of yesterday let us see what we are made of; and only Eleanor knew of Joey's plans to confront his past and understand it so as to lay it to rest.

He wished to open up the back of the timepiece and see its workings; he knew only the face of the clock and his own cracked expression in its reflecting glass. It would never be enough for him to understand the timeline after the car had hit him as he crawled down the dark country road; he had to work out how the harmonic oscillator had vibrated at that particular frequency to put him on all fours in the dirt verges just before midnight and divine why the driver had left him for dead. Nothing happens by pure chance; there's an oscillating tuning fork in everything, sending ripples forth that decide the months and years and decades that follow.

Joey wanted answers only the driver of that old Austin motorcar could give. Only once this had been dealt with, would he be ready to kiss goodbye the museum home they had shared on Chambois Close.

Eleanor's spirit would travel with him wherever he ended up: maybe he would turn his hand to becoming a watchmaker's apprentice, channelling time in a tiny shop full of tuning forks and pendulums, like the widowed Michel Descombes; maybe he would set up his own gym and train people in the ways and methods by which he had improved his own physique; or maybe he would serve his time and then disappear from all the physical triggers of the past that would decay and fade, unlike the memories he carried with him. Dreams, unlike the physical world, were left untouched by time.

So, now, Joey would enjoy, for one last afternoon or maybe one last week, the home that Eleanor had created for him, as she scribbled away in solitude at all hours when her darling son was finally asleep. The driver of the Austin was coming; he would be here soon, maybe today, maybe tomorrow, but there would be a reckoning. The driver would want answers for the break-in, the smashed-up salon, and the Polaroids that Joey had mocked up with the broken furniture from the garden shed.

The driver's name was Samuel, a ghost blown in from the century before, from the 1990s. He had left no trace; the only clue he'd left was the hole caused by his vanishing act. As the poet James Fenton had written so peerlessly, "It is not the houses. It is the spaces between the houses. It is not the streets that exist. It is the streets that no longer exist."

It was not the teenagers who stayed in that small patch of Kent; it was the teenager with the unique, soft Scots brogue and the girlfriend who resembled Winona Ryder; the teenager who left in the night, whose absence was remarked upon in every school corridor, if not in the smudged print of the local newspaper. Samuel was the missing man.

Where is Your God Now?

You see, people here didn't disappear in those days before Folkestone became a trendy old dear. Once you were born here, you were busy booking your plot in Cheriton Road cemetery, a tidy space hopefully far away from the ivy and brambles that had grown wild since Queen Victoria's reign.

For an extremely well-liked boy of 18 to disappear like the burrowing rabbits on The Warren, well, something must have happened, and Joey had connected all the dots as he recuperated in the sun room, his injured face slathered in witch hazel and Eleanor's soup tureen on a table by the lounger's side.

There were many hours to wile away until Terry, the landlord of The East Kent Arms, had passed on to Joey and his mother what he'd learnt from his barmaid – that on the night of the accident, Rhona had ordered a taxi home for her friend Sam, who had been getting wasted all day at the pub. And now the teenage boy had gone back to Scotland apparently, without a leaving party or even a word of farewell; Rhona had been trying to comfort his girlfriend Nena, who had shorn off all her hair and taken to sleeping with every barfly and boozehound who shambled into the pub. Nena had become the shame of Sandgate; Sam had upped and gone.

Why had Sammy left? Rhona asked. It went against all the plans he'd told her of that summer, on his many journeys on the monorail between her bar and the bar-billiards table. His future would be minted in Folkestone, he'd confided in her, whether sober or drunk, and Nena would be his equally young wife, the "princess of my existence". Something had happened to smash his sureness of purpose into pieces. Rhona was convinced of that.

And Terry now believed that the young lad Sam had been the driver of the car that had mown down Joey a while earlier. "A driving licence is a privilege, not a right," the moustachioed landlord had told Eleanor in the kitchen.

"That fool has obviously scarpered. Our generation used to stand up and be counted, not head for the hills at the first glimpse of trouble. He comes from a good family. I knew his grandfather – took hold of that cabin down by the Lower Leas, set up a summer home there with his bare hands. This fool Sam isn't worthy of his parents or grandfather. Look what he's done to your handsome boy, Ellie. Can't find the bugger now."

Joey had heard it all through the kitchen hatch into the sun room, and as soon as he was fit again, he had walked across Folkestone in the rays of late winter and spoken to Rhona herself in The East Kent Arms. He'd slunk in, even though he was only 13, and nabbed her while she was poaching a cigarette; he said he was a friend of Terry, who had told him everything when he'd come over with a film for his mother to watch. Rhona had informed Joey that the teenager had gone back to somewhere in Scotland with his parents; he had driven a brown Austin 1100 called The Flying Pig during his last few months in Sandgate and Folkestone.

Nena, his abandoned girlfriend, newly orphaned, had been in a couple of nights before and poured a pint of Thatchers cider over the bar billiards table in the far corner. She'd caused a scene, calling the regulars "wanker tosspots". As Rhona escorted her up the road to the salon she'd just opened, Nena revealed she didn't know Sam's present whereabouts or the address of the Berwickshire farmstead. The frenzied young lass had wished Sam a hot hell for disappearing. Her punky hair smelt of gin and vodka, and the back of her salon was a mess of empty bottles; she'd been sleeping like a dog in a bundle of cloths on the couch there. Nena was fast getting a horrendous reputation in town. "What a smash-up, boy," Rhona had concluded. "My brother Tom is now in Italy; our little band has just broken up over the last months. It's all gone to shit. Tommy hasn't heard from Sam either, and they were the best of friends. They played billiards and hung out by the old Rotunda on the beach. It's very sad and strange how things fall apart. Joey, you ought to enjoy being a teenager and feeling free. Nothing lasts." And then Rhona finished her shift and hopped on the back of her friend Harry's motorbike. The next time he saw her, pink-haired in a pale-blue tux, she was reading the eulogy for Harry after he'd lost his life on that very machine.

And so, over the long, nothing years, Joey had charted every possible course of the Flying Pig from The East Kent Arms to the spot where the Austin had collided with him. Aside from his mother and their films, it became his only obsession – he concocted myriad theories about Sam's eventual destination, far away from his loved ones and from the East and West Cliffs and the Bayle of Folkestone, driving ever further in his brown Austin 1100 until the wheels deflated and the metal powdered away upon tarmac roads that helter-skeltered up into the sky.

It wasn't punishment enough to know that the popular boy with the shock of sandy hair had been driven out of town by his cowardice. Joey wanted Sam to know what it was like to feel stranded in the middle of nowhere with no route back home. It was pure chance that, on his first visit along the Leas down to Sam's cabin, Joey had found the Jiffy bag on the front step. He had taken it away, steamed open the envelope on the hob at his bedsit, and placed the Polaroids inside that he'd taken at Chambois Close, deliberately mysterious and open-ended enough, defying explanation.

This was the trap into which Sam would fall – human curiosity should do the rest, and sooner or later, the front doorbell would chime and the man who had so dented his teenage years would be there standing at the door, expecting the grungy man in the Polaroid. It was indeed Joey dressed in a fair approximation of the clothes he'd been wearing that night as a drunken 13-year-old on that road out of town. The beard was just a little disguise to hide the scars on his lower face; it had come out rather well in the photographs.

Joey had two decades' worth of questions to put forward to the mystery boy, although he knew how he'd come to be crawling on the unlit country road, mud in his mouth and plastered to his hair.

Before the accident, he'd been working evenings at the garage in Alkham; the money from tidying up the accounts every six months would help his mother pay for her diabetic treatment and mean she could be more selective with the writing work she took on. No more evenings would be spent writing up property particulars, pimping out her prose for a few pounds.

Joey was very proficient with numbers and he was also quietly infatuated with the garage owner's wife. She would fix him up with sausage-and-egg suppers as he sorted out the garage books. On the night when everything changed, Mrs Hampton had called him over from the desk in the back porch to sit and watch Coronation Street with her. Her husband was always under the ramps fixing a tractor at that time of year; Sid had to service the cars and farm vehicles of 100 villagers on his own, so Joey seldom saw his dusty face around town.

Mrs Hampton was unusually happy as she and Joey talked over the voices on the television. Her breasts were wondrously full in her thin cornflower-blue blouse tonight. After a few minutes, she shifted. "I'm having some tonic water," Mrs Hampton said. "Would you like a glass?"

Joey had never had that drink before, but he didn't wish to appear like the 13-year-old boy he was, so he nodded and watched Mrs Hampton disappear back into the kitchen to fetch the tonics. He vainly tried to focus on the soap scenes playing out on the TV screen, but his mind kept racing back to that straining blouse and the possibility the thirtysomething woman within it, who formed his night-time fantasies, was making a play for him.

From there, he recalled the car-washing scene in Cool Hand Luke where the frustrated wife had entranced the gangs of passing convicts, her bust pressing against the suds on the vehicle's windows, a smile of satisfaction on her face, fully aware of the carnage she was creating among the desperate men. What on earth was going on here?

Mrs Hampton reappeared at the doorway, carrying two tall glasses of something she'd called slimline and a slice. A third button on her blouse had come undone, and Joey looked away for another point of focus.

"Here, have a try of this. Slimline tonic is an acquired taste, but you ought to get used to it, now you're a teenager. How tall are you now, Joey?" She sat back down next to him on the two-seater sofa with the Delft print. He could smell that she'd reapplied her perfume in the kitchen.

"I'm 5ft10 now, Mrs Hampton. I've grown a few inches since summer. Put on a couple of stone as well." He winced as he tasted the tonic, but it was fine enough.

"Well, that's a good height to be. Little Sid always finds it hard to reach the airer in the kitchen, and I have to get out the steps to help him." She yawned and switched the TV off with the remote. "How's that glass going down, Joey? Do you like the taste?"

"It's lovely, Mrs Hampton. May I have another?" He raised his glass and she took it.

"Yes, yes. I'm glad you like it. It's quite a bitter drink at first, but it's almost like your taste buds relax and open up so it all slips down quite nicely." She got up and slinked back into the kitchen, sashaying for the benefit of his observations.

Joey looked down at his lap and then back up at the empty, grey screen of the television, in which he could see the Aga and the pan rack framed by the kitchen's pine doorway. The undulating form of Mrs Hampton then reappeared large in the reflection, filling every side. Joey turned his head and saw that her red-and-pink floral bra was now visible, the blouse open to the waist, pushed wide by the fully round weight of her breasts. She was grinning, with her head cocked to one side and her corn-blonde hair tumbling down onto her slender shoulders. She nodded.

"Mrs Hampton..." Joey started, but she put her index finger to his lip, handed him his tall beaker once again and nodded for him to drink up. This time, Joey realised that the notes of citrus and alcohol were coming from the drink itself, not her perfume. There was a heap more vodka in this tonic, and his tongue almost flickered with its sharpness. He'd downed more than half of the contents, though, and in his mounting panic and nervousness, he finished the glass. "Mrs Hampton, I can't drink alcohol. I'm not 14 yet; I'm 13."

"You're old enough for me. You please me, Joey. You're not going anywhere right now, are you?" She was sitting rather too close to him, her left hand brushing his right thigh, and Joey pointedly looked the other way through the darkness of the window. There was precious little light from the moon tonight; there was no guidance anywhere, and Joey's throbbing head was making the lounge furniture recede and draw nearer as if it was floating on the dark-brown sea of the carpet.

Joey placed Mrs Hampton's ringed hand on her own thigh. "I have to go now. I'm going to be late, erm, and I have to walk... go to the bus stop on the A260. Mum's expecting me at 9. Thanks for the sausages and thanks again for the tonic." He dizzily got up to leave and realised his grey school trousers were noticeably tenting.

Joey fled. As he ran through the kitchen, he could hear Mrs Hampton laughing drunkenly from the sofa. He put on his black brogues and bolted through the slalom poles of

Where is Your God Now?

umbrellas and sticks in the porch and into the void of the garage yard, scrabbling in the mud and the puddles that had formed that hour in the drive.

The whole place was barely lit by the ghost of the moon. Joey slid into the mud, his hands clawing at the matted grass, his knees sodden and sore; how would he explain his state, dirty and drunken, to his mother? Joey's balance had gone, the vodka seeping through his body, coursing through his veins, and he had no way of calling off its chase. His head was bobbing and he realised his glasses were still on the ledger book at the desk he'd been working at before all this nonsense started.

Where was the road? Why weren't his legs working properly? Why did they fold under him like those of a felt puppet? Joey had to keep moving in the direction of the main road, past poor Sid's motorcade of rusting saloon cars and pick-ups in the weeds, broken mourners clutching broken flowers; Joey had to head onwards, or else the alcohol would begin to send him under its waves, and he, trapped under the sheet of glass, would never get home. The mud had even got into his mouth, and his tongue tasted of metal and mulch.

Even all those years later, when asleep on his cot in that bedsit high up above the streets of Folkestone or napping on his mother's sofa waiting for the driver to return to him, Joey could taste the granules of that metallic mud and feel it stagnating on his tongue. It was his petrol.

My name is Luca; I live on the 17th floor.

The curved roof of the recently built terminal at Southend Airport, once London's third-busiest airport during the golden age of travel, emerged from among the conurbations. Somewhere on this erstwhile base for World One bi-planes sat a Cessna 172-SP, of which Luca would be the sole passenger. After placing the two trolley bags in the two seats at the back of the cabin, the plain-clothes pilot guided the beaming and thankful Italian into the space beside him.

"It's wonderful to have a bit of company – you're doing me a favour, Luca."

"I am?"

"Yeah. It's a pleasure to help out a mate of John's."

The pilot was a great deal more buff than he was, though probably only a few years younger, and Luca was delighted that such a manly specimen was thrilled to be whisking him away to the motherland. He settled into his seat. "I feel like Pavarotti. I have never been up in a private plane. It's so small."

The pilot smiled as he ran through his checks before take-off. "I'm not sure I could carry Pavarotti what with those enormous two trolley bags of yours." He spoke into his headset and adjusted his Wayfarer shades. "Golf-Charlie-Whisky-Alpha. Ready for departure." He looked over at Luca. "So, you're going home?"

"Yes, yes. I'm going back to Turin to see my brother, but I live in East London. It's been my home for several years."

The pilot broke into a wide smile. "You are one of John's Whitechapel set. It's been all a bit busy out there. John told me everything, about how discreet you are and what a trusted ally you are to our little set of friends. You can talk freely to me, Luca. I'm Tom, by the way." His high, mellifluous speech went soft. "I work for John's business partners in Turin."

Luca considered this for a moment; was it all a test by John to see whether his vow of silence over the old man and the girl had been forgotten? Was the councillor behind Milena's dodgy drug overdose? Unsure, he decided to change the course of the conversation. "Ah, so you live in Torino then?"

Tom seemed well aware of Luca's diversionary tactics. "Yes, I own a palazzo on the Via Carlo Alberto. I've lived there for years. I've done it up and settled down with a true Turin woman. It's fair to say that she keeps me on all ten toes." He looked over at his passenger again. "Listen, I know all about the death of that pair of perverts, Luca. I know it must have been a shock for a man of culture and refinement such as you to see such events. John has informed me of your difficulty in accepting what happened. You now understand why it had to happen, right?"

Luca looked out across the ancient airfield from the Cessna's tiny passenger window, the green and grey smudges of outfield and empty runway refracting in the blobs of condensation. This luxury was coming to him on someone else's bill. "I understand why now, yes, Tom."

"Well, I can give you the picture in Italy. The people of Turin are growing older and older, there and everywhere. John's friends, as you know, are heavily involved – no, instrumental – in improving the standard of healthcare in London. And I look after the retired ex-pats in Turin, mainly the English, the pink-faced ones, a great number of whom are really beyond any hope of physical improvement. I'm in my late thirties, and things are starting to go wrong, you know what I mean?"

Luca nodded. "Look at me, Tom. Out of shape."

"Well, we're of similar age. You know how it goes: I can't run the same splits I used to; I can't run a half-marathon in 80 minutes any more. We all get to the age when we need to sort out our affairs so that our loved ones won't become mired in admin and death duties. I'm not a pilot by trade, but a lawyer for the elderly; my work dovetails very neatly with John's work in Whitechapel, Greenwich, all across London."

"I see." Luca looked at Tom's benign features and tidy, tall bouffant of chestnut hair; he didn't fit in with the goons who had offed the elderly gentleman on that spartan square of grass.

"In fact, when John and his partners hear of an acquaintance who wishes to enjoy their autumn years in your beautiful home city, away from the miasma of East London, then I introduce them to Turin. I tidy up their concerns so that their last years may be spent drinking Barolo in the trattoria rather than freezing to death in a high rise overlooking the Tubes and taxi jams. The whole network of friends improves people's lives in the years and decades when they most need calm and reflection."

Luca looked at the control yoke, joystick and toggles on the Cessna's instrument panel. "I get the point of it all, Tom."

"Now, John has explained to you how at risk these operations were because Signor Renaldi and his daughter were compromised and about to raise false allegations. Have you heard these?"

"I have not."

Tommy started the plane's taxi left into the spaghetti of tarmac. "Well, Signor Renaldi was, as you know, making a mistress out of his own daughter, who herself was the unloved product of a fling with a Krakow prostitute. But as well as this, he was alleging that John and our friends were bringing about the early deaths those clients of ours who had made new lives for themselves in Turin. These clients also became friends of mine, dear friends, and Renaldi's slurs were destroying my memories of them, along with my hard-won reputation. Renaldi was a rival in private medicine. In the clinics and surgeries that have been set up all across the east of the capital, John's good work had tried to improve the wellbeing of these people who had worked all their lives to maintain London and its very fabric. Some were engineers, others were nurses, others were teachers – all were cared for right up until the point where their life quality was beginning to deteriorate. John does a great deal to make sure that the medical staff who are recruited to the shiny new surgeries agree to a fair percentage of pro bono work. These friends of ours are not always wealthy, although the majority are, and a proportion of their money gets siphoned into a kitty that everyone can access when ill. Renaldi's suggestion – that guys like me were hastening their demise for financial gain, having won their trust and gained access to their personal accounts – is as abominable to me as the details of how he treated his own daughter as his own personal concubine. Would you trust a man who lies with his own offspring? I cannot even bear to tell you how far gone into wantonness the pair of them had sunk."

Luca nodded, but he was with each passing minute hoping that Tom would tutor him in the ways of piloting a plane. He sighed: "Sometimes, I am grateful not to have brought a son or daughter into this angry, polluted world."

"Ah, come now, man. I don't wish to spoil your trip. I just want to tell you that I am a man you can trust. You're either on the side of John or you are rubbing shoulders with the devil. You see, we're all working for the greater good, not for greed. You must understand that as a countryman of Garibaldi himself." Tom was guiding the plane to the tip of the runway but talking at ten to the dozen.

"Garibaldi is a father of Italy." Luca wanted to launch into one of his lusty speeches, all gesture and sonorous declamation, but the tiny cockpit was barely large enough for his bulk when he was static, let alone when he had become a windmill of oratory. He sat stock still.

Tom started: "You'll have to excuse me for not reeling it off in Italian, but here goes. Don't laugh if I get it wrong, Luca – 'I can offer you neither honour nor wages; I offer you hunger, thirst, forced marches, battles and death. Anyone who loves his country, follow me."

As a swelling pride rose in Luca's chest at the words he had memorised for 30 years in his native Italian, so the nose of the Cessna started to lift into the brightening sky of late morning. "That speech. It's always felt like comfort to me. It makes a home of everywhere that's not my true home. I carry that speech in my heart."

Tom was looking straight ahead, but he could feel the strength of Luca's smile to his left. "We all have the sense of being dislocated from our true homes. Why, I was telling my best friend only yesterday that I feel like an interloper in Turin, even after all these years. The carnival of life weaves around the streets that I look upon as I eat my breakfast, but the scenes might as well be on the big screen. I'm like the projectioner that nobody ever sees, observing everything that lies before me but unable to join in the shared experience. I'm behind the glass, boxed in, a spectator. There's no interactivity, even with Claudia around."

"She's your lady?" Luca looked at Tom's profile and reckoned Claudia must be a real beauty, a princess of all Piedmont.

"Yes, Luca. I find her inscrutable. I do speak Italian fluently."

"Good man!"

"But I miss certain inflections, Luca, the grace notes. Claudia is from the oldest family in the region; she has little time for explaining all the little Braille bumps my hand misses. She's an elegant lady, but I wish I understood her better. I really want to be part of the carnival, Luca. I want to immerse myself completely, but Claudia has no desire to tutor me. Do you know just how frustrating that is?" Tommy now looked across and met Luca's unerring gaze.

He smiled: "You can always act as my go-between, Luca? What do you reckon?"

Luca looked at his new friend. "What do you mean, Tom?"

"I mean, you could work away trying to make this wonderful angel whom I adore more comprehensible to me. A translator of the ways of a woman – how does that title suit you?" Tom chuckled. "It'd be unpaid – well, paid in dinners out."

"I get you, Tom. When I'm not with my brother Gianfranco, I will help you how I can. I'm only around for a week, but I will be your go-between." Luca smiled and then elaborated. "We're going to see a performance of Vivaldi, the day after tomorrow – The Four Seasons."

"Wow. At the Teatro Regio, yes? Well then, you, Claudia, Gianfranco and I must go as a four, dear boy. Just booked that after seeing it advertised in La Stampa. Wow. How great is that? We're all going to the same event." Tom looked across again. "And to pass the time till we land in Piedmont, I'm going to give you your very first flying lesson." He pulled the control yoke out from the instrument panel. "This is going to be fun for both of us, Luca. I knew John's friend would become a friend of mine. It always works that way."

And then the SP-172 turned towards the English Channel and away from all the concerns of the capital.

Where is Your God Now?

Grand plans.

Cadwick was scanning the room, taking in the burnished woods and the creaking leather dining chairs, but The Grand was without the busy waddle of his brother, Rufus. He must be networking or chatting to his partner, Leon, the head receptionist. Nena had gone to powder her nose in the ladies' cloakroom, down and back and to the left in the basement, and Cadders ruminated upon their conversation over main course.

It was agreed that the best course of action would be to gather as much information as possible about the suspect before involving the rather bottom-heavy policing of PC Stuart – he certainly had the right stride for a constable, but as Nena had noticed, he wore the expression of a low-wattage soul to whom everything seemed like an idea of no little genius. His boots far outweighed the contents of his cranium.

Quite what this information would consist of was yet to be discussed, but it would be enough hopefully to stop the harassment through break-ins and unwanted drive-throughs. Cadders was a little tired of all the upheaval; he had to find a new lady to squire around town, and this mystery was getting in the way a bit.

Nena had suggested a rota of stakeouts of 33 Chambois Close, chiefly to counter the rumblings of boredom felt by the pair. If the trio did a little bit of sleuthing each, none of them would end up too jaded. Was all this meant to assuage the very real sensations of violation and intrusion? What had started as a fine excuse for a brisk walk and elongated chats at Loaf was now rapidly in peril of becoming a chore. Instead of feeling inspired by the fresh revelations, Cadders' natural buoyancy had been slightly deflated. He had been certain that unearthing a suspect would be a herculean task. PC Stuart was still without a CCTV image of the mystery figure's face or a single fingerprint. Instead, Jacqui's little bit of tittle-tattle had solved the riddle. Her endless nattering had succeeded before Cadwick could impress his friends with his deductions and doggedness. He felt cheated and more than a bit annoyed.

The only tough aspect of the manhunt had been explaining to the idling mind of PC Stuart that Nena had not pulled off some insurance stunt; that she had not cajoled one of her pals to shove the Skoda estate down Military Road and into her salon in order to claim on a business that might be on the verge of failing. Nena wasn't as shifty as Cadwick – he had once dipped the paws of his childhood cat in the paint he'd spilt on the new carpet when he was redecorating his bedroom, partly to avoid his mother's anger, partly to spare her a few thousand pounds under the terms of the house insurance.

Nena was not exactly insolvent, despite the constant keeling-over of her aged clientele, but it was only when she had flashed a PDF of her bank statement before the constable's eyes that PC Stuart had relented from pursuing his hunch. He'd let out a sigh and taken his shiny size 12s back out of the salon door.

The stakeouts of the rather dilapidated 1930s semi-detached house would take place over a period of one week. Jacqui's friend had mentioned that the son was a regular visitor; he would come alone every few days as if in a hypnotised trance and leave on his own with watery eyes and a shuffle to his walk.

We three Musketeers would rotate every three hours of daylight. Each would take a single shift every day from the vantage point of Cadwick's trusty old Mercedes saloon – the reprobate had never been sober enough to string together a dozen or so driving lessons and a test at the end of them, so I would have to park the old gal a hundred metres from the house's front door, by the junction with Warren Way. I could then use my birding binoculars rather than to take a chance by parking any nearer – the East Cliff was lively enough with school runs for Cadders' black Merc not to rouse attention. It could stay parked up all week on the neighbouring street.

Nena had agreed to double up on shifts from time to time as a female presence would seem less suspect in suburbia than a single man sitting there, fingertapping to music from the Merc's elderly radio. The following day, we would reconnoitre the gentle hills on the other side of Folkestone to find the ideal spot to park the car.

"Cadwick, a penny for your thoughts?" Nena came up and rested her hands on his shoulders.

"Just thinking about what we were talking about. I think it's meant to be sunny but cold early tomorrow, so we should walk over to East Cliff in the morning. Do you have workmen at the salon tomorrow?"

"Not tomorrow, no. I'm waiting on the glass to arrive and be fitted, but that's a couple of days off." Nena sat herself to Cadwick's left and browsed the dessert menu. "I really hope the son pops into the house sooner than later."

"I'm just grateful that we can have a cheeky sup in the car. It won't be going anywhere for five or six days at most. I'll leave a chiller box in the rear footwell."

"Good call."

"Perhaps you could join me for my first couple of stints on stake-out?" Cadders smiled. He always consoled himself with the fact that he would rarely drink alone.

"If the delivery of the glass isn't delayed, I will."

"Cheers."

"Did you manage to find a photo of this guy Joseph?" Nena put down the menu.

"He has no online presence, Nena. You know what a devotee of Facebook I am, and I could not find any trace of a Joseph Harkett on any social media or microblogging site. Just lots of fan pages for that A-Ha singer Morten Harket. And it's not him."

"No digital footprint? That's odd." Nena had herself come up empty-handed when she had searched for me on social media recently, but she kept silent about that to Cadders.

"From what is known of Joseph, he lived as a recluse during his schooldays. He wasn't at any of the schools around here, and Rufus confirmed that he's neither on the electoral register nor in the phonebook. He has no criminal record, no club ties and no hobbies – there's nothing really."

"Nothing? Fuxache."

Cadders sighed. "Well… He was devoted to his mother, and she never married. She was an occasional contributor to the local media, but she too shunned any social contact, either digitally or through clubs and societies."

"What a pair."

"I know, right? Jacqui's chum said that the son looks wholly different this year – he's swapped a rolling tubbiness for an almost military leanness."

"On a mission, perhaps?"

Cadders winked at Nena. "Joseph has cropped, light-brown hair instead of a bleached-blond ponytail. Along with his utter invisibility online, his new physique might hint at a man on a mission, yes."

Nena jumped in. "Well, we have been saying that the photo-dropper is very likely to be the same person who let the estate car slam into my shop…"

"It's quite likely, or there may be two people working in tandem, which is something that my brother posited." Cadders scanned the room again, but Rufus was missing from the clusters of white-hairs. "Where is he? He's meant to be on shift, and neither the maître d' nor the head maid has seen him."

Nena was tapping into Google on her smartphone. "Nothing, is there?" She looked up to see Cadders watching the whole room. "Your brother's probably showing one of his informants to their room of favour." She paused. "You know, I always feel slightly non-standard being in this room when I know that my Mum could never have dared visit here in full regalia. They would've thought she was one of the serving staff gone rogue."

"I know. Thank the Lord, there's been progression. Ru's always kissing his fella."

Nena half-smiled. "Anyway, back to this case of ours, I don't think it's a duo."

"Why the hell not?"

"Come, Cadders. This chap Joseph doesn't sound like someone who can call up a cadre of assistants on WhatsApp. Unlike you and your little monkey fingers."

"The son is a Luddite and a loner, yes."

"Cadders, I mean, even Sam's mad drunken aunt is on Facebook – but, for a guy in, what, his early thirties to live as if it's 1955 is quite unusual."

"But it's in keeping with the image of Joseph as a quiet monk-like man…"

"… who makes a weekly pilgrimage to his dead mother's house. Nice!"

"Nena, it was probably his childhood home. You make him sound like Norman Bates. Have a heart, gal."

"I have no heart, just a black void, Cadders. You know that."

Her friend harrumphed. "Well… People find solace in what doesn't change – this guy with the house he grew up in; you with your salon, and Sam with his family cabin off the beaten track."

Nena laughed: "You're saying I'm like that loner psycho?"

"In some way, yes," Cadders smiled back. "I mean, we all hang on to physical items, don't we?"

"I suppose."

"Nena, I do it, too. Relax." Cadders smirked. "That old Merc of mine was bequeathed to me by my late uncle Freddy. I don't drive – and he didn't drive either, so it has only 25,000 miles, which is not bad for a 1974 motor, but it's not about that. It acts as a comforter."

"But I would think visiting the house in which one's beloved mother had recently died would bring back gloomy memories, no?" Nena was still scanning her friend's face.

"Well, everyone acts differently to loss. When Freddy went, I was almost relieved because he had been ravaged by motor neurone disease. It got to the point where he had become a shade of the force-of-nature he once was. And look at me – now I'm looking forward to sitting in his old motor, breathing in the old wood and leathers, and raising a beaker to his memory. The car hasn't gone anywhere since 1975, for God's sake – Freddy merely used it as a receptacle for any books that wouldn't fit in his house. The Merc was an immobile library!"

The pair of them hunched up with laughter.

"Yes, I get what you're saying, Cadders. When I think about loss, I always think of my friend Harry. His death was sudden, and he was only 22, so it took a long time for us, his friends, to fill some of the hole that the crash had opened up. We didn't have any real photos of him; no one had smartphones back then, so we took an oath that everyone should meet at Radnor Park every June 25th and share stories in the absence of any physical mementoes."

"Was Harry the biker boy?"

"Yes, he rode a superbike, and died a few years before you and I met."

"Yes, I remember."

Nena spoke softly: "It was almost written in the stars. Harry was the only one of us who was going places; in fact, his job at the BBC meant he had to commute, and that in turn meant that he was always on that bloody bike, even at half-past midnight in the furious winds. Harry told me he felt like he had a contract with fate – he couldn't see its terms and conditions nor its length, but he knew it was unbreakable and had to be honoured. He was a fatalist; I tried many times to get him to spend his TV money on anything else, even a flimsy sports car instead, at least something that might protect him in a crash, but that Honda carried memories for him – he'd bought it at 18 with his first pay packet and convinced his parents to stump up the huge insurance costs. So, Harry would never sell it. Like my salon and your old Merc, it was his talisman, but it brought him only his doom. You wouldn't believe how many mourners there were spilling out along Cheriton Road; some of them were the celebrities he acted as publicist for." Nena stopped and looked away.

"Yes, it's always the worst of times when people die young," said Cadwick softly. "I always try to look after the ones left behind. I scoop them up. You can't do much for the dead except remember them and see that their graves are well tended."

Nena sighed. "The sadness comes from never knowing what Harry might have achieved and what adventures we would have had; for someone who had matured far more quickly than anyone else in our gang, he was also a chilled-out dude, the guy with the best jokes at the worst of times. He was never fazed by anything. I see Harry as this wonderful thriller that's missing its final two-thirds, a tantalising opening chapter left hanging there. How might his story have developed? Would he have moved to the capital for good? You know, sixteen years on, I still wonder at times how Harry might've reacted to certain situations that have happened in the years since; but I do know that he would be there every weekend at my salon, fixing it up, toiling away even at the end of his long working week in London. His commitment to himself and his mates was ferocious – I remember when he came and sat with me one Christmas because he had seen me going off the rails after Sam disappeared, and we watched videos of all those Eighties Brat Pack films back to back in my little room. He said I was like Mary Stuart Masterson." Nena laughed. "Pre-eternally wise was our Harry. These starboys and glittergirls who are taken from us too soon seem to cram several marathons into their single minute here; they hold their breath to dive as deep as they can within their allotted span. They know nothing of their fate. It's the survivors who suffer the what-ifs. The unanswerable questions buzz around me like wasps; and, sometimes, I get stung. I wish I could make hard copies of the pictures my memory keeps of Harry. I would like that."

Cadders spoke: "He sounds like quite the man. I still hear his name mentioned fondly around Sandgate; he'll live as long as he's spoken of. No one like that ever truly dies, you know. 'Speak of me so I shall live on.' To die young is to be remembered at one's most vigorous; that's comforting. It's sad for the ones left behind, though. 'Death is as near to the young as to the old; here is all the difference: death stands behind the young man's back, but before the old man's face.'"

Nena wiped away a tear with her napkin and then placed the cotton square on her right thigh once again. "He was quite the chap, Cadders, but Harry was undone by his own memories. He had this skein of sentimentality that ran right through his very able self. It compromised him; it was the jag that would cut him down. I told him that he should sell that bike, that it was nothing but a hobby, that it wasn't fit for bombing up and down the M20 every day. He didn't listen. I said Harry should have hung it from the beams of his cottage as a memento of his first pay cheque. I don't like thinking of how he was alone that summer's morning up on

Wrotham Hill. His final moments were in solitude. There was no other vehicle involved, so he died from his chest wounds on the verge. Perhaps he was never conscious. Maybe the rising sun had tricked him; I don't know. It doesn't matter anyhow. Looking back or looking away sometimes leads to you getting flung from your course. Sentimentality chains you. I tried to remember that. I fear that Sam and I are a little hog-tied by our own souvenirs; you see, your Merc, a car you can't drive, is ironically not going to leave you stranded from your future. However, the salon and Sam's cabin may prove millstones that pin us to Folkestone and scupper our hopes and dreams."

Cadwick spread his palms across the mahogany table. "Now, look here, Nena. It's a bit early to set yourself and Sam up as When The Wind Blows types; the salon and cabin don't need to be your bunkers. I know it's not your intention to remake the world at large or to own a string of salons across the county, but neither do you fit the profile of a Mrs Havisham, formerly Miss."

"I have responsibilities, Cadders…"

"The salon isn't going away. You don't always have to live and work there – you could aim to simply use it as a workplace and set up home with Sam in that village you love. Where is it again, Nena?"

"River. The village down towards Dover, where the abbey is." Nena had often told Cadders that if that rural adjunct to the great port had been just a tad livelier, then she would have already set up her home and business there.

"You could easily commute from River to Sandgate, gal – it's only four miles or so by car. I think there's a bus, too. I see it around St James's."

"Yep, there's one."

"Nena, I know you see your salon as the museum of your life, but you needn't actually live there."

Nena chuckled.

Cadders continued. "Why should it be any different to the Merc? A car that I sit inside once a year to flick through Freddie's old photobooks? Just work at the salon."

"You're right, you little bastard."

"You don't even have to do that, you know. Just visit it, Nena. Use it as a place for contemplation. Everybody needs a little spot away from the world. No one's always ready to face other people, to face the future. You do need a little piece of the past to hang around."

"I know. But it's not that simple. It will prove tougher to separate Sam from that cabin of his than for me to leave the salon. I can still smell his mother's perfume on certain linens, as if she's simply nipped out to pick up some dry-cleaning."

Nena smiled. "But it's going to take Sam a decent stretch of time to say goodbye to that whiteboarded crate. I hate the place – the wind seeps into every nook and cranny late at night and it's like a marsh round the back where the water settles. Even without a madman hanging around in the dark, I'd hate it – but I would never say so to Sammy."

"We don't choose our madeleines and our Rosebuds – rather, our mementoes find us in the fullness of time."

"You sound like Jerry Springer, you tit." Nena smiled again. "Except you… You said you don't own a single item of your father's bequest?"

"I have no fond memories of that dread bastard. He even gave me this meatball of a nose. I was shipped off to prep school before my last nappy had dried on the airer. I scarcely saw him. I saw plenty of my mother in floods of tears at the foot of the stairs, mind you. I remember wishing my arms would grow long enough to hold her."

"I never knew it was that bad, Cadders. No wonder Penny hugs you so tightly. You were her hug."

"I did used to comfort her, even though I was only five. That happened whenever Father was out at the massage parlours. So I didn't keep a thing of his – it all went to charity or to Freddy; all the smoking pipes, his cricket bat, his old Roberts radio, the whole lot. Even at 13, I knew that the man was a wrong'un and that not one of his belongings would ever mean a thing to me, not then nor as a man myself. I chucked his .22 rifle off Radnor Cliff into the gorse; Age Concern didn't want it, funnily enough."

"However in control you feel you are, the rug always gets shifted, doesn't it? I suppose we then just cling on to whatever control we can possess over our lives. Opening the salon every day convinces me that I have a certain purpose, that I'm a woman with some semblance of a plan, that I am not cashing in any chance of developing into a proper adult female for another beaker of the hard stuff, even though from a glance at the back room, it is obvious to everyone that I'm a drifter in the game of life."

Cadwick looked at her, the front window of The Grand framing her youthening profile to perfection. The pink moon was almost her halo, holding her face in its glow. "Everybody has a reason; nobody truthfully has a clue. I don't think grabbing a banker's case and sitting on the train platform every morning at 6.53 puts one in any greater control of one's destiny. Ineluctable fate, and other people's ways, will always team up to shaft you."

"There's always a knife in the woodwork..."

"Always. Maybe shunning all hopes and ambitions is the best. Nobody can derail your dreams if you never pay them any notice, much less speak of them as your 'life goals'. We're all of us bouncing around on the same patch, but I'm more than happy for people to regard me as a waster without purpose. What I take from life is the sensation, the delights of the inner-visions, the interior world I can access with the assistance of my dear, dependable friend in a glass. Denial as a form of control is pleasing to me in certain ways. I'm not confusing that with abstinence, though. I shall always sail on liquor's swirling ship!"

Nena smiled. "When all of this is over, and he's over his grief, then I'll suggest living together to Sam."

"In the cabin, Nena?"

"No, I find that place spooky."

"No wonder, with all the intrusion…"

"It's not just that, Cadders. If his parents' spirits are anywhere, then they're entwined in that arts-and-craftsy bed of theirs. Like John and Yoko without the drugs and peace symbols drawn on card. A pair of conjoined souls. You can probably hear Alistair and Sandy at sunset, slotted together like a yin-and-yang symbol."

"Just the taijitu of us," Cadders sang.

"Eh?"

"Just a crap pun of mine on the song Just The Two of Us. The yin-and-yang symbol is the taijitu, you see. Anyway…"

Nena shook her head in mock disapproval. "Here we are having this deep-and-meaningful, and you wreck it all in that clever-clever way of yours by punning on an old song."

"Sorry!" Cadders tapped his knife with his fork.

"Stop that. Anyway, where was I? You've broken my train of thought as usual. Yes. You've never seen a more loving relationship than that enjoyed by Sam's folks, I tell you."

"Well, you should try to outdo them. When all this is done, when PC Plod puts the frighteners up this Joseph chap in whatever way the law eventually rouses itself to push through, just imagine you and Sam in a cottage in River, him dropping you off at the salon and then driving up to the cabin to write that novel he's always outlining to us."

"His plotless thriller without violence or any suspense?" Nena laughed. "His anti-thriller of sorts? Sam could be a kept man. He could type away on his dad's Olivetti, and then nip into Sandgate to treat me to poached eggs on toast at the cafe. The cabin could become his writer's retreat; he could summon the shade of his father to help with the proof-reading – and his mum could rustle up a phantom chicken-and-leek pie to fuel his creativity."

Cadwick called over the waiter. "Now you're being facetious, Nena."

"I'm just a bit pissed, old fruit."

"Your Wise Uncle Cadders had divined something from the tannins in that Malbec he had with his starter – his fellow Musketeers are going to live in a higgledy-piggledy house full of laughter and love. And lots of typing."

Nena bowed her head to Cadders. "I'm sure it'll happen in time, but not yet. First, I must have the tarte au citron." She turned to the waiter who'd appeared on her left. "Plenty of whipped cream, too, please. Cadders wants the tiramisu." Nena looked at her friend who was nodding. "And a large limoncello for us both, please."

And with that, the friends began working out what cottage Nena and I could hope to afford in the little village of River.

The fratellis.

Gianfranco, just as his much-loved brother, was childless, although it was not for a lack of trying. His partner, Monica, had already decorated the spare room a startling primrose, partly in readiness for Luca's stay, but primarily for the baby she craved as company. Gianfranco was forever at the university, helping the foreign students to settle into Turin, a benevolent uncle flicking from Spanish to French to English as if fiddling with the long-wave tuner on a radio. In his absences, Monica had become well skilled at DIY. Her pale denim dungarees were not only splattered with primrose, but with brilliant white after attending to the skirting-boards, and there were residues of clay grey after sharpening up the kitchen.

Looking up from dunking her brushes in a bucket of white spirit, Monica saw the unmistakably hefty silhouette of her brother-in-law-to-be through the frosted glass of their front door, the graphite smear of a passing yeti. A shower was setting in down Via Monte Rosa, so she took care to usher Luca and his usual heavy-duty wheeled bags inside. He always brought too many gifts – it would make her feel uncomfortable – but he was a good man.

"Monica! You've been painting again?" Luca was always overjoyed to see his childhood friend, whom he had introduced to his brother way back in the early Nineties.

"Yes, Luca."

"You never stop, do you?"

"Your room looks very fresh now, brother, but, please, come in and warm yourself up with a glass of something. The weather has been deteriorating. It's getting worse with every hour." She led Luca down the 19th-century mosaics of the entrance hall into the kitchen with its stainless-steel rails on which hung large stainless-steel pans and utensils.

"Gianfranco's not here, but he's not at the university either for once."

"So, where has he got to?" Luca leant back on the warm clay curvilinear walls of the pizza oven. This was a most impressive home; co-habitation brought out the best in people, and this house was an example of that.

Monica broke the surprise: "He's waiting for you at the trattoria. Been there a couple of hours now."

"I'd better go soon then."

Monica smiled: "Andrea has called in some treats for you. He had to take a taxi to ferry all the wine over there."

"Has he now?"

"Yes, so I don't expect the pair of you to be coherent by midnight."

"You're not coming?" Luca loved Monica as a sister, but there was much to catch up on, and he silently hoped the two men would have time together. Gianfranco would not believe the upturn in his brother's fortunes, much less that he had taken a private plane into Aeroporto di Torino-Caselle as its sole passenger.

"No, you go it alone. I see that it's boys' catch-up time," Monica replied in her singalong Italian. "It gives me time to catch up on my welding." Her chief hobby was creating wall baskets in glass and lead for the flowers that Gianfranco would liberate from the university gardens. Although he was handsomely paid, he considered this a perk of his role as liaison officer, and it gave Monica something pretty with which to fill her jardinieres.

After a swift slug of Disaronno Originale and a slow change into his new blue houndstooth three-piece, Luca waved goodbye and started on the five-minute stroll to La Taverna dei Mercanti, past the skeleton trees, past the wettened cars and past the property of Luigi Grassi, who had pioneered prefabricated private housing in northern Italy in the 1920s. A philanthropist and city councillor,

Grassi was Luca's kind of Italian, a civic-minded polymath and autodidact who'd seen Turin as a fitting resting place.

Luca had promised to call Tom when he had liberated himself from his luggage at his brother's, so the two new friends could meet up and introduce Claudia and Gianfranco to one another. They could then all go to The Four Seasons in a few days. Tom had suggested to Luca that the socially connected pair – the fashionista and the faculty head – were most likely aware of each other. Luca, for his part, was intrigued to set eyes upon Claudia, this princess of Piedmont.

Tom and Claudia were to join the brothers sometime after dessert, by which time the pair would be getting through their fourth or fifth bottle of vino tinto. Gianfranco had a tendency to hold his wine more successfully than Luca could, because of the many soirees he attended on university business, black-tie drinks when insobriety was frowned upon but the glass flute was never empty. Gian would always match his Barolo with a similar amount of water. Luca, however, was accustomed to drinking alone; his only marker of inebriation was the hangover afterwards, and how difficult the walk into the post office became the next day.

Andrea's tiramisu had slid down easily, and a line of empty bottles stood around its white china bowl; Luca had loosened his tie and hung the blue waistcoat on the back of his chair; and Gianfranco had related the tale of the Andalusian students who had invited him back to their wonderful house near Parco del Valentino for sardines, anchovies and sherries. He told his brother he had returned their hospitality with a bash at Jose Feliciano's Light My Fire on the guitar. The sloppy rendition brought back fine memories of his own student days in Turin. Gianfranco had won a place reading Italian history at Universita di Bologna but had chosen his home city instead; it was, after all, when the chronicles he most treasured were written, and where the love of his life resided.

Luca called Andrea for a snifter of Limoncello and prepared to bring his brother up to speed on his freshly minted life within councillor John's circle of friends. "It sounds as if we both are enjoying the finer things that life may bring, Gianfranco. The leather seats of my plane were empty but for myself and a charming English pilot. He will drop by in an hour or so. Tom lives in Turin, you see – he squires this woman called Claudia around town, and she sounds like Gina Lollobrigida reborn."

"Well, I'll be interested in meeting them soon. I don't find the English adapt so well to our Piemontese way of life." Gianfranco chuckled. "Though they would keep up with us here." He flashed his hand around the ring of bottles. "The Spanish are far more Italian in their outlook. The students integrate well. Their rhythms are also southern European."

Luca smiled. "Tom has been here for almost two decades. He still feels like an outsider, though, so I thought… Perhaps you might help him integrate a little better when I've headed back to London?"

"We'll see, brother." Gianfranco also smiled.

"Anyway, Claudia sounds high-born to me, and I don't think integrating Tom into Turin life has been her concern. Anyway, we shall see what transpires in an hour. I like the guy; he shoots from the hip."

"So, this Tom, he arranged your flight over here? I know he was the pilot, but you've only just met him, right? You didn't pay him out of your own pocket, did you? That's an indulgence too many." Gianfranco looked at Luca's ornate three-piece suit and sighed a little. His brother was forever pushing his pay packet in the search for the accoutrements of a gentleman.

"It was a present, Gian; relax."

"I'm very relaxed, Luca."

"Anyway, the flight was a gift from a new friend, a London politician and aesthete called John."

"Oh, yeah?" Gianfranco leant in.

"Yes. John used to run clubs in Soho in the Eighties and now he uses his contacts and cash to improve healthcare in the capital."

"A good Samaritan!" Gianfranco looked over at Andrea cleaning the fingerprints off the trattoria's front door.

"Listen, Gian. People yap all the time on social media about what wonderful, kind souls they are. Time-rich and truculent, they criticise the very ones trying to make a difference. Yes, perhaps they do so in atonement for past misdemeanours, I grant that. But their critics do nothing. They can't be bothered to improve the miserable lot of their fellow citizens."

"Most people keep their charity quiet, Luca."

"Well, John is a man of actions, not moaning words. He does things. You wouldn't believe the favours he can call upon. I've seen it these past months. People bend their backs to help him in any way they can." Luca moved back, so Andrea could set down the limoncellos and a jug of water in front of him.

Gianfranco brought his own chair nearer to his brother's. "And when people help him out, they do so because of his kindness or because they are afraid of him?"

"Why would they fear him, Gian?"

"You said it. This John comes from Soho. So, he has probably enjoyed all the illicit pleasures of nightlife and then had some Damascene conversion somewhere along the line."

"Come now, Gian…" Luca was getting fed up.

"What provoked that change? Suddenly John goes from being Giorgio Moroder to the new Luigi Grassi?"

"That's hardly the case, Gian."

"Why the change? Why is John nice to you? You don't get anything for free, my brother. There's nothing free in this world. What does he expect from you in return for the private plane trip, eh?"

Luca rubbed his eyes. This conversation was not adhering to the course he had foreseen. He was cursing himself for not predicting that Gianfranco would approach this new information as the university man he was – fearful of disruption, pragmatic and cynical, the very things Luca himself was not.

"John, John is a generous man, Gian. Even when he ran his nightclubs, he tried to get black acts and DJs good wages – there was still a lot of racism around in the late Seventies – I think, I know, that he has always championed the underdog. John did everything himself. And when he was no longer youthful enough to maintain the hours, he became an administrator, specifically in healthcare. And his wife Jeannie had died of cancer, horribly. It was a change in careers that met his need as a people person."

Gianfranco rested his hand on his brother's right shoulder. "Listen, Luca, as long as you are aware that this John might ask for a favour, then I'm all right."

"He might use me as a translator, yes."

Gianfranco removed his hand. "You should have perhaps brought John to Turin instead of one of his buddies, you know?"

"For what reason?"

"Luca, I perhaps have a few questions for him, not his chauffeur." Gianfranco paused. "I'd like to check out this John before you get too pally."

"You can, in time," Luca muttered without believing it would ever happen. "But you can see that a man of restless energy might make the switch from London nightlife to becoming a councillor?"

Gianfranco nodded. "Yes. You were talking about Grassi and his housing revolution earlier – maybe John has a similar civic drive, you know, maybe he needs to focus his energies on something at all times. And maybe you interest him because you have always had a big heart and this sense of community."

Luca smiled. "I believe it is rather like that. John loves my company and my stories from Italian history. He's not a homosexual either. He's lived a life as well. John's just a person who loves life and those who embrace all its vicissitudes and variations. There's nothing more to it than that, Gian. We bonded over our love of Barolo anyway. He has cases of the stuff at his place."

Gianfranco eased up. "Ah, I like a man who realises the healing properties of the grape."

"That he does!"

"And it sounds as if John has provided you with a family of sorts at long last in London. Luca, I don't think Patty and your colleagues are the answer – you have the excuse of the language barrier for working in a post office. To be English and to do so must mean a limited horizon." Gianfranco paused. "I'm not sorry if that sounds snobbish."

"I know you're a meritocrat, not a snob." Luca looked down at his limoncello.

"Right. That Patty is not going anywhere. Why her? I don't know why you form these attachments and obsessions."

Luca sank his limoncello. "Patty is not my concern any more. I guess I was just lonely and in need of attention. I'm starting to realise how exotic even I must appear to these friends of John who have spent their entire lives within London's borders."

"Well, London is a big place. I do worry about you getting inhaled into its labyrinthine airways. If you have a support network of guys like John, it's not so bad."

Gianfranco looked away, a little teary-eyed again, just as he'd been on Skype.

"Hey, my brother. There are other people, not just John – councillors, nurses, the people who run everyday London – and all of them have been unrelentingly kind to me, asking nothing in return but a few tales. We hold parties in the tower block; they are like resident soirées. You know, everybody knows one another, so there's never any rift or trouble."

"Good. Nice to hear." Gianfranco's smile returned and he took in his brother's gleeful expression.

"Yes. It's good, Gian. We all share the same front door, the same lifts – no one shits on their doorstep, as we say in England."

Gianfranco stopped. "I didn't realise these people were your neighbours. That makes a difference."

"It does, Gian."

"Was the guy who came to fix your sink a neighbour? The African?"

"No, but he's a friend of John – Asgar. He is always with John."

"Like a PA?"

Luca laughed again. "No, like a butler. He drives John's car. I admire him for his energy and loyalty. John has given him and his family so much in return. I like the set-up in East London, where everyone chips in and donates their expertise."

It was Gianfranco's turn to chuckle. "What, pray, is your area of expertise?"

"I'm still working on that, dear brother. John really wants me to act as a sounding-board for his plans for expansion and improving healthcare. I think the fact my English is not native helps – if this Italian understands his pitches and his presentations, then the residents of East London will not be confused by it all."

"So, you mean to say you act as the lowest-common denominator of listener?"

Luca chuckled.

"Well, there's a role, I suppose, brother," Gianfranco said. "I'm not sure it's a good use of your years studying Francesco de Sanctis and Vincenzo Gioberti, is it?"

"I still have their words in my head and my heart, but modern life requires something different if I am to get along in a foreign land. My neighbours are surprised that I hold a Masters and a doctorate, but they can only hear the slip-ups I make in a foreign language and the fact I work away in a grotty post. They are only misled by facts, not prejudices. Anyway, I plan to wear this new three-piece on my days off as a badge of my civility." He laughed. "If I stay silent and let the suit speak for me, then I find the ladies of London town are intrigued. I remain almost wordless and let my eyes back up what my suit is saying."

Gianfranco grinned. "Let me raise a toast to a very smart bit of thinking."

"Anyway, more importantly, I'm just glad the antenatal check-ups were all clear," Luca said. "I cannot wait to be an uncle, a teller of our history."

"Are these your friends? The tall man and the showgirl?" Gianfranco was looking at the trattoria's front door. Tom and Claudia had arrived, looking fit for dinner at Arcadia with its lofty gallery ceilings on Piazza Castello Galleria Subalpina, not Andrea's homely trattoria with its wine jugs and treetrunk-like candles.

Claudia was not properly dressed for the squally weather, the wind shunting a small white cardboard box outside from pavement to pavement. Her silk kimono of midnight blue was wrapped around a little black dress that ended 10cm above her knees, and Tom was vainly trying to warm her up in the cradle of his right arm. It was Claudia who swooped through the door first, leaving her beau to struggle with the antiquated iron latch. A man across the street was watching their entry.

Claudia was at the tableside in one stride, her Louboutins coming to a stop noiselessly. In formal tones, she asked: "Are you the friends of John?" and, not waiting for a reply, she added: "I am delighted to finally make your acquaintance." Then she held out an immaculately manicured hand, flush with the largest garnets and emeralds. "I am Claudia, daughter of Massimo Paganino, patriarch of the most established and venerated family in all Torino. And you are?"

"I'm Luca, friend of councillor John. And this is my brother Gianfranco, de facto proctor of the University of Turin..."

"However, he is not the appointed proctor, is he?" answered Claudia. "I am very close friends with the real proctor, the one who was sworn in last year." She paused. "Does your brother often masquerade as other people?"

Gianfranco interjected: "I work with Gianni every day, and he would not mind me being introduced to you as the de facto proctor. I carry out the lion's share of his university duties, as he covers for the vice chancellor."

Claudia smiled contemptuously, but Gianfranco continued: "I feel that this introduction has started on the wrong foot, Claudia. I know of your father, Signor Paganino; he made a very welcome contribution to the new student block in the Milan quarter."

Now it was Tom's turn to attempt to restore the atmosphere of conviviality. "Now, Claudia, dear, just settle and enjoy a glass of something." He took off his black suede overcoat and handed it to a waiting Andrea. "Two bottles of whatever Luca and Gianfranco have been enjoying, please."

"We have brought in the finest Barolo for the evening, sir," Andrea replied. "All paid for."

"Well, then, let me settle any tab that remains…"

"There is no tab, no money needs to be paid. Gian and Luca are my oldest friends. This place is as much theirs as mine. We are brothers." And, with that, Andrea turned and disappeared between the aluminium fly-curtain that separated the parlour from the kitchen.

Tom was standing, fixing his shirt collar, when he caught sight of the face of the man watching from the other side of the street, his features very faintly lit by a mobile phone screen through the glass boils of the trattoria's front window. The shadowy shape then immediately moved behind the arthritic arch of a plane tree.

Tom craned his neck forward, then sat down and turned around to Luca on his left side. "You see that?"

"What?"

"No, it was nothing. Just a lone walker." Then Tom clapped his hands in precisely the same manner as his boss, councillor John. Luca took it all in. "This is a real treat," Tom beamed. "You needn't have, Luca, but I shall ply you with cocktails at the Teatro Regio."

Luca grinned. "It's a deal, Tom. I was telling Gianfranco about the good work that councillor John does for the people of the East End of London. The new surgery over by Aldgate East looks like something out of a James Bond film." Luca paused and smiled at his brother. "Gianfranco is civically minded as well, always pushing for better student accommodation; it's so important when his charges are mostly from other countries. Even England." And then he laughed.

"Well, John's work makes life better for the other end of the age spectrum, I guess," said Tom. "I haven't seen the Aldgate East surgery, but I had a minor operation on my right Achilles at a place of his in Mile End last year."

Claudia piped up. "You should stop jogging around everywhere at your age in those shoes of yours. They're meant for Astroturf, not jogging on the banks of the Po. You're not 21 any more. You're 39."

"I know that, dear. However, I must remain fit to squire the princess of Piedmont from beauty treatment to dress fitting, and then to her couch." The other men caught the sarcasm of Tom's words, but Claudia simply nodded away, her eyes closed as if dreaming of her giltwood chaise longue, an army of stylists toiling away at her face and fingertips. Truth is, she was bored of all the pleasantries.

"Of course, such beauty must be maintained," exclaimed Gianfranco. "You wouldn't let the Roman Palatine Gate slide into disrepair, would you? Young minds must be nurtured, just as ageless beauty should be preserved. This is the key to our betterment."

Tom chuckled. "You're reading my mind, my friend. All the money I have left over once I've attended to the fair Claudia is spent on my apartment. I bought it a long time ago and I have crafted every square millimetre, every nanometre. It's my baby, a thank-you to the people of Turin. I have renovated what was once a ruin so that future generations may enjoy it."

Luca beamed. "The people who come to our city always bring something to it. Torino Open City. My brother here knows many of the English; he can introduce you to them."

"It will be my pleasure," Gianfranco added. "There's always a party going on."

Luca grinned again. "Isn't that why we all go to university? For the good times and the drinking?"

"And the betterment of ourselves," his brother finished.

Andrea brought over the latest pair of wine bottles, and two glasses for the Englishmen and his lady. "There is plenty more in the cellar. And I don't plan on closing any time soon."

Tom took a bottle and read the label. "Cordero di Montezemolo Monfalletto. This is not the cheap plonk, is it, boys?"

"Tom, we always create an occasion here whenever Luca comes back to his mother city. He was telling me about the flying lesson you gave him, high above France?"

"Oh, yes, Gianfranco. It was as much a treat for me to have a passenger in my little plane as it was for Luca to take the controls. He was good – maybe he can learn properly, fly away from the post office."

Claudia had finished her glass in no time. "You are always flying people you barely know from London to Turin."

"Friends," said Tom through a grimace.

"And yet I never see these so-called friends again, Tom. They are like ghosts as soon as they reach our city. Where do they go to, my love?"

Her man looked a little shaken by this interjection. "They go all around the region, my dear. They travel to Asti for the fizz, Alba for the truffles, the Langhe hills. The kind of people who leave London for Italy are intrepid enough to explore all of Piedmont, not just its wonderful capital." Tom addressed Luca directly. "In fact, when I have dropped you back in London, I'm coming straight back with an elderly barrister who's settling in a villa on Lake Maggiore in the north east. He's no 'ghost'. He must recuperate after a wrist operation."

"Lucky devil,' replied Luca. "If I could retire anywhere, it would be the Borromean Islands. But I don't have a barrister's money." He laughed as he hogged the second of the bottles. "I must rely on the kindness and beneficence of friends to sate my appetites. Good shout this, Gian."

"This wine is truly the nectar of Bacchus himself, isn't it, Luca?"

"Where did you get this from?"

"That's my secret, as guardian of the university cellars, Luca. One of the many perks of being the de facto proctor is liberating those bottles that do not suit the palate of the chancellor and his immediates. For no reason of taste, Signor Bigetti does not hold with this Barolo. I believe it was a political decision on his wife's part."

"Well, Signora Bigetti has let her politics deprive her palate of a special grape," said Tom. "Each to their own. I've never got on with the humble pig. I just picture it slathered in mud when I try to tackle a breakfast sausage."

"You continue to eat those English sausages, Tom," countered Claudia. "I can find nothing good to say about English cuisine. Were I ever to come to England, I would need to freeze-dry some of my mama's meals, or else die of poisoning and obesity."

Tom laughed. "There is little or no chance of you ever deigning to come to my country, so I won't be fitting a makeup cabinet to the back of the Cessna." He patted Claudia on the shoulder of her kimono and smiled. "I'm not about to whisk the city's main jewel away. Turin can keep her Elgin Marbles here safe," he whispered.

Luca was smiling, but he couldn't help but find the dynamic of Tom and Claudia's sparring-rich relationship a little outside his definition of a coupling. Claudia kept her eyes down in the manner of Lady Diana, Princess of Wales, and this, in unison with her habit of near-whispering from the corner of her glossy lips, made her unfathomable. Claudia appeared to present the world with a beautiful mask, wonderful to behold but sorely lacking in communication.

There were several Claudias who were born and bred within the old city limits, but the majority slipped away in the direction of Rome, either in the passenger seat of the latest Ferrari or on the express train with a change of clothes and a gargantuan case. It was their choice, and he called it the traditional diaspora of the sumptuous females. Good luck to them, thought Luca – this was not London, where women were gaining their rightful claim to equality. Turin was a decade or two behind in granting options to women who were quite content to act as the matriarchs and engine rooms of the traditional Torino families.

Rome was the place for the quick-minded and ambitious; others, such as Gianfranco himself, found in their Piedmont home a familiarity and warmth that the capitals of Europe largely were without. Turin itself, the fourth-largest Italian city, was well aware of its place in the scheme of things, reacting to events elsewhere, but, not for more than a century, ever kick-starting change itself.

When Rome became the capital of the Kingdom of Italy in 1871, and later the Italian Republic, so Turin concentrated on preserving himself as the cradle of Italian liberty, rich in culture and history, a grand old dame looking south to its elder but facelifted sister on the shores of the Tiber. Rome was always in flux, and no doubt Claudia, a creature of no little leisure, would find the capital's constant quest for pertinence most tiresome. Claudia was Turin through and through, thought Luca. Her confidence and defined parameters were most admirable.

"Luca, Luca, you seem away with the angels, brother?" Gianfranco was clicking his fingers at a point some 30cm in front of the daydreamer. "Tom, we've been drinking for some hours, so we'll act as pacemakers – you go ahead with the wines."

Tom was still nursing his first glass, musing on the man he'd spotted across from the trattoria. Anyway, Claudia was protective of his health and form, if not his spiritual wellbeing, so she'd stop him from chugging the wine. That, at the same time, didn't stop Claudia from enjoying a liquid dinner, swapping a proper meal for two or three large beakers of Barolo. She was a happy drunk; in fact, Tom wondered if his life would have been rosier if she had slowly slid into a light form of alcoholism – not the stage where the washing machine rattles with half-bottles of vodka, but that point where the corkscrew needs a colleague or two to divvy out the labour.

Tom poured out the remainders of the wine bottle. "I've been dancing around the idea of donating the money to a local society. It's been in my mind for some months. Do you have people who help your English students to settle in, for instance?"

Gianfranco smiled. "Now you are trying to oust me from my duties, Tom?"

"No, no. I didn't mean that."

"I know, I know, Tom." Gianfranco smiled.

Tom continued: "When my best friend, Sam, and I arrived in Turin in a hot rush at the end of the Nineties, we didn't know our arse from our elbow. There were a great many differences between Piemontese society and that back home in Kent, and Sammy in particular was forever shunted from no-hope job to no-hope job. I had something to do, via councillor John; my father used to knock around Soho with him back in the day, so he gave me a liaison job with ex-pats who needed legal counsel and paid for me to study for a law degree. But for him, I would have been totally lost. I suppose that's your role at the university – to shepherd the lost sheep who arrive from foreign climes."

"I try my best, but the university has enough resources. Tell me more about our mutual friend John and your work for him." Gianfranco's gaze was fixed upon Tom, who seemed rather taken aback by its force.

"Well, there's not that much to add to what's been said and to what your brother has probably told you. I came across to reduce the risk of John's English friends here being preyed upon – rich retirees who spoke next-to-no Italian. My best friend would help with their day-to-day acclimatisation and sort out rental homes or property to buy, if they hadn't a place here already. Sam doesn't speak much Italian, but he really knows how to find a bargain – and the old boys love him because he has a regal mien."

"Mien?" asked Gianfranco.

"Sam has the air of royalty – until he opens his mouth, and a lilting Scots brogue comes out, rather than the usual plummy tones. Anyway, John entrusted us both with the care of his circle of friends who came to Piedmont, often to recover in the healthy air around Lake Maggiore. There were a couple of settlers here in Turin, but the Brits who could afford it normally chose a little living space by the lake, though away from the ski slopes, given that most were pushing 70. In time, I pushed for a part-time role, since the flood of arrivals slowed down to a trickle and I wished to invest my money in my own business. This is slightly different to John's; I focus upon wills and legacies, rather than prolonging and upgrading the lives of the elderly. Much gets lost in translation from language to language, from jurisprudence to jurisprudence. I try to catch that slippage. And now that Sam's gone, I tend to spend all my time on drawing up wills. I couldn't begin to tell you where the best property bargains are to be unearthed, but I can make sure that those who are on the way out shore up their assets and make provisions for any loved ones they are to leave behind."

Gianfranco relaxed his gaze and looked at Claudia. "And so, Tom, do these ex-pats tend to have loved ones in London and England?"

Tom stiffened up and set down his glasses. "That depends on the case, Gianfranco. The nuclear family is no more, and many of my clients do not wish to make provisions for family. The flight from London is often caused by a breakdown in relations. However, for every case such as that, there are a brace where I contact the dependents and sort out bequests. Is this an area of the law that interests you?"

"I am interested in all things to do with family, I must confess." Gianfranco tapped his brother's shoulder. "This is my best friend. I'm glad Luca has found a friend-set worthy of his learnedness. London is not a place that appears too forgiving to the solo traveller. The king of one country becomes a clown in another if he doesn't know the right lingo or possess the right contacts."

Tom picked up his wine and held the glass to the light humming from trattoria's ruby pendants, stealing a quick glance at the street outside. Nothing stirred. Tom considered the contents of his goblet for a moment and brought the Barolo back down. "We seem to be agreeing on the importance of men such as John and yourself. Any place can become a home with the correct pastoral care. You need the right network of confreres, too."

"That's very true," Gianfranco nodded.

Tom gave him a weak smile. "I wouldn't be so suspicious of a man like John. He counts the Mayor of London among his trusted pals, as well as Luca and me. His wealth was not built upon nefarious activity, but rather upon hard work and the seizing of opportunities. John caught the scent of every nascent musical craze and invested in land that was rotting away in the Seventies and Eighties. Blame the ghettoisation of the East End, not dear old John with his biscuit-coloured suits. A lot of the places that used to be dens of iniquity are now providers of private and public healthcare. Do not confuse the workings of Shoreditch with those of Sicily! He's not Don John."

Gianfranco smiled. "I am just naturally cynical. Ask Luca. When our mama used to give us the day off from weekend chores to go and swim in the lakes, I would ask – "so we have double the work to do tomorrow?" Sometimes, I guess people just want to hand out reward for hard work, to allow us all to swim freely in the waters, to feel the sunshine on our faces, to enjoy nature while we can."

Tom nodded. "I wish you could meet John, but he rarely travels anywhere any more. He has these plans to go for a full MOT, blood transfusions at some Far Eastern spa, but they never amount to much."

"So you and your friend Sam acted as his adjutants in Italy?" Gianfranco asked. He caught Luca yawning in the corner of his eye.

"Adjutants is a rather militaristic word, my friend."

"Lieutenants? Fixers?" asked Gianfranco.

"'Lieutenants' is also militaristic. And 'fixers' has the ring of gangsterdom. We were more like glorified PAs."

Gianfranco raised an eyebrow.

"I don't mind the feminine tones of that, far preferable to any laddish, matey, macho bollocks, Gianfranco."

"Noted, Tom." Then Gianfranco turned sideways as his rapidly atrophying brother began to yawn. "Say, Luca – another round of limoncello? Sherry? You're not pacing yourself here."

Tom smiled; Claudia maintained her withering thousand-yard stare.

"Ah, the joys of no responsibilities, Tom – my brother was always to the manor born. He used to drag the nearest cushion under himself and say 'night, night' for the rest of the day. It's true that we never escape our true nature – I would be buried in books while Luca spent his pocket money at the patisserie."

Luca jolted awake and wiped down the corners of his mouth. "It was a long trip, apologies. I need a revivifier, yes. Maybe a sherry? Surprise me, Andrea."

The trattoria owner, who resembled a soaked young Einstein, had taken a seat next to Tommy during his long defence of councillor John, although he spoke almost no English. His response to the conversation around him was largely a collection of pantomimic tics, so he jumped at the chance to leave his seat and disappear behind the fly curtain once again in an impossibly extended hunt for a Lustau Amantillado de Sanlucar Alma.

Luca was keen to involve Claudia, her heavily mascaraed eyes still fixed on a point on the table just north of her glass. Her English was more proficient than his own, and yet she didn't display the same verve to make use of it, to improve it. "Claudia, I know your father, Signor Paganino."

"Well, he is very well-known around the city," she murmured.

"He was, and perhaps still is, the president of a little arts club of which I was a member before my move to London. Is he still organising Visconti film seasons over near Parco Dora?"

Claudia looked up, registered the over-eager cherubic features of Luca and set her glance back down on the table top with an exquisite ennui. "He doesn't like the way that district has changed – it's gone from the Fiat factories to flophouses for skaters – so he doesn't leave the apericena of San Salvario."

"Send him my best wishes," replied Luca, chastened. "I'm forever grateful to your father for getting me into films like The Damned. Visconti was dying from underexposure – he was called a dinosaur. We have much to learn from his portraits of decadence gone mad."

"Have we?" Claudia scanned the table of empty bottles, the empty china bowl with rubbings of tiramisu, and the causeway of shot glasses. "If there's a lesson out there about decadence, it seems we all rightly chose to disregard it."

Luca and Gianfranco chuckled at their indulgence.

Claudia remained stony-faced. "My father likes to view Turin as the powerhouse of Italy, not as a spruced-up, post-industrial party zone. Where was the fight against globalisation? The workers just gave in, and now we have art collectives and cathedrals to industry that host those crappy sound-and-light shows."

Gianfranco was not amused. "What were we meant to do? Just let everything wither away, not bother with repurposing the fine architecture that remained."

"We needed a bit of patience," Claudia answered.

Gianfranco scoffed at this. "And how long would the factories have stayed gathering dust as they waited for the return of the blue-collar workers?"

"A few years. It's all a cycle."

Gianfranco shuffled his chair forward and stared at Claudia. "The answer is, they were never going to come back. So we have grand arts spaces instead of factories."

"Whoop-de-do!" Claudia interjected, sarcastically.

"Well, it helps. My students can put on plays and dance spectacles that honour the way Turin drove our country for years. Pragmatism has kept our city vital, even though the game has changed. Surely Signor Paganino has himself applauded this reversal of fortunes? As a former patron of the arts?"

"My father," Claudia began sternly, with all the hauteur of one of Visconti's contessas, "my father was never a patron of fads; he was a preserver of the same traditions that made Turin great. He walked the boulevards in his youth and recruited those men who also believed in the city's primacy, before even Rome."

"He's a great man," Luca slurred, quietly.

"If we all had shared my father's civic pride back in the Eighties," Claudia continued, "then the Fiat and Paracchi factories would still be thriving. Several hundred thousands of our brothers would not have been expelled south or overseas. Is it any wonder my father has given up on the wider city, decades after Turin gave up on herself?"

"Market forces did for the city…" Gianfranco started.

"My father barricades himself in our family home. This "new" and "revitalised" Turin is a sham – like a grande dame dressed up in punk clothes, pretending she's a cool, edgy student. No, the way she holds herself betrays her true nature. Leave this faddism to cities like Hamburg or Berlin or Barcelona. My Turin is still there, but it's limited now. The Piemontesi draw strength from within." Claudia pointed to the sherry that Andrea had brought to the lazy Susan in the centre of the round table. "I mean, what is that piss?"

Andrea looked confused, but Gianfranco exploded at her rudeness. "Turin is an open city now. We were the first to expand the outlook of all Italians. No one wants to live in a museum, decaying, dusty, of no purpose. The Piemontesi were being left behind – all their futures hung on Fiat, on Michelin; all our youths left Piedmont and were too naïve to thrive even down south; and all their meals were soaked in butter and garnished with truffles. Great dinners perhaps they were, but who wants the same dish of agnolotti Piemontese for two centuries or more? Now we have plentiful options on how we chose to live, we can pursue many careers within these city walls, we can eat our risotto with lemongrass and drink Spanish sherry, and men like Luca can wing their way abroad to the most dynamic city on Earth and thrive. How is all that a sham, Claudia? Adapt and survive – all the burgeoning cities in the world have had to take this phrase as their shibboleth, and Turin is no different. It angers me when I see people moaning about my students bringing their "ways" into our city. What does that mean? These young people are not the same as the former European rulers laying down their modes of thought and telling us how we had to be, under the cosh. We can cherry-pick from a marvellous bouquet of influences now, we can create a design for living from a wider template. Turin is a laboratory now, not a factory, no, but not a museum either. You should take your father and walk arm in arm through Barriera di Milano, where, instead of its broken windows and cobwebbed doorways, the Docks Dora boast artists creating wonderful glassware and artworks. The warehouse hums with creative endeavour. Your father will be full of civic pride once again. The grande dame has thrown her mansion open to the poets dying in the gutters outside. You cannot fail to feel proud of that. Turin Open City is born again."

Claudia said nothing for a few seconds and then announced she needed to powder her nose. Tom got up to pull out her chair, his eyes still fixed on the plane tree outside in the shadows, and Andrea led her to the top of the basement stairs and gave her directions. The table was still silent when he returned to his seat. He charged the men's glasses.

Tom could now understand why he had never integrated himself fully into Torinese society. The city was still fractured, some 30 years after most of the factories had closed their doors, and there were many who were hibernating in the false hope that the glory days would return. Those street scenes of families waltzing in their finest garb were just as much a period piece as Tornatore's Cinema Paradiso. It wasn't real. Through his closeness to Claudia, he had been colluding in this denial of reality, perhaps not hibernating himself, but certainly not exploring those areas off his jogging course.

Tom had never once stepped foot inside the Museo Egizio to see for himself how the Egyptian artefacts in the archaeology museum now shimmered with light in mirrored rooms that had been remodelled by Dante Ferretti. The very ancient was now housed in the ultra-modern; the present day was protecting the priceless treasures, the ages-old Drovetti sarcophagi, the Books of the Dead and the Kings Assembly, all recast and served by 21st-century artistry. Hadn't this credo been replicated throughout Turin? Wasn't this credo behind Gianfranco's own efforts to refresh the old modes of thought with young thinkers from abroad? Turin was still a powerhouse, ranked third in the Italian economy behind Milan and Rome, but she was not as powerful as she had been. New blood might revive her once more.

Tom now addressed the university man. "Gianfranco, would you be kind enough to show me this cultural regeneration one afternoon? It sounds similar to what's been going on in my humbler home town on the south-east coast of England."

Gianfranco nodded. "I would be delighted."

"Thank you."

"Tom, I have students who play football in Parco Dora and others who play baseball in the Campus Luigi Einaudi near the river. It's a lively city. We'll show you a very good time – and perhaps Claudia if she's of the mood."

Tom smiled. "Claudia is more adaptable than she first appears."

Gianfranco nodded. "She argues her case well. From the opposite side of the debate, I can see that she is a very educated woman, well versed in the history of our city. I can make friends with anyone who can hold up one end of a debate. It's a dying art. Blame Twitter."

Luca piped up. "It's all lost in the text-speak nowadays. It's all 140 characters or fewer. You can't put across your views in a micro-debate." He got up uneasily from his chair. "Gentlemen, please excuse me. I need a comfort break and to wash my face." He threw his napkin onto the table and into his sherry. "Be right back."

As Gianfranco and Tom planned an expedition into Barriera di Milano, and Andrea pretended to comprehend with a nod here and a raised eyebrow there, Luca descended into the basement with its pink bougainvillea flock wallpaper and sat on the wicker chair beside the door to the single washroom. He could hear Claudia inside, coughing into the paper handtowels.

When she emerged, Luca stood up. "I didn't mean to... I mean, I meant what I said about your father."

Claudia smelt of lavender and had reapplied her makeup. "Thanks. And I'm sorry to enter a debate about our home city with your brother when we both clearly love Turin." She looked around the stacked chairs and tables in the well-lit basement. "Are all these ever used? There must be another 20 seats down here, and yet your friend Andrea seems to be the only waiter, as well as the chef-patron."

"It's never open down here. Andrea is a one-man band – well, his wife does the accounts. I don't come back as often as I should. I'll come more often, I say, and I never do. But now, now I feel spooky. London feels spooky."

Claudia sat down on the first step and looked at Luca's suddenly crestfallen face. "But at least you've tried to make a life in England. I've never even left Torino. You should be proud to have made a go. Is that what you say?"

"Your English is better than mine. And you have never been to London, or England. I don't feel a lot of good about myself right now, and my home is really here." Luca paused as a wave of nausea swept over him. He leaned forward a little in the wicker chair, the rolls of his thick waist pressing through its curved arms. "I love the city, don't get me wrong, but sometimes London is too harsh. I look at it with eyes of wonder, you know, but my eyes see things that they don't want to see. And my mind doesn't stop. My mind is like the waves."

Claudia saw his eyes begin to water. "Would you like to talk about it? Because we don't know one another but we're compatriots. Tell me, so perhaps I can help you?"

Luca wiped his right eye with the cuff of his shirt. "Thank you. I need to get this off my chest because it's been all I have thought about for ages. Let's switch back to Italian."

"Go on, Luca," and Claudia held her hands on her knees.

"Well, I can explain this more easily now. My life has been actually very good for the past few months, but it's come at the expense of my morals. Gianfranco and I were raised in the correct fashion by our mama. I have been silent and I have received rewards for not speaking, and now I must tell you the horrendous events I witnessed this year. I saw the deaths of an old man and his daughter, one beaten in front of me, the other snuffed out at a party, John's party…"

Claudia's eyes widened. She moved to hold Luca's hand, but it was grasping his bowed head. "Was John involved in these murders, Luca?"

"I don't know. People around him die – overdoses. The old man was taken away in a car the councillor uses, and he told me not to say a word about the Polish woman who was killed in his flat. Their blood was not literally on his hands, Claudia, but he was the one who told me to be silent. And in return, he watered me, he fed me, he confided in me and he arranged for your Tom to fly me here. I don't have a lot of money, you see; I live a financially precarious life; and I feel my silence has been bought. I am aware that I have played along with all this but it sits so heavily on my soul, Claudia, that even during the moments of indulgence, even as I sup the finest Barolo and dance with all the young girls who adore John, I have this flashing images of the old man there in the dirt, blood in his white hair, just a bundle of clothes, kicked into lifelessness; and that poor young woman, snuffed out just a moment after she was laughing and carefree… And that frail little bird Milena."

Claudia was still. Her hands gripped her knees and her mouth was agape. After half a minute, she spoke. "Luca, I have long suspected there's a darker side to Tom and John's business dealings, but this, this is incomprehensible. Are you sure that John is involved in murder? Tom idolises him, and although I don't like the sound of him, this flatterer and networker, John is well respected in London. Tom tells me of all the awards he wins; he even has an honorary doctorate somewhere. Are you sure he didn't just panic? Tom has never mentioned any wrongdoing."

Luca brushed the sweat from his forehead and wiped it into his suit trousers. "I don't think Tom knows the full story," he said. "And John didn't touch those two people. I didn't see him order anything to be done to them. I just saw him after the Polish woman's suffocation and he just acted as if it was normal. John told me the old man and his daughter were sleeping together and that they were deviants who wanted to blackmail him and his business partners. They were rival operators, who wanted serious money and to derail plans for more practices. I don't know why."

"Yes but that doesn't warrant their murders? Why kill them? Are you scared?"

"I am only scared of speaking out, because life has been good to me since I've been silent about all this, and the same thugs who killed the old man and the girl could easily hurt me or end my life. That's what I am facing – the war between my conscience and my survival. And I am the king of convenience." He chuckled but then stopped himself. "Most of the time, I reason that I can't do anything – I'm just a post office worker in a strange, foreign city; John and his friends are in its engine room. I swear there were police officers at some of the parties in John's flat. They have his back. Who would listen to a fat idiot like me?"

"I'm listening to you. And I'm sure that Tom would help you if he knew the seriousness of what you're telling me now."

Luca's face whitened even further.

Claudia held his hand. "As I said, I swear on the Bible that Tom has never mentioned any wrongdoing. You know, I sometimes see the passengers he brings over to Italy in his Cessna; they aren't ghosts, just nearly dead and very old. He doesn't bring corpses to Turin. Tom's story stacks up. But I don't know this John. And, you know, some party people overdo it."

Luca stared at Claudia. A calm settled over his face. "You know, all this." He paused to collect his thoughts. "I'm just making this up. There were no murders. I, I was just overreacting to a beating I saw on the lawn outside my block. This old man was getting a kicking from some youths who wanted his wallet. I helped him up – he was groggy but told me his name was David – then I called the police. They came immediately, took statements from me and David, but they didn't catch the guys. Claudia, forgive me. I'm telling tales. I'm just very drunk. I was bullshitting because I wanted to appear interesting to you."

Claudia looked confused, but he did look pickled. Luca continued, weaving together a different story, stitching a new hide with which to save his own skin. "What I mean to say is that the old man didn't die; nor did the girl," he lied. "In fact, I saw her at the Polish salon just before Tom flew me over. Her name is… Marlena. She waved, she waved at me on Commercial Street. I walk past the salon every day and sometimes stop in to chat, so she knows me. You see, I lied about the killings just now. I'm just very drunk, Claudia. I am just very tired, too. I'm blabbering and I just wanted to speak to you as you're very beautiful." As evidence of what he was saying, Luca slumped forward and fell between Claudia's knees. He lifted up his head to her hands and kissed her left fingernails.

"Luca! Ugh. You are drunk. You're just a swine." She got up from the step and kicked out at the back of his head as he clawed at her little dress and kimono. She brushed off his clammy hands and hissed, "Get off me!" and then raced back upstairs into the parlour so Tom could take her home. She claimed to the table that she had been vomiting up wine for the past ten minutes.

Luca picked himself up from his disgraced slump and walked into the washroom. Taking in his perspiring reflection in the black moisture spots of the circular mirror, he told himself: "Ah, you. You may have just offended the prettiest girl in all of Turin, Luca, but you have just saved your skin, dear boy. Adapt and survive."

Luca turned on the cold tap and cupped its water into his face. He would have to excuse himself and come up with a plan for missing the Vivaldi concert – he couldn't face Claudia again. Luca would offer his ticket for the Teatro Regio to darling Monica and blame his hangover and a little gout for his change of heart. And on the flight back home on Saturday in the tiny Cessna, he would assure Tom that his mind was still set on silence and on protecting John's family of friends. He was just a lush, that's all, he would say, and apologise for pawing at Claudia if she were to reveal this to Tom.

That would be for another day, however. Scanning the drops of water running down his flushed cheeks, Luca whispered to himself, "It will all be fine," before shambling back upstairs to pick up his suit jacket and head home with his brother.

Into the warren.

"Just edge up as close as you can to the corner, Sammy. That's it. Let's get a good look at the front door." Nena was director of operations, in the passenger seat of Cadwick's elderly Mercedes 280E, its hubcaps originally the same black as the bodywork but now tarnished to anthracite grey. "Have you got the birdwatching binoculars?"

I parked up and leaned over to the back seat. "Here you go." I handed Nena the binos. "Are you going to sit with me for all of my shifts?"

"Of course. We can talk a bit more about River, yes?"

I looked at her. "Are you sure about moving out of the salon?"

"I'll still work out of there. I won't need a house with an outbuilding. I'll hop on the bus every morning."

"I might be able to drive you into Sandgate, depending on the job I get. I've put my hat in the ring for a couple of property agent jobs. Cadders says it should be a doddle finding me a post, given how much experience I gained out in Piedmont."

"Getting the bus will help me get into a routine," Nena said. "I think part of the problem has been that I can just tumble out of bed and go downstairs in about a minute. So I've become a bit slobbish."

I laughed. "Yes, I'd noticed that – even Tommy is tidier than you…"

"Well, I'll sort it out. I'll probably turn the back room into a coffee and waiting room, so I can get rid of the sofa and put in another couple of basins. I can hire a girl to work part-time, someone from the local college who wants to do salon work. Cheap as chips."

I nodded. "You need a website as well, which I can sort out for you. That'll increase the salon's profile and pay for the extra pair of hands."

"Good idea, Samuel."

"I think we need only a two-bed in River; it's not like we'll have any family to stay with us, just maybe a Cadders too drunken to roll into a taxi."

Nena smiled. "He's on the next shift, so I'm going to sit with him as well."

"Hussy!"

"The salon glass is coming the day after tomorrow, so that's when I'll open up again, as soon as the men have left. So, I'll do all day today and tomorrow in this tired old jalopy." She looked across the vinyl and chrome of the elderly lady. "Do you think Cadders would let us use her?"

"I think that boy would give us his houses if we only asked. What a good friend to have. I know how he feels, or has felt, about you, and it's all fine with me."

"Really?" Nena studied my face for signs of falsehood.

"Yes, of course. He's taken care of you, and vice versa – you were free from any responsibilities when I came back. I mean, I see Cadders as a kind of chaperone to you – all those nights you could've been fending off guys in the bars around here, you were actually semi-comatose at the back of the salon with him. He kept you single and childless and neatly pickled in gin so you're even more lovely than when we used to arse around town in the Nineties."

Nena laughed. "You have a very strange way of looking at things, Sammy; your mind's like a Catherine Wheel, shooting off these sparks. I don't think I've ever had a dull moment in your company."

"Oh, you most certainly have."

"I mean, look at us – staking out a house in the type of car that an American detective might drive." She looked down into the footwell. "Swap the gin and shortbread biscuits for a hip-flask of whisky and some doughnuts and we're there, Hutch. It's a strange road we walk down, isn't it?"

"We were never cut out for a normal life. Tommy used to say the very same to me. 'Why is it that you've ended up in Turin, Sammy? You never wanted to travel, you never wanted to learn another language and culture. I see you wandering around the city like the eternal tourist. You ended up here because you're my best friend.' I suppose most things are decided for us. If my best mate had been Harry, not Tommy, then I might've at least stayed in Britain, but I too might have died out on the M20. Our plans are always dependent on our nearest and dearest; they are not our own. I wouldn't be here in this car if it weren't for my parents dying and leaving me the cabin. I wouldn't be here with you. I'd be in Turin, probably sitting with Tommy on that bench again by the Dora Riparia, talking bollocks and watching the sunset dip."

Nena reached over and held my left hand in hers. "Do you miss Tommy?"

"I only miss him when you're not here. I think he'll be over soon enough. He's ended up in this situation because he always does what's expected of him."

"I would have thought it's the very opposite?" Nena asked me.

"No, he was always expected to break away from it all and to have a beautiful woman. Don't you remember all those times we'd be in the pub and Tommy would disappear to go to a better, livelier party? You'd turn around, and he and Harry would've gone. Tommy seemed to have a portal – he could teleport from Sandgate High Street to The Leas in the blink of an eye, like a column of air you couldn't grab hold of. I found it exasperating. In Turin, he had no other place to go to, so the opposite was true, but until he found Claudia, or rather it was suggested that they find one another, Tommy was forever bouncing around, trying to please him, her, them, you name it. It's why he always gets clients – they can see he'd work a 25-hour day just to please them. Claudia recognises this and gets him to act as her butler. Tommy knows she's like a trophy; trouble is, the rest of the world gets to see the best of her. Tommy just catches her without her make-up and designer threads every morning before he heads off. It's the queens she hangs out with who get her smiles. She's perhaps the sharpest gal out there. She always achieves what she wants."

"So you think Tom dragged you away from your rightful destiny, Sammy?"

"No, I think he helped a friend in need and, in return, he expected me to act as his side-man. It was my own fault I didn't come back here sooner. My lethargy kicked in, and to keep pace with Tommy, at work and play, was frankly exhausting. I should have found the energy to make a break, but you know how it is when your work and living arrangements are just handed to you."

Nena took her hand away to draw a porthole in the side window's condensation; the heater was taking care of the windscreen. "The salon was what I'd wished for, and it worked out for me for more than a decade. And yet I would still be in that back room at 60, now the same age as my clients, perhaps the gin would have caught up with me, and perhaps Cadders would've met his girl and moved her into his west London pad. We always assume that the people around us will meld seamlessly into our great plans, but the truth is, they're more likely to change our destiny, which is what happened to you and Tommy. He showed you that the grass is not always greener – these stunning women can bring trouble too, and no one can play the role of the eternally young boulevardier for twenty years. Something's gotta give in all things."

"I arranged much of my business by phone and then the internet, and I rarely ever went to the viewings themselves, not that it made the blind bit of difference. All the old boys and girls fell in love with Italy within the first day and often accepted the very first place that I arranged for them to view. Once you build up a network of trust with an agent who speaks good English and knows your requirements to a tee, then it all becomes very robotic. And I didn't have any distractions, just my cot in a quiet corner of the palazzo."

"So how did you spend all those years, Sammy?" She looked frightened.

"Doing nothing. My folks would visit and tell me it had been six months since I'd last seen them; then we'd Skype and when they came over and stayed at the Piazza Carlina, they'd think they'd seen me last week. It's the same with everyone – these gadgets and apps close down the space and distance between us all and create false realities. My parents felt like they were just around the corner, after all the conversations we'd had using Skype and FaceTime."

"God, I wish we could have done that. I guess Alistair and Sandy never lost their son, though?"

"No, we were always in touch. They knew exactly where I was, that I was somehow thriving, with a secure job and a rent-free roof over my head. And we chatted every other day. I think to know that one's son is safe and well is all any parent truly desires. My folks had busier social lives up in Berwickshire than I did."

"What's happening to the farmhouse now?"

"This whole palaver with the break-in and the car, all of that, has meant I've not done much," I said. "I know that my folks' best friends are staying there for the next couple of months as they are selling their own place and it's all in limbo. They're paying over the market price, but I couldn't stop them, so I'll use that cash to market the farmhouse and get it sold on. It's too far away from us here, and I have all my memories wrapped up in what's in the cabin. I don't know why that is; it just is. We don't choose our memories, do we?"

"We can at least make use of all that lovely furniture in the new place."

"Aye, Nena. Once I've bought the house, I'll hire some Duns removal guys to bring it all down here, but the farmhouse can go. I'll give Mimi some money as she needs all the help she can get, and the rest will go as a float and on repairs to whatever cottage we decide to do up. I can't live in a modern home; that one thing I will make clear."

"You love your old ladies, don't you?"

"I hope you're not being self-deprecating again. You could pass for 30 if you smiled a bit more." I grinned as I surveyed the empty road ahead. "Here's a bit dull."

"Well, it's better than Cheriton. The East Cliff is for families and it does have nice views, but I couldn't live here; most of the houses aren't old enough for me. I need something pre-Edwardian, something with a raft of tales in its rafters. We should get a tumbledown cottage that breathes with us, that grows old with us."

"So you don't want a project?"

Nena chuckled and watched a young mother guide her toddler across the front of no33 Chambois Close. "I want a sensitive renovation of something with a history, something that will keep your firecracker mind occupied and keep you away from the sofa of your lethargy. You know me – I want the bloody pink moon on a stick."

"Having not paid rent for years, Nena, even on my meagre salary, commissions and tips included, we should be able to bag an old lady by auction. Cadwick has been sniffing around River since your conversation with him at The Grand. With a couple of hundred grand to buy a cottage outright, and another hundred thousand to sensitively renovate the place, we should be able to get a three-bed home. I can use the third bedroom to write that novel that I've bored you and Cadders to death about." I laughed. "Everyone's a writer these days. 'Blog this, review that – God, you're brilliant, babes.'"

"You should base your book in the realities of living in an old city in Italy. That way, I can guess at the mysteries of your life between 18 and 38. Which bits of the novels are fact and which bits are just feverish fiction? It could be your way of subtly divulging the saltier details to the woman you're about to set up home with? Aren't the best debut novels all semi-autobiographical?"

"I wouldn't know. Surely that's the task of the reader – to winkle-pick the fact from the fiction? I don't buy into the idea that a novel is like a naked person stripped of all disguise – there is such a thing as a double-bluff, and there are many ways of subtly wrongfooting the readers. They are entering a world where this old Merc can be transformed into a gleaming red Ferrari, a car that once carried Grace Kelly to a mystery date with Prince Rainier. The only way to know that something is fact is surely to live it, to be there when it happens – even television footage can be doctored, and we live in an age of fake news. Just as my folks lived content in the knowledge that I was surviving and physically all right, so we all live with what facts are given to us. But we should challenge those truths, shouldn't we? And it should be enough for you to know that I've survived. My future will be lived by both of us. You'll be right by my side; you share the same covenant. Isn't that enough?"

"I'm not desperate to unearth and experience all that's happened to you since we both left school. Only I'm convinced that it might help me to live a better life with you." She looked across at me.

"It might also screw things up if we're too hung up on the past we've spent living apart. Why does everyone always assume that the 'other life' would have been better? I thought we'd agreed at Loaf that our separation might have spared us from killing one another? We were too young, and now we're sitting here in this old car, both fit and healthy, without any encumbrances. And by that, yes, I mean 'kids'."

"I suppose I won't ask you any more questions about Turin…"

I cut her off. "Yeah, right – now you're going to be creeping into that third bedroom and sneak-reading the skeleton of my novel for clues as to what the hell I was up to on my great Italian adventure, aren't you?"

"As if I could do that without you knowing."

"Well, I might just switch on my bullshit generator and make the whole book an unbelievable work of fiction. I'll recast myself as a clone of Jacqui but with 44D tits. And I'd be the advisor to the Obamas, a former NASA astronaut who can turn paper into gold, and all of the shit."

"Stop it now. I get the point." Nena paused. "Tell me, Sam. Aren't you going to be bored by switching housemate? From Tom the great roisterer to Nena who's spent two decades in a 70 square-metre box in Sandgate?"

"I've been living in a small room in the windowless corner of Turin where absolutely no one likes to show that they've spent even a minute learning English. The Piemontesi are very insular."

"I want to go there soon. I want to see your little dog basket in Tommy's boy cave of an apartment." Nena laughed. "Good Sammy can have a Bonio."

I put my palm on her denim thigh. "I'm sure you and I will be hopping over there in Tommy's little Cessna SP-172 soon." I paused. "How do you manage to keep in such shape without doing any exercise? It's one of the marvels of the Western world how standing up with a pair of scissors and pickling yourself with gin have left you with the body of an amateur runner."

"A liquid diet has a great deal going for it. And plus, we've been hiking all over the hills of coastal east Kent for several weeks and you've been using my body as an amusement park, to quote Seinfeld. That's bound to keep a gal fit."

"You mustn't tell Tommy how we've managed to shed the timber," I said. "It would crucify him to think all those lonely miles around the Po may have been unnecessary. He could have joined us at the bar for a gin n slim and then worked off the booze calories with some hussy in town. He should've gone up Tontine Street and got himself some tail."

"So that's where you ended up with him last week? I did wonder."

"No, we went to the titty bar, not the prossie parlour. Don't worry, darling." I slapped and gripped Nena's thigh, and she let out a tiny gasp.

"Don't touch what you can't afford." Nena scanned the road ahead and saw absolutely nothing. "You know how I said I'd be right here with you today and tomorrow? Well, I'm currently reviewing that promise. They don't show these boring interludes when the Hollywood hero is on stake-out."

"It would make for a very dull thriller if they did. At least it's only three hours at a time." That was more than enough for me.

"I've promised to do nine today. Shall we break open the gin? It always has the effect of compressing time into a manageable chunk for me."

"It's only 10am, Nena. You're going to have to cut down on the pop when we're doing up our tumbledown cottage by the river, you know."

"OK, Dad!"

I half-frowned. "Nothing gets done when the booze starts flowing. We're about to get very busy indeed. I hope you know that?"

"Yes, Dad!" Nena was laughing.

"I need you to be clear-eyed when you come back from the salon. I don't want Cadders getting you hammered and then pouring you into the back of a cab, so I receive a puddle of a partner in River. Is that understood?"

"Yes. I'll lay off the juice until Cadders starts his three-hour shift." Nena then spoke in a babydoll voice. "I promise, daddy, I promise." She stopped her poor attempt at a Yankee accent and looked down the bonnet of the black car. "We didn't see anyone fitting Joseph's description yesterday, so he's due to visit today, right?"

"Yes, it's pretty clear he'll show up at some point today, Nena."

"He's going to stick out when he turns up – it's been largely mums and kids this morning. Some 6ft of muscled oddball will stand out."

I squinted through the windscreen. Nobody was around. "I expect your shift to be the busiest, from 3pm to 6pm; the school run, people coming home from work. We're just seeing mothers returning from school and the shops."

"Sammy, I'm glad you don't want to be part of this world."

"If you promise to put an end to getting pissed every afternoon, Nena, then I'll promise that we can go to a rescue centre. We'll get a little furry shit-machine that will take my place. I know which vow is going to be easier to keep."

Nena snorted. "That's true. Cadders and I are well aware of our drunken days. It's written in the very backbone of the contract we drew up together years ago, like the vein of shit that runs through a prawn."

"You cannot hole up in the bunker of your back room. If you think that, without parents, you're just this atom bouncing around in that little fortified box, then the world will always scare you. We have to be proactive now. That's why we're here waiting on our chum Joseph to return home."

"I've been getting bored of it all – it's no longer fun to surf a hangover all day. And I can't vouch that Cadders is going to be around here for ever – he's convinced that he'll be married within a year, and then it's off to Kensington for the little man and his spouse."

"How can he be so sure?" I was genuinely puzzled.

"Public-school confidence?"

"I mean, Nena, he's a wonderful chap, and if he makes it his year's mission, then I suppose so, but it all involves a lot of luck."

"That's true."

"Finding someone who isn't a) an enormous arsehole, b) available, and c) into you, is such a vast undertaking that even those who devote their lives to Tinder and Match.com end up chasing shadows."

Nena sighed. "Rather sweetly, Cadders is unswervingly convinced that your return is a herald of good times for all three of us Musketeers. It might be a formerly Rubenesque old classmate of his…"

"Didn't he go to an all-boys' school?" I interjected.

"Okay, all right. Maybe a Rubenesque former work acquaintance, or perhaps a waitress he was chasing who has seen the light and who now views our dear friend as the perfect amalgam of every chivalrous hero of the silver screen. I don't know. Cadders just has this ingrained belief that if he works hard enough at something, then it will come good. It's probably a public-school thing. You see it in the politicians we have, their eyes unblinking and their opinions cast in titanium. Cadwick has that conviction, but he uses it in his pursuit of the ideal woman."

"It's also brought him a good deal of cash…" I chuckled.

"Well, that's another story. You don't want to know what a king shit his father was. I do believe, though, that Cadders will find his Queen Guinevere soon. He's persistent and he plays the percentages game like a maestro – he gives himself every chance in all of his pursuits."

"Have you met his female friends?"

"They've largely moved to London, so, no, I haven't been introduced to them. I don't go up to the capital; the Smoke and I don't get on. There's a sense of entitlement shared by the place and its inhabitants – people park their cars wherever the hell they like and sometimes don't wait for them to stop before getting out. It's heavily polluted, literally and figuratively; I couldn't breathe. I'd always feel like a failure, like the backroom staffer peeking through the velvet drapes at the most impossibly glamorous party of the well-connected and well-dressed. I think London has to happen to you at an early age when you have the energy to meet it head on, or else you will tire quickly and its great big foam-roller will swallow you up. You're entering a game of roulette whenever you cross the M25 – success or sadness; salad days or slumdog times. You never know. A great city feeds on the energies of its inhabitants and then when they are sapped, it feeds on the inhabitants. Tommy acted as your buffer – his energy would've protected you from any attempts Turin made to swallow you up whole."

"It's quite easy to fly under the radar in a bustling city, as long as you have an income and a bed. But I wouldn't have survived without Tommy. He is splendidly resourceful and tireless."

"And he must know the type of women whom Cadders runs after – you know, the posh types who've lived a life?"

"Yes, Tommy has a ring of people in London. It's how we got our clients in the early days before Claudia introduced him to the Italians. We helped out the English, the East London set, and there were always young women, even if 95 per cent of our clients were geriatric. You know, property agents in Greenwich, will executors in Hackney, London Fields, and such like? But whether Tommy's going to go to London any time soon is debatable. I got the feeling after our lads' night out that he wants to come back to Folkestone now I'm here and split his time half here, half in Turin. He sees some business in the regeneration of the Cultural Quarter, whether it's the bricks and mortar or the preparation of wills for the aged population. I don't know. If Claudia realises how homesick he currently feels, then she may pay him attention for once, and then all bets are off – he'll stay in Turin. He is easily wooed, is our Tommy."

"His energy has always been used to start projects, if not always to see them through to completion, hasn't it?"

"He has high hopes, but life gets in the way, Nena." I stopped and shook my head.

Nena put her hand on my leg. "You and I always reach the same point when we look back. It's either Harry's bike crash or your incident with our friend Joseph, Sam. The two events stand out like roadblocks or wellsprings or both. They're always in view, whether we look backwards and into the future. It's like we're standing on a roundabout, and those two totems, Harry's Honda bike and your Flying Pig, are the only two vehicles circling it."

I nodded. "We can always cross the road and leave it all behind. There's certainly no helping Harry, and my own situation could have been a great deal worse. Head away from the past." I looked at Nena. "Ah. Come on, gal. Don't well up. Things happen for a reason. There has to be a plan for everything. That duality – the good and bad, the fortunate and the unlucky – it all depends how you view it. There are very few things in life that are wholly bad and wholly unfortunate. My parents dying brought me back to you; even Harry's death granted him an immortality of sorts. He'll still be spoken about in a hundred years because all his famous friends bought him that huge tomb, a kind of mausoleum. I couldn't believe that. It'll be on the tourist trail now. Maybe death spared him a decline in fortune.

We'll never know. But as I was saying to you earlier, the future can go two ways, and we can give ourselves a chance. And I live in the present, because the past is immutable, and the future depends on too many factors for me to corral…"

"Stop." Nena hushed my train of thought and made a note of the time on the Merc's dashboard clock. "10.17am. He's here, Sammy. That must be him. He's quite a unit." She brought the binoculars up to her eyes. "He's a big old boy. Look!"

I took the binos and watched the tall, muscular man with cropped hair walk across Chambois Close as it curved away downhill and towards the car. "We'd better move the Merc opposite the house or we'll lose him once he goes into the house."

Nena grabbed back the binoculars. "We can view him through the big lounge window. Start the car. Park up opposite, and then we'll discuss what we can do."

I fired up the Merc's straight-six engine, and the old car slowly wobbled into position. Joseph had entered the front door and was visible in the lounge window, his back to the pair of us, holding a cushion in his right hand. He was looking down at what must have been the sofa. I wasn't looking forward to confronting the hulk.

"It's best you keep hold of the binoculars, Nena, view him past me, so he can't see you."

"He can't?"

"No. Push your seat right back and look past my headrest. I'll look straight ahead. You tell me if he moves or leaves the room. Tell me what he's up to now."

Nena brought the binoculars to her face again. "He's walking towards the far wall of the lounge and now he's dropped down. He must be on a sofa."

"What are we going to do? There's nothing to be gained from just giving a description of him to PC Stuart. What- what evidence do we need?"

Where is Your God Now?

Nena was still training the sights on the spot above Joseph, the patch of wallpaper below which the young man was probably lying down. "If you go in…"

"How am I meant to go in? What's my excuse?" I asked.

"Joseph must know who you are. He's been to the cabin, he might have seen your name on the Jiffy bag, and he'll have Googled it."

"You're scaring me now, Nena."

"What can I say, Sammy? He's obviously followed you or us at some point from the cabin right up to the salon. He may have been stalking us since the moment you and I bumped into one another on Military Road." She paused. "He'll know enough to guess that you're Sam, and he'll probably have questions for you."

"I'll certainly have a few for him as well. Should I take this for protection?" And then I opened my blazer to reveal the butt of a pistol.

The colour drained from Nena's face, and then mine. I'd screwed up.

"How- how did you get that?" Nena tried to grab at my blazer. "Give it to me. You idiot. You can't have that. Where the hell did you get it from?"

I obediently handed over the firearm to her and, holding the black handle between her thumb and index finger, Nena gently dropped it, so it slid into her tote bag. I looked back at the house. "Listen. This guy is obviously crackers, so Tommy popped into some pawnshop the other week and got this for me. He knew the owner."

"Oh, that's OK, then," Nena said, sarcastically.

"Look, Nena. It's a last line of defence. I wouldn't shoot first, you know. I've never fired a gun before." I rubbed my forehead. "I really don't like the look of this Joseph fellow. I was expecting some pallid geek, not an Army bruiser who looks like he squat-lifts 200kg…"

"You're almost the size of him, Sammy…"

"The guy is like a caged pit-bull, all that unused muscle, all that energy just coiled up, day after day, sitting in that empty house, thinking of his dead mother and dreaming up a ton of shit about me."

"Sammy, come on…"

I spoke quickly. "Can you imagine all the hours he's spent with no one to mouth off to? It's been festering for almost twenty years, Nena, and now he's got himself into insane shape to mete out some justice. Kick my skull in. He must be the boy I hit. Think about it. He's the right age."

Nena frowned from behind the binoculars. "I thought you said he was a traveller?"

"I guessed he was, yes. But it would make sense for this Joseph to be the boy, doesn't it? His mum is no longer around to rein him in. Joseph has probably been planning this day for a year. Think, Nena – a year, ever since Mrs Harkett passed away. I have been his obsession. That's why he's been training."

"Listen…"

"No. Please listen to me, Nena. All bets are off for a guy who would let a car smash into your salon. He could have killed the three of us. He didn't care. You can't talk sense to a guy prepared to risk another's life." I brought my hands down hard onto the Merc's steering wheel. "That gun could save us!" My fingers were stinging.

Nena let out her breath at last and stared into my eyes. "I'm hearing what you're saying, but if you enter that house with a gun, then things are going to go south very quickly indeed. You will not have any control of the situation. This isn't the right form of proactivity. Sam, you understand?" She looked across at the house. "Listen, I'll go around the side and take the pistol with me. The kitchen window and the door overlook the driveway on the side. I can hear everything and I can react if Joseph starts to get aggressive. But this isn't the right time for a gun. Go and knock on the front door, and I'll be outside the kitchen entrance." Nena leaned over and kissed the side of my head. "You'll do the right thing, baby. But stay calm."

I opened the driver's door and got out, walking at a diagonal across the road's soft camber to the pavement before No33. My heart was thumping to the march of my own footsteps, and my eyes were fixed upon the metal-framed window for any signs of movement within. There was none. I fumbled in my pocket for a stick of chewing gum. There was none.

Up the brick-paved drive I walked, trying to move with a purpose that was in utter opposition to my wavering mind. On reaching the front door, I looked back to see Nena go around the bonnet of the car, across the road and tiptoe up the other side of the driveway where the unkempt hedge marked the boundary with the neighbours. When Nena had silently traversed the paving and taken up position to the left of the kitchen door, she nodded to me. I ducked back in front of the entrance, grabbed the ring knocker and forced myself to rap the door hard with it.

Within seconds, Joseph was standing before me. His hair was cropped, grown out from a self-administered session with the clippers. A red Y-shaped scar dropped down the side of his small nose to an emotionless mouth. After another few moments, Joseph spoke in a light, measured and well-educated manner: "Ah, Samuel, you have come at last. Come in, come in," and he led me, his nemesis, down the hallway and into the very kitchen shown in those Polaroids that both of us knew so well.

Cabin fever.

"I was sorry to hear from your brother about your gout, Luca. I guess it's the cost of having fun – the downside of a love for the finer things in life, eh?" Tommy was doing his instrument checks. Luca had tried to get on a commercial flight back to England after the farrago at the restaurant, but Monica had convinced him that Tommy meant him no harm after Luca's saving lunge at Claudia.

"I suffer for my love of the red wine," muttered Luca. "I get these crystals in my blood – it's impossible for me to get around sometimes." He looked out of his passenger window and wondered whether someone had told Tommy that he'd pawed at his woman. He decided to test his fears. "I give into my appetites too easily. Always have."

"Well, it was pleasure to meet Monica at Teatro Regio and talk a bit to her, and Gianfranco has kindly offered to whisk Claudia and me around the Museo Egizio when I'm back from England. I want to know everything about the wonderful city of Turin, your wonderful home. You have a lovely pair of people there. I am just sorry we couldn't get together at The Four Seasons." Tommy paused. "Golf-Charlie-Whisky-Alpha. Ready for departure."

Tommy hadn't taken the bait. "Even the word 'whisky' is making me feel ill. I must stop drinking," whined Luca. "I can't remember the end of our evening at the trattoria."

"Don't worry, old bean," Tommy reassured the man hunched in his passenger seat, "there's nothing to report – Claudia was sick for a while downstairs, and you came up and told us Monica was expecting you and Gianfranco before one o'clock."

"That's good." Luca inwardly thanked his Lord.

"It was all fine, Luca – Claudia is just a bit 'feast or famine' when it comes to drinking. She absolutely adored the LSO performance, especially the 'Spring' concerto, no1 in E major, and she got on very well with Monica, who is very much from the same set of Torinese. You know how it is, Luca."

Luca silently dropped his interior persecutions. "I feared that I had offended your lady with my drunkenness…"

Tommy chuckled. "Ah, she is used to the advances of men, my dear boy. Even the postman follows in her trail like a puppy dog. Claudia doesn't take offence at an inebriate pawing at her legs; she's inured to all that and has been since she was 13. Christ, how often do you think such a woman has to fend off guys in the street? She has all the shrugs, insults and street-fighting skills of a mafiosa."

Luca was confused at Tommy's calmness but carried on looking straight ahead. "Many times, I'd wager."

"Yes, every single day. Over dinner, Claudia always tells me of the latest hilarious attempt to get her in the sack, and we laugh about it. Whereas another man might storm out and pace the streets at night looking for the guy who had tried it on with her, I just shrug my shoulders. It sounds like you were so squiffy, you just fell into her legs in a forward roll. Do you think your friend Andrea has any CCTV footage of that?"

"I could ask?"

"I'm joking, dear Luca. I would imagine you have been castigating yourself for the past three days about your indiscretion, haven't you, so that is punishment enough." The Cessna was now picking up pace on the runway at Turin Caselle Airport, and Luca wondered when he would next be back in his city. Tommy continued as he pulled back on his controls. "What you should really worry about, Luca, is blabbering to Claudia about what you have seen in London…"

Luca now switched his head towards Tommy. "I don't know what you mean?"

Where is Your God Now?

"You know exactly what I mean, Luca."

"I don't know…"

Tom's voice went low. "Claudia knows exactly how John has built up such a tight ring of trust. Just as I tolerate her flirting and endless trips to Milan, so she is well aware of the things John and I have to do to keep our operation going. Do you think my partner of three years is in the dark about the disappearances of people like you who fail to keep quiet? You know who her father is, after all."

Luca looked back out of the window, wishing he could float down the 1,000 metres to the soil below and try to hide under the shield of the loblolly pine trees. "Tom, listen, I thought I had thrown Claudia off the scent by pouncing on her." He sighed and caught his worried face in the window's reflection. "I knew all of this was too good to last. I knew I'd screw it up. I always make life hard for myself."

"Well, you're going to have to face John and try to reassure him, aren't you? I know he has tried to keep you safe from other people with interests in East London. John has tried to save you from yourself. So, stop with the self-pity – you were made very aware that your silence was your protection; once you'd talked, then that protective bubble disappeared. You've had lunch with John 13 times in the past few months, and that's the only stipulation he has made. He could have had you silenced all those weeks ago – you didn't see Asgar watching us all from opposite the trattoria. I saw him; that's when I knew John was not convinced of your silence. You're trying to protect yourself now, but that is futile. You've pissed outside the pot and now you're going to have to crawl and beg John to throw his cape over you once again."

Luca spoke in a mixture of Italian and then English. "Then let be me killed and join Signor Renaldi and the Polish lady. And dear Milena. I'm not going to beg for mercy from a cold-blooded killer. John is going to murder me anyway; he'll have me killed. I say that compliance is for cowards. I don't believe that Signor Renaldi was a monster; he was probably about to reveal the sinister operation run by John and people like you. A lot of barking little lapdogs."

Tommy smiled. "You've discovered your bollocks at long last, Luca. OK, you can make your escape at Southend; I'll let you run on your porky little trotters and I'll call John and tell him of your plan. You'd be better off begging, you know?"

Luca's blood was up. He could only imagine at how many lives had been snatched away and how many families broken up by John's constant search for personal gratification and business success. "I hope his money and wealth make him happy…"

"Oh, John's a very happy boy," Tommy interrupted. "But you, you get your rest, Luca – you're gonna need it…"

"No, you listen to me, Tommy. I'm going to die in my footsteps, but I hope the ghosts of every soul John's had killed return to haunt him, and their mothers, their fathers, their sons and daughters." Luca carried on in Italian: "Men like you disgust me; you're no better than a whipped dog, beaten till it's tame. You probably disgust yourself; that's why you surround yourself with these beautiful girlfriends in airless apartments high above the strada. You make ghosts of people. I bet those so-called friends you claim to have helped to relocate in Turin never left the airport."

Tommy chuckled again. "I understand your Italian. How very perceptive of you. All that you say is so – the same man who has silenced all those old buffers will have you too, before sunset, Luca. Except this time, there'll be no pillow over the face, no gentle drugging – and we're not going to get our hands on your money. He'll do it for fun, to silence a Torino rat who should've recognised he was onto a good thing. John will use his every last penny to exterminate you. He'll probably do it himself, as you're the only sod in poorer shape than he is. Look at the state of you, all puffed up when it's hopeless." He laughed.

"All these threats don't frighten me now. I'll get to see my mama again and regain my self-respect. There's nothing you can do to touch me. I'm back on the side of Good – we are each of us angels with only one wing, and we can only fly by embracing one another."

Tommy laughed hard enough to make the tiny plane shiver slightly. "This is going to be a long flight. I might kill you myself, you mawkish mound of mother love. You're going to have a half-hour head-start, then I'll get you culled, from snout to tail, Luca."

Luca mouthed goodbye to the Italian Alps and closed his eyes. "All the money you make can never buy you forgiveness. Imagine that poor girl's real parents back in Poland – I have. I spent weeks and weeks thinking of how they're coping with their daughter's disappearance, how they must curse themselves for sending their darling off into the jungle, how they know it's futile to even try to drum up any interest among the policemen who are in John's pocket. I'm just another lost soul. I should never have left Turin. I fooled myself that people like John ever had a genuine interest in me. Those clinics are fascist hangouts. Those parties are just Nazi get-togethers."

"Will you ever put a pipe in it, Luca? I'm not recording all this, you know? It's all lost to the thin air outside. I don't give a shit about you regaining your conscience." Tom paused. "What the hell do you think you'll achieve? Where is your god now, Luca? You're not even going to get a home burial – there won't be little boys in black suits holding flowers and weeping for you on the marble steps."

"I don't need that." Luca looked down at the clouds.

"And Gianfranco and Monica will never find you – they'll need a pneumatic drill to unearth you. You'll become part of the concrete foundations at another clinic— all those zimmerframes tapping away on top of you, all those old people being preserved until their wills have John's name on them. That's what I do. I'm the adjustment bureau. I make sure their cash isn't spunked away on some dog sanctuary or another wet-lipped ponce of a nephew. There's a little bit for John, a little bit for Justyna, a little bit for me, a little bit for the sergeant, a little bit for the mayor, a little bit for John again, a little bit for the party crew, a little bit for John's mistresses, a little bit for my home renovations. Signor Renaldi probably paid for the marblework in my parlour. Ha! Think on that."

Luca tugged at his seatbelt. "If I could jump out of here, I would... I know what a bad person is, and I don't want to even breathe the same air as a man like you. It disgusts me. You disgust me."

Tommy was still looking straight ahead. "I don't suppose sleeping with a prostitute like Justyna disgusted you, did it? How does that sit with a good man like yourself? What would Gianfranco say if he could have seen his piggy little brother sweating away on top of a whore in some stranger's toilet? I'm sure John can dig out the tapes. Gianfranco won't ever seen his brother again; well, he'll see him there on CCTV, begging his dick to get hard and sniffing cocaine off the cistern. I'm going to enjoy hanging out with Gianfranco and Monica and gradually seeing them crumble."

Luca stared at the side of Tommy's head. "Don't."

Tommy chuckled "We can always find someone who'll drop off that memory stick at Via Monte Rosa; we can always pay someone to give them false hope that you're alive and that you've been silent out of choice. Gianfranco and Monica will now always think they offended you. No one will look for you. You're one of the ghost people now. Oh, and good luck trying to get a signal at Southend

Where is Your God Now?

Airport. I've nobbled your phone anyway. You might as well try to cosh me with it." Tommy paused. "Don't do that, or I'll snap your neck like a breadstick."

"All this will catch up with you one day…"

"Well, I fancy my chances, Luca. Next year, I'll have survived for twenty years without being caught. I'm just an elders lawyer, Luca, ferrying a porcine Italian back into Southend."

Luca did a sign of the cross.

"If you draw attention to yourself at the airport, then I vow to go around the Via Monte Rosa and kill your brother, his partner and their unborn baby tomorrow. White spirit and paint are highly flammable." Tom paused to eyeball Luca. "So, you're going to get into the back seat of that Merc and keep your head down and let yourself be taken to the café. Then you'll wait in the refrigerator room until John works out a plan. We might chuck in a bowl of chips for you." Tommy laughed and looked over the Alps. "Not gone so great for you this week, has it, Luca? It's not been one of your better weeks, has it? Oh, Claudia's father doesn't care for Fellini any more. He treats me as a son, and I send him a little present every Tuesday – the masseuse almost makes the oxygen tube shoot out of his nose! That's how we grease the wheels of power."

Luca started to mutter the Lord's Prayer and when he was done, he thought about attempting to wrest control from Tommy and direct the Cessna into the mountaintops. At least then he would be forever in his land. He was not strong enough, though. "You asked where is my God? He is always with me. I can see him in the head of a daisy. He shall punish you in the next life, the world we cannot see with our eyes. He is the Great Commander, not some councillor with a Messiah complex. He is the one who chooses who truly lives and never dies. John will realise this as well when his dying day comes. He's just a man of corrupted ideas. He has no protection against my God's will, and neither have you. You both shall burn for ever."

Tom grinned. "Then I'd better make the most of my money and Claudia when I can. Luca, it's a lot easier for you now to pipe down. I'm a 39-year-old atheist and I've sent more men to meet their maker than I've had years on Earth. You wouldn't believe how many people put their faith in the same truisms as I do. You are literally a dying breed. It's rather sweet that you hold to these beliefs in the very moments you are utterly helpless. It's only for my own sake that I don't dump you into the snows below. I don't want to destabilise old Wendy now – these Cessnas are delicate old ladies. And as you know, I always look after the futures of delicate old maids."

"I…" shouted Luca.

"No, shut it. You've said your piece, so shut the hell up. You can sleep now and try to sleep in the café chiller, although Asgar will not like the fact you've been blabbering away. He will see you as a block to his wife and kids getting that house over in Poplar. He won't like that. He was in the special forces, that boy. I think he used to pop people's eyes out and use them as gob-stoppers. Something for you to chew on, Luca, as you sleep, so get sleeping."

The kitchen-sink drama.

"I would offer you something to drink, but I have only water here, and I want you to speak and focus on your words." Joey was leaning against the kitchen counter, side on to the kitchen window, with the door to the driveway behind his left shoulder. Nena was just outside, with the pistol in her tote bag. She could hear us speaking in the kitchen, but their words were largely muffled.

"I'm not thirsty, and I won't be staying long…" I stood in the doorway between the kitchen and the hallway, facing Joey and the outside door at the other end.

"You'll be staying as long as I have questions for you." Joey put his hand into his right jeans pocket and brought out the butt of his own gun. "You've had almost twenty years to figure out what you might say to me; I expect all my queries to be answered properly." His voice was almost plummy, with the soft Rs of the upper classes, and his back remained ram-rod straight. He was without expression, as if addressing a court-martial; the scar on his face wasn't long, but it was an angry red.

"You're the bearded man in the Polaroids." I noted how Joey had become even more stripped since they were taken. A vein throbbed on the side of his bull neck.

"You can see the beard up there on top of the cabinet next to you – and more pertinently, I'm the 13-year-old you knocked to the ground on Alkham Farm Road in 1998. Did you even stop to check I was not dead? Did you hell…" Joey snorted and grinned to himself.

I looked out of the kitchen window, above the stainless-steel sink to my left. "You were moving. I mean, I hear you murmuring drunkenly as well. You stank of vodka and you were caked in mud. I was only 18 myself." I could still smell that alcohol years on.

"I didn't ask your age then. It's of no interest to me what your circumstances were, although I can guess you were drunk too. That's why you didn't stop to help a boy whose face had been ripped apart by the bumper of your car…"

"Now, steady on. That scar is pretty small. I don't think you are remembering things correctly here." I moved into the kitchen, but Joey raised his heavy left eyebrow to warn me of the danger of coming any closer. He was staring right through me.

"Samuel, lie upon lie – that's all your past has for proof. I hope I've tugged the comfort blanket of bullshit away from you. How has it felt to come back to absolute chaos?"

"You can imagine…"

Joey grinned again. "Why should you have any crumb of comfort when you left me there alone in the road like roadkill?" He fished the gun out of his pocket and held it up, six feet in front of me. "I have the control now, Samuel. It's my call now."

"There's no need for that. My conscience is clear." I was keeping my breaths as steady as I could.

Joey laughed. "Really? Your conscience's clear, is it? Then you must not have much of one – or else you've covered up any shame with the drift of the years. Is your conscience buried under your memories? Is it lying there under yet more boozing? Is it hidden under constant activity to fool your mind into not contemplating the past?" He nodded towards the gun. "I intend to use this today."

"Steady on, Joseph." I paused. "I have come here expecting you to reveal yourself as the boy. Would I do that if I felt I was totally to blame? That night, I went to fetch help and my best friend came to you 20 minutes later."

"Twenty minutes? It was an hour at least," Joey had stopped smiling.

"As if you had any concept of time that night. You were crawling in the road like a drunken dog. You were on all fours, plastered."

"You ran over me with your car!"

"My friend Tommy even went to the hospital the next day to check on your progress, and you'd gone. You were not dying, you were not even unconscious, but you were drunk enough to have little clue of how long it took help to come. Face it – you wouldn't expect a boy to be crawling in the road at that time of night, or at any time of day." I gripped the counter for support.

"I was trying to run away – the woman had plied me with the vodka."

"Oh yeah?" This was a new excuse.

"Yes. The mechanic's wife was molesting me. She spiked my drink." The gun was still trained on my head, but Joey was at least blinking now.

"Now surely that's the greater of the crimes here? Did you go round her place and point a pistol at her head?" I took a pace backwards, so my back was pressed against the other counter in the mirror image of Joey's position. "No, you didn't. So why are you pointing that gun at me now?"

"An oh-so-clever man like yourself must realise it is the victim who gets to call out a crime and judge its seriousness. It's up to me to choose who is the offender here, Samuel."

"That scar reminds you of me. But what about the woman with the drink?"

"I wear these scars on my face like a victory band – they show all I had to overcome in the aftermath of the criminal act perpetrated by you, Samuel. I could deal with the drunken pass made on me by a lonely and lustful woman, but I couldn't get to grips with the callous actions of a drunk piloting a one-tonne block of metal..."

"Come now, Joseph, you're being melodramatic..."

"Don't you tell me how to act! You know, when it gets cold, when it's winter and the winds blow across the East

Cliff, these scars contract like metal straps. When I hear a sudden noise behind me, I jump in fear. I haven't touched a drop of alcohol since I was 13; in fact, I never had a proper childhood after that day. When you and that girl of yours were probably pissing around in the park, my mother was rubbing witch hazel into my wounds, a single mum ferrying her only son, her only relative, from consultant to consultant, trying to find a way to make his life normal again. The very smell of the alcohol in the witch hazel made me dry-heave. I could remember the terrors of that night, day after day. You smell like you've been drinking for the past 18 years. You still a toper? Do you still drive around pissed, knocking over kids and then leaving them for dead in the road? The shame is all on you."

I sighed and rubbed my eyebrow. I was dealing with an irrational man. "How do you know I was drunk? I was scared like you."

"Your car was travelling at 20mph on the wrong side of the road."

"Bullshit."

"No, fact, Samuel. I'd come off the left verge, from the direction of the garage. I went back there a couple of days after the hit-and-run. I could see my tracks still there; it hadn't rained. I should have taken a photo, but I was 13. And I didn't have a mobile back then."

"No copper would have done me for hitting you when you were crawling down a country road… He might have arrested the mechanic's wife for grooming a minor, though."

"Well, he would have arrested you for drink-driving, and that's why you drove off and got your friend to sort out the mess. You got him to drive me to the hospital and then hang along to check I wouldn't raise a fuss. And yes, Samuel, you're right – it wouldn't have looked good for me

Where is Your God Now?

to stink of vodka. Who'd believe a teenager except his mother?"

I looked down to the lino. "And you're now pursuing this vendetta because? I know your mother passed away almost exactly a year ago. Would she want this for you? To be pointing a gun at the head of a stranger who actually fetched help for you? We all have scars." I rolled up my left shirt-sleeve. "There's a knife wound." It was an old mark from a metal hinge.

"You probably earned that in a bar fight. My nightmares drown in a dark brown. Every night, I taste the mud in my mouth, the smell of the blood across my face – it leaks into my eyes and nose. The mud covers everything. I feel like I'm bound in wet plaster. I can no longer breathe. It masks my mouth, and then when I wake up with a jolt, I can see every scar, a reminder that all this actually happened. As for my mother, she let me play my funny little games. I told Mum that I would plan a graduated revenge. I didn't want you to find any comfort when you decided to come back to Folkestone. It was my mother's final act; she gave me the money to put my plans into action. I didn't dream this all up in the past months, but in the long decades of loneliness. Can you imagine how my scars sprained my mother's heart? She only wanted me to feel free, to be happy, to be normal. I'm not normal, Samuel." Joey paused. "I want to harm you, not quickly, but torture you by degrees. I'd sooner shoot off all your fingers than put a bullet in your brain. I'm intractable. You're done, matey. You're trying to negotiate with a wrong'un. I'll taste your blood, not the mud now." The gun began to shake.

I raised my palms. "Look at yourself. Are you ready to be a killer? No, you're not. I can tell from your voice that you're an educated man – your mother was a writer and probably instilled in you a love of culture, right?"

"Shut the hell up, Samuel!" His voice was quavering.

"So what do you want from me, Joseph? To maim me? Because if you kill me, you instantly become ten thousand times the monster I might have been that night. You'll be running until they find you and lock you away in prison. The authorities aren't going to hit you with manslaughter, but with premeditated murder. You haven't thought this through."

Joey took a step closer to me as his gun wavered in his hand. His face was drained of blood, and sweat ran from his crop of hair. "What I want is revenge, and that's what I'm getting now. I want you to feel what it's like to face your death. The Skoda crashed into your bird's salon; the furniture being shifted around that shitty little cabin you have by Radnor cliffs – that's all minor stuff. I'm prepared to go to prison for a lot more. I'm prepared to do years, not months – I'm ready to spend decades in a small, windowless room because I'm used to it now. I've grown accustomed to being on the outside of everything. The only good memories I have are of my mother, and she is just a spirit now; I cannot make any more daydreams with her. I can close my eyes and dream. I can do that anywhere – in a cell, in my bedsit, in a hospital bed, in the lounge here. I don't need much. I have nothing to lose. I'm invisible now."

I stared again straight at the sweating man-child. I felt some compassion and empathy for Joey; I too had felt like an outsider before I'd bumped into Nena and restarted our great romance. "Joseph, you never know what your future holds for you. You are young, you are handsome, and you obviously have enough money stored away to pursue this vendetta against me. Why draw a line under any happiness you may have? You might find someone to replace your mother, someone as fine as she was, you might have kids and your mother might look down upon grandchildren..."

"Might, might, might... could, could, could," Joseph thundered. "I don't have the social skills or the appetite to bother with people. You snatched away all my love for others. After the accident, our friends stopped coming to the house. I would snap at everyone who came. Even my mother's swinging mood wasn't as bad, and she was suffering from Type 1. And now I want all the pain that I felt to be foisted upon you. I want it to weigh you down. I want you to thrash around like a bug under a glass and then I want to slam that beaker down on you and paralyse you. I want your brain to work, to stew upon what you've done, but I want your body to be immobile. You'll be just a hunk of meat with a diseased brain dwelling upon all your wrongs, whirring away night and day inside the prison of your lifeless body." Joey paused. "Nena will have to nurse you, like my mother did me."

"Please, think about this, Joseph." I held my hands above my head. "This is an assault on your mother's memory."

"Don't mention my mother, you bastard," and Joey pulled the trigger and I fell onto the lino, bleeding from the side of my head. I could hear blood rushing into my ear, the sound of the sea covering a beach.

Moments later, I saw Nena burst through the side door. She slid slightly over the lino, brandishing the pistol, and she emptied its six bullets, bang, bang, bang, there, right into Joey's back. The boy slumped forward. He was dead immediately, his blood mingling with mine four feet away. Nena ran over to me, cradling my head, as an angry buzz began in my skull. I blinked the blood away.

"Oh, Sammy. God. Speak to me." She dug away at my hair and her finger felt what seemed like a hole-punch mark in my right ear, near the lobe. "He's caught your ear. It's only a nick. There's a lot of blood though." She wrapped her scarf around my head like a bandana.

I raised myself onto my elbows and looked past my feet at the mess of blood that leaked out from Joey. He didn't move, his legs sticking out and his chest blown forwards. I wheezed: "I'm ok. I'm ok. Just the one shot. He only fired a pellet at me." I clutched the cotton to the side of my head. "My ear is on fire."

Nena didn't reply. She was rocking backwards and forwards and whimpering to herself.

Evening things up.

"I'm on my burner, John. Yes. I'm back in Essex. Pavarotti's sung like a canary. No, just to Claudia. I knew he would. You get soft on your projects, John. It's your weakness. The Italian guys told you so, and I did as well. You also got soft on that nurse who was stealing morphine from the clinic. Yes, I've disabled his phone and thrown him into the back of Asgar's Merc. No, calm down, calm down. We've been through bigger scrapes than this. Asgar's going to drive Luca around the M25 until we work out a plan. Asgar won't do him, no – and tell him I spotted him outside the trattoria. Rubbish." Tommy rubbed his head as he sat on an oil drum outside Southend flight control. "I'm thinking, I'm thinking. We could use the usual crew, but it's going to be impossible to get them out to East London or anywhere before tonight. The Merc will run out of petrol by then. No, that was a joke. Don't worry, John. He hasn't talked to anyone. I whisked him through the airport. He has no means of communication; I gave his smartphone a drink of water. He's not going to make a dash out of the back seat at 80mph on the M25, and no one can see him in there behind the black glass. He's done." Another call was coming through. "I'll call you back, John."

And us, we were back in the Merc on the driveway to the side of the kitchen. Joey was rolled up in the kitchen lino in the boot; rather than try to clean the oceans of blood, we had just taken it up and used it as a body-bag, carrying it a couple of metres to the car's huge boot. Nena was now trying to fit my bandaged head under a beanie hat she'd found in one of the upstairs bedrooms, having staunched the flow of blood with some New Skin and cotton wool. The buzzing had subsided, though my ear was stinging.

Nena turned to me. "So you're going to ring him then? Let's hope he can help us. He owes us one."

I pulled the Merc out of the driveway, rounded the bend and parked up on Warren Way, well away from the school gates of Martello Primary. "Yes, I'll call Tommy right now." I fished for my mobile from my dad's old Barbour jacket. Thankfully, both of us were blood-free now, my drenched black jumper transferred over to the dead man.

I punched in Tommy's new number; his last missed call had run out the magic six times, telling me he had a fresh burner. "Hi, Scooter. Listen, where are you? OK. It wasn't a foreign ringtone so I guessed. The girl and I are going to have to get out of the country, and we're going to have to meet you wherever your plane is." I paused as Tommy replied. "It's there? Perfect." I then listened for more than a minute to my friend's staccato instructions. Nena reached to grip my left thigh. "No, I can't with her around. You're going to have to get the guy to bring him to the clinic site and then he can drive the pair of us over to you. Stay at the airport. I'll do it, I'll do it, but you have to get the pair of us away this afternoon and sort us out with the change of details and a place to crash. Right, I'll see the guy in 90 minutes from now, and then we'll get it to you an hour and a half after that." It was now reading 11 o'clock on the car dashboard. My ear felt like it was being cauterised off my head.

I hung up and turned to Nena. "We must go to Whitechapel right now."

"East London?"

"Yep. I've rearranged with Tommy to send us a driver – we can dump the car at a building site there. Then we'll be taken to Southend airport, where Tommy and his Cessna are waiting for us. You said you wanted to see where I spent the past 18 years? Well, here we go, a bit sooner than expected, eh, but needs must." I put my hand in Nena's, which still rested on the thigh of my jeans.

"Can I stop off at the salon and pick up my passport and things? What about the Merc?" Nena looked at me. "Cadders loves this car. It was his uncle Freddy's."

"Honey, there's currently a dead man in the boot, and the lino will only stop a fraction of the blood draining into the carpet. Cadders loves this Merc, but I'd wager he loves his liberty even more. We'd be handing the smoking gun to him; he's the licensed owner and he won't be able to verify his whereabouts, so bang goes any alibi. Plus, he's been talking to Rufus and all his brother's spies about Chambois Close for the past week. We can't do anything that will implicate our dear friend."

"So, no goodbyes? I guess…"

I cut Nena off. "He's not going to hear from the pair of us for a while; the Musketeers have been disbanded. You'll have a new identity waiting for you in Turin." I squeezed Nena's small right hand and rubbed her fingers with mine. "It'll all be fine, but we can't look back. We can't delay and we must get to London by half noon. I'll then drive the car to be disposed of, and the driver and I will pick you up outside the Blind Beggar pub 15 minutes later. I won't be far from you, but we cannot use our mobile phones any more. Give me yours." I paused. "I love you, darling."

Nena unlocked her hand from mine so she could give her iPhone to me. "We did put the pistol with the body, right?"

"Yes. And remember, there won't be any visitors to the house so we have time to get away."

"Are you sure?" Nena was near-choking.

"Listen. I checked the neighbour's house the other day, and it's a vacant possession. No one lives in a house with a cracked front window, and there are no fresh footsteps around the front footpath – even the postman's given up on them. There are lots of vacant possessions around here, so another to the list isn't going to be noticed. And Joseph was a loner; the street will just think he's stopped coming round to the place. Think about how hard it was to find anything on him – he lived just as much under the radar as we do. It's been a year he's been grieving, so anyone will think he's moved on, perhaps gone somewhere else with his money. No one grieves for the invisible."

Nena's face was wet with tears. "You seem very calm, Sammy. We've just killed a man. I've killed someone." She wiped down her face. "I'm never going to see the salon again, am I?"

"Well, never say never, but we need a lot of breathing space. The fact your place is still being done up, it will help your absence not appear so noticeable, eh? And only the Coupers and you really knew I was back, but I have to think about how we're going to manage Cadders."

I steered the Merc out of Warren Way and headed for the A260 and A259 roads out of town and onto the M20 towards London. "Nena, you have to see this all as an unexpected vacation. We'll be gone at least two months, but if we play our cards right, it won't be permanent. A lot depends on today, darling. Just focus that redoubtable mind of yours on having as little contact as possible with the world outside this car's windows. We have enough fuel to get to London, and Cadders won't be at Chambois Close for another hour, so we can visualise this Merc as a hiding spot for the next 60 minutes or so."

Nena buried her head in her hands. "What will Cadders say when he finds no sign of us and no car? You know how he is. He'll go running to his brother, and then Rufus will get a dozen people scouring the town for us. Rufus and Cadwick are bound to drop the ball; they are. It's in their nature to tell stories and to share, to over-share."

I shook my head as I drove. The thoughts were coming fast. "No. These public schoolboys all learn to be discreet –

it's something in their upbringing, being shuttled between school and uninterested parents, having only a few personal effects in a trunk at the end of their bed. They learn to compartmentalise their lives – I mean, you've never even seen Cadwick's friends – and it's why they end up as CEOs and ministers, or in the secret service. I've met quite a few of them, retired and packing themselves off to Turin. The old buffers are perfectly happy to live in a single room in the guts of a big old villa by the lake. It's programmed into them to be hush hush, on the QT." I paused. "Listen, I'll send Cadders a text from your phone before I bin it up in Whitechapel. I'll say that we're tailing Joseph up to London so it's all in hand and he can hold fire on any stake-outs at Chambois Close. Then later this afternoon, I'll ask him to manage the repairs to the salon as we're tracking Joseph over to France and we'll be several days at least. I'll give him my second mobile number, a burner I have. We can pretend to be around St Malo, following Joseph as he stays at his 'uncle Jeremy's'. I'll keep it vague but fairly frequent. As long as Cadders has a little text here and there and thinks the Merc is parked over somewhere for the long term, he won't worry about us for the next week or so; he only sits in the car once a year. We can then formulate a plan where, perhaps, Joseph disappears into the French interior, and we head off for an extended holiday, beyond the reach of all communications, somewhere with a low population density, no mobile phone service, somewhere South American, possibly. We can cite the stress of it all for our getaway among the rainforests. We'll write that in a long letter to Cadwick, and tell him the Three Musketeers are recharging our batteries, ready to redouble our efforts to entrap this Joseph fellow. We must mention him, so Cadwick believes the guy's alive as well. We're both off the grid anyway, when it comes to social media, family and employers. I have a ton of ready cash in Turin so we needn't touch any English accounts. You're paid up at the salon. No mortgages, no social life – it could be perfect for us. You just need to be cool. We'll change our hair and go shopping for a new look in Milan at the Galleria Vittorio Emanuele. I'm rolling in money out there, all at hand. And we'll have Tommy as our Passepartout. He'll be thrilled that we've come over."

I swung the car through the roundabout at the bottom of the A259; in a minute or so, we would pass the end of the road where all the lies began, that night almost twenty years ago when Joey crawled into the road and collided with the metal bumper of my Flying Pig. Where had his vengefulness got him? I thought. It had led him to his own destruction – he had looked back and obsessed about a moment in time when no one was really in the right. It had been not the end of the beginning for Joseph, but the beginning of his end. He had placed himself in a moment from where there was truly no escape except death. Joseph had rattled the cage of a killer, only to die at the hands of a saint; he had refused to focus on anything other than that night on the farm road in the absence of his mother, and now he was in the carpeted boot of an old Merc, his spirit hopefully with Eleanor's, far above the ribbon of the A259 as it wound its way uphill.

All this was an irony not lost on me. And neither was it lost on me that where once I had fled without much reason to scarper, now I was an accomplice to a murder committed by the person I loved most of all. There was no chance of the pair of us ever explaining away what had happened in the kitchen of no33 Chambois Close or how a woman without any police record had shot a bull of a man half-a-dozen times in the back; even PC Stuart would catch the scent of retribution for the loss of Nena's salon and vow to take down those who would take the law into their own untrained hands.

We had stepped on Joseph's turf and if we had known him to be the man behind the break-in and the runaway estate, then we should have alerted the police, not confronted a troubled soul who was brandishing just a fake pistol, with his back turned to his killer. Better to leave no trace of a victim and no trace of his killing; there would be no seed from which the oak of justice could grow. Where is the justice here anyway? Whose story is right? I believed Nena had been absolved of any wrongdoing in the moment that Joseph had sent that Skoda estate smashing into her home. It could have killed her. Tough justice had been meted out to the maniac.

"Nena, look right. That's the lane where I knocked over the boy. 'So as it was in the beginning, so shall it be in the end,' but now I have you with me, and that is all I need." I tapped out I LOVE YOU in Morse code on Nena's right forearm.

A couple of minutes later, the Merc was picking up her skirts and hogging the middle lane of the M20 as it carried us on the run to our new life.

Farewell to Luca.

Upon seeing me on the corner of the Whitechapel High Street and Vallance Road, Asgar parked his own black Mercedes up in Durward Street, around the back of Whitechapel station. The fat Italian in the back of his car had fallen asleep in resignation after two hours of reciting prayers and hollering in vain against the black rear windows. Luca's bloodied fingernails had torn holes in the car's tan leather seats.

"You must be Sam?" the tall man asked, without offering his hand to me.

"Yep. Luca's in the back?" I replied, and on Asgar's nod, I walked to the Mercedes, parked next to a large recycling bin. I quietly opened the rear door. Within half a minute, I was back outside, flexing my right hand. The Italian had a snapped neck now.

"Right," I said. "Take the body to the clinic in Mile End and drop it into the furthest foundations. A cement truck is there and will come over to screen you as you deposit the fat man. The foreman has prepared the site – no CCTV and so on. I told the Bishop of Wells. Be swift and be silent. Then come back here. I'll be on the corner of the high street again; you'll take us both to Tommy at Southend airport."

Asgar nodded again. "All that Italian was doing my head in. He then said something about being 'trapped in the balance of God's plan' and then he fell asleep." With that, Asgar slipped into the driver's seat for Luca's final journey, his chauffeur cap stashed in the glovebox.

An hour or so later, Nena and I were at Southend Airport, thankful that Tommy had brought along some wet sandwiches of thick margarine, cream cheese and sad-looking lettuce. There wasn't anything in the way of catering at this once-busy airfield.

"You're looking far more sober than when I last saw you, Tommy." Nena was a bit perkier now we were ensconced within the snug cabin of the Cessna, but still she wondered if the last breaths of Joseph had stuck to her like incriminating Post-It notes and if a stray smear of blood was on her clothes. Then Nena reminded herself that this wasn't all some booze-addled dream of hers, and she was far from the cocoon of her salon.

Tom couldn't see her frown. "Well, I heard you turned a man into a human pepper pot." He paused. "I'm sorry. I'm such a tactless bastard; I blame the solitude up here." He paused again. "Hey, I'm glad you caught the guy who's been turning both your lives into a living hell. Don't look back, I say. Sammy said you shot him in self-defence, but we'd best not leave the police force with any material to magic up a miscarriage of justice. People disappear every day like smoke." He stopped again.

"What did you do with this Joseph's body, Sammy?" Nena whitened and looked out of the window, half-hoping Joseph had found peace at last, half-hoping his body would never be discovered. It was how I had first felt, all those years ago.

"We stashed him in the lino he fell on and then humped him into the boot of our friend's Merc. The car is in the long-term; the corpse is encased in concrete in that site over in Mile End. It's the safer way. I thought about leaving Joey in the boot, but we'll be gone for some time, won't we, so the hoy would attract all sorts of attention to the Merc."

"Hang on – you used the clinic? That's hilarious. Asgar is dropping our cargo off there as well. The foreman's going to have a right old busy Tuesday afternoon. It shouldn't cock up the clinic's foundations. Can you imagine if the bloody thing slid away in ten years' time? The rozzers would be swarming all over it like pigs in shit." Tommy started laughing.

"What the hell are you boys on about?" Nena was feeling a bit queasy as the Cessna SP-172 continued its steady ascent over the North Sea. "You're both really casual, considering what we've just done. What's up with you?"

I looked at Tom and sighed. "Nena, there were a lot of once-great men who were having a hard time facing the fact that their days of heading a FTSE-100 business were very much behind them. They had no family and were not longer able to enjoy the wealth they had accumulated for their retirement. I have seen guys living in a single room in a 20-bedroom mansion. So I assisted their demise – overdoses, suffocation, carbon-monoxide poisoning, all manner of endings. Joseph's death doesn't faze me at all – what glory days awaited him? And if he thought he was ready for prison, then I very much doubt that." I turned to Tommy. "In a scenario where I'm staring at a firearm for five minutes, I'm not going to shed any tears for the bloke holding it. I tried to reason with him. The pellet could have lodged in my temple or eye."

Tommy now addressed Nena over his shoulder. "You did the right thing. That nutter could have maimed our Sam for life or could have killed you earlier when he let that estate car smash into your shop. How did he know you guys were in the back room? Joseph set up his fate by pursuing vengeance to an unreasonable degree. You shouldn't castigate yourself for defending the love of your life." He looked right to me. "Everyone chooses the ending to their story, don't they?"

I picked up the thread. "Nena, we know all this will be confusing for you, but we are enablers. The decision to end life is not ours."

Nena was taking it all in. "Do these clients pay you for the actual act itself?"

Tommy took over. "No. Obviously, we get a commission for finding them a property, which goes to Sammy here, and I get paid for all the transportation of themselves and their goods, and of course, for sorting out their last wills and testaments. And then, of course, if they wish to thank us for our services – we even sort out gardeners and home helps, doctors and pharmacists – then they can, and often do, make bequests to us in those last wills and testaments. It's a very neat solution to finding themselves beyond the help of the NHS or, in 99 per cent of the cases, beyond the abilities and resources of private healthcare."

Nena was growing increasingly relaxed, which surprised her a little. She had always been a fatalist but had never held an opinion about assisted suicide. "So you operate a kind of ersatz hospice then? Is that the best way to describe what you offer? I suppose being out there around the lakes at the foot of the Alps, waited on hand and foot, and all of that, is a better option than what you could possibly hope for in London, eh?"

I looked over my right shoulder, slightly relieved. "It's not a hospice, dear. These are not well men, no, and they've only a year or two to live. We have never, for instance, had a fellow under 65, so don't worry about us acting as God and executioners, as well as executors of wills. We have a very strict code of conduct and we liaise with colleagues who are caregivers in London and the home counties to make sure that everything has been done to cure these people of their maladies and longstanding medical complaints. Nothing is left to chance. Given these men's status and great wealth, they will have tried every option and accepted every possible cure."

Tommy joined in. "These aren't lusty young tigers, Nena. We rarely deal with married men. It's almost all widowers or those who have devoted their lives to business and civic life, you know. Our friend in London, John, The Bishop, vets them all – they place all their faith and confidence in him, just as you have entrusted Sam and me with establishing your new life in Turin."

Nena smiled. "Well, let's see how long we're out in Turin for. I will be surprised if I spend 18-19 years out there, even if the mountain streams flow with gin." Nena looked at the two of us in front of her. "I am very grateful to you both for whisking me away from that shitty situation over in Sandgate. In the darkest moments, you find out who your friends are. But I can't make promises that Turin is going to grow on me, or that I shall win over the Piemontesi people. I've been living under the seashell all my life. This is only the second time I've left the country, and I do so without my belongings, my passport or any money at hand."

"It'll be set up for you," Tom replied softly. "All you have to do is live in the present, live discreetly and live with the fullest trust in us both. This is your new gang; maybe you'll find others into which to charm your way. You haven't met Claudia."

Nena chuckled. "No, but I've heard plenty about her. She'll think of me as a weird gender-fluid tomboy. I'm everything she's been warned about by her mama."

Tom laughed. "She'll definitely see you as a project. Please don't take offence if you spend the first week of your life in Turin as the subject of Claudia's beauty therapy. She's a very smart and capable woman, but her belief is that we all should maximise our outward appearance. It has, after all, brought Claudia a fantastic life and a great deal of patronage. However, you can hold conversations with her about the opera, about the history of Europe, about the great film directors and about the industrial life of Italy. Claudia always surprises people. If you ever meet

Where is Your God Now?

her family, the curtain lifts – they're a family of industrial heavyweights and political thinkers, and all of that has breathed its way by osmosis into Claudia herself. She has taken on the temperature of all those years swimming in the family pool."

Nena nodded. "I don't think it's possible for a woman not to become an all-rounder in the modern world. And anyone can reach out and touch every situation in every country on every continent. That's the way it is."

"We all are global citizens, etc," I agreed. "It's very, very difficult these days to live off the grid," I winked at Nena, "but it's not impossible." Nena smiled.

She looked across to the other back seat of the SP-172. "Whose bags are these anyway, boys?" Nena had Luca's two trolley bags as her neighbour. "Bit tatty, aren't they? Are they yours, Tom?" I knew they were the Italian's.

I looked across at Tom. "They're Tommy's, Nena. I keep telling the bastard to buy a fresh pair of wheelie-things, but he spends all his money on expensive pants and that missus of his. Eh, Tommy?"

"I have a sentimental tie to the bags. I might stick a paper face on them both and pretend they're my kids. It'll give me some company on these trips I make to and from Turin. I get so bored up in the skies that I find myself chanting lists on the way over to Blighty. It's only half the time that I can count on an entertaining old boy to rattle on about his Aston Martin or the pert arse of his Mexican maid. The rest of the hours I'm up here, all alone in my tin can, way above the streets and houses."

I coughed. "Major Tom – back it up. Lists? What lists?" Both of us boys sensed that this was a fine time to break away from further investigation into our Torinese activities, and we both were in no mood for Nena's philosophising.

"Oh, just alphabetical lists of bands – ABBA, Badfinger, Counting Crows…" Tom laughed. "I'm surprised I don't send myself to sleep. You get it too, Sammy – the obsessive whirling of the headgears at night, the windmills of my mind. In your absence, I've been running further and further with less and less to occupy my thoughts, so I begin breaking down my runs into ever more impossible splits and databases. I sprinted down the side of the Po, counting the trees and then counting the shrubbery, until I couldn't figure out if my mind was palsying because of the overload of information or the aerobic exercise. I'm grateful for the presence of both of you." He paused and smiled at me. "Anyway… I've sorted a temporary place for you; it's outside Turin, nearer Asti, right by the nature reserve, so you'll get oceans of peace and quiet and very few questions. Shag away in silence."

"I'm intrigued," said our guest from the back seat.

"We have people out there all the time, Nena – every one of them English and without a swearword of Italian on their tongues – so you and Sammy can compose yourselves and work out how to press on after this morning's events. It's a late 19th-century Liberty-style house about 3km from Asti, and you'll have about 3 hectares of private land, should you want to ramble in the nude and fire up a barbecue by the pagoda. It'll be your oasis. You can hike in the Monferrato and Langhe if you're missing the Leas and the East Cliff, Nena. There won't be many old biddies, and the Italians aren't so keen on dogs and cream tea, you'll discover. I'd advise against any socialising until Sammy and I work out how to compartmentalise things with an additional bod on the books."

"It'll all be fine, Nena," I assured my love, although I didn't know my hope to be true. "Tommy and I have had twenty years of making things work out there. One can pretty much live in any developed country without too much scuttle shake – your bank won't even know where you are. Everything's on direct debit?"

"Yep," Nena confirmed. "I must be the easiest person in the Sandgate community to make disappear – owns own home and business, orphan, childless, friendless, has no hobby other than getting shit-faced. I'm a kidnapper's dream. I'm skinny enough to put in the post cheaply. And it seems I have a very rich and ice-veined boyfriend, who has a very well-heeled best mate with contacts to die for. I'm a lucky girl, am I not?" She was beaming now. "I just have to keep convincing myself that I attacked Joseph in defence of my love and myself. I just have to keep murmuring that beneath my breath until my psyche absorbs it and quells my conscience. I'll make him my nemesis."

"He was very definitely your nemesis," I confirmed. "His terror campaign against us was in fact a very long suicide. Don't forget, Nena – Tommy had been so concerned for both of us that he'd bought that firearm for me."

Now, we had to make do, to turn our backs on our River dream and to head away, in my case for a second time, against our wishes, eschewing our boltholes. We deserved pity, not punishment, and certainly not imprisonment. The law in England was nonetheless always tough on the victims of the primary crime. We'd done well to get away, and in the absence of a body, then there would never be any crime. Joseph would never be found; the clinic into which he was now fused by tons of concrete would never be touched or demolished. It would stand as a beacon of hope and help thousands of people. We had right on our side, and we had the protection of good men and women on every side. Fear not, Nena; don't be inclined to be afraid when all is safe, my sweet love. You deserved all my care and protection, and you'd forever receive it.

I drew my right hand back onto Nena's knee. "Joseph ranted at me, 'lie upon lie is what the past has for proof'.

What do you reckon, Tommy? Bicep tattoo? It's a keeper. And so are you, Nena, my dear."

"These private displays of affection are fairly unsettling," joked Tommy. "I can see myself taking over the role of Third Musketeer and Platonic Observer from Cadwick. How has he reacted to his two best people fleeing the motherland?"

I brushed down the thighs of my jeans. "Cadders believes we're currently tailing Joseph to the St Malo flat of his uncle. I texted him from Nena's mobile phone, but it's now in the pockets of the dead man; Cadders believes Nena dropped it into the Thames by accident during a thrilling chase over the Millennium Bridge."

"And the Merc?"

"That needs a thorough clean, and then perhaps Asgar can drop it down to Folkestone? Your boys in Lewisham will be able to valet it free of evidence, I assume?" I grinned, as I knew I was asking a great deal of my best friend.

"This is an irregular situation, and you've paid me back already, so yes, I'll sort out the Merc. Keys in the exhaust?"

"Yep. The Merc's in Whitechapel obviously. It's really the front seats and, of course, the boot that need your boy Milo's greatest attention. Nena and I will treat you tonight to the best meal we can concoct from whatever's at hand, Tommy."

"Lovely – beans on toast?"

"Probably, possibly, my old mate. You are now the Third Musketeer, and we promise to keep any PDAs to an absolute minimum."

Tom smiled. "I won't be able to join you tonight, I'm afraid. Claudia's father has asked me to review a Letter of Intent he has drafted for some Arturo Martini sculpture. You know how Signor P is – it's always, "I want it done yesterday, and you owe for some minor good deed I did you." He has an astonishing power of recall when he needs something from someone he's helped in the past. For a man without a smartphone or even a Filofax, and with a real thirst for the grape, Signor P is always on top of Outstanding Favours…"

"That'll be your father in law one day," I laughed. "You'll be his consigliere."

"He's not a Mafioso, Sammy, just the eternally grumpy paterfamilias of a clan of hot-heads, staring down the world from his corner seat at that café with the mermaid beckoning locals inside. It's all his kingdom – every piazza, every park, every palazzo, every pizzeria. You see, old bean, I just have an exeat to scratch out a living as the man spears another plate of ravioli with his fork and nods his approval."

"And after three years of living with his daughter, Signor P will demand a certain question of you, Tommy."

Tommy sighed. "Yes, and, at that point, your presence in Italy will make my life rather more three-dimensional, and your new home near the woods will grant me an avenue of escape. What's good for you is always good for me, young Sammy. It was always so."

"You and Signor P will make for a frightening union of grace-and-favour types. He'll send you his chums, bored with life and confused, nay frightened, by this world of micro blogging and tweets and algorithms – and you'll treat his daughter in the manner to which she's accustomed. Helping Claudia should help your business."

Tom stopped grinning. "Our business, you mean?"

I sighed. "Look, I'm present but not involved; so regard me as a sleeping partner, Tommy, there to extend a modicum of advice to you. Nena is going to need me around. Isn't that right?"

Nena spoke from the back. "In a nature reserve, well away from the city, with no communication with the outside world, no friends and family, and speaking only

English, yes, I'll be rather dependent upon you." Nena continued. "And anyway, wasn't it our grand design to nest somewhere? I don't mind if it's River or rural Piedmont, or whatever. I just demand that you don't rocket off again. I'll be keeping an eye on this plane and its cargo."

"Not too closely, I hope," muttered Tommy, and Nena looked again curious to the type of people who had sat in her very seat in the cramped rear of that plane. I knew it was nigh on impossible to imagine some septuagenarian of infirm health tolerating the hours and hours of flight, when even she was perhaps starting to daydream that Tommy's bags were a chiller bag full of spirits. It had been almost a day since her last drink, and her hands were starting to become encased in that light sweatiness; a sign her liver was in confusion. She was no doubt missing the bodywarmer of her gin, especially now she felt like part of an overaged Bonnie and Clyde. There was nothing to do up here but chat. "How did you learn the language?"

Tom coughed. "It came from just being around people, so that option won't really be available to you. I'm sure Sammy here can slip in a few bons mots when you're padding around the house. His Italian is actually serviceable when he can be arsed to try it out."

"It's moribund, dear boy!" I replied. "I get by on hand gestures and smiles – remember when I bought the Lancia off a dealer using just frenetic waving and signals? TWO DOORS." And I made the hand motions, laughing at my own physical comedy, like an utter fool.

"That was a memorable day, Sammy," Tommy paused. "Nena, I'm sure you will work it out – there's a TV in every room of the house because the old boy who lived there for the first half of the year wanted the company of television screens, if not actual living, breathing human beings."

Nena interrupted Tommy. "And what happened to the old boy?"

"Well, he passed on in his sleep, darling," Tommy answered. He then quickly looked across to me. "He had sleep apnoea – he used to drift in and out at times. We'd got him a specialist, but the dodgerer was in his early Eighties. Good innings. Old leader of Tower Hamlets council in East London. He carried a copy of Wisden cricket annual with him and kept reciting bits of Tennyson in this restrained whisper. Very odd…"

"Passed away in his sleep, or put away in his sleep?" Nena looked out of the window.

"No, Ronald was not looking for an assist, Nena. Don't worry – it's not like that. It was actually harder to keep him on this side of things than to let him die. He had a load of call buttons and panic pulls all over the place, and we set up a baby monitor of sorts, didn't we, Sammy?"

Tommy laughed, and I took up the tale. "Mad old Ron gripped onto life so tightly that even his forearms were white. God knows why. He seemed built of cobwebs and dust and powered by his far-right ideologies…"

"I thought these men were friends of the community, people your boss took a shine to…" Nina interjected.

"Not all of them, darling," I muttered. "Some were brought over here to lessen the damage to the socialist plan we had in London. Ronald was a roadblock to any idea of the greater good – he was like a Pinochet. In fact, he was the very spit of Pinochet, with his little fascist moustache. All the far-right military nuts have those vague top lips, don't they?"

Tommy jumped in. "Unwaverable in their beliefs, but reticent in their grooming? Franco, Adolf, Pinochet, Ronald – all of them unwilling to upholster their top lips with a confident forest of facial fur. It's worthy of a thesis. Perhaps you two could get on that as you start your bed-in? You'll have to find another amanuensis apart from me, though – I'll leave you to your shagging." Tommy chuckled and scanned his instrument deck. "I'll try to find a bar-billiards table. It'll be like the old times in the East Kent Arms before Sammy knocked over that boy like a kingpin…"

"Tommy!" Nena cried. She ran her fingertip against the bag next to her, remembering all the day's events and Joseph's slow forward slump onto the kitchen lino. "You have to ruin things, don't you? I was beginning to forget this morning."

"It was self-defence, darling." I tried to break it up. "Anyway, I wouldn't mind a bar-billiards table. Tommy, you can store all your boys' toys at our house, and, Nena, I can teach you the rules of the game. We can wile away the hours with a spot of chess, some Cluedo, all of that."

Tommy chuckled. "I still think you should write your thesis on how the facial hair of the dictators is diametrically opposed to their commitment to their bananas policies, or something. But yes, I'll sort out the lounge and turn it into a common room of sorts. It'll be my housewarming gift to you."

And as it was at the beginning.

Two hours later, Tommy's Lancia dropped us off at the house. The Liberty style of the late 19th century had developed from the spread of Art Nouveau across Europe, and Italian architects had fully embraced the casting-off of restrictive traditions. The property near Asti was rather too large for me and Nena to rattle around inside – God knows how old Ronald had managed to make a home of it – but its capacious grounds offered us real seclusion and a feeling of protection from an outside world we felt had little sympathy for us. Nena had been crying on my shoulder in the car; my grey T-shirt was streaked with tears and mucus.

Above the time-flecked front double door, some three metres in height, were floral motifs of the Liberty style, which took great inspiration from the grand department store in London. Twenty heavy oak windows on two storeys surrounded the hefty entrance, twelve on the first floor and eight on the ground floor, with eight facing to the front. The façade was of stone, painted a shade of terracotta, with a box tree either side of the front door, which seemed to me to stand like a pair of stout doormen. Once inside, there was a voluminous, open-plan living area with two sofa beds, a rustic dining table with space for eight, and a rocking chair made of tired wicker. The style of furniture was French, with a random scattering of Ronald's belongings here and there, antique curios to remind him of Blighty, of the days when his estuarine bark held people's attention and corralled them with fear.

To Nena, the house resembled the ski chalets she had seen on the back-room TV in the salon, reality TV that had made her vow never to brave the slopes; to me, the familiarity of the place was a comfort blanket after an interminable day. Ronald had been one of my most demanding clients, although I had always admired the tranquility of the house, a ten-minute drive from Asti.

In this spot, the only neighbours would be the occasional visitor to the regional fair of truffles in Montechiaro d'Asti camping in the unfenced hectares or the Montferrat oenophiles who pitched tents after getting sloshed on Barbera d'Asti and Ruché. Earlier that year, I had to turn up to move the campers on before Ronald reached for his .22 rifle with tremulous hands and peppered their canvas tents with pellets. The old boy had spat his froth over me.

"The bar-billiards table could go here?" Nena laughed, pointing to a dusty alcove that would have to be commandeered for storage. "It needs a feminine touch, this place – it looks like the sort of pad that swallows up a minibus of Cadwick types, bent on drinking the region dry of red and then indulging in homoerotic rough 'n' tumble on the hessian rug."

I agreed: "I can imagine Cadders chasing the chalet girl around the wingback and pinning her to the fridge like a pretty magnet; he'd be on his tiptoes."

"I hope he's OK."

"He's tougher than us." I paused. "This place needs a little love. It does feel like a frat boys' den. I had 18 years holed up in a boys' pad, frankly alone. Now, I don't mind being cooped up," I chuckled. "I know what it takes to succeed as a couple. It's not about sweet harmony – that's a bonus my folks enjoyed. When we were teenagers, we thought it was all about sweet harmony. We were simply playing at the game of being adults, doing the things we thought grown-ups in love do. Remember when we went for that awful meal on Valentine's Day, must have been 1997, and I was dressed up like a penguin and ordered a minute steak, and you looked like a Speech Day mum? Well, it was inauthentic – we hadn't lived yet. We hadn't gained the weight of years, of solitude and separation, the broken dreams, the lost friends like dear Harry and the concrete disappointments."

"Have you been preparing this speech?" Nena began to weep again, but from happiness, not guilt. I couldn't have found the words except now, in this moment of calm.

"No, it's off the cuff. I promise you, Nena. Romantic life really is all about finding your rhythm as a couple, a beat that no one else can ever sense. Then you can live in a pigeonhole like this far away from the concerns of others."

Nena sniffled and then joined into the thought: "And if the outside world can't dance along in our merry song, well, sod them."

"My world began and ended at the farmhouse gate back in Berwickshire, under the wing of my folks. And now it begins and ends now at that big Italian front door. The ruins of the world will strike me unafraid, Nena. This is where we were meant to arrive at the end of our first final journey," I said.

Nena nodded and looked around the room, perhaps picturing how we could make it our River vole-home, a place where I could write and she could fuss on me.

"It's quite different to the cabin and the salon, isn't it, gal?" I finished tinkering with the fuse box and reading of the meters. "I'm quite glad Tommy has left us to our own devices. Bed calls us. I'm absolutely shattered by the day's events."

Nena's face darkened, her lips pursed. "You were playing it very cool today, Sammy. I mean, I want to know, but I don't want to know."

I closed the fuse box and walked over to my companion. "Close your eyes and hold my hands… It was only important that you knew – the number doesn't matter. I've never fired off a gun, for instance, or stuck a knife in someone. And I wish you hadn't today. What's done is done."

Nena took a pace back. "I know, but I keep getting these flashbacks to the kitchen and the weird collapse of Joseph's body. You don't see people fall like that in the movies." Nena slumped down into the hard wicker of the rocker.

"Treat it as an unreliable memory, a fiction," I urged as I sank into the soft velour of my own chair, facing Nena. "Look to the future, and forget even today. You can't reach back and touch it; you can't re-position the pieces. You can only create your own account for yourself." We couldn't carry more weight.

Nena sighed. "It's going to take some time. I guess time passes slowly out here in the mountains."

"It will pass. And everything will become normal again, like in the Nineties."

Nena swept back her hand and took in the ragbag of furniture in the vast room. "I know I had to do what I did, but the deed is something that 99.9% of people will never do, and I was forced into it. I wouldn't have fired if I thought you and I were safe."

"We weren't. It was simply an unfortunate set of circumstances," I said. "We now have to make best of the situation, and we have to live in hope of a brighter future. As my mum used to say when the farmhouse was getting whipped from all sides by the winds, "it will get brighter later". You know the Nick Drake album?"

"Didn't he kill himself?"

"Something like that, a few years after, but the album was called Bryter Layter," I replied. "Now if even Nick Drake can see the sunny side of the street, then so should we. This is a lovely place."

"It is," Nena said.

"And Tommy knows what's best for us – and he has seen to it that the Merc will be valeted and Joseph will never be found. The dead have to deal with one another; even the good ones, like my folks or yours. It's just the way it is. Let's go upstairs and hibernate in that big old brass bed. Let's not think upon things we cannot change. Madness lies in that direction, darling, and we should go in this one."

And I led Nena by the hand through the echoing lounge, up the curved staircase to our new bedroom, and she ran her trailing fingers along the oak balustrade, happy at last to have reached a sanctuary. How she loved me. In the couch of one another's arms, there would be no more canvas-wrapped nightmares for me, nor companionless evenings for Nena, dead to the world on her vinyl sofa.

The following morning, the pair of us would be found by Tommy, in the chair of one another's limbs, in an everlasting quietness, the duvet wrapping us together to be carried away somewhere beyond human sight, where all our erstwhile crew would be waiting for our arrival – my father in that battered wax jacket of his; my mother fussing with her primrose-yellow cap; and Harry revving up his beloved Honda motorbike. The dreams that had kickstarted my final sleep, entwined with Nena in every way, had now become our new alternate reality, one without an end, one without seams and one without windows.

Their friend Tommy, shaking, in floods of tears, would then switch off the gas heater he had set up by our bedside table; he would open all of the twenty windows to dispel the silent clouds of carbon monoxide and coax in the scent of bougainvillea; and he would then remove his dust mask to make the planned 10am GMT call to councillor John.

With that, the house was now clear for Gerald's stay, once his wife's money had hit Tommy's account. It was all a process, planned and executed, step by step, with all the detachment and precision of a chemistry practical.

Meanwhile, Tommy had a personal contract to honour, via a jeweller's on Via Giambattista Bogino, an act that would set up his new life as Claudia's fiancé and as the consigliere of her father, Massimo Paganino, the close friend and partner of councillor John. The circle was almost perfect now, and the stray splinters on the wheel had been buffed away. Tommy had tried to protect his best friend, to find a way in which my new life could co-exist with his own old ways, but there was no solution, except to send me off in long-desired happiness and companionship.

And we lovers, me in my one-euro boxer shorts and Nena in that Minnie Mouse T-shirt of hers I so loved, which had been with her during all the years of loneliness, would be together for ever more, under the floorboards of the pagoda, next to Ronald and his faithful .22 rifle.

About the Author.

After his Classics degree at Gonville & Caius College and his journalism qualifications in London, James joined The Mirror Group, breaking onto the set of the James Bond film The World Is Not Enough for a string of exclusives.

He subsequently spent years on the party circuit, chatting with Andrew Motion, Joanne Harris, Dame AS Byatt and others. He then compiled the Critical List for The Sunday Times, including new books. James edited the columns of AA Gill and Germaine Greer; and wrote TV previews for the Sunday Telegraph magazine.

The creation of a graphic novel series about the bibulous actor Sir Ronald Timberlaine Clutterbuck and his one-way feud with Sir Alec Guinness led to two successful Kickstarter campaigns and an appearance at London Comic Con.

The idea for the novel Where Is Your God Now? sprang from James's love of fiction concerning (false) memory; from novelists such as Dame Daphne Du Maurier, Patrick Hamilton, Philip Roth, Zadie Smith and many others; and the locations came from failed house-hunting in Folkestone and Sandgate, something that seemed to stretch for years.

James now lives in a sleepy market town in Kent with his Spanish wife and their devoted PA, Beaulieu the King Charles spaniel.

Printed in Great Britain
by Amazon